the
darkest
corner
of
the heart

the
darkest
corner
of
the heart

LISINA CONEY

PAGE
&
VINE

Page & Vine
An Imprint of Meredith Wild LLC

Paperback ISBN: 979-8-9877583-5-9

CONTENT WARNING

This book contains themes of alcoholism, drugs, profanity, death, and explicit sexual scenes.
Recommended for mature readers only.

Dear readers,

Nothing I could ever say or do will be enough to thank you for making my dreams come true, but I'm stubborn enough to keep trying.

This book is for you. I hope it reminds you that hard times won't break you—they will forge you.

AUTHOR'S NOTE

The events of this book take place seventeen years after the ending of *The Brightest Light of Sunshine*.

This is an independent story with different main characters, which means you don't need to read *The Brightest Light of Sunshine* in order to enjoy this story (although you will find spoilers for *The Brightest Light of Sunshine*). But if you want to learn about Maddie's childhood from her brother's perspective, you are more than welcome to pick it up. Who doesn't want to read about an intimidating tattoo artist falling for his little sister's sweet ballet teacher?

I hope you enjoy Maddie's story as much as I loved writing it. It was about time she got her own happy ending.

chapter 1

MADDIE

I was four years old when my mother sent me to the hospital with an open wound in my head.

Yeah, ouch.

To be fair, my memories from that day are foggy at best—an empty bottle of whiskey on the floor, a sharp coffee table corner, the sound of my mother's drunken screams.

Then, nothing.

If I had to guess why I was the lucky winner of such a fun childhood, I would tell you some people are just born with it. Bad luck, I mean.

Hazel eyes stare back at me in the mirror before I slide my gaze away from the scar marring the right side of my hairline. I have much bigger and more pressing issues to worry about now than a past I can't fix.

Kyle presses play for the fourth time in a row, and Tchaikovsky's harmonic notes fill the room. My friend's voice drifts over to me. "Let's do it one more time for good measure."

He doesn't bother asking if I'm ready to go because he already knows the answer is always a "hell yes."

As the music flows within me, I tune out everything else; Kyle dancing behind me on the barre, the bustling Norcastle streets below the high-rise studio, the curious stares from the office building across the street. I had the choreography—the whole six minutes—memorized on the first day, and now the movements are second nature.

Adagio, turns, plié, tendu, rond de jambe, petit allegro, grand allegro, repeat.

I feel free, reborn in my dark-blue leotard and pink tights, as I always do in the studio.

My wings aren't on my back—they are on my feet.

The music ends, and another Tchaikovsky classic begins, an extra pas de deux I'll be filming with Kyle for his own audition, and I ignore the way my leg whines in discomfort.

One day. Just one more day of practicing, and then I can finally rest.

When we're done, he lets out a breathless sound that resembles a choke more than an actual word. "Okay," he says, wiping the sweat off his brow with the back of his hand and looks at me like I've grown a second head. "You want to go again, don't you?"

I shrug because the truth is I could. I want to and I could, but Kyle has been dancing with me for hours. He looks a second away from passing out and not waking up for three months straight. So I smile at him and say, "I'm cool. I think we're ready for tomorrow."

"Damn right we are." He claps me on the shoulder as he passes by to retrieve his phone from the plug-in speaker he brought to the studio.

He's right—I was born for this, and so was he. There is no doubt in my mind we'll nail the audition tape tomorrow. And when we get called in for the in-person audition next month—not if, *when*—we'll nail it again. Because that's what we do.

Dancing is all I was ever born to do.

"I rented studio fifty-four at ten in the morning tomorrow, remember that," he tells me again, as if I'd ever forget.

He gets an eye roll for that. "I'll be there at nine thirty. Don't forget your leg warmers." I point to the ground before he rushes to put them inside his bag. "Bring me a snack tomorrow, pretty please? One of those peanut butter bars you make." I give him the puppy-dog eyes that always work on my brother.

"Sure," he says. But he's too busy browsing through his daily twenty-something chat requests to look my way. All from a new dating app he swore he would never sign up for, the liar. I smirk on the inside. "See you tomorrow, Mads. Love you!"

"Love you too." I blow him a kiss, but the heathen doesn't spare me a second glance as he waves goodbye, his eyes glued to a six-pack on his phone I can see all the way from here.

Whatever. Kyle has been one of my best friends for the past four years, and I couldn't love him more. Which is a good thing because I'll be seeing more of him from now on.

A few days before we graduated from The Norcastle School of Dance, we got an email from The Norcastle Ballet with exclusive invites to an audition.

A freaking audition for one of the most prestigious ballet companies in the whole country.

Pinch. Me.

I did nothing but stare at the white wall of my studio apartment after reading the email, wondering if this was yet another joke from Mr. Universe himself. It had to be.

How else could *I*, the little girl with the neglectful mother and absentee father, even be considered to join the ballet company of my dreams? Me, who only made it through childhood unscathed thanks to her much older brother, who raised me when it wasn't his job?

For some reason, I caught the eye of a recruiter, and they wanted me. *Me*, who danced because it's always been the only way I could see the light. The only way I could *breathe*.

But the minutes passed by, and nobody jumped out of my closet, laughing and pointing a mocking finger at me while yelling, "Hidden camera!" so eventually I came to terms with my new reality.

And then I cried. God, I cried so much. It wouldn't have

surprised me if my family had heard me all the way from Warlington, the city I grew up in, hundreds of miles away.

When we video chatted after I had calmed down, my eleven-year-old niece, Lila, cried with me until we both had no more tears to shed. My brother called us dramatic, but I saw that sneaky tear roll down his cheek too.

A day later, I found out Kyle had been invited as well, and we got our heads right into it, coming up with different routines and moves we could film for our tapes. Tomorrow is the big recording day, and although I could perform our choreography in my sleep, I won't risk it.

So, instead of leaving with Kyle, as I probably should after hours of rehearsing nonstop, I get my phone out of my bag and press play.

Sure, auditioning doesn't mean I'm going to join the company, but it means everything to me that I even get the opportunity to prove once and for all that I can make something last.

As the music starts, I rub my right leg, ignoring how it's starting to feel a bit sore, and go once more. It's nothing a hot shower and massage won't fix later.

Ballet has been a constant in my life since I was a little girl. I took my first lesson when I was four, and since then, I've been working toward my ultimate dream—get a BA in ballet, join a company, and make a career out of my passion.

Seventeen years ago, I made a promise to my first ballet teacher, Grace—who is now my sister-in-law—that I wouldn't stop dancing for as long as it made me happy. For as long as it made my heart feel lighter. I've kept that promise all this time.

I won't stop, not ever. And if rehearsing for twelve hours a day is the price I need to pay to live my dream, so be it.

The music ends and starts again.

Adagio, turns, plié, tendu, rond de jambe, petit allegro, grand allegro, repeat.

I'm not going to fail because I didn't practice enough. I'm not going to miss this boat. I've been lucky enough to be offered my dream career at twenty-one on a silver platter, and I'm not going to waste it.

Hanging out with my friends can wait. Seeing my family can wait too.

My phone pings, but I ignore it. It's probably one of my brother's daily reminders.

"Slow and steady wins the race," he says, always the wise man who, like me, had to grow up too fast. "We all believe you can do it. I believe in you more than anything, you know that. You got this, princess. Don't be too hard on yourself."

"I know, Sammy," I tell him every time, hating but loving the protective side of him I grew up nestled in.

I promised to visit them in Warlington after graduation, but then the audition happened. They understand, always the supportive family, and I try not to focus too much on how guilty I feel every time I go back home. I don't want to make myself their problem again. I don't need them to—

Not now, Maddie. Stop that thought before it even starts. Concentrate.

Adagio, turns, plié, tendu, rond de jambe, petit allegro, grand allegro.

Yet that gaping hole inside my chest opens a little wider anyway.

I'm loved. I'm appreciated. I grew up with a roof over my head, food on the table, a family that wasn't made up of a mom and a dad but of two people who fought tooth and nail to make sure I was cared for.

My brother loves me. Grace loves me. My niece loves me.

I have money in my bank account.

I have friends and a college degree.

I have everything I could ever ask for and then some more.

And that is the problem, isn't it? That is the damn problem.

One moment I'm trapped inside my head, counting my blessings so I don't get lost in my nightmares.

And the next, my future is gone.

A sharp pain pierces through my leg, and my ankle gives in.

I fall like my limbs don't belong to me, like I'm no longer in control of the body that has given me so much.

"Fuck, fuck, fuck. *Fuck*," I hiss, breathless, as I wrap my fingers around my right ankle and yell in pain.

This isn't right. This isn't supposed to be happening.

No, no, no...

I wait, hoping to wake up from a bad dream, but the pain radiating through my leg tells me what I refuse to acknowledge. I'm not asleep.

Tears fall to my feet, and grief crashes into me at once, like a brutal tidal wave.

I try to move, but it feels like someone is slicing my ankle with a sharp knife.

I cry and scream for the light that gradually extinguishes until I'm left in total darkness.

I cry for the little girl who wanted nothing but to believe something in her life would last, something she could build and cultivate for herself.

And I scream.

And scream.

And then I feel nothing at all.

chapter 2

MADDIE

"Come on, princess. You need to eat something."

If I make any sound as a response, it's completely involuntary. I don't want to be awake today.

Of course, half-assed answers never work with my older brother.

He finishes making a cheesy omelet (my comfort food) in the small kitchen of my studio apartment and turns to look—glare—at me, crossing his massive, tattooed arms over his chest. "Don't you dare grunt at me, young lady." He's only half joking.

I give him another grunt because, again, I don't want to be awake today, and he knows this. I lived under his roof for fourteen years, after all.

Normally he doesn't like it when I'm being too irritable, so the fact that he only sighs and sits next to me in bed tells me everything I need to know.

I've missed a once-in-a-lifetime opportunity, and I should feel sorry for myself.

And I do. More than anything in this world, I do.

He places a warm hand on my shoulder. "How's your ankle feeling?"

Like shit, Sammy. It feels like shit.

A shrug is the only response he gets, and the guilt starts eating me alive once more.

I'm never this difficult, not with him. I love my brother more than life itself; I don't take for granted the sacrifices he's made since the day I was born to a mother who wasn't ready for a baby. He's always been a brother, a best friend, a father, a protector to me. I would be lost without his love and support.

But...

Without another word, he goes back to the kitchen and grabs an ice pack from the freezer. He wraps a cloth around it and places it over my ankle as I look out window and wallow in the quiet Norcastle morning.

The sky is clear, the birds are chirping, and sunshine filters through the white curtains Grace gave me as a housewarming gift. On the windowsill sits another one of her gifts—the coolest flower vase, shaped like a woman's bust. Sammy thinks it's horrifying. Ha.

"Your appointment starts in an hour. You should eat something before we leave," he tells me in a patient voice. "I know you're nervous, but I got you the best physical therapist in the East Coast. Doctor Simmons has years of experience working with athletes, and they've all fully recovered. You'll be in good hands."

Today is my first day of rehabilitation for my posterior ankle impingement. And no, this isn't a nightmare—I've pinched myself more than once to check.

I'm lucky I don't need surgery, I guess, which means the recovery process is supposed to be faster.

But it doesn't matter, does it? I'm not getting into The Norcastle Ballet. Auditions are an exclusive, one-time thing. If you miss your chance, that's it. They don't hand them out like candy, and I'm not getting a second shot at it.

"I'm not hungry." My voice sounds rough when I speak, maybe because I haven't uttered a single word since my "good night" to him last night. There's not much to say, anyway.

I also don't care about this Dr. Simmons person—no matter how good he is, he won't magically fix what I so stupidly messed up. But Sammy doesn't need to hear that.

My brother takes a deep breath—one of his frustrated ones—and runs a hand down his face. Perhaps it makes me a shitty sister, but it's only now that I notice the heavy bags under his eyes and the tiredness all over his features. My heart sinks.

I'm being an asshole. An ungrateful, inconsiderate asshole who gets more love and support in her life than she could ever ask for but still complains about what she doesn't have.

After I hurt my ankle at the dance studio, I could barely move. Luckily, Kyle was still around the area and took me to the emergency room.

Let's just say, neither my brother nor I have very good memories of the last time I was in the ER. Open wound to the head, anyone? Yeah, that wasn't a fun day.

The hospital called him, and he drove for hours, nonstop, until he got here. He thanked Kyle and took over from there, driving me to my apartment and staying with me for the past few days. Buying groceries, cleaning, changing my ice packs and compression bandages, calling a rehabilitation center... He did it all.

Sammy left his wife and daughter behind to take care of me at the drop of a hat. He left Inkjection, the tattoo parlor he owns, in the hands of my uncle Trey and canceled all his appointments because I refused to listen when my leg started giving me trouble.

I didn't listen. And now...

Now everything I've built since I was four is gone.

Serves you right.

"Sammy..." My voice is small as I hold out my hand, reaching for him like I did so many times when I was a kid. His features soften as he wraps his tattooed fingers around mine. "I'm sorry."

He only shakes his head, as if I wasn't a total mess. "Nothing to be sorry about. I'll always be here for you."

"I know, but—"

"Shh..." He squeezes my hand and gives me one of those reassuring smiles that always manages to put all my fires out. It doesn't work today. "I don't need you to apologize. I only need you to eat. Will you do that for me?"

I nod because that's the least I owe him. Sammy squeezes my hand one last time before he grabs the plate with the cheesy omelet, and I almost tear up from the smell alone. "Here." He sits back on the bed and passes me the steaming plate.

I take my first bite and zero in on the bags under his eyes again. It's undeniable that, despite the exhaustion clouding his face these past few days, my brother is a handsome man. We may not have had the best luck with our parents, but we can't complain about our genes.

At forty-seven, his muscular build is pretty much identical to how it looked when he became my guardian seventeen years ago. His frequent visits to the gym certainly pay off, even if he's all sweaty and stinky when he comes back and tries to shove my head and his daughter's under his armpits. He's so gross.

Both of his arms are covered in ink, and so are his hands, knuckles, and the side of his neck, as well as some skin on his back and legs. It's safe to say my love for drawing was passed down by him. I might not be as talented as my brother—he's the most popular tattoo artist in Warlington for a reason—but I'm not half bad.

I mean, I designed the tiny butterfly he tattooed on my ribs last summer, and it looks amazing, so there's that.

Aside from a few gray hairs here and there—that he insists Lila and I are totally responsible for—it looks like my brother hasn't aged a day.

"Do you want to take a quick nap before we leave?" I ask him with my mouth full, something I know pisses him off, but I also know he won't scold me for it today. "You can take the bed while I read on the couch or something."

He shakes his head as I suspected he would. I love my brother, but he can be a stubborn ass sometimes. He's been sleeping on my pull-out couch for the past week, which is definitely not comfortable enough for any six-foot-three man. "I'm good."

I arch a skeptical eyebrow, not buying it. He only ruffles my hair and takes the plate from my hands once I'm done. "Want another one?"

"No, thanks." However... "Can you get me a chocolate bar, please? Second drawer." I beg with a pout and everything. It's common knowledge in our family that as soon as any of us—Grace, Lila, or me—give him the puppy-dog eyes, he's a goner.

Hey, it's not my fault he's a big softie underneath all that harsh exterior. I might as well take advantage of it.

"This thing has no real nutritional value and you need that to recover, but fine," he says, giving in after some more puppy-dog-eyeing. See? It works. "But only because I want you to eat, and right now I don't care what."

"Sure, sure." I make grabby hands as he brings the chocolate bar over to my bed, and he laughs. It's the best sound I've heard in days.

My phone buzzes on my bedside table, and my heart drops. I know who it is because he's been texting me nonstop for the past week.

I ignored Kyle's first text, then the second, then the tenth, hating myself a little more every time as I let the ball continue to grow. I'm not ready to face him just yet. I have so much on my plate right now that thinking about Kyle too is unbearable. And if that makes me a shitty friend...

Well, there you go. Something else to add to the list.

Bad daughter? Check.

Ungrateful sister? Check.

Terrible friend? Check.

"Come on, peanut. You need to get dressed, or we'll be late."

Pushing the guilt away, I instruct my brother to pass me the clothes I want to wear from my wardrobe, and I insist on using my crutches to get to the bathroom by myself. Once I call out that I'm safely inside the shower, my mind plummets to the dark pit I haven't been able to crawl out of for the past few days.

After I got injured, Kyle had to find a last-minute partner for his audition. Sandwiched between all the unanswered texts he sent me, I read that Polina had luckily been available. If Kyle had missed his chance because of me, I would've never forgiven myself.

Relief crashed into me when I learned he'd managed to film his tape, which was a good thing.

Because he got accepted for an in-person audition at The Norcastle Ballet.

I should've called him to congratulate him because truly, truly, I'm proud of him. I know how much he's struggled to make it as a male ballet dancer among unsupportive family members and "friends" who would laugh at the sight of him in tights. Assholes, all of them.

I was there for Kyle when he broke down two years ago after he came out to his family. His father didn't accept it at first. I wanted to be there when he celebrated his most important milestone yet, one he'd fought so hard for, one we shared—but I'm ignoring his texts instead.

I might be twenty-one, but I can't seem to grow up.

Tears roll down my cheeks, and I place my head under the shower, hoping the hot water washes them away. But it won't wash away the truth—I could have been celebrating my spot in the audition, maybe, if I had listened to my body. Now my body is making sure *I* listen to *it*.

"Princess? Are you okay?" The concern in my brother's voice tells me I've been in the shower for too long.

"Yes! Just finishing up!" I call out, rubbing my eyes and hoping they don't look too red and puffy once I get out.

I only shampoo my hair once, forget about conditioner, wash my body, and get out as swiftly as this stupid ankle will let me.

It's not like I don't have a plan B. Since there never was any guarantee of passing the audition in the first place, I had already looked into other dance companies I could join. However, because auditions are off the table until I recover completely, Grace suggested that I take a ballet teaching job in one of the nearby studios. I never envisioned myself being a teacher, but I need to do something with my life. Right?

My brother isn't pressuring me to take a job or anything, even though I have one. It's not much, only a waitressing gig I take a few nights a week to help cover my expenses since I live away from home and all.

He's already sacrificed enough, and he has Lila to look after. Plus, now my rehab. It's too much.

Until I decide if I want to pursue a career in choreography or teaching, or until I can join a dance company, I need to work if I don't want to go back home to Warlington. Which I don't because I love it in Norcastle.

I *belong* here. I can feel it.

Monica, the manager of the bar I work at, promised me I could have my job back as soon as I recovered, but I'm still not going to get paid for at least two months. I'm lucky that my family can financially support me while I sort everything out, but it doesn't mean I like it.

"Princess?"

"Coming!"

The time to feel sorry for myself is over. At least for now.

Once my hair is half dry and I put on some of my most comfortable clothes, Sammy and I leave for the injury rehabilitation clinic. At least my building has a working elevator so he doesn't have to carry me down seven floors—because he would totally do that. My brother knows no limits when it comes to helping the people he loves, even if he ends up with the short end of the stick.

The drive to the clinic is silent for the most part. Grace texts me good luck on my first day of rehab, and my stomach drops. Because that's where I'm going today. Not to the dance studio, but to a rehabilitation clinic.

I destroyed my whole career at the age of twenty-one, and there's no coming back from it. And no matter how great this Dr. Simmons is, he won't be able to fix that.

chapter 3

MADDIE

My first thought as we enter the injury rehabilitation clinic is about my mother.

Years ago, she'd hop in and out of other kinds of rehabilitation clinics.

I was sixteen when I finally confronted my brother about our mother's troubled history with alcohol. Not that I hadn't overheard him and Grace talk about her issues before, but I didn't find out the real extent of her past until we had the "Mom's intense headaches" conversation.

Needless to say, she didn't exactly have migraines.

I don't blame Sammy or Grace for disguising the truth when I was younger. What was the alternative? Telling me that my mother used to forget to pick me up from school and ballet lessons because she got too drunk to remember she had a daughter to take care of?

Yeah, right.

Now, as I take in the pristine white walls, clean floors, and smell of antiseptic in the air, I wonder if she ever felt as trapped in one of those clinics as I do now. And I've only been here two minutes.

We reach the reception desk, where I tell a smiley lady my name and what I'm here for.

It still feels surreal to say it out loud. Posterior ankle impingement. Sounds painful, doesn't it? I can confirm it hurts like a bitch.

"Please, take a seat." She gestures to the waiting room with a manicured red nail. "Dr. Simmons will see you shortly."

My head goes back to my mom as I follow my brother to the waiting room.

Learning the truth so many years later wasn't easy, but I understand why they didn't talk to me about it sooner. I was nowhere ready to hear about my less-than-ideal family life.

Sammy told me that, when our mother's brother passed away unexpectedly many years ago, she became a ghost of the woman she used to be. She drowned the voices in her head with alcohol, and little by little she drowned herself. Then she met Pete, and I was born not even a year later.

Pete, a father who never played with me, never took me anywhere, never even hugged me. *Stupid Pete.*

I try not to think about him too often because the mere mental image of my father turns me into a person I refuse to be. Bitter, angry, hateful. That's not me. That's not who I was raised to be.

Despite growing up neglected by my mother, I've never hated her. Sammy was afraid I would, but I couldn't find the energy. Three years after I started living with my brother and Grace, my mother got out of rehab for good and, apparently, has been clean ever since.

I cried when I heard the news, afraid I would be taken away from my brother and his girlfriend.

I know, right? What kind of child has a meltdown when learning her *mother* is coming back for her?

Luckily, both Sammy and my mother decided I was better off living with him. I was happier and had a better chance at a bright future if my family life didn't change.

I still saw my mother a few times a month when she would take me out for pancakes or to play in the park, but those visits didn't help to bring us closer. I'm sure she was devastated about it, but I... I barely knew the woman. I wasn't attached to her. Even when I lived with her and Pete, my brother came by every day and always took me to the park and for ice cream, so I've always gravitated toward him the most.

I can't long for a mother I've never had. A mother I haven't seen in a year.

"Are you nervous?" Sammy's knee bumps against mine when we sit.

"Jittery," I deadpan.

He sends me a look, a silent way of telling me to behave. I think he should give me a free pass today.

I was supposed to be working my ass off to nail an exclusive audition for my dream ballet company today or, at the very least, crying about not having been accepted. I was still supposed to be able to dance, to *move* my leg. Not... Not this.

Now my body is an empty shell of grief and unfulfilled dreams I'm not sure I'll ever bring back to life.

"Don't sulk," Sammy mutters under his breath. "Dr. Simmons will have you back on the stage in no time. At least you don't need surgery."

Fine. That would've been way, way worse—I'll admit as much. I try to tell myself that, as far as careless accidents go, I didn't get the short end of the stick, even if it feels like it.

But all attempts at convincing myself that I'm fine, that this is nothing I can't climb my way out of, aren't enough. I'm not in the mood to count my scarce blessings right now. Not when—

It's the "Maddison Stevens" that snaps me out of my thoughts, but it's the deep voice saying it that has my stomach plummeting.

I turn my head in the direction of the man standing only a few feet away, and I crane my neck up, up, up, because he's so tall he surely must experience a different kind of weather up there.

When I don't respond, too busy staring at this mountain of a man who has just walked into the waiting room, my brother elbows me softly in the ribs.

"Here! I'm here," I call out awkwardly, my voice only slightly higher than usual.

I feel my brother's eyes burning a hole into the side of my face as I stand, probably wondering why I look so worked up all of a sudden. But I'm too stunned to speak, my throat going dry for reasons I don't even want to entertain.

I'm used to being around tall men. Sammy is six-foot-three, and Kyle towers over me too. But this guy is on a whole other level.

At what I would guess is around six-foot-five, he narrows his impossibly blue eyes at me and frowns. He *frowns*.

I ignore the uneasy feeling settling in the pit of my stomach and grab the crutches Sammy is holding out for me.

"Are you Maddison Stevens?" There goes that low voice again, asking me the simplest of questions I can't seem to answer like a normal person.

My mouth feels too dry. "Yes."

It's not that I find him attractive or anything. It's not that. And sure, I might have taken in his short dark hair, his big—way too big—hands holding a folder between his thick fingers, and how the navy blue scrubs he wears contrast with the dark brown of his short beard, for a little longer than it would be appropriate. But it's not every day that I get to see a real giant out in the wild.

He's imposing. It's just that. He's intimidating. Handsome, too, all right, but...objectively.

And okay, let's say I found him attractive. *Hypothetically*. If I had to guess, I would say he's around thirty. I'm not saying that makes him decrepit, but he's definitely old for me. Not like that matters anyway.

"I'm James Simmons," he introduces himself, stoic and—yep—still intimidating. "I'll be overseeing your recovery."

So *this* is one of the best physical therapists in the East Coast. He doesn't smile, and for some reason I find it odd. Aren't doctors supposed to be friendly and all that? Maybe this guy didn't get the memo.

His icy blue eyes don't linger on me as he turns to Sammy, now standing by my side. "Are you her father?"

"Brother." Sammy shakes his hand, and indeed, this James person is a couple of inches taller than him. Which is impressive because my brother is the tallest man I know by far. "Nice to meet you."

"Likewise," he answers, still in that same deep but almost bored voice. "I've got it from here. We can go now if you're ready, Miss Stevens."

Miss Stevens. Why have those two words just sent a thrill down my spine?

Actually, I don't think I want to answer that.

I manage to get out of this giant-man-induced lapse in judgment and turn to my brother. "Will you be here when I finish?"

His smile is soft. "I'm not moving an inch, princess."

A tiny sense of guilt takes over again before I can stop it.

He wants to be here. You're not making him stay.

But is that really the case? Didn't he just upend his family life in Warlington because I was careless and injured myself?

"Miss Stevens?" That authoritative voice manages to add a nonverbal layer of *stop wasting my time* at the end of his question somehow.

Or maybe I'm reading too much into this man's every little action.

"Ready. Yes," I blurt out, because apparently, I am unable to form a single coherent sentence in front of him.

With one last look at my brother, I turn to face Dr. Giant and give him as much of a sincere smile as I can manage. "We can go now." There it is, one full sentence. I got this.

Without another word, he gives my brother a nod and turns around. To his credit, he doesn't speed down the empty hallway, but he doesn't walk beside me either.

We reach a miniature hospital type of room, which I assume is his office. Two huge windows with blinds occupy one of the walls, and different graphics, anatomy posters, and diplomas hang all around the remaining three.

"Take a seat, please." He gestures to a treatment table placed against the opposite wall from a small desk and a couple of chairs. He doesn't spare me another glance, focusing instead on typing something into his computer.

Okay, then. It would do me well to remember I'm not here to make friends. I'm here to get back on track as soon as this stupid injury will let me.

Holding on to my crutches a little tighter, I make my way to the table as slow as a turtle. I'm not particularly clumsy, but I'm paranoid the slightest contact with any surface will set back my recovery process. What if I make it worse? What if I end up having to need surgery because I keep on being careless? No, thank you.

Because, if I can't dance, what can I do? What do I even have to offer?

Nothing makes me breathe as easily or feel as complete.

I could never live a fulfilling life if my days didn't consist of stretching on the barre and learning routines.

How would I live?

The dark spiral of my thoughts only becomes more violent when I reach the treatment table.

He wants me to take a seat. It should be simple enough, but... I... I can't.

I set my crutches aside and feel the soft fabric of the cushioned table under my fingers. *Breathe in, breathe out.*

Tears prick the back of my eyes, and I remind myself I'm not alone in this room. Ever since Sammy came to look after me, I've restricted my crying sessions to my showers. I don't like bawling my eyes out in front of anyone, let alone a complete stranger who doesn't seem to like me all that much in the first place.

You're fine.

I'm here, on the right path to healing my ankle, and I'll be fine. My brother is right outside if I need him.

That's the problem.

"Miss Stevens?" His voice comes from somewhere behind me, but I don't want to turn around. "Can you get on the table by yourself?"

I could. A few days ago, I could. When I had a working ankle and a purpose. What do I have now, besides self-pity and regret?

I don't want to tell him that no, I can't get on the damn table. This isn't about him. This is about how my own body feels like a prison. How my limbs feel foreign and heavy when, just a few weeks ago, they helped me fly on the dance floor. How I was on my way to make my dream happen, and now...

Now I can't even push my body weight up.

"Let me help you." Looking over my shoulder, I spot him walking toward me, only stopping when there's a small gap between us. He smells good—like wood and spice and some fresh-scented shampoo. *Stop it. His smell is none of your concern.* "Here."

Huh?

My eyes drop to his hand, that massive hand that is now holding some kind of step stool.

For me.

Oh.

As he leans in to place it on the floor, embarrassment clouds my thoughts. Why does the fact that I need a step stool to get on the table make me feel so weak?

"Grab my arm for support."

Dr. Giant offers me his forearm, and for a second, I don't know what to do with myself. I mean, it's not like he's asking if I want to hold on to him or if I'd rather climb the two steps alone. He's *commanding* me to do it. It's as if he knows I'm useless, which wouldn't be too far from the truth.

There's a slight tremble to my fingers as I wrap them around the firmness of his naked forearm. The hairs on his arms tickle my skin as I slowly make my way up, praying he doesn't feel how clammy my hands are getting.

As soon as my butt touches the table safely, he extracts himself from my koala-like grip with ease, sets aside the step stool, and slides into the rolling chair in front of the computer.

I lace my fingers together and stick them between my thighs, begging this tingling sensation to go away. And then Dr. Giant, this man who is already way too attractive for his own good, reaches into the pocket of his scrubs and takes out a pair of glasses.

And he puts them on.

Goddamn it.

My gaze darts toward the ceiling, suddenly finding it fascinating. It's lost its original white color, and I suspect that lightbulb will need to be replaced soon because it doesn't blind me in the same way the lightbulbs in the waiting room did. His office—

"All right. I would like to ask you a few questions before we begin," he says, breaking the tension in my shoulders.

I drop my gaze toward him and those evil glasses. He's turned sideways toward me, but his attention remains on the screen.

My throat is dry. "Sure."

He goes straight to the point. "How did you get your injury?"

"I hurt my ankle while dancing ballet." It's funny how the reminder feels more painful than the actual injury. "I think I pushed myself too hard, and it just...gave in."

He doesn't react, doesn't comment on my careless behavior. He doesn't chastise me for not taking good care of myself either.

I get nothing, and I can't tell if I feel more relief or unease.

He types something in and asks me another question. "Does the pain travel or stay in the same area?"

"It never travels above the knee, and my toes don't hurt."

"Does the pain get better or worse if you move your ankle? And in what positions?"

"It stays the same."

"What was your functional mobility status prior to your injury?"

At his question, my stomach turns with nausea. All the optimism my brother tried to make me feel this past week at the fact that I don't need surgery melts away as the reality of my situation settles in.

I can't dance.

I lost my chance to join The Norcastle Ballet.

An uncertain and cold future unfolds before me, a future I want nothing to do with.

"Miss Stevens?" Those blue eyes watch me carefully, and I'm quick to snap out of it.

"Yeah, yes. Sorry. I, um, recently got my BA in Ballet Performance and was supposed to audition for The Norcastle Ballet." *Don't cry, don't cry, don't cry.*

"You were a professional ballet dancer, then?"

It's the *were* that almost makes me sick. I swallow back the lump in my throat and say, "Yes." It only comes out half-raspy and with no tears. That's a win in my book.

His eyes linger on mine for a beat too long, and his jaw clenches in a weird way. I don't know why I think it's weird. Maybe because it's paired with that look in his eyes. Kind of soft, kind of not.

The moment breaks as he types something in on his computer again. "What is your goal?" he asks then, catching me off guard.

I blink. "Goal?"

"With physical therapy," he clarifies. To be honest, I haven't thought much about what I want to get out of PT besides going back to who I used to be. So, I tell him just that. "We'll see what we can do."

We'll see what we can do.

I get that doctors aren't supposed to give you false hope and all that, but he could watch his words a little more carefully. Make them sting a little less.

After making me feel like shit—not like he's even noticed—he takes off those glasses that make him look too good and stands, moving closer to where I'm sitting. "In this first session, we'll focus on measuring what impairments could be affecting your injury, and I'll trace a treatment plan from there."

I only nod and take off my shoe and sock.

I'm not expecting his touch to be so gentle as he palpates my ankle, looking for who-knows-what, but I try to pay it no mind. So what if this is the most physical contact I've had in months besides hugs from my brother and dance partners? Pfft. Big deal.

Hating myself a little more, I glance at his profile for the tenth time since I walked in and try not to think too hard about why I can't seem to take my eyes off this man. This *older* man.

His short but thick beard doesn't stop me from noticing the sharp edge of his jaw, or its tightness for that matter. Why is he so on edge? I'm the one suffering from a life-altering injury *and* his grumpiness.

I let out a deep sigh, feeling more frustrated with myself than anything else, and he notices. "Does it hurt?"

"A little, but I'm fine."

A grunt is the only answer I get.

We move on to some range of movement measurements and some tests of strength. I like that he takes his time explaining every exercise, even though I barely understand a thing. He says nothing that isn't strictly necessary and doesn't try to make small talk, which is fine by me.

Closing my eyes, I lose myself in the familiar darkness. I find comfort in knowing all I have to do is exist right now, in this room, as I'm lying on this table while he massages my ankle with such unexpected gentleness.

In the distance, the clock ticks, and voices drift from under the door as other physical therapists and patients walk by. The smell of antiseptic isn't so strong now, unlike whatever shampoo Dr. Giant used this morning. That minty scent could wake up the dead if he got close enough.

"That'll be all for today." His gruff voice pulls me out of my almost sleepy state. I can't believe I was about to call it a night right here, at ten in the morning. "I can confirm your ankle won't need surgery, and we're looking at around a six-week recovery plan. You'll come to the clinic four times a week, then perhaps two. We'll see how you progress."

Still somewhat groggy, I sit up as he moves back behind the desk. "Okay."

I put my sock and shoe back on and grab my crutches, only to set them aside when I realize I can't use them to get back on the ground. I count to five in my head to avoid thinking how pathetic this is. How pathetic I am.

"Could you...?" I start, dying a little inside. He slides me a confused look, and I point to the stupid stool with my chin. "So I can climb down."

He gets the stool and lends me his arm again. *Don't focus on his muscles. Don't you dare.*

I do. I do dare, and I only regret it a little bit.

Once I can stand on my own and hold my crutches again, he moves back to his desk. "You should rest as much as possible, so avoid going out for now unless it's strictly necessary, or it might take your ankle longer to recover."

My breath hitches at the mere possibility of messing up rehabilitation too. What would happen if I did? Would I... God, would I not be able to dance ever again?

"I will send you an email later this morning with a list of

proper care instructions and our treatment plan for the upcoming weeks so you know what to expect."

I swallow. "All right. Thank you."

For the first time since we entered this room, he looks at me. And I mean, really looks at me. It may be all in my head, but his jaw seems to lose all that tension from before and his voice sounds a little softer when he says, "Take care, Miss Stevens. I'll see you tomorrow at nine."

chapter 4

JAMES

A drop of sweat clings to the side of my neck as my feet hit the treadmill in a fast, steady rhythm. The console indicates I'm well past my usual thirty-minute mark, but I keep running. A poor attempt at getting yesterday out of my head.

In my five years as a physical therapist, I have overseen hundreds of patients in all kinds of different physical and emotional states—cheerful and motivated, calm and quiet, tired and impatient. I'd never seen anyone look utterly defeated.

Until her.

The clock on the far wall of the gym lets me know my shift starts in an hour and a half, and I've yet to jump in the shower and feed the two gremlins upstairs. With a hint of restlessness still dancing inside me, I hit the stop button and use a towel to wipe the sweat off my face and neck before heading to the elevators.

The in-building gym and the city views from my unit are what sold me on this place years ago. At times like this, when my head gets too loud but my schedule doesn't allow me to get lost in the bustling streets of Norcastle even to go to my nearest gym a couple of blocks away, I know I've made the right decision.

The second I open the front door, I'm assaulted by loud, angry meowing.

Another one of my right decisions.

"Hey, hey." I shut the door behind me and head for their food closet, carefully so as to not step on them as they circle around my legs. "Calm down, tigers. I fed you right before I went to the gym. Let's tone down the drama, yeah?"

The loud meowing continues—a clear *shut up and feed us again, Dad.*

"All right, all right."

I grab Shadow's dry food and Mist's wet pouches—he was born with a dental disease, and the vet had to take all his teeth out, sans his fangs, shortly after I adopted him two years ago. He still gets into daily fights with his brother—who I adopted at the same time since they both lived in the same animal shelter—and eats just fine, so he doesn't seem to mind his condition at all.

Shadow rubs his black fur against my leg when I crouch down to fill both of their bowls. "There you go." I scratch him behind his ear before getting back on my feet. "All set. I'll clean your litter box before I head out."

Maybe the fact that I have one-sided conversations with my cats is an early sign that I'm losing my mind. It's definitely an indicator that I should go out more, spend some time with humans who aren't Graham or my patients, but I can't be bothered.

I haven't been bothered for a long time, for reasons I'd rather not think about today. Or at all.

Once I make sure their litter box is clean and their water fountain has enough water, I take a quick shower, get dressed for the day, grab my car keys, and drive to the rehabilitation center.

She's my first patient of the day.

My brain fixates on that inconsequential fact during the twenty-minute drive, as I greet the rest of the staff, as I set up the equipment, as I pull up her file on my computer.

Maddison Stevens. Twenty-one. Ballet dancer. Posterior ankle impingement.

What her file fails to mention is how she zoned out when she realized she couldn't get on the examining table by herself, how her hand trembled as she held on to my arm, how I could tell it killed her to ask for help to get back down.

Working out this morning has done shit for me because my head is still too loud.

My watch marks five minutes until she gets here, and I remind myself to get a grip. I specialized in sports injury rehabilitation during my master's degree, a calling I felt deep in my bones after what happened. It's probably that, the reminder of what I—

A knock at my office door stops my train of thought before it derails.

"Come in," I call out, my voice sounding too stiff and business-like. I don't bother correcting myself.

Her long brown hair, pulled into braid that falls over her shoulder, is the first thing that catches my attention as she walks in, holding on to her crutches.

"Good morning." She gives me a smile that doesn't reach her eyes. "I'm a little early today. I hope that's okay. My brother thought traffic would be worse."

A small part of me is curious about why her brother is the one taking care of her while she's injured and not her parents. That tall, tattooed man who was with her yesterday had to be in his forties. She's twenty-one, so that's a big age gap between siblings. I wonder what prompted that, if their parents—

None of your goddamn business.

"You're good." I put on my glasses as she walks up to my desk. "Did you get my email with the treatment plan?"

"Yes, thank you. It was very...um, informative." She pauses. My eyes are fixed on her file, the one I've been mindlessly scrolling through since I got here, but I know she isn't done. And I'm right. "So, six weeks of recovery."

There's a hint of something in her voice, something that sounds a lot like misplaced hope. A disguised plea for me to tell her that no, that six weeks is too much and she'll be fine in two. That she shouldn't worry about her ankle because she will go back to the stage in no time, as if nothing had happened.

But I can't.

"Six weeks, if everything goes well," I confirm with a nod, not missing the way her breath hitches. "Let's get started, Miss Stevens. Come over to this wall and take off your shoes, please. You can leave your socks on."

I motion to the wall next to my desk. She follows my command, clearly unsure, but does as I say. After she removes her shoes and places her crutches against the examining table, I move to stand next to her.

"We're going to do some isometric holding today." I'm pretty sure she has no idea what I'm talking about—and it's not her job to understand. But not informing my patients of what we're going to do has always felt wrong to me, so I keep going under her confused stare. "See that step stool over here?" I gesture toward the low, black step stool placed against the wall. She nods. "We're going to use it to get your muscles to turn on."

Her nervous fingers toy with the end of her braid. "Will it hurt?"

"It shouldn't." If her little frown is any indication, she doesn't really believe me. "You may feel some cramps, but that's completely normal."

"Okay," she mutters, glancing down at the step stool. "So do I just get on it?"

"Only the tips of your feet should be directly on it—your toes and about an inch of your feet past them."

She takes one careful step after another until she's on top of it, her hands braced against the wall. "Like this?"

I look away from the way she's nervously pulling her lip between her teeth. "Yes." It comes out so unexpectedly rough, I have to clear my throat before I continue. "Don't press down too hard. Just stand there in a normal, horizontal line. Hold that position for thirty seconds."

We repeat the same exercise four times, and I confirm that her ankle is responding well. Her lack of complaints tells me she's doing okay so far, too. "All right, now let's do it on one foot."

Her head snaps up to me, eyes wide. "One foot?"

"You will be fine," I reassure her, catching the way her step falters before she holds herself back up. "I'm here, Miss Stevens. I won't let you get hurt."

Her dark eyes remain on my face for a beat too long, as if she were waiting for divine confirmation of my words, before she nods. "Thirty seconds again?"

"Let's do one-minute holds. We'll repeat it three times."

Her barely there smirk catches me off-guard, and I find that I'm unable to look away from the upright tilt of her lips. This time, it looks genuine. "What if I told you I'd rather sit down and do nothing for the rest of our session? Would you let me?"

"If it's any consolation," I start, crossing my arms as she holds her position on one foot, "I have some sit-down exercises planned for later. I'll do all the work, so you can stare blankly at the wall if you want to."

"I'm leaving you a five-star review just for that." Her voice is a weird mix between tired and teasing. "Is the minute up?"

I glance at my watch. "It's been ten seconds."

A quiet groan escapes her, but she says nothing else. Silence falls over us, and even though I'm never talkative during sessions with my patients, today I wish she would give me something. A thought, a worry, anything.

What the hell are you saying?

"Let's switch to your right foot now," I tell her when the minute is up.

Uncertainty is written all over her face when she looks at me. "This is my injured ankle."

"I'm aware." My voice is a mask of cool, stiff hardness. "One minute."

I can tell she isn't happy about it, but she doesn't protest. She's scared of hurting herself again, it's easy to see that, but I meant it when I said nothing would happen to her while I'm here—taking care of her physical health is my job. And I'm damn good at it.

Twenty seconds go by, then thirty, and I don't take my eyes off her foot. She's wobbling a little, but she's holding on to the wall in front of her, so I'm not worried about—

"*Shit, shit, shit,*" she hisses, losing her balance on the step stool.

My hands shoot up to grab her hips as my heart skips a beat. Her body leans into mine, my mouth just inches away from her ear as I mutter, "I got you."

The warmth of her skin seeps through the tight T-shirt she's wearing, making my palms tingle. I pull away once she's safely back on the step, relief crashing into me at the loss of contact.

"Thanks." She sounds breathless, her cheeks flushed, her hand placed over her heart. Taking a deep breath, she shakes her head and places her hands back on the wall. "This wouldn't have happened if you'd let me sit down and stare at the wall, you know?"

I make a noncommittal sound at the back of my throat, resisting the urge to chuckle. "Let's do one more minute on your other foot."

"You're serious?"

I arch an unimpressed eyebrow. "I didn't let you hurt yourself, did I?"

A tired sigh is the only answer I get, and I don't say anything else either. The rest of our session remains incident-free, mostly coated in silence. She lets me guide her foot, tells me when it hurts or cramps, and keeps her promise of staring blankly at the wall while I work.

I don't like the void I see in her yes. Not one bit.

After I go back home after a long shift and feed Shadow and Mist, I find myself in the gym downstairs for the second time today, despite my muscles groaning in protest. Because, as I see it, this is my only option—work out until I reach the point of exhaustion.

Until this strange edginess inside my body goes away.

chapter 5

MADDIE

Sammy leaves at the end of the week, and not because he wants to. I have to kick him out—kind of.

It means everything to me that he stayed for so long to take care of me, never once complaining about my shoe-sized studio or how uncomfortably he spent his nights on my pull-out couch. He cooked, shopped, and cleaned, all while keeping a smile on his face and asking if I was okay every five seconds.

But two weeks is enough. He has a wife and a daughter to go back to, not to mention all the missed appointments he needs to catch up on at the tattoo parlor. My uncle Trey—who's not my real uncle, but Sammy's best friend—has been handling Inkjection on his own just fine, but my brother is the boss. He has to be there.

As *she* would put it, "You can't hold your brother back. It's unfair, and you're a grown-up."

No matter how much time passes, I can't get her voice out of my head. It's always there, whispering in the back of my mind everything I'm doing wrong for myself, for my brother, for Grace, for Lila, and even for my mom.

It's because of *her* words, the reminder that still stings, that it feels a little easier to say goodbye.

He gives me a big bear hug at the door of my apartment. "We'll come and visit you as soon as we can." He means Grace and Lila, who I haven't seen since graduation more than a month ago. "Call me if you need anything or if something happens."

"I will." I won't. Nothing is going to happen, and I don't want him to leave everything behind again for me when I can take care of myself now. Kind of. "My ankle feels better already."

That much is true. I'm by no means cured, but so far, rehabilitation is going well. I don't know what kind of black magic Dr. Giant is practicing on me, but it works. We did some flexibility exercises yesterday, and even though it's still weird to let a stranger guide my body like that, I've grown used to his touch.

But I'll never say that out loud. Not in a million years, and not if I want my brother to preserve his sanity.

"Still, you should rest as much as you can." When Sammy pulls away to look me in the eye, concern and exhaustion mar his face. "I love you, princess. Please, call me or Grace if anything happens."

"I'll be fine, and we'll see each other soon. Don't worry about me."

He ruffles my hair before pressing a lingering kiss on my forehead. "That's impossible."

A chuckle escapes me, a rare occurrence these days. I barely remember the sound of my own laughter. "You're such a dad."

"I *am*. Is that supposed to be an insult?"

"For you, yes," I tease him.

It feels weird, like a betrayal to myself that I'm feeling joy when my future has gone down the drain. But it also feels right that my brother would be the one to make that light at the end of the tunnel flicker back to life, even if only for a single second.

"I love you, Sammy. Drive safe." I hug him again, inhaling his familiar scent that always takes me back home no matter where I am. And these days, I need his comfort more than anything—but I have to let him go. *She* was right about that.

"I love you more. You take good care of that ankle, yeah? If Lila finds out you've been careless, you'll never hear the end of it."

I smile, recalling my niece's bossy nature. "Doesn't sound

like a bad plan to me."

None of us know where it comes from, since both Grace and Sammy are as easygoing as they come, but I've always found it funny that she's a little firecracker.

Lila is such a small thing, having inherited not a single one of my brother's tall genes. She still has a lot of growing to do, but I wouldn't be surprised if she stopped at five-two or five-three like her mother.

She has Grace's blond hair, but the rest is all my brother—the mannerisms, the smiles, and even their eyes look the same.

She's the sweetest kid, and she always manages to put the brightest smile on my face. I miss living with her the most—I miss her every day, especially how she always tiptoed into my room at six in the morning, claiming she wasn't sleepy anymore and wanted to watch something on my tablet while I slept next to her.

Lila coming here to scold me would be a blessing more than a curse.

"I'll text you when I get home." Sammy kisses my temple again. "And one last thing—don't worry about money, please. Order as much takeout as you want and call as many Ubers as you need, yeah? Don't hurt that ankle now that you're recovering."

I nod, resigning myself to the fact that I'm back to being a leech. At least I could cover my own expenses when I worked, but now... Now I'm an inconvenience once more. The eternal sacrifices my brother has to make.

"I love you, princess."

"I love you more."

He shuts the door behind him, and I let out a deep breath. Just like that, I'm alone in my apartment again. This is what I wanted, wasn't it? To live and let live.

I take a moment to bask in the silence. And then the darkness comes back all at once, as if Sammy had been keeping it at bay and now that he's gone, the spell shatters into a thousand cutting pieces.

I should be back in Warlington right now, celebrating the success of my audition with my family or organizing summer trips with my friends. Instead, I'm stuck with this...this unbearable heartache until time offers me a cure.

My friend Beth, who I met in college two years ago and is now one of my best friends, is coming for dinner tonight. If I don't cancel on her, it's merely because she promised to bring food from my favorite Chinese takeout place down the block. It may make me sound like the most terrible person on the planet, sure, but I don't want to spend any more of my brother's money if I can prevent it.

So I sit on my bed and stare at nothing, think of nothing, as life passes me by.

All this nothingness feels oddly comforting.

***

"Guide your toes up toward your shin as far as possible. Good. Does it hurt?"

I shake my head.

"Hold it for ten seconds."

My first week of rehab is coming to an end, and Dr. Giant is still an emotionless grump—no surprise there. But the fact is that whatever he's doing to my ankle works wonders, so I put up with it. It could be voodoo magic for all I care. At this point, I'll take anything with a smile.

And speaking of smiles, I have yet to see an upward tilt of this man's mouth. Maybe the muscles on his cheeks are stunted or something—that would explain a lot.

A little bit of fondness won't make my ankle heal faster, but since this is one of the only human interactions I have these days, it would help me feel less like shit. Not that he knows about that, obviously. And I doubt he would care.

After a few more stretches, we move on to the BAPS board, which has slowly become my own personal hell on earth. It doesn't make my ankle hurt, but it does make me feel self-conscious about my balance—or lack thereof. It mocks me because I can't for the life of me manage to stay on top of it for five seconds, when two weeks ago, I could walk on my toes. *Barefoot.*

"Can we switch exercises?" I dare ask after ten minutes on the stupid board, unable to stand this any longer—no pun intended.

I flex my knees to avoid losing my balance, and when his attention shifts to that movement, I internally curse myself.

"I would advise against it, since you clearly need to work on your balance."

Clearly? *Clearly?*

Oh, he's going there. All right.

I bite my tongue, forcing the verbal lashing to die down my throat, and say nothing. I've lost the battle. It was never a fair match in the first place.

Yes, he's the physical therapist, and yes, he knows best, but... There's always a but, isn't there?

But you're a failure.

But you did this to yourself.

But you will never be as good at ballet as you were before.

But you will never join TNB because you've lost your one and only chance.

But. But. But.

The list goes on and on, and it never seems to end.

My left ear starts ringing, and all traffic in my brain stops as if ambushed by a red light.

My chest constricts, all air sucked from my lungs, and my stomach turns.

The nausea hits me out of nowhere.

A fraction of a second before I lose balance and make my life even worse, a strong pair of hands lock on my forearms and keep me steady.

"Miss Stevens?"

I know that voice.

It's gravelly and distant, and I've heard it before.

I cling to it with shaky hands and labored breaths, hoping the sound will lead me above the surface.

My eyes are open but unfocused, and I can't see.

You'll never recover. You'll never dance again. Everything fades. Everyone leaves because you don't try hard enough—

"Listen to me," that voice commands again. The fog clears just enough to do as it says. "You're getting light-headed, but you're fine."

Light-headed? Is that what this feeling of emptiness is about?

As if the past few minutes had been nothing but a product of my imagination, the darkness fades away at once. My eyes manage to focus again, taking in the overwhelmingly bright lights of the room, and reality hits me.

I'm at the clinic.

The hands holding me for balance are a man's hands, big and strong and firm.

"Easy," that voice says again, and my brain finally makes the connection it's been searching for.

I blink up at Dr. Simmons. My throat is dry and my tongue feels like it's made of sandpaper, but I can't swallow. When I glance at my feet, I notice I'm back on the ground and not on the BAPS board anymore.

"What—"

"You were having a panic attack."

A panic attack?

No, I don't have those. Not since—

"Sit down." Dr. Simmons lowers me to a chair with so much gentleness I could cry. A few moments later, he comes back with a bottle of water. "Here. Drink this."

With my mind on autopilot, I do as he says. The cold liquid runs down my throat, unclogging the lump that didn't let me breathe, and before I know it, I've finished the whole thing.

"Do you want some more?" he asks.

I shake my head, my gaze still lost somewhere on the white wall in front of me. I hear him shuffling around the room, moving stuff, but I can't find it in me to move my head or my eyes.

"I'll be right back."

He disappears behind me, and I know he's left the room when the door opens and closes. Maybe I would find it disrespectful that he's left me alone after a panic attack if I wasn't so...so *burdened* already.

I miss my brother so much. The fact that he isn't here anymore to look after me, that he won't be picking me up from the clinic and making me dinner tonight, makes me want to burst into tears.

I could go back to Warlington with him and Grace. They would find me another rehabilitation clinic there, and I could be home with Lila.

You're an adult. Stop running to your brother for everything. He's done enough for you.

The door opens again, footsteps getting closer until Dr. Simmons reappears in front of me. This time though, his hands aren't empty.

"I hope you don't have a nut allergy," he says before handing me a snack bag full of almonds.

My hands have a slight tremble to them as I grab it. "Where did you get these?"

"They're mine."

My eyes snap up to his.

"You can have them. I always bring more snacks than I end up eating, anyway."

Heat rises to my cheeks. "I'm sorry. I can't... This is..." *Full sentences, Maddie.* "I really appreciate this, but I don't want to eat your snacks. I swear I'm okay now."

He sits on the chair opposite to me, our knees touching, and just...watches me. Leaning forward, he rests his elbows on his legs and clasps his hands together. "Humor me, Miss Stevens."

I'm spared of making that decision when my stomach rumbles. "Just a couple," I warn him.

His chin dips once.

I open the bag, pick up an almond, and bring it to my mouth. The crunching sound fills the room, but somehow, it's not uncomfortable.

He doesn't speak again until I've eaten six of them. "Tell me how you're feeling."

I give him my default answer. "I'm fine."

A beat of heavy silence passes between us. Then: "All right. Now tell me how you're really feeling."

I should've known he wouldn't buy it. I shift on my chair, itching to end our session earlier like he suggested.

"I zoned out for a bit, but I'm okay now" is the next and best thing he's getting. Then I add for good measure, "Same time on Monday?" I'm desperate to shift the conversation away from me and how I'm feeling. Away from that nothingness.

I start to think he's frozen into place from his lack of a reaction, but then he says, "Yes."

I get up from my chair, mortified at the fact that I just had a panic attack in front of him. Or that I had a panic attack *at all.*

"Thanks for the almonds." I give him the bag back with a small smile. He takes it wordlessly, his eyes lingering on my face as if he were waiting for me to freak out again. "I'll see you next week, then."

It kills me to think I'm making him uncomfortable by simply standing here, forcing him to be in my chaotic presence for a second longer than necessary. So maybe that's why I hurry to the door when I shouldn't, and maybe that's why his voice startles me when he says, "Careful, Miss Stevens."

Yeah. *Careful.* Let's tell that to the Maddie from two weeks ago.

Right when I think I'm finally free of this mortifying situation, his voice startles me again.

"Let me walk you out."

No way.

"You don't have to," I'm quick to say, because I couldn't possibly feel more self-conscious right now if I tried.

First, he has to help me up onto the exam table, then I have a freaking panic attack in his office, and now he feels obligated to walk me out because he doesn't trust me not to faint in the middle of the hallway? Because I'm so weak now that my body can't perform simple tasks without making me look like a fool?

Dr. Simmons sends me a look that leaves no room for arguments. "As my patient, you become my responsibility the second you step into this building. It's my obligation to make sure you get to your family or your ride safely if you don't feel good after a session. You've just had a panic attack."

Like I need a reminder.

The no-bullshit tone of his voice tells me this is a fight I'm not going to win, so I let my shoulders fall and say, "All right" as my embarrassment levels skyrocket.

He doesn't bother with small talk as we exit the clinic together. I'm not in the mood to do anything but go home and binge-watch *The Office* for eight hours straight so I can get some much-needed serotonin in my body.

"This is my Uber," I tell him, pointing to the white car waiting for me right outside the clinic.

He tips his chin down once, those cold eyes on mine. "I'll see you next week."

And when he's quick to put a hand on the car so I don't hit my head as I climb in, I tell myself it's something he does for all his patients.

***

My phone rings as I'm brushing my teeth that night.

After my session with Dr. Simmons, I came straight home and did nothing all day. Some of my friends asked to come over and watch a movie, but after what happened this morning, I wasn't in the mood.

Sammy texted me today, as he always does, to check on me. I didn't tell him about the panic attack, and I *may* have been a little cold through text, so I'm fully expecting that call to be him.

But after rinsing my mouth and grabbing my phone from the couch, I'm staring at Unknown Caller instead.

Huh.

I usually ignore these kinds of calls, but this time I don't give it a second thought before I pick up. I need a little thrill today. "Who is this?"

Silence.

"Miss Stevens."

That voice.

"This is Dr. James Simmons, from the injury rehabilitation clinic."

No. Way.

My heart does a little somersault—who am I kidding? A *ginormous* one—and blood rushes to my face as I will myself not to sound like an idiot. "Dr. Simmons, yeah. Yes. Of course. Hi. Hey. What's up?"

What's up? Really? Are you dumb?

"I was calling to see how you were doing after what happened this morning."

"Oh." I blink, taken aback by how...sweet I find that he cares. I'm probably not getting any special treatment, but it still makes me feel things I shouldn't. "Well, I...I've been resting all day."

Which is another way of telling him that my life is as boring as it gets.

"That's good." How can a voice sound gentle and rough at the same time? "Is your ankle giving you any trouble?"

"None at all. The BAPS board and I don't get along, but I will admit it gets the job done."

A sound suspiciously similar to a snort reaches my ear. "Glad to hear it." Then he adds something that gets my breath stuck in my throat. "This is my work phone, so if you have any questions about in-home care, just give me a call. I'm also available after five and on weekends."

I gulp. "I... Okay. Thank you."

There's no use in saying that I wouldn't want to bother him because I know what he will tell me—that it's fine, that this is his job, that his patients are his priority.

"Have a nice weekend, Miss Stevens."

His deep rumble makes my head tingle in a weird, not entirely uncomfortable way.

What the hell is happening to me?

"You too, Dr. Simmons." I hesitate. "Thanks for calling. I really appreciate it."

A pause. "It's nothing. Give me a call if you need me."

Need him. Why is my brain stuck in those two words?

"I mean it, all right?" he presses.

"All right," I mutter, struggling to breathe normally.

The last thing I expected today—or *ever*—was to get a call from my closed-off, grouchy physical therapist checking in on me after I had a panic attack, yet here I am.

When we hang up, I notice it's only a few minutes after five. Did he call me right after his shift ended?

I sit on the couch and stare at my phone, debating whether what I'm about to do is the stupidest thing ever.

In a sudden burst of courage, I unlock my screen, check my

recent calls, and add his phone number to my phone under "Dr. Grump."

chapter 6

MADDIE

Day ten? Fifteen? Of not speaking to Kyle is going as expected—terribly. He's sent me several texts since my injury, but I haven't dared to open them yet. It's been three days since the last one, though, and I can't say I'm surprised he's stopped. I'm the worst friend ever, after all.

But the whole mess with Kyle is only a pebble in my shoe compared to the text I woke up to this morning.

My mother wants to see me. After a year of no contact, and even longer of not meeting face-to-face, she's now decided it's time to barrel into her daughter's life, acting as if nothing was amiss.

"Hey, princess." My brother's voice greets me from the other side of the line. He sounds happy, which is a shame because I'm about to ruin his mood for the rest of the day. Or the week. "How's that ankle?"

"Better. I can move it a little," I respond. It hurts a bit today, but I don't need to worry him further. I love Sammy, but he's such a dad. "Are you at work?"

"I'm on my lunch break."

I already knew this, but I wanted to confirm.

"I'm tattooing Aaron again, so he won't mind if I stay on the phone a little longer."

Aaron is Grace's older cousin, although they grew up as close as siblings—I call him Uncle Aaron for a reason.

"What's he going for?" I ask as I adjust myself on the bed.

After giving my pillowcase a quick sniff, I make a mental note to call one of my friends to help me change the sheets because this is getting gross.

"Hanna's footprint on his chest," my brother says.

Hanna is Aaron's third child and only daughter, born four years ago, and she's the most adorable thing I've ever seen. She definitely gets her stunning looks from my aunt Emily though, no matter how much Aaron insists she's all him.

"That's cute." I clear my throat and decide I don't want to keep stalling. "Hey, guess who texted me today."

The air shifts. We aren't even in the same state, but somehow, I feel it. My brother knows.

A loud sigh drifts over to me. "Mom?"

"Yep."

Another sigh, this time a little louder and a lot more frustrated. "What does she want?"

My fingers find a loose thread in the blanket I usually throw over my bed. "She said she wanted to meet but didn't tell me when or where."

"What did you answer?"

I gulp. "I haven't. Yet."

My palms start sweating, and I remind myself my brother isn't going to chew me out for this. Ever since he became my legal guardian when I was four, he's made sure I saw our mother whenever I could. He never spoke ill of her in front of me, never tried to pit me against her. It's always been important to him that we had a good mother-daughter relationship, despite the circumstances.

He stopped trying, eventually, and I can't blame him for it. I'm at fault for that. She made sure I knew that crystal clear.

"What do you want to do?" His voice turns somber, and I internally curse myself for it. I knew I was going to ruin his good mood, but I can't not tell my brother. Without him I'm lost.

"I don't know," I mutter. When it comes to my mother, I can't seem to tell right from wrong. My head and my heart are too tired to make the effort. "What do you think I should do?"

"I won't tell you how to deal with this, Maddie. This is your life, and this is your relationship. I don't have a say in it."

He called me Maddie.

Maddie.

I haven't heard my name on his lips in... I can't remember the last time my brother didn't call me "princess" or any other of his endearing nicknames. Why does it feel like he's just stabbed me in the chest?

I get that he's pissed about our mother not having contacted us in a while, and I know he's not angry at me, but... *Fuck*. Maddie?

"Okay." I swallow past the uncomfortable lump in my throat. "I'll let you know what I want to do when I decide."

"Don't be upset, peanut. What's wrong?" His voice turns softer, less frustrated, and it makes me feel a little better.

"Nothing," I lie, and I bet my left arm he can smell the bullshit a mile away. "I'm just exhausted. It's been a long week."

He hums like he knows I'm not telling him the whole story. To be fair, I don't think I know it myself. "So physical therapy is going well? Is Dr. Simmons as good as they say?"

He's good with his hands, all right.

Wait.

No.

Stop, Maddie. He's like, a hundred years old.

"He's...great." I clear my throat and hope my brother is too tired to notice my voice sounds a bit higher for some inexplicable reason. "He's really good. Progress is slow, but I'm optimistic."

"That's what I want to hear," he beams.

My mouth tilts up just barely. "We'll talk later, okay?"

"Okay, princess." He hesitates. "Whatever you decide about Mom..."

"I'll run it by you."

"What? No." He almost sounds offended. "What I was going to say is that I'm here for you no matter what you decide. We all are, all right? Do what's best for you, and don't think about anyone else."

I gulp. "I'll do that."

"Good." He doesn't sound too convinced, but he doesn't press either. "Text me later. I love you."

I pinch the bridge of my nose, a massive headache coming out of the blue and blinding all my senses. "I love you too, Sammy."

And just as if my mother been summoned by a strong force of the universe, not even five minutes after ending the call with my brother, my phone buzzes with a new text.

> **Mom: I'll be in Norcastle Friday. Are you free for dinner? You pick the place.**

I intertwine my fingers to stop my hands from trembling. It doesn't work.

***

Something that used to surprise my therapist back in Warlington was that, despite having been only four, I remember quite a few details of my time living with my parents.

I recall the smell of my mother's cheese omelets—my favorite food from childhood—and the sound of alcohol as she poured it into a glass every night. She thought I was asleep when she did it, but I always ventured out of bed for a while because I wanted to find out what adults did while kids slept. I was never too impressed.

As for my father, no happy memories remain. Mainly because we made none together, or as a family of three for that matter.

Something I do remember about him, though, is his face. I've never forgotten it because I still see it in my restless dreams.

Pete is—or was, I don't know if he's still alive—a few years older than my mother, and it showed, despite my mom not being the most healthy-looking woman her age. Drinking so much took its toll on her in more ways than one.

My father was tall—but not taller than my brother—and balding the last time I saw him, with a limp body. His crooked nose, as well as his thin lips, gave him a mean look that was pretty accurate to what lay underneath the surface.

The strong smell of smoke that always clung to his clothes, and the way he wore socks with holes in them inside the house. I remember him being at home a lot because, from what I've been told, he used to lose his jobs often; that didn't mean he ever made time to play with me. He never paid me any attention at all, as if I were just another cockroach under the fridge he was too lazy to kill.

Despite his obvious dislike for my father, Sammy never bad-mouthed him while I was growing up. He wanted me to have a good relationship with both of my parents, even if at least one of them didn't deserve it. He wanted me to have that choice, but his efforts didn't pay off.

I hate Pete with every fiber of my being. Not only for what he did—and didn't do—to me, but also for the way he treated my mother. How he neglected her, and how he made her already decaying mental health even worse.

A mother that is about to walk in any minute now.

Monica's Pub is the only place I could think of to have dinner with my mom. I feel safe here, my former workplace, and Monica knows enough about my relationship with my remaining parent to step in if I give her a panicked look. She never asks too many questions either, which is a plus.

Agreeing to meet her is probably not a smart idea. As Dr.

Simmons insisted, I should be resting as much as I can, but my mother is too unpredictable for me to let this opportunity pass me by. Who knows when the next time she remembers she has a daughter will be.

And yes, technically I could text her sometimes too. I used to do that—until I went ten months without a reply and didn't see the point in reaching out anymore.

There's a fine line between being a good person—a good daughter—and being foolish.

I fidget with the menu between my nervous hands before setting it aside, not knowing why I picked it up in the first place. I know every dish by heart.

"You good, honey?" Monica sets a glass of cold water in front of me. She's in her late forties, has a blond perm, and is by far one of the coolest, most selfless people I know. I lucked out the day she hired me to be a part-time waitress here because she "liked my energy."

I manage a small shrug. "I could be better."

She opens her mouth to say something else, but she doesn't get the chance because the door chimes and my mother walks in.

Here we go. Showtime.

Larissa Callaghan looks around the pub, her eyes full of disdain like it physically disgusts her to be here, and I mentally slap myself for not thinking of this sooner. According to my brother, she's been sober for the past few years, but what if she's one of those people who relapses as soon as she sees a bottle of whiskey?

I'm such a shit daughter.

"We can go somewhere else," I blurt out when she reaches my table, the first words I've spoken to her in a year.

My mother lowers herself into the cushioned seat in front of me with far more poise than I remember her ever having and gives me a small, lopsided smile. "This place is fine."

She sets her bag next to her, and it's only when she notices I haven't uttered another word that she clears her throat. "How have you been, sweetie?"

I wrap my hands around the cold glass just to feel like I'm holding onto something solid. "I'm in physical therapy for my ankle." Straight to the point. Ice broken.

A barely there frown appears on her forehead before she notices the crutches at my side. She gasps. "Maddie! What happened to you? Are you okay? When did this happen?"

An uncomfortable feeling crawls up my spine, and I shift on my seat. "I injured myself while dancing a few weeks ago."

There's no point in telling her about the audition I missed. It's not like she's ever been that invested in my education, and it would lead to too many questions I don't have the strength to answer tonight.

She shakes her head like she can't believe it. "You said you're in physical therapy for it. Is it working?"

"Yes." That is one truth I couldn't be more grateful for.

"How come you're in Norcastle?" I change topics before taking a sip of water to clear my clogged throat. She lives in Warlington, just like my brother and Grace.

"I'm not staying for long," she says as she flags down one of the waitresses. "Dave had to come here for business, and I convinced him to stop by today so I could see you."

My stomach twists unexpectedly. "Who's Dave?"

Monica arrives to get our order before she can answer. I ask for the usual—a burger with extra cheese—and my mother only orders an iced tea. "You don't want to order anything to eat with that?" Monica asks, swiftly looking my way.

My mother gives a tight smile that doesn't reach her eyes. "No, thank you. Just an iced tea would be great."

When she suggested we meet up for dinner, I didn't think I would be the only one *actually* having dinner. But okay.

Once Monica leaves, my mother turns to me. "Dave is my boyfriend, honey. We've been together for a year. He's the cook in the new restaurant I started working at, and we just...clicked, I guess. He's getting a promotion, so he had to travel for a training course, and I came with him. You know how it goes." She lets out a small chuckle as if anything she's just said is funny. It's really not.

My mother has proved time and again that she has horrible taste in men. Not because she picks the ugly ones—that would be the least of her problems—but because she always ends up with the assholes. My father is very much included in that category. He might be at top of it actually. Although Sammy's own dad might be number one, seeing as how he abandoned them before my brother was even born. That couldn't have been easy on our mom, given how they were only sixteen.

She never lasts long with any of them either, but the consequences of their asshole ways do. My brother says she's never loved herself enough to set any kind of healthy boundaries. I agree, and I'm grateful that I was raised in a very different environment.

"He's a good man," she adds when I say nothing.

I just nod. Nothing nice would come out of my mouth, and it's not like she would listen anyway, so there's no point.

A couple of minutes of awkward silence pass by until she asks, "So, um, you graduated a few months ago, right? Have you found a job yet?"

I take another sip of water. At this rate, it will be empty before my burger gets here. "I'm figuring it out," I opt for, which is better than confessing I didn't listen to my body and now I'm paying the consequences. "I work here sometimes."

Her trimmed eyebrows shoot up at that. I've never seen them done before, and it surprises me to see her look so polished and collected. But I refuse to think this is it, the moment she decides she's ready to get her life together. It never is.

"What is it that you do? Waitressing?"

I nod. "The owner is the woman who came by to take our order. She's a good boss. I always get out on time, and it pays as well as you'd expect. The tips are good." It feels weird, I've just realized, to have a face-to-face conversation with my mother after so long. "But I'm not working right now because of my ankle."

"I see."

A few moments later, Monica arrives with the iced tea and my burger. "Enjoy." She winks at me, and I only manage to give her a sad excuse of a smile in return.

"If you don't mind me asking," my mother starts as I take the first bite. "How do you pay for rent if you're not working right now? Do you live with roommates, or...?"

She knows the answer to this. She does, but she wants me to say it for some reason.

I chew slowly, taking my time before swallowing my food with some more water. And then I say what she wants to hear. "Sammy pays for it."

Her lips thin at the mention of my brother's name. I don't know why, since it's the exact answer she's looking for. The answer she knew she was going to get.

"Business must be going well, then, since he can financially support his daughter and his sister." There's a hint of bitterness in her voice, almost as if she hated the idea of her own son being successful in life.

I don't know what happened between them for our mother to have turned so bitter toward him, or if anything's happened at all, but I don't like it. I'll always be on my brother's side, which is why I refuse to reveal any details about his life.

"Yeah." If she's only meeting up with me to fish for crumbs about Sammy, she's going to leave this pub very, very disappointed. "How's work?" I ask her to shift the focus of our conversation.

It works. "Luckily, great. It's tough to find a job at my age, but I'm happy at the restaurant for now. It doesn't bring much money to the table, but it's fine since Dave and I split the bills."

Since...

Another headache starts building up. If she and this Dave guy split the bills, it means they are already living together. Is she going to let another man dictate her life?

I bite into my burger again and decide to ignore that comment. I don't have the mental strength for a confrontation.

Maybe meeting her tonight was a mistake. Am I really risking my ankle's recovery for a mother I barely know? For a mother who doesn't seem to learn?

Her words from four years ago assault my head before I can stop it.

You never gave your mother a chance, Maddie. You pushed her away.

"I'm glad you're doing well," I say, banishing the demons in my head. But it's not a lie, it really isn't. Even if she's never been the greatest mother, she isn't a bad person. She isn't evil. She just... has some issues. It would be amazing if she acknowledged them and worked to fix them like she did with her alcohol problem, but I don't have a say in that.

I eat in silence while she sips on her drink and looks around the pub, and I wonder what she's thinking. She might be wondering why I work here, in this dark place that smells of greasy food and pine-scented floor cleaner, but it's not like she has any room to judge. Just because she has trimmed eyebrows now doesn't mean she's moved up in the food chain or something.

I feel bad for being so judgmental for all of three seconds—until she opens her mouth.

"Are you sure you want to work here? This place looks..." She glances around again and shakes her head. "I don't know... sketchy. Maybe you should find something else, like a cute coffee shop downtown or something."

Swallowing the last bite of my burger, I try not to snap.

"Sketchy how?"

I've worked at Monica's Pub since I turned nineteen, and sure, it might not look exactly cozy, but it's far from sketchy. Monica loves this place and always makes sure both her clients and her staff are happy and in a safe, fun environment. Not once have I ever felt in danger while working here, not even when the older men get a little too drunk and flirty.

I can defend myself—Sammy and Grace made sure of it—and everyone here knows not to mess with the staff anyway. Monica won't hesitate to kick them out of one of the cheapest bars in town, which is the last thing they want.

And it hurts, it really stings, that my mother of all people would judge where I work. My brother, I would understand, but even he agreed having a job would be good for me.

So why is my mother, someone who barely knows me, suddenly pretending to know what's best for me? Suggesting that I find another job?

This is laughable, if only I had it in me to find it funny.

"It's too far away from everything," she explains.

I bite my tongue and only say, "There's a metro stop two minutes away." A metro stop that leaves me a block away from my apartment. It doesn't take me longer than fifteen minutes to get here, tops.

"Yes, but I assume you end your shift late at night. The metro can be dangerous, and it's full of...strange people sleeping there and everything."

I count to ten in my head. *Now* she worries about my safety?

Where was this concern when she left an empty bottle of alcohol on the floor the day I tripped over it and had to be rushed to the ER with a bleeding head?

Where was this concern when she would leave me alone at home for hours, while she thought I was asleep, to have a few drinks at the bar down the street?

But I bite my tongue again. My brother raised me better than to lash out at people, even when I think they deserve it. He isn't here, but I still don't want to do something that would disappoint him if he found out. I wouldn't put it past my mother to call him and reprimand him for the "poor way" he brought me up—as if it had been Sammy's job to take care of me in the first place.

"Monica knows this," I explain, aware that it will fall on deaf ears. "She lets me leave earlier, when the metro is still somewhat crowded."

She purses her lips, like that's not good enough, when Monica's shown more concern about my safety in the two years I've known her than my own mother in twenty-one.

"I don't know, Maddie. It still doesn't sound safe to me. Maybe you can switch shifts so there's still daylight when you leave?"

"I only work here part-time, and I make a lot of money on tips. People barely come here during the day, so it wouldn't make sense."

"How about..."

I don't hear the rest of it. My brain tunes her out, unable to focus on anything else but him.

I don't understand how I haven't spotted him until now, but he's right there.

Right there.

And his eyes are directly on me.

Dr. Simmons is here.

Shit, shit, shit.

I look away, but it's too late.

He's sitting with who I assume is a friend, a man who looks around his age, and the shock of seeing him dressed without his scrubs is too much. I mean, I'm not blind. I can tell he's bulky under his PT attire, but now it's all the more obvious. That black T-shirt is about to burst from how stretched it sits across his chest, and his arms are easily bigger than my head.

Arms I touched.

A sexy, model-like Dr. Simmons is a sight I didn't need to see. Sexy as in, *objectively sexy*. Of course.

It's difficult to see his mouth since it's partly covered by his short beard and the bar is so dark, but I swear his lips are pressed in a thin line. *Great, he's pissed.*

I mean, obviously. I don't think his range of emotions is too wide.

"Maddie?" my mother asks as she waves a hand in front of my eyes.

I blink. "Sorry." I'm not sorry at all. At least not for tuning out our conversation. "I... I need to use the restroom."

She gives me a strange look but nods, and I grab my crutches as quickly as I can manage. It's humiliating, I realize as I walk away, that he's seeing me. Outside, when I should be resting. If he scolds the hell out of me on Monday, I will totally deserve it.

Passing by the bathrooms, I push the emergency exit at the back of the bar with my shoulder and walk outside. It's dark, but nobody comes back here except for the rest of the staff on their smoking breaks. I take breaks, too, even though I'm not a smoker, but only because it's unfair that they get to kill their lungs and chill for a few minutes, and I only get to work. Yeah, not happening. If they can avoid drunk old men for five minutes every hour, so can I.

I rest my head against the brick wall behind me and take a deep breath through my nose.

I should've known meeting my mother wouldn't be easy, and now on top of that, Dr. Simmons knows I've been ignoring his instructions. *Great.*

A panicky sensation clings to my lungs, one I'm too familiar with but have spent years avoiding. And I'm usually successful— except that day at the clinic.

It's one of the two things I've always kept from my brother, my panic attacks, if only to not add one more weight on his shoulders.

Exhale. Inhale. You're grounded. You're safe. You can leave your mother and call an Uber if you want. Nobody is holding you hostage here.

Knowing that I have a way out of the situation usually helps, but it proves to be a bit more difficult tonight.

I hate to say it, and I don't want to put all this blame on her, but I can't ignore my feelings either.

Her sudden concern for me has triggered this response, and now my chest feels like it's burning and drowning at the same time.

I'm wondering how that's even possible when the back door opens.

And Dr. Simmons steps out.

Into the dark alley. With me.

Shit.

He doesn't say anything, but he sees me here. I know this because he stands away from the door, only a few feet from me, with his hands in his pockets. He doesn't look my way.

Having him here calms my nerves, or maybe it's just that I don't want to embarrass myself by having another panic attack in front of him.

Either way, my brain forgets about my mother and chooses to focus on a much safer, yet also dangerous thing—his smell.

I've been around that wood and spice aroma and that fresh-scented shampoo fragrance so many times I could probably identify him from the smell alone, eyes closed and in a throng of people. And that's why I suspect I've gone insane.

The invisible clock between us ticks by, and he still doesn't say a word. To be fair, neither do I. My mother may be thinking I'm locked in the bathroom or have a severe case of constipation, but I don't care. I'd rather be out here, standing in silence next to my physical therapist in a dark alley.

"Are you okay?"

His voice startles me. One would think I'd already be used to it, and I am, just not outside the clinic. It's so deep and rough, he should consider getting those vocal cords checked out.

I'm surprised he cares enough to ask and that my ankle isn't the first thing he mentions.

"I've been better." I'm too tired to come up with a lie.

He doesn't reply to that, and I find his broody silence oddly comforting. I get the impression that he doesn't ask too many questions, like Monica, and that's exactly what I need right now. Someone to just...be here. To listen and then act like I didn't say a thing. I need the exact opposite of my brother. I love him to death, but he can be overbearing.

Dr. Simmons still doesn't look my way as he asks, "Do you have a way to get home?"

My heart stammers inside my chest, wondering why he's asking and why it sounds like he'd offer to drive me if I said no.

Don't be stupid.

"I do," I say, my throat dry. "But thanks for asking."

He grunts something under his breath. "Are you sure you're okay?"

No. "Yes. I'm fine, really. You can go back inside with your friend."

I glance at him with what I'm hoping is an easy expression on my face. His, in turn, is all hard edges and unreadable stares. "Apply some ice to your ankle when you get home. It might be swollen." A pause. Then: "Come find me if you change your mind."

And just like that, without a spare glance or a goodbye, he turns around, hands still in his pockets, and leaves the way he came.

And me?

I've never been more confused.

chapter 7

MADDIE

Two days after my seeing my mom for the first time in months, my brain is still going in circles about her awkward concern. About how, at some point, I felt like I was having dinner with a stranger.

Maybe meeting her wasn't what I needed when I was already feeling low about my injury, but I can't find it within myself to regret it. Not exactly.

What I'm sure I'm about to regret is entertaining this conversation.

"You need to get laid."

What I need is for my best friend to set down that glass of wine and drink some common sense instead, but alas.

"I can't exactly move right now, you know?" I say, reaching out my hand until my fingers wrap around some salt and vinegar chips. They are the superior flavor—I don't make the rules.

Beth arches a blond eyebrow at me. "Your point?"

I shake my head in amusement and focus on chewing down some more chips.

An hour ago, a loud banging on my front door woke me up from my nap. Afraid it was a murderer on the other side, I'd stayed in bed and held on to my crutch for dear life, ready to use it as a weapon if necessary. But I was being too dramatic.

"Maddie! Open up! It's your favorite Sagittarius!" I'd recognized Beth's voice immediately, but I still wanted to kill her for the heart attack she'd almost given me. The only thing that

saved her was the wine—that I couldn't drink because of my medication—and the two bags of chips that I was absolutely going to devour.

Beth graduated with me, but she decided last minute that professional ballet wasn't her calling. She made a brave decision and rejected the life of castings and ballet companies, and she focused on teaching instead. She has a job at a local dance studio, which she loves, and I'm proud of her for having found her path.

I wish I could say the same about myself.

"Trust me on this one," she insists, a mischievous gleam in her eyes that red poison is responsible for. "I know exactly what we should do."

Why do I feel like this won't end well for me?

"We need to find you a hot date," she concludes.

And the reason Dr. Simmons's chiseled jaw flashes in my head at the mention of hot will forever remain earthed.

I point to my ankle with an exaggerated gesture. "This won't exactly help me meet anyone." Not that I want to in the first place.

"And that's what dating apps are for."

Oh, no. Please, no.

"Give me your phone."

I let out a nervous chuckle. "Are you kidding? I'm not going on a dating app, Beth. I don't want to get murdered."

"Pfft. You watch too many crime documentaries, Mads. People meet online all the time. There's a thing called 'sending your location to your friends' or even 'having your friends sit at a nearby table the whole time.' Kyle and I would totally go with you."

She's also a close friend of Kyle's, and I'm grateful she isn't taking any sides. Beth knows better than to stand in the middle of a fight, although *technically* we aren't even fighting. I'm just dumb.

And I'm also not sure Kyle would want to keep being my friend in the first place after this, but I don't say it out loud.

"That's not the point. What if he's a weirdo? Or a catfish? I don't want to waste my time with someone who may not even be real."

Beth lets out a deep breath, as if *I* were irritating *her*. That's a funny one. "Making a profile won't hurt. Plus, it will be fun. You could use some fun these days, Mads. There's this new app, Heart Swap, and it's blowing up for a reason."

"Isn't that a Pokémon thing?"

She slaps my arm. "Focus. What do you have to lose?"

Let's see—I lost my chance to follow my dream career, I injured my ankle, I just had a disastrous meeting with my mother two days ago... I guess Beth is right. What do I have to lose? More of my sanity? I don't have much to spare.

"Fine. Whatever." I give in, which makes her squeal with excitement. She reaches out her eager hand, and I give her my phone, which she knows the password to. "But you're doing all the work. I'm too tired to type."

"Oh, don't worry. I was already going to."

Her eagerness is contagious, and despite hating the whole online dating idea, I find myself invested in choosing my most flattering photos minutes later.

With Beth's help, I finally opt for three pictures—a casual, smiley one my brother took when I visited during Easter break this year, one in my ballet outfit, and another one with my late dog Rocket.

My brother and Grace adopted him from a shelter a year after I moved in with them, and he loved Lila and me with all his soul until he passed away. I miss him every day, but thinking of him doesn't hurt anymore. He lived a good, long life, and he'll always be part of our family.

Once we get my profile description ready with a bunch of my hobbies, I ask, "I'll see men of all ages here?"

She nods. "Yep. There's no age filter, which means you'll see everyone geographically close to you that is older than twenty-one

THE DARKEST CORNER OF THE HEART

because that's the minimum age to sign up. *Unfortunately.* Boys are dumb—you need a man. Someone who's like, thirty-five."

My eyebrows shoot up in surprise. "Thirty-five?" I'm not sure about seeing someone that much older. It feels forbidden, and it would give my brother an aneurysm if he found out.

But Beth only shrugs like it doesn't matter. Maybe it doesn't. "Why not? You're a responsible and mature woman. You know what you like and what you want to do with your life." That last part might not be entirely true, but I get what she's saying. "Your boundaries are healthy and firm. I really don't see the problem. Don't you want a man who also knows what he wants? I don't think college boys are for you."

Perhaps she has a point. I didn't date anyone while I was in college, although I've had a handful of hookups here and there. My only relationship was in my last year of high school, and while he was a sweet guy, I couldn't see myself with him long-term.

It's not like I'm looking for a husband or anything right now. I'm not even looking forward to any kind of date, but if I had to choose right now, I wouldn't want a boy. I'd want a man who has himself figured out. I refuse to endure a human-shaped headache, not even for a night.

"We'll see," I concede.

Maybe being with someone that much older would be too weird. I mean, Dr. Simmons must be around that age, and—

Don't think about him.

Yeah, I probably shouldn't.

It doesn't help that I'm nervous about our upcoming session tomorrow since it will be the first time we'll see each other after that weird encounter in the alley behind Monica's Pub. I bet he's ready to give me the lecture of a lifetime for not staying at home to rest my ankle.

Beth taps something else in and then says, "Oh my God! It's done!" She squeals and cuddles up next to me, passing me the phone. She points at the screen, where a profile that isn't mine has appeared. "You'll see the different men here, all within a few miles from your location. You can check their photos and bios, and if you like them, you have to swipe up. If you don't, swipe down."

Sounds simple enough. "What happens when I swipe up? Can I just...talk to them?"

"No, to chat with someone, they'll have to accept your invitation."

I think I get it now. "So it has to be mutual?"

Beth nods, and I redirect my focus to the screen, where a shirtless twenty-two-year-old Max stares right back at me. I swipe down at once, which makes my friend gasp. The dramatics.

"But he was so hot! And you didn't even look at the rest of his profile." She pouts.

"Any man who has a shirtless photo of themselves on their dating profile is a big no-no," I say. "I'm not looking for a random hookup."

"What are you looking for, then?"

Honestly? "I have no clue, but definitely not a one-night thing."

"Well, you may want to think about that for a second. Some guys could ask you."

"It wasn't even my idea to do this." I swipe down on yet another shirtless picture. It's concerning the amount of defined abs I've seen in the past minute alone. "But this is fun, I'll give you that."

"I knew it," she beams.

We spend the next five minutes swiping down, despite Beth's complaints.

"But he has the cutest dog!"

"What do you mean, he looks like a player? He's only wearing his cap backwards!"

"Okay, that was totally a mistake, Mads. When have you ever

seen an eight pack?"

"This is pointless," I say after minutes of mindless browsing. "These boys are clearly looking for something I'm not interested in."

"Fine, no packs of any number for you." Beth snatches my phone from my hands, and I let her be.

It was fun at first, but it's obvious that online dating isn't for me. Plus, I'm not entirely sure I'm as ready to get out there as Beth thinks I am. I'm too much of a mess, too much too lost. Dragging down an unsuspecting man with me wouldn't be fair.

"*Oh.* How about him?"

I'm not ready to see another arrogant smile or staged picture at a ski vacation, but when I turn my head, all blood drains from my face.

My palms start sweating, and my heart beats like a war drum.

"He's thirty-one, likes normal things like hiking, and... Aww, he wrote 'hanging out with my two cats' as one of his interests. Too bad there are no pictures of them. I bet they are so cute."

Yeah, no way this is happening right now.

No. Way.

"Should I swipe up?" Beth asks.

"No!" I snatch my phone right back, managing to keep my ankle in place by some miracle. I scan my screen with sharp focus to check that my eyes aren't playing sick tricks on me.

They aren't.

Oh, God, they aren't.

This is Dr. Simmons's—James's—profile.

He only uploaded two pictures, but he looks terribly handsome in both. I hate him so much.

He's hiking on some trail in the first one, his blue eyes covered by dark sunglasses. He's sporting a black T-shirt similar to the one I saw him wear the other night, and now I can take my time ogling his massive arms openly like the biggest creep in existence.

In the second picture, he's sitting at some kind of wooden bench in front of a small fireplace outside. It looks cozy. He's holding a bottle of beer in his hand and looks mildly annoyed at whoever is taking the picture.

He isn't smiling in either of them, but his attractiveness stands out, nonetheless. It must be that beard. It should be illegal for facial hair to fit a person so well.

"You're interested, aren't you?" Beth asks in a conspiratorial voice as she nudges my arm. "I think you should swipe up. He looks a bit grumpy, but it adds to the sexy."

I can't argue with her on that.

No, stop. He's your physical therapist. This is inappropriate. Go get some bleach for your eyes so you can unsee his dating profile.

Only...I can't. I'm physically incapable of not looking at it. He's listed some other interests in his profile, like hiking, being in nature, and going out to eat at various restaurants. And I've just confirmed his age too—thirty-one. That's a whole decade older than I am, and I don't know how it makes me feel. All I know is that it shouldn't send this stupid thrill down my spine.

"Why aren't you saying anything? Do you know him or something?" Beth asks, taking my phone again to get a closer look at the pictures as I internally curse myself at her question.

Because I'm mortified. Not because he has a profile on the dating app, but because he's been nothing short of professional with me, and I can't for the life of me stop staring at his pictures like I have a right to. Beth finding out about my confusing feelings for *my physical therapist* will only make things worse.

So even though I hate lying, I end up saying, "It's just that he's too old for me."

That's not it at all. Before today, I already suspected he had to be in his early thirties, and that didn't stop me from appreciating his attractiveness. Not once.

I'm such a mess.

"We've talked about this." Beth rolls her eyes. "I have a feeling, Mads. A strong one. If you don't swipe up, I will."

My heart does a cartwheel inside my chest. "You wouldn't dare—"

"Done."

My stomach drops to my feet. This can't be happening to me. "Tell me you're fucking joking."

Beth shows me the phone with a proud smile I intend to smack off her face right about now.

She isn't joking.

"I bet you're his type too," she muses out loud, oblivious to the hell she's just cast upon me. "He looks like he'd be a beast in bed. I want all the juicy deets if you go on a date with him."

I swallow, but my throat remains dry. "Is he going to get a notification that I swiped up?"

Don't say yes, don't say yes, don't say—

"Yes. He wouldn't get a notification if you swiped down, though. That'd be mean," she explains, but my brain is barely listening anymore.

I swiped up on Dr. Simmons on a dating app.

He's going to get a notification and see what Beth did.

I can't look at him on Monday.

I *can't.*

With no short amount of frustration, I come to terms with the fact that the shit show that is my life has just added a whole new season.

***

Like a total fool, I convinced myself all through Sunday that Monday morning would never come. That, by some strange miracle, all those articles about the world ending that never got the date right would suddenly become true and a huge asteroid would hit our planet, wiping me and that stupid dating app from existence.

But Monday morning does roll around, no catastrophic event kills me or my embarrassment, and I still swiped up on Dr. Simmons this weekend.

Technically, *I* didn't do anything, but it's not like that would make a difference. It's done.

I barely slept a wink last night, worrying about what he would say to me when I entered his office. Would he call me out? Or just ignore the whole fiasco? That would be the professional thing to do, right?

I swear the ride to the clinic feels faster today, and during the trip, I try to convince myself one more time that he probably didn't even see it. Many people get tired of dating apps and end up uninstalling them without actually deleting their profile. Their information is out there, and people keep swiping up and down on them, but they never find out because the app is no longer on their phones. That can happen, right? I'm too scared to google it.

Holding my crutches a little tighter this morning, I greet the lady at the front desk and make my way—very, very slowly—to his office. I don't care if I'm a couple of minutes late. I'm waiting to see if the ground decides to swallow me after all.

After the awkward dinner with my mom on Friday night, I thought my biggest concern come Monday would be the realization that we don't seem to be in a better place than we were last year. Or the year before, or the one before that. And even if my brother has always encouraged our mother-daughter relationship, I still feel the guilt eating up at my conscience for not telling him about our dinner. I tell Sammy *everything*, especially when it comes to our mom. It's just that... *Ugh.*

How do you tell your brother you might not want to see your mother again because she managed to make you feel like shit in under an hour?

When I returned to our table after my brief interaction with

Dr. Simmons—who was nowhere to be found at the bar—I told her I was tired and that I was going to call an Uber. She didn't object, and she didn't try to set up another dinner either. I can't say I'm disappointed.

What I wasn't expecting was *this* to be the cause of my anxiety. A huge mistake, a total disaster I don't know how I'll recover from—or if I ever will.

But I need to stay calm. I'm probably blowing things out of proportion.

At least that's what I tell myself until I step into his office and the air shifts.

Dr. Simmons, who I now know looks ridiculously handsome in casual clothes and has two cats, doesn't look at me differently or for longer than usual, which only manages to confuse me even further.

Am I imagining this? This...zapping electricity in the room?

Maybe it's just my nerves. I shouldn't listen to my judgment right now. It's poor, at best.

"Good morning," he greets me. Not enthusiastically, but that is to be expected. He types something on his computer and gestures to the exercise mat on the floor, not looking at me. "We'll begin shortly with some stretches."

If I thought our session would be awkward, I would be a hundred percent right.

I'm excruciatingly aware of every breath he takes, of the pressure of his fingers on my sensitive skin, of the tightness of his jaw every time he's about to ask me a question. As if acknowledging me is the last thing he wants to do.

And I don't die inside when he touches my back to correct my posture during one of the exercises. Of course not.

Dr. Simmons avoids my gaze as much as I avoid his, which only fuels my suspicion that he knows about the dating app fiasco. He's a man of few words on a normal day, and I don't expect him to bring it up at all. It's on the tip of my tongue to do it myself, because only fifteen minutes have gone by, and I can't stand this tension any longer.

Sure, what happened is mortifying and not my fault, really, but there's an itch inside me begging to be scratched by clearing the air. For hours I've been dreading facing him in today's session, and now I want to talk about it? I must've hit my head this morning when I woke up.

Halfway through the session, we move on to some strengthening exercises that involve him touching the back of my ankle, and for a second there, I think I might pass out. Seriously, I can't take this anymore.

More than anything, I want to apologize for crossing an invisible boundary and making him uncomfortable, even though, if we're getting technical, it was Beth who did it. But still, every time I picture his face after he read the notification, I want to puke.

There's only one small problem, one thing that makes me stop in my tracks. What if he really hasn't seen the notification? What if he doesn't use the app anymore and I make a fool of myself for nothing?

My headache heightens, and it only gets worse when he dismisses me half an hour later. "That'll be all for today."

I have seconds to make this decision. Pressure never gets to me onstage, but when it comes to dealing with daily situations, dealing with normal people and saying actual words, let's just say I could use a lesson or two in self-control.

And so, I blame my lack of proper training for my next words. "I'm so sorry."

Slowly, too slowly, he turns his head. His eyes pin me in place, and I have to swallow past the sudden lump in my throat.

Well, I guess I'm doing this.

Mustering all the courage my dread has left behind, I let it all out. For better or for worse, here it comes.

"About the dating app." I swallow again because the ice-cold look he's giving me right now could freeze an entire continent. It's definitely frozen my sparse confidence. "I... A friend swiped up, and I'm sorry if it made you uncomfortable. I would've undone it if I'd known how. I'm sorry, again." I'm rambling. I know I'm rambling. Oh, God, this is bad. "We were just joking around. I didn't mean anything by it. It wasn't like...a serious thing or anything. But I'm sorry anyway."

A second goes by.

Five.

Ten.

And finally, *finally*, Dr. Simmons blinks.

Are his cheeks flushed?

"It's fine," he says, shattering my world with just a few words. *It's fine.*

That means he saw the notification. That means he uses the app. The dating app.

That also has to mean he's single, right? Unless he's an asshole, but I don't peg him as one.

And why am I focusing on his love life right now when I should be putting all my efforts into getting a new identity and fleeing this country?

"I'm very sorry," I insist.

At this point, I'm not sure what else to say. Maybe I shouldn't have brought it up at all.

Dr. Simmons lowers himself down into his rolling chair, types something on his computer, and takes his sweet, sweet time responding. "You're good."

"My...my friend swiped up on you." I feel the need to clarify once again. It's very important that he knows this, I decide. "We were just playing around. I didn't even want to sign up or anything."

And now it sounds like a lame excuse. I can never win, can I?

I hate everything.

"So why did you?" he surprises me by asking.

I shrug, even though he's not looking at me. Holding my crutches, I answer as I walk up to his small desk, "My friend said I could use some fun." Which is sad to say out loud, now that I think about it. "I just didn't know *that* was her idea of fun. It really wasn't. Fun, I mean."

He grunts—was that a grunt?—under his breath and adds nothing else. *Okay, then.*

Before he inevitably dismisses me, my eyes dart to the small pile of books on his desk. Most volumes have boring titles with words such as "physiology" and "fibromyalgia," which I'm sure are fascinating for the professionals in the field, but they don't catch my attention.

However, that one mandala coloring book sure does.

"I didn't know you liked mandalas," I blurt out in a hopeless attempt at changing the topic.

It doesn't work.

"Why would you? I didn't put that information on my dating profile."

What. The. Hell.

"Relax." He eyes me carefully from behind his glasses. "I'm just messing with you."

Him? Messing with *me*?

I clear my throat, unsure of what to say now. Luckily, he makes that choice for me. "I'll see you tomorrow. Your ankle is recovering as expected, so keep resting."

I don't know if that's a jab or not. After all, he knows I haven't been properly resting my ankle. He saw me at Monica's Pub, which neither of us seems to want to bring up for whatever reason. Works for me—I've suffered enough embarrassment to last me a whole decade.

But I still ask, "Are you sure it's fine? I'm really sorry if I crossed any boundaries."

His deep voice sounds serious—and tired—when he says, "Miss Stevens, it's okay. Stop apologizing."

I swallow. "All right. Well, I... I'll see you tomorrow." I give him a small smile and turn around, heading for the exit.

I'm pretty sure my mind is playing cruel tricks on me, because I swear I feel his scorching stare on my back the whole time.

chapter 8

JAMES

Fuck.

How did I get myself into this mess?

All throughout my Monday appointments, I can't get it out of my head. It's engraved in the deepest cavities of my brain, lurking, waiting for the most inconvenient time to make its presence known again.

There's only one person to blame for this fiasco, and that would be me.

I had to mess something else up.

I believed her when she told me she hadn't done anything on the app. Something in her voice, usually so firm and confident yet so meek then, told me it was true. But her explanation and the apology she didn't owe me haven't made this uncomfortable feeling go away.

They don't erase the fact that my nerves came close to combusting when I received the notification on my phone a few nights ago.

And that, in itself, is a damn big problem.

To think that this situation could've been avoided in the first place, if I hadn't been so careless, is what grinds my gears. Graham, my closest friend, forced me to sign up for the dating site a month ago under the premise that I was, and I quote, "a lonely and grouchy motherfucker," and I needed to "fix that shit with a good fuck." He might have been right, but that's not the point.

I admit I have used the app once before, shortly after he set up my profile. I'd been getting notifications of swipe ups here and there, and I'd always let them get lost among the dozens of notifications I get every day, but that one day my judgment slipped through the cracks.

I didn't like how looking at all those requests made me feel—like a piece of meat on display. I should've deleted the app, I know, but then one of my patients came in for their appointment, and I forgot about it.

Until that day.

"Cat's got your tongue or what?"

I take another sip of my drink, not even bothering to answer. Graham has been around long enough to recognize my moods and not give a crap about them. But I've also been around long enough to know my friend never lets things go.

He mimics me, taking another sip of his beer, and nudges my arm. "What's eating at you now?"

I down the remains of my bourbon and ask for a glass of water. This is only the second time I've been to Monica's Pub, but apparently, it's the perfect place to grab a low-key drink without being disturbed by the corporate America assholes in the city. And Graham swears by it. It's dark, moderately quiet, and nobody looks at you when you walk in, so it works for me.

"I'm fine." The words taste like a sour lie, and they remind me of her excuses. She didn't *zone out*. She had a panic attack, and I don't take that shit lightly. I know sadness when I see it, and the sight of that raw pain in her eyes still haunts me.

It shouldn't.

"Nah, you're not." My best friend watches me closely, trying to decipher everything I'm not saying out loud and never will. "You talked to your brother yet?"

I take a sip the second the waitress places the water in front of me. "No, and I'm not going to."

"James—"

"I don't wanna hear it."

"I'm just saying—"

I set the glass on the table with a little more force than usual. "Fuck, Graham. Drop it."

He knows better, so he does. I let out a frustrated breath, running my hand through the beard I know I need to trim soon. "Sorry. I didn't mean to snap at you, man."

"No, I'm sorry I brought it up," Graham mutters before bringing his beer to his lips.

I shake my head. "It's okay." It's not the first time he's had to put up with my asshole ways, and it won't be the last. To be fair, I've also been putting up with his shit since college, so we're pretty much even.

"Want to order some nachos, or are you good to go?" he asks, back to his nonchalant self. Graham is a computer engineer at a top-notch firm downtown and, just like me, not the biggest extrovert. But his wife, Sarah, is working the night shift at the hospital tonight, and he didn't want to be alone. As for me, I needed to unwind. *Badly.*

"Darling! Oh, look at you! How are you feeling?" the waitress that was just in front of us exclaims out of nowhere, her big eyes glued to someone behind us. "We miss you."

A prickle of awareness jolts through me and settles in the pit of my stomach, and I know. I just do.

Now it makes sense why I found her at the back alley of the bar the last time I was there. Why she went to what I'd assumed was an employees-only area. "*We miss you*" must mean she's part of the staff. Or used to be.

"I'm not doing too bad." Her voice drifts over to me, and my ears start ringing.

"Oh, honey, you didn't have to come. You should be resting at home," the waitress adds, and I couldn't agree more. What the hell is she doing here?

It takes all my willpower and then some to stay right where I'm at and not turn my head.

"I was craving one of Matt's burgers," she says, her voice sounding much lighter and full of life than I've ever heard it. Sure, we've only had a handful of sessions together, but this is a contrast to the girl I see at the clinic—a girl with a permanent cloud above her head who now sounds like the sun is shining just for her. "And I needed to get out of the house."

"Maddie, your ankle..."

Yeah, exactly.

"Don't worry about it, Monica. I took an Uber here, and it doesn't hurt much."

That *much* hits me right in the gut. Because what does that even mean? I've treated injured dancers before, and I know they're used to pain, but is that hurt at a one or at an eight?

I hear a heavy sigh behind me. "Fine. Come on in, then. I'll get your order in a minute." My muscles tighten with tension as I hear the unmistakable sound of her crutches drawing closer.

"James?" Graham nudges my arm. "You in there?"

I blink. "Yeah, what's up?"

"I asked if you wanted to call it a night."

Five minutes ago, I wouldn't have hesitated. I've had a bad day, a bad week really, and I almost didn't accept his invitation to come here in the first place. Now, however, I don't think it would hurt if Shadow and Mist were alone for another hour.

"I don't want to go home yet," I tell him, a weird feeling settling in the pit of my stomach. "Let's grab something quick to eat."

"Fuck, yeah," he beams. He flags down the waitress—Monica, apparently—and asks her for a basket of nachos and another beer.

While he's distracted, I steal a quick look at Maddie. She's sitting by herself in one of the booths on the other side of the bar, her back turned to me. That gives me a chance to scold myself for even paying her any attention in the first place.

It would serve me well to remember that, outside of the clinic, what she does or doesn't do is none of my business.

But as Graham goes on to tell me something that happened at work this week, something he's texted me about already, my mind drifts off to a few days ago.

I'd just gotten out of the shower to clean off the sweat from my workout when my phone lit up with a single notification. Only one, which was strange because I have this annoying habit of not deleting any app I download, ever.

"Maddie has just swiped up on you!"

Maddie is a common enough name to not have her face pop into my head as I read the notification. And yet.

I remember how I stood there with nothing but a white towel wrapped around my waist, staring at the dark screen on my bedside table, and hearing nothing but that one organ hammering inside my rib cage.

It had to be a joke.

After leaving a small puddle of water under my feet on my hardwood floor, I mustered the courage to unlock my phone and look the unfunniest joke in the history of the universe in the eye.

I didn't look at her profile beyond the first picture. I didn't scroll left, right, or in any other direction. I didn't read her profile description. I only allowed myself to look at that twenty-one for a second.

Her age is no secret to me, but the reminder did me good.

"All right, man, what is going on?" Graham's question pulls me back into the present moment. When I look at him, he's frowning.

"I don't know what you mean."

"You're scowling."

"Your point? I always scowl."

"Not like this, you don't." My friend scans my eyes as if he were looking for something. Something he's not going to find, if I have any say in it. "You're distracted, so what is it?"

"I'm not distracted," I lie.

"Like fuck you're not. I know you like a brother, James, so tell me what's up."

Graham is a persistent motherfucker if I've ever met one, and after years of friendship, I know there are certain things I can't get away with. One of them is lying to him when he can read me like an open book.

"Forget it," I try one more time.

"Ah, so *something* is bothering you," he says with a smirk. "I knew it. Just tell me, man. I'm gonna find out anyway."

"Doubt it," I mutter.

I love Graham, and this isn't about him or anybody else but me and my fucked-up head.

"Whatever. Just trying to help." He shrugs as he eats the last couple of nachos in the basket. "Ready to go?"

I can tell he's pissed, but what am I supposed to do? Tell him my twenty-one-year-old patient is here when she's supposed to be resting at home, and all I want to do is go up to her and ask her to stop being so careless? That I can't stop staring at her for some goddamn reason? Yeah, fat chance of that.

Her burger comes, and the waitress, Monica, takes the seat in front of her to keep her company. Then our nachos are gone, our drinks are gone, and Graham's already taking care of the tab. He wants to go home, and I should too. I fucking should.

As I make my way to my car, I remind myself she isn't my problem outside of the clinic.

I remind myself I probably crossed some kind of boundary when I went outside to check on her the other day, for reasons I don't even want to think about.

I tell myself that time and again, but I end up waiting in my

car for an hour until she exits the bar anyway.
I only drive away after her Uber does.

chapter 9

JAMES

Unknown: We need to talk

Two minutes after Shadow wakes me up, meowing for breakfast as if I haven't fed him in years, my day is already ruined. Because of course it is.

I barely slept a wink last night, my mind fixed on the fact that I should stop going to Monica's Pub with Graham if I don't want to lose what little I've got left of my sanity.

There was no need for me to stay in the car for an hour after I parted ways with Graham. I could've argued I was just waiting for my alcohol levels to come down, but I'd only had one drink and I wasn't drunk—not at all, or I wouldn't have gotten in the car in the first place.

Twenty-one. She's twenty-one and your goddamn patient.

It's Mist meowing next that gets me out of my head this time, and I reluctantly start getting ready for the day.

That text haunts me at the gym, in the shower, and on my way to work, but I'm keen on leaving it unanswered. Just like the other seven he's sent me.

He can go to hell for all I care.

I greet Barbara at the front desk as I sign in, and I manage to keep my shit together during my session with Maddie, but only because she barely speaks a word. Long gone is the bubbly girl I overheard last night at the bar, and it's none of my business where she's disappeared to.

Despite her outings to the bar, her ankle looks good. Everything tells me she's been resting, and at the end of our session I let her know as much. "Recovery is going as expected." I make a point to keep my voice as flat as possible. "You should be able to take short trips in moderation, but avoid stairs."

I catch her nodding in the corner of my eye. She hesitates, moving closer to where I'm sitting. I keep my gaze trained on my computer screen. There's nothing there but a spreadsheet I opened on accident and don't need to check right now at all.

"I..." she starts before clearing her throat. She tries again, and I don't like how small her voice sounds. How meek. "I wanted to apologize."

That photo of her bright smile I refused to look at for more than two seconds on her dating profile makes my hands start sweating. "You're good."

"I know. That's not... That's not what I want to apologize for. This time."

Slowly, I turn to look at her, curious as to what this apology she doesn't owe me could be about. "What is it?" I ask, not because I'm particularly interested but because I can tell she needs a push.

Indeed, she doesn't hesitate. "That night we saw each other at Monica's Pub. I wanted to apologize for not following your instructions. I should've stayed at home." She's doing this. All right. "I was... I was scared going out would set me back on my recovery."

Something akin to a grunt escapes the back of my throat. "Your ankle is fine."

She stays silent for a few seconds, and I lock my eyes on the spreadsheet again. I get where she's coming from. She's scared her carelessness might have cost her the recovery she so desperately needs.

I've been there. I recognize that darkness a little too well.

"I wanted to apologize anyway."

"Okay."

But she still doesn't leave. Maddie stays rooted into place for a few more moments until she reaches into her tote bag and gets something crinkly out of it. "Here."

I look at her again. At her extended hand, and the piece of paper she's holding in my direction. At the... *Wait.*

"This is for you." Her voice comes out shy, unsure, and the shaking of her fingers is almost imperceptible. But I see it. "It's silly, but... I've been apologizing to you way too often, and I thought you'd forgive me faster if I gave you this."

It's—

It's a mandala.

She's giving me a mandala.

I didn't know you liked mandalas.

She noticed the coloring book the other day, didn't she? And thought it would be a good idea to make me one?

Fucking hell.

"Did you draw this yourself?" I manage to ask. "By hand?"

Something warm and *wrong* stirs inside my gut. Heat climbs up my neck, and I know I'm blushing like a damn schoolboy.

"Yeah." She releases her grip on the drawing, and I place it on my desk, unable to look away from it. "My brother is a tattoo artist, and I've always practiced my drawing skills with him. I sketch when I'm stressed, and I thought... Well, thinking of apologizing again was kind of stressing me out, so I made this for you."

Speechless. I'm speechless.

"I should've stayed at home," she continues. "But my mom called and... Well, it was important that I met with her. I don't see her much. I also went to the bar the other day because I wanted a burger and some fresh air, but I took a car, so I barely walked.

I used to work there, too, and my boss is like a friend to me, so I wanted to see her."

I can't even find it within myself to mask the relief I feel that she didn't spot me last night. If she knew I'd waited until she got into her ride safely, we would be having a very different, very awkward conversation right now.

I also make a point to ignore the comment about her not seeing her mother much. The less I know about Maddie—*Miss Stevens*—the better.

The mandala is the safest thing I can focus on right now. It's made of a circle with some kind of flower in the middle, and if I didn't know she'd made it by hand, I would've mistaken it for one of the mandalas of my many books—it's that stunning.

"Your brother is the man who came with you on your first appointment?"

"Yes," she confirms. "He's the tattoo artist."

"You've never considered following in his footsteps?"

I don't know why I'm asking. It's not like I care. I don't want to get to know her better. She's my patient, my decade-younger patient, and there are boundaries I'd never cross. Unnecessary kinship with a patient is one of them.

"Oh, no way," she says with a chuckle. The sound makes me look up at her, at that small tilt of her lips. "I'm not that good. I've always preferred ballet, anyway." Her smile falters at that last sentence, and I remind myself I'm here to take care of her physical injuries, and that's it.

"Thank you for the mandala," I say as a form of dismissal. My next patient will be here any minute, but even if they weren't, chatting with her isn't a good idea. "I'll see you tomorrow."

I can tell my sudden brush-off has taken her aback, but she doesn't miss a beat as she flashes me a bright smile that isn't totally genuine. I only stare at her in response.

"Sure, yeah. See you, Doc."

Doc. That's a new one.

An eternity passes before the door clicks shut behind her, and only when the ticking clock on the wall is the sole sound in my office, do I allow myself to run a hand over my tired face.

Her mandala stares at me from my desk, daring me. On a whim, I shove it inside my backpack and refuse to think about it for the rest of the day.

***

MADDIE

I order an Uber after my appointment with Dr. Stick-Up-His-Ass.

He's earned that one.

Maybe it's the mortification I felt when giving him the mandala, or maybe it was how quickly he dismissed me and the realization that hit me right afterward—we aren't friends.

I thought I saw a blush on his cheeks when he saw my drawing, but with his dark stubble... The more I think about it, the less sure I am. I wouldn't be surprised if I made him uncomfortable, so I tell myself this is going to stop. I tried, and he seemed to appreciate the mandala, kind of, but that's it. No more gifts for him. No more friendly attitude toward him, no matter if it goes against my instincts.

The driver stops in front of The Norcastle Ballet twenty minutes later, and it dawns on me that I don't know what I'm doing.

Why did I put in this address? Why didn't I just go home?

I shut the car door once I'm safely holding my crutches on the sidewalk and watch as the Uber speeds away.

Breathing in through my nose, I dare to take in the building where all my dreams were meant to come true. I was supposed to come here for my audition and hopefully to work later.

Kyle got accepted.

Beth told me last night, and I couldn't be prouder of him.

Of course he made it, because he's the best, and I knew this place was for him. I knew they would see the star he turns into whenever he dances.

The most mature and compassionate part of me knows I need to speak to him. I really do. He isn't to blame for my childlike behavior. I need to get it together and give him the apology he deserves.

I think of texting him for about five seconds before I decide to be honest with myself—I'm not ready, not yet. He's been nothing but an amazing friend to me for years, and it isn't his fault that he got accepted into TNB and I didn't. It's not his fault, damn it.

So why does it hurt so much to think about talking to him? Hearing him tell me how incredible it is to be living his dream? A dream we shared and now only one of us gets to experience.

My eyes zero in on a nearby sandwich shop, and my stomach growls in response. Okay, then, eating I can do. Plus, Dr. Simmons said I could take short trips and it wouldn't affect my recovery, so I feel a little less guilty as I, once again, do everything but rest.

Ten minutes later, I'm sitting at a nearby park, munching on a tuna sandwich. The neoclassical-style building of The Norcastle Ballet looms in the distance, but not too far away I can't see it, reminding me of the contrast of where I should be, versus where I actually am.

When the questions about my blurry future start piling up and the guilt and the anxiety make it impossible to breathe, I take my phone out of my bag and dial a number I should've called days ago.

"Yes, sweetheart?"

Grace's voice calms me down at once. Aside from being my ex-ballet teacher, my brother's wife is one of the people I love the most in this world.

She's my go-to person to talk about my issues, and I feel calm knowing she always has an answer. But then I remember why I called her in the first place, and my nerves skyrocket once more.

"I had dinner with my mom on the weekend," I blurt out.

Silence greets me from the other line.

"Okay," my sister-in-law says after a moment. A sister-in-law who feels more like a mother than my actual mother does. "I'm guessing you haven't told Cal."

She calls my brother Cal, not Sammy. His name is Samuel Callaghan, but everyone calls him Cal except for me. I guess Sammy just stuck when I was little because I found the name funny, and I don't feel like changing it now.

I swallow. "No."

"Okay," she repeats in that soothing voice I've missed so much. I know what she's not saying, though—that my brother will be upset I've kept this from him. "What did you talk about?"

And so, I tell her. About David, or Dave, or whatever his name is. About how she's suddenly worried for my safety, how she frowned upon my job as if she had any right to. About how she'd made a face when I told her Sammy paid for my living expenses in Norcastle.

I let it all out in the same breath, afraid I'll lose momentum if I stop, while she listens and doesn't interrupt me once.

When I'm done, the last thing I expect Grace to do is to let out a deep, almost frustrated sigh. "Your mom..." she starts, but she seems to hesitate. "Your mom has been through a lot, but it's not an excuse. You don't deserve this weight on your shoulders, Maddie."

I look up at the midday sun, hoping the light will keep my tears right where they are. Not rolling down my cheeks, basically.

"I'm not sure I want to see her again," I mutter under my breath, shame coating every word. This is my mom, damn it. I shouldn't be feeling like this. "For... For now," I add to convince myself that I'm not a monster. Not fully. Not like *she* insinuated I was.

"You don't have to," Grace assures me in that firm voice she uses when Lila refuses to eat her broccoli. And as if she's just read my mind, she says, "Listen to me, Maddie. I don't care that she's your mom, that she's family—if you don't feel comfortable around her anymore, you don't have to see her. For now, or ever again. You're an adult now. You're the only one who can make that decision."

I let out a shaky breath I'm very aware I've been holding but my body wouldn't allow me to release. "Thank you."

"You don't have to thank me, sweetheart. I won't be upset if you decide to cut her off, and your brother won't either."

I'm not so sure about that. "But he..." I squeeze my eyes shut. Damn it, these tears are not coming out. "He tried so hard to keep the peace. He—"

"He tried, but your mother didn't, and there's nothing you or he can do about that." She cuts me off, her words freezing me in place. *Your mother didn't.* "She made her own bed, and now she has to lie in it. If you don't want to see her again, she shouldn't blame anyone but herself. Not your brother, and definitely not you."

Grace has always been the voice of reason in our family. While Sammy gives great advice, sometimes his overprotectiveness gets the best of him. This doesn't happen with my sister-in-law. If you mess up, she'll tell you. And if something isn't your fault, she'll work her way through your thick skull until you see it too. That's what she's doing to me right now, and I know she's right, but...

"But she's my mother," I mutter, because at the end of the day, it all comes down to that undeniable fact. No matter how much she deserves less effort from me, there's a small part of my heart that withers just thinking about how selfish I'm being. She might not be the person I need, but my mom tried. I saw it in the way she'd take me out for pancakes on weekends or to the mall after my ballet lessons, even after I'd already moved in with Sammy and Grace. She wouldn't have bothered if she didn't care about me. "I know she loves me."

"That's not enough," she tells me softly, as if she is afraid her words will break me. I'm not completely confident that they won't. "Sometimes love isn't enough. Sometimes people have to *show* you that you matter, and you do. You matter to all of us, Maddie. Don't ever forget it."

I gulp, tears now running freely down my cheeks. "I won't." I quickly wipe them away with my sleeve. "Thanks, Grace. I'm just... I'm not having the best week, I guess."

"Did something else happen?" she asks, concerned.

I hesitate. "No."

Very much like my brother, his wife doesn't buy my lies either. "I can tell something is up," she insists. "Are you going to tell me, or do I have to guess?"

Her teasing brings a smile to my face. "Take a wild guess."

"Mm." She pretends to think about it. "I think I got it."

"Doubt it," I say, still smiling through the remaining tears.

"Does it have to do with a guy?"

After so many years of knowing Grace, I'm still convinced she has some kind of weird psychic powers.

"Kinda," I admit, hearing her chuckle in the background. "It's weird. It's not that I like him or anything—"

"Sure."

My heartbeat picks up. "Beth and I did something stupid, and now it's awkward between this guy and me. I don't think he likes me very much anyway, so yeah."

"First of all, who wouldn't like you? You're a gem. And secondly, am I allowed to know what that stupid thing is all about? Or is it too humiliating?"

"It's definitely humiliating." I sigh, scooting back on the wooden bench. The sun hits my face, and I close my eyes, letting the heat dry the tears on my skin. "Beth thought I needed to dip a toe into the dating pool, and somehow she convinced me to set up a dating profile on some app. Long story short, I swiped up on someone I know, and now it's awkward between us."

There's no way I'm telling her this "guy" is my physical therapist. Over my dead body.

Grace, the traitor, full-on laughs. "Yeah, that's pretty horrifying."

"Thanks," I deadpan.

"Oh, Mads, you know I'm just joking," she says, and I can still hear the remains of her laugh. "Did you talk to him about it?"

"I apologized for swiping up because, well, it wasn't even me who did it," I explain. "He said it's fine, but I don't know."

"If he says it's fine, then it must be. Is he acting normal around you?"

If normal means grouchy, then... "Yes."

"There you have it. All's good, then."

I snort. "Love your positivity, Gracie. I needed it today."

Her voice softens. "You can call me anytime, sweetheart. I promise I won't tell your brother about the dating app fiasco."

Phew. I love Sammy, but he can be an overprotective papa-slash-brother-bear sometimes. Who am I kidding? *All the time.*

Deciding to change topics for my sanity's sake, I ask her, "How's the new book coming along?"

When I first began therapy as a kid to cope with my parents' abandonment, I wouldn't open up. I couldn't understand my own feelings, lost in the loud voices in my head. Because even though I'd always loved my brother, going from living with my parents to moving in with him permanently was confusing for a four-year-old.

Until my therapist tried a new approach.

It was through books, and characters that were dealing with the same issues as me, that I finally started healing. There was one story in particular, a story about a little fox who went to live with his older sister in the forest after her parents left on a very long hunting trip, which helped me come to terms with my new reality.

"It's going well," she tells me. "My deadline ends in two weeks and I'm running on caffeine and little hours of sleep, but I can't complain."

As my progress in therapy moved along, Grace took her career as a children's author to the next level. She teamed up with several therapists specializing in bibliotherapy to write self-help books for children and young adults.

We have a whole collection of her books at home, all of which Lila knows like the back of her hand. From consent to fear to adoption, Grace has written about many difficult topics in a way that children and teens can understand and relate to.

To put it simply, Grace is a true angel on Earth.

I smirk. "Please tell me you have Sammy on coffee duty."

"Coffee, laundry, groceries, dishes..." she lists before letting out a happy sigh. "I don't think I could do it without him, if I'm being honest."

"Husband of the Year," I tease, knowing if that was a real award, he'd win it every year. My brother is too good for this world, and I'm happy he ended up with a woman who deserves him as much as he deserves her. "We'll video chat over the weekend, yeah?"

"Of course. Take care of that ankle. I love you."

"I love you. Tell Lila I love her too."

"She's at school now, but I'll tell her when she gets back."

I smile, picturing my niece's sparkling eyes when her mom tells her she talked to me today. I miss her the most, that pip-squeak. "All right, I love you all."

"We love you too, Maddie."

When I hang up, a new resolve settles in my bones. Maybe Grace is right. Maybe love isn't enough, not if that's all there is to the feeling.

When people don't go out of their way to show you that you matter to them, is it really love? Or just an empty word?

And am I really showing Kyle that I love him, that I appreciate him as a friend when I can't swallow my own pain and apologize?

I gather all my trash to throw it away and hold my crutches tightly as I make my way out of the park. I need to talk to Kyle, and I refuse to let this situation go any further.

Getting my phone out of my bag, I scroll down his unanswered texts, feeling like shit for ignoring him, and type him a response that is long overdue.

> **Me: Hey, Ky. I'm sorry for the radio silence. I understand if you hate me, but if you don't, I'd love to invite you over for pizza tonight at my place so we can talk. Let me know.**

He doesn't reply right away, but I don't let it bother me. I went days without acknowledging his existence, so it's only fair.

Now that short trips are allowed, perhaps I could talk to Monica about taking a couple of shifts again. I could stay in the kitchen and wash the dishes, no problem, and use the money to stop living off my brother again. It won't be much, but at least I'll have a reason to get out of my studio.

A new, light feeling bubbles in my chest, and for the first time since my injury, I feel somewhat optimistic, despite the uncertainty.

But as I turn to head for the taxi stop, a prickling sensation travels up my spine, and I stiffen.

A sudden urge to run away invades all my senses, and I know.

Call it intuition, a sixth sense, but I just know.

Somebody's watching me.

The park is crowded with men and women dressed in suits, out on their lunch breaks, so I don't feel particularly threatened. A busy road is right there, and so are multiple shops and buildings. Nothing is going to happen to me here, yet I can't help but feel that something is very, very wrong.

Not with me, but *around* me.

As discreetly as I can manage, I scan each and every one of the faces I see. There are too many people walking around, most of them in a rush, to tell much of anything.

I don't make eye contact with anyone, and nobody is blatantly staring at me, but I want to get out of here. *Fast.*

Luck is on my side as I spot an empty taxi right away. I rattle off my address to the driver and don't peel my eyes off that park until we drive away.

Someone was watching me. I'm sure of it.

chapter 10

MADDIE

When I texted Kyle earlier today, I didn't expect him to answer. Well, that's a lie—I knew he would reply because he's a ray of sunshine, but I didn't expect him to accept my invitation. In a way, I wasn't ready.

And maybe that's why I now find myself with fidgeting fingers resting on my lap as Kyle and I stare at the pizza box that got here five minutes ago. I still haven't said a word, and neither has he.

Not awkward at all.

Silence consumes my apartment until, finally, I gather the little dignity I have left and say what I've been meaning to tell him for weeks now. "I'm really sorry, Kyle. I didn't mean to go MIA."

Then Kyle does something I did *not* see coming. Not in a million years.

He smiles.

Just a tiny one, but it's there.

"It's okay," he says, one hand reaching for the pizza box and opening the lid. The delicious smell of cheese and pepperoni blinds all my senses and gives me that small dose of serotonin I've been lacking. Or maybe it's his forgiveness. "How's recovery going?"

"My recovery?"

"Yeah." He takes a big bite of pizza and speaks with his mouth full. "Are you seeing any progress yet?"

Why isn't he calling me out for ignoring him for the past few weeks? Why isn't he telling me I'm a horrible friend and he never wants to see me again? That's what I'd deserve.

"It's going well." My words are laced with skepticism. Surely he'll go off in just a moment. It's coming. "How's...work?"

I hate myself for not being able to say *The Norcastle Ballet* out loud, but I almost had a mental breakdown earlier from just looking at the building, so there's that. Kyle, however, scans my eyes like he knows the truth I'm hiding behind them.

"Maddie," he starts, and I already know I'm not going to like how this ends. I blow out a breath as I dump the pizza slice I've just grabbed back in the box. I don't have an appetite anymore. "I understand how you're feeling. I promise I do."

We're doing this.

"We shared that dream, and then you got injured and lost the chance to prove yourself. I'm so sorry it happened, Maddie. I'm so incredibly sorry you're going through this, but..."

"But I've been a shit friend," I deadpan. There's no heat in my voice, not even frustration at this point.

I'm the worst—plain and simple. The notion that I hurt my friend, one of my best friends, because I was selfish enough to let my injury blind me is something I will never forgive myself for.

"No, you haven't," he says firmly, but I don't believe him. And because he must see that in my eyes, he adds, "I knew you'd come around eventually, and I knew you'd realize this wasn't the way to act, and that's all that matters. I'm not mad at you, and I don't think you're a terrible person, Maddie. Not at all. I just think you were hurt in more ways than one and didn't know how to handle it well. Everyone deserves a second chance."

"I'm so sorry" is all I can say, even though words could never be enough for the pain I must have caused him.

He shakes his head and takes another bite, as if me ignoring him for weeks wasn't that big of a deal. "People go through things. I get it. Just promise me next time you'll talk to me instead of going

MIA."

"I promise." And I mean it. He's giving me a second chance, and I'm going to make it count, even if I don't think I deserve it. "It wasn't about you, Kyle. I promise it wasn't. I'm so proud of you. You're a star, and I can't wait to see you shine on that stage."

He smiles at that, genuine and warm. "Thank you, Mads. You'll get your chance to do the same sooner than you think. You'll be back onstage before the year ends, I'm sure of it."

I shrug, not really feeling like raining on his parade. We both know if you miss an audition for TNB, that's it. You're out.

I'm never going to be his dance partner again, but I'll be cheering him on from the audience. That's for sure.

He drops all conversations about ballet and my injury after that, and it's not until he starts talking about a disastrous blind date he went on over the weekend, that I realize something. Something major, and probably something I should've worked out a long time ago.

I'm tired of feeling sorry for myself. Of being a downer, of telling myself my future is over just because I missed an audition.

If Kyle hadn't been such a compassionate angel, I would've lost one of my closest friends because I got blinded by my own darkness. I didn't even try to fight back the intrusive thoughts, and that's what kills me inside. Because I'm not a quitter. I'm not one to run away when things get tough. Sammy and Grace raised me to shine, yet I'm dimming my own light.

Kyle is right—I'm not handling the aftermath of my injury well. At all. I'm not doing myself or my loved ones any favors by making this cloud over my head even heavier. Because, when it finally pours down on me, I'll drown.

Sure, my current situation is far from ideal, and I'm allowed to mourn a future that isn't in the cards for me anymore, but I still have options.

When I recover in four weeks, I can go back to dancing.

Maybe I'll get into a master's program and find a new path. And if not, I can always turn to teaching jobs like Grace suggested.

My life isn't over, damn it. I refuse to wither away when I'm only twenty-one, and I still have so much about the world and about myself to discover.

I don't want to be pitied; I just want my heart to be calm. And the first step to achieve that is to come to terms with the fact that my present doesn't look like I envisioned it, but it doesn't mean it has to be terrible.

I refuse to keep living in the past.

***

"Again," his deep voice says. A commanding rumble I'm so used to by now. "Good. Again."

I let out a shaky, tired breath as I follow his commands. Turns out Dr. Simmons, my ankle, and resistance bands aren't a good combination. Who knew?

It doesn't matter that I've been focusing on this particular exercise for ten minutes, on the way my toes bend when I move my foot backward again and again. Today, for some reason, I can't keep my mind pinned in place. And so it drifts.

Not only is it returning to my missed audition—the traitor—but now it also makes sure I don't forget about the whole I'm-pretty-sure-someone's-watching-me moment at the park. For my own sake though, I pretend it's all in my head. I think I've watched too many crime shows.

But hey, it can't rain every day. Because after much begging and assuring Monica that Dr. Grouchy had given me the thumbs-up—he hasn't—I finally convinced her to let me take a few shifts at the bar.

I can't wait tables for obvious reasons, but she liked the idea of me washing the dishes while sitting on a stool well enough to allow me to do it three times a week. It isn't much, but it's far better than sitting at home.

"That's it. Once more."

I'm momentarily distracted by the warmth of his touch dripping into my skin as he guides my ankle the way he wants to. He isn't looking at me, doesn't seem to share this weird ache in my chest that expands every time his skin grazes mine, and it's easy to get consumed by the voices in my head again.

I thought getting my job back at Monica's would help get my life back on track, but so far it has done nothing but remind me of how stuck I am.

I try to stay positive; I really do. But it's difficult to keep going when the pressure of doing something with my life weighs down on my shoulders every single day, during every waking moment—I don't have a plan, and it's driving me a little crazy.

Nope. Stop feeling sorry for yourself. We don't do that anymore.

"Again," Dr. Simmons instructs.

He must notice my head isn't into it today, because I swear he growls under his breath right before the warm weight of his hand settles between my shoulders. His gentle touch is a contrast to his mean scowl. "Keep your back straight."

The shiver that has just traveled down my spine has nothing to do with the sound of that deep baritone caressing my ear. Absolutely nothing.

I tell myself his hand doesn't linger on my back for a bit longer than necessary, that I'm just imagining things because I'm delusional.

When he takes a step back, watching my ankle from a safe distance again, my head goes back to its favorite pastime—overthinking.

Sure, I can't exactly move normally, but my head is still on my shoulders, working at its full capacity. I could come up with a step-by-step plan.

Maybe my immediate future doesn't include The Norcastle

Ballet, but it can include...something else.

"Well done. That should be all for today."

Dr. Simmons's voice brings me back to reality. We've been doing some exercises with the resistance band for the past hour, and although I hated them at the start of the week, by now I'm humbled.

For the first time in who-knows-how-long, I can actually feel my foot gaining strength. I shouldn't be surprised that he can do his job so well, but damn, he's an actual magician.

The smallest ember of hope reignites in my chest.

I follow him to his desk, barely relying on my crutches at this point. I'm still a bit on the fence about letting my foot touch the ground just in case I mess it up, but I've been slowly regaining that confidence by walking back and forth in my studio.

When he sits on his chair and a sudden frown mars his strong and—*fine*—handsome features, a weird feeling sits in the pit of my stomach. Only, this time, it has nothing to do with my small, not-crush on him.

This isn't like his usual pissed-off-for-no-reason frown. This is a you-won't-like-what-I'm-about-to-say kind of scowl, and it makes my skin crawl.

"Tomorrow at nine?" I ask, as if we hadn't been meeting at the exact same time for the past three weeks. Not-so-deep down, I know this is a poor attempt at distracting him from whatever made him frown so he won't tell me.

It doesn't work.

"Take a seat, Miss Stevens. Please."

Ah, shit. Swallowing, I don't sit down but lean on the treatment table instead. "Is everything okay?" I'm almost too afraid to ask.

He sets those big hands on the desk, his fingers laced together, and starts, "As you know, we're halfway through your recovery process and everything looks normal. However."

I'm not ready. I'm truly not.

He makes a thoughtful face I don't like one bit before he continues. "You mentioned you had plans to join a professional ballet company in the near future."

It's not a question, but I still give him an answer. "Yes." I did. Before it all went to hell, I did.

He makes another weird face I don't like, and bile rises in my throat. It's barely noticeable, but the way he turns his mouth to the side just slightly is very obvious to me.

For better or for worse, he isn't one to beat around the bush.

"That level of skill might be too aggressive for an ankle that has just recovered from an injury like yours."

He's not saying what I think he's saying.

He *isn't*.

"From a medical standpoint, it would be wiser to avoid such high-risk activities for at least a year. Preferably longer."

The small ember of hope whooshes out of my chest.

Dies.

Gone.

Just like that.

He's not... He's not saying...

"What are you saying?" I manage to ask through the thick fog clouding my brain. I must have misunderstood. *Surely.*

"You should be able to return to ballet progressively." He eyes me carefully, as if he's afraid I'm about to start bawling my eyes out. He isn't all that wrong. "In your case, that progress will take twelve months or, as I said, a little longer. You can start with easy, nonaggressive routines next week, and we'll see how your ankle reacts to that."

One breath in. One breath out. I can do this. I can have a civilized conversation about my health like any adult would.

I won't start crying in front of him, damn it. My crying sessions are restricted to my shower so I can let it all out in ten minutes and be done with it for the rest of the day.

"Just to be clear," I start, licking my lips that now feel like sandpaper. I need water. I need air. I need the last month of my life to disappear from existence. "I can't dance for a year?"

His cold gaze moves to my lips for a whole millisecond before his eyes land on mine again. "No, that's not what I said. You can return to your activities progressively, starting next week. But you won't be able to perform at the same capacity you did—let's say, when you graduated—for at least a year. Just to be safe, I would advise eighteen months, and then we'll see."

And then we'll see.

I'm about to pass out. Or throw up. Possibly both.

I'm not sure how I manage to do it because I can barely feel my body anymore, but I ask him, "Can I have some water?"

A minute later, there's a sealed bottle in my hands, and I gulp down half of it in seconds. Dr. Simmons still hasn't said a word, and his eyes haven't moved from my face.

Once I put the cap back on and set the water bottle on the treatment table, I stare at him. And he stares at me.

"Miss Stevens, I unders—"

"What am I going to do now?" I blurt out, catching both of us off guard.

I don't miss the way his frown deepens, but there's something else in his eyes now. Something I don't like. Something that looks a lot like pity.

"I'm sorry. I... I don't know why I just asked you that."

I grab my bottle and my tote bag, heat climbing up my cheeks. I can't believe I just said that to him.

I wouldn't call myself a super private person, but I'm not one to vent to strangers either. Or practically strangers, I suppose.

"Miss Stevens."

Our eyes meet, but I'm already on my feet with no plans to sit back down. "I'm sorry. I understand, ah, everything you said. Eighteen months. I won't put any unnecessary pressure on my ankle. Thank you. I'll see you tomorrow, Dr. Simmons."

"Our session isn't—"

"I'm sorry, but I really need to go. I'll see you tomorrow."

Later, when I get my free pass to cry in the shower, I'll think about how I'm going to face him in our next session. Right now, though, I need to get out of here if I want to keep bringing oxygen to my lungs.

I won't be able to dance professionally for eighteen months. Maybe never again, if he thinks my ankle could be compromised.

The cold morning air caresses my face as I exit the clinic, and I wait for the pain to hit me. The frustration, the anxiety, the guilt. But nothing comes.

My chest is a void, and I feel...

Nothing.

chapter 11

MADDIE

There's a small chance I've completely lost my mind. Just a tiny one. Because who storms out of a doctor's appointment like I did this morning? Who can be so blatantly disrespectful?

Ugh. I groan as I scrub the pot until my elbow screams in agony. This stupid grease isn't coming off, and I'm two seconds away from bursting into tears.

So much for staying optimistic, I know. In my defense, I've had a terrible morning, so I think I'm allowed to cut myself some slack.

A meaty hand comes around my shoulders and takes the pot away. "You're gonna dislocate your shoulder at this rate, kid," Matt, our cook, teases me as he also grabs my sponge and finishes the job for me.

I let out a deep breath and reposition myself on the stool Monica gave me earlier. My back is killing me, but I'm not complaining. My paycheck will be enough to pay for groceries, and even if I'll still have to ask Sammy for rent money, at least I'll contribute in some way. For now, this is all I can do.

It's not enough, and you know it.

Nope. No. Everything is fine. I'm at work, and I'm all right.

"Here you go." Matt gives me a gentle smile as he passes me the sponge and the clean pot that is ready for use again. "What's eatin' at you tonight? You look like you'll bite my arm off any second."

I give him a sheepish smile. Matt has been the cook here for ten years, and he's an adorable man. Although one wouldn't necessarily use that word to describe him at first, seeing how he's as big as a brick wall with a mean scowl that rivals Dr. Grouchy's. We use his intimidating looks to our advantage when the drunk men around here need to get kicked out.

"This week has been...a week." And it's only Tuesday, so go figure.

He knows about my missed audition, so I understand the meaning behind the sad look he gives me. "You might be a small thing, but you're stronger than all of us combined, kid. I have no doubts your future will be bright."

With one pat on my shoulder, he goes back to making burgers and sandwiches, but his encouraging words stay with me, making me feel better about today's fiasco.

I don't want to recall how immature I was this morning, but it's difficult not to when I've embarrassed myself in front of Dr. Simmons more times than I can count. There's only so much my poor ego can take.

The dating app still haunts me, and then there's the mandala too. I still can't decipher whether he appreciated it or thought it was weird, but I make sure to think about it nonstop for the next hour. Because of course I do.

I can choose to be happy and look at life in an optimistic way as much as I want, but deep down, I know that's not me. That's not what I deserve to feel.

"Maddie?"

I look up, meeting Monica's eyes. "Yes?"

Can she tell I'm on the verge of yet another mental breakdown? Probably. If she notices anything, though, she doesn't say.

She glances behind her shoulder, her eyes full of suspicion, and my heart rate picks up.

"What's going on?"

She comes inside the kitchen, shutting the door behind her. "A gentleman came in asking for you," she says, and I freeze.

"Who?" I try to get a glimpse of said gentleman through the small window separating the kitchen from the bar, but I don't see any familiar faces. "Did he give you a name?"

"He said his name was James."

James? Who—

Oh.

Oh, no.

No way.

My boss arches a suspicious eyebrow. "Do you know a James?"

"Um, yes." I grab a nearby cloth and dry my hands with it. "Could I...?"

"Go speak to him." She looks back at the bar, and when her eyes find me again, there's something in them I don't like one bit—amusement. "Jeez, girl. That's a fine man if I've ever seen one. If you don't want him, maybe tell him I'm available?" she jokes, which makes Matt grunt.

He and Monica can hide it as much as they like, but it's painfully obvious they've been...ah, involved for a while. Honestly, I'd rather not know.

"It's not like that," I mutter as I grab my crutches, my heart beating so damn fast I can barely concentrate.

"Sure." She gives me a look like she doesn't believe me, throwing me a wink before leaving the way she came.

Somehow, I manage to block all my thoughts as I make my way to the bar. Neither the bachelorette party that can't stop squealing as they take shots nor the music around me distract me—he's impossible to miss.

The first thing I notice is that he's trimmed his beard. It's not completely gone, but it's shorter than it was this morning. Then, my eyes land on those bulging biceps not even his black sweater can hide, and my pulse rises to my throat.

I tell myself I don't need to look at the massive hand wrapped around the can of root beer, but then I do exactly that.

He studies me as I approach, like I'm prey he can't wait to sink his teeth into.

I must be coming down with a fever.

Once I'm standing next to his booth, which he isn't sharing with anybody else tonight, I swallow and gather all the courage I didn't even know I had. "What are you doing here?"

The question is simple enough, but it takes him a while to answer. He takes a sip of his drink, and this time I succeed at not zeroing in on his plump lips. Because I can have self-control. Sometimes.

He doesn't say anything. Instead, he takes something out of the back pocket of his jeans and places it on the table.

It's a piece of paper I'm way too familiar with.

The mandala, the one I drew for him, the one I thought had made him uncomfortable, stares back at me. And it's *colored*.

He worked on it. At home. Or at the clinic. I don't know. Does it matter?

"You colored it?" It's beautiful, in dark tones of blue and purple. He did a meticulous job, I notice, which I find endearing for some reason.

"I did." When I muster the courage to look at him, his eyes are already on me. "It was too beautiful not to."

Wow. Okay. Wow.

"Th-Thank you. For saying that." I feel my cheeks heating up by the second. "I love how it turned out."

I really do. We're not friends, and I'm not exactly sure why he's showing me this, but I'll take it. Because, as a sudden warmth spreads inside my chest, I come to the realization that I feel appreciated.

How can such a small gesture make me feel something so... complicated?

But I suppose he isn't here only to show me the mandala.

He confirms my suspicions when he asks me to sit down across from him, and I only do it because I don't want him to be worried about my ankle.

"Miss Stevens," he starts again, but I cut him right off.

"It's Maddie." I'm surprised by the firmness of my tone. "We're not at the clinic."

Turns out he doesn't drop the grouchy act when he's off the clock. "I'm aware."

He leans over the table, his fingers laced together, and speaks in such a low voice, it makes my legs feel a bit like goo. *You're so dumb.*

"I might be breaking a rule or two by seeking out a patient outside the clinic, so this conversation never happened."

I nod. "You were never here."

"Good girl."

Oh, hell.

I know I'm probably overreacting and it's just the way he talks. He means nothing by it, and it shouldn't mean anything to me that he's praising me like that. I'm not that desperate to be told I'm a "good girl" or whatever.

So even if it does feel good, shame forces me to bury the feeling deep down, under thick layers of denial.

The man in front of me slides me a look I couldn't have missed even if I tried. Under the dim lights of the bar, he looks dangerous, forbidden, and I feel like a deer caught in headlights.

He locks those icy eyes on my face and says in that husky voice I hate and love so much, "I don't make a habit of speaking to my patients outside of work."

For a moment, I wonder if it was his presence I felt the other day in the park, but then I remember he had another patient to see to after I left, so it couldn't have been him. Plus, the way I felt at the park... This isn't the same.

When Dr. Simmons looks at me, my stomach turns a little and my legs feel weaker, but I never feel threatened or endangered.

It wasn't him that day at the park, and it only manages to make me even more anxious. I've learned to always trust my gut with these kinds of weird feelings, so if he didn't follow me to the park that day, who did?

"Yet here you are." I give him a smile that is probably too tight, but I'm too nervous to do better. "Why?"

He doesn't say a word for a moment, but I watch his jaw twitching with tension and his shoulders squaring up as if he were about to enter a fighting ring. In his mind, maybe he is. "I wanted a drink, and I remembered you worked here."

My arched eyebrow tells him I don't believe any of that. "You know I can't wait tables right now, so you came here for what? So I can wash your glass once you're done?"

I can tell my sarcastic tone riles him up, and it makes my smile a little more real. Who knew poking the bear could be so fun?

I'm not dumb. I know he didn't come here because *he wanted a drink*, and I'm not going to let him think he's fooled me.

"You're already here, and I'm not going to report you," I tell him, pushing him to talk. "So you might as well be honest."

"Honesty." He pronounces the word as if he were making fun of it. "Fine, let's all be honest. Why did you storm out of the clinic this morning?"

My back doesn't tense up at his question, of course not. "I didn't storm out. I had to leave."

He doesn't buy it. "Right after I told you about the not-so-good news of your progress? You didn't seem to be in a rush before then."

Just be honest, Maddie. For once in your life, don't hide behind lame excuses nobody believes anyway.

I lean back and wipe the sweat off my hands on my leggings.

"Trust me, Doc. You don't want to hear about it."

"Why am I here, then?"

I shrug. "To have a drink—you said so yourself."

I know I'm being difficult, but what is the alternative? To open up about years of insecurities and trauma to an almost-stranger who also happens to be my physical therapist? Is it even ethical to do such a thing?

His fingers tap along the wooden surface of the table, and he lets out a frustrated sigh that is barely audible. "You told me you had plans to join a ballet company in the near future, and now you're upset because you think you won't be able to do it anymore. Correct me if I'm wrong."

He's going there.

I shift on the cushioned seat and stare past his shoulder, watching our regulars stroll in and out of the bar. I could get out of here right now if I wanted to. The choice is mine. I don't have to talk about this. He won't force me to stay, and if he did, it wouldn't last long with Matt and Monica around.

But I don't want to flee. For years I've tried to keep this down, to not bother anyone with my intrusive and not-so-intrusive thoughts. God knows the last time I opened up to someone, it didn't end well. Not at all.

For one, Dr. Simmons... Well, he's asking. I doubt he knows what he's getting himself into, but if he gets the full Maddie nervous breakdown, it'll be his fault.

Aside from being my physical therapist, he's nothing to me. No one. And he could transfer me to someone else if he didn't want to treat me anymore, so it's not like I'd be left stranded without him.

I have quite literally nothing to lose. A bit of time, maybe, but I'm used to that.

So I swallow, but the lump in my throat doesn't go anywhere. "You're not wrong."

"Okay," he says slowly, kind of softly. "I understand how you're feeling. Do you have a plan B?"

He *understands*? Why? How? One look at the discomfort on his face is enough to bury my curiosity, though. Now's not the time. Maybe it never will be, and that's okay too.

Since we're already talking about this—"this" being my worst nightmare come to life—I give myself the freedom to massage my temples and look a little more on the brink of a mental breakdown than before.

"No. I have no alternative. I mean—I do. I have a few, but none that I truly feel passionate about. None that I feel...called to pursue, if you will. At least not right now."

"There are no other options for you in the ballet industry?"

"Oh, no, there are. It's just that..." I might as well just let it all out, right? I mean, he asked. "I've worked really hard to join this one ballet company for years. It's very prestigious, and sometimes it felt more like a dream than a real possibility, but a few weeks ago, they invited me for an audition. I injured myself while rehearsing for that audition, and now...now it feels like I have no future. I-It's fine. I'm just overreacting."

All right. I did it. I told him without shedding a single tear. That's a win in my book.

He asks the question of the century. "Why do you say you have no future?"

I shrug. "I've worked all my life toward this one goal, and now it's gone forever. If there is a future, it doesn't look too bright to me."

"You can't audition again?"

"No. Auditions are exclusive and only accessible through an invite. They barely hand out any in the first place, just a few a year. I missed my chance."

Saying it out loud still feels surreal.

He leans over the table a little more and pins me down with

one of his hardest stares yet. I swallow down the urge to squirm under it. "Your future isn't gone. That's bullshit. How old are you?"

I have a feeling he knows, but I tell him anyway. "Twenty-one."

"Twenty-one," he repeats, a strange shadow passing over his eyes. "Do you really think your future is gone at *twenty-one*?"

"In ballet, yes." And that's the problem. That's why I was in such a rush to make it. "Ballerinas join companies at my age or even younger because they tend to retire in their mid-thirties. It's not a long career, and I'm already wasting half of it."

"You're not wasting anything. You're recovering from an injury so you can return to ballet safely in a few months. You're not the first professional ballerina to get an injury like this, and you won't be the last. I've seen athletes fully recover from worse."

"Thank you," I tell him honestly. "I appreciate what you're trying to do. It's just that I..." I shake my head. "It's fine. Forget it."

"Tell me."

Shaking my head, I rub my eyes and say, "I'm just tired of life being so damn difficult, I guess. Welcome to adulthood and all that."

I really don't want to get into it. Opening this can of worms now, plus the other one... *Boundaries, Maddie. Remember those.*

He doesn't smile at my poor attempt at lightening the mood. Oh, no, his scowl stays very much in place.

"Life is hard sometimes, but it doesn't mean you have to live it miserably."

"That's easy for you to say," I mutter under my breath before I realize what has just come out of my mouth. My eyes widen in horror as I trip over my words. "I don't know why I've just said that. I'm sorry. God, I'm being such an asshole. You are just trying to help, and I—"

"Stop apologizing," he demands in that deep, cutting voice of his. "I don't want to hear another apology come from your mouth.

I don't need them."

"But I said—"

"You're having a bad day. I get that," he assures me calmly, so calmly I want to start crying.

"Why are you being so nice to me?" I can't help but ask, my voice not much louder than a whisper.

I need to understand why this grouchy man is going out of his way to make me feel better. Why he came here to ask me what's wrong.

But if I expected a long and heartfelt explanation, I don't get one. He simply leans back and says, "Because I've been in your shoes."

That's it. No further elaboration, and I don't ask for one either. He's done enough for me today.

I swallow. "Does it get better?"

His gaze travels lazily from my eyes to my mouth and then back up. Why that triggers an erratic response from the stupid organ in my chest, I don't want to know.

"Some days are better than others." I can't help but notice he didn't say yes. I guess I should appreciate his honesty. "Everything happens for a reason. Focus on that."

I almost snort. Unless the universe's reason is to kick me in the ass, I understand nothing.

"You have options," he insists.

My only response is a long sigh.

"I know you don't see them now, but you will. Don't punish yourself for something you can't change. You are talented, and you are determined. I have no doubts you'll find your calling."

He thinks I'm talented and determined? And he just told me to my face?

I'm not used to this version of Dr. Simmons. To this slightly less grumpy, almost kind of sweet version. But I like it. I like it a lot.

"Thank you." I give him a smile he doesn't return. "For everything. I have...a lot to think about."

"Just doing my job."

Yeah. Right. "I doubt giving words of encouragement to your patients is in your job description."

Something that resembles a grunt escapes him. "I guess it isn't." Silence stretches between us for no more than two seconds, but it feels like a lifetime. And then he says, "I'd better get going."

He's not subtle at dismissals, I've noticed. It almost makes me smile.

"Sure. I'll see you at the clinic." I grab my crutches and stand up, but he doesn't. I think he may be waiting for a second or third confirmation, so I look down at him and say, "This conversation never happened. No need to worry."

He keeps his face neutral, as unreadable and cold as always. "I'm not worried about that."

But he's worried about something? I don't feel like I have the right to ask, so I keep my mouth shut. When he stands up and towers over me by at least a whole foot, I tell myself he doesn't smell good at all.

I press my lips together as he reaches for a bunch of bills to cover his tab, way more than what that root beer is worth. He slides me a look that reveals nothing and says, "Take care of that ankle, Miss Stevens."

He's retreating, drawing that line once more. I don't feel embarrassed for having vented to him, but only because he asked. He's not my therapist, and we shouldn't turn this into a habit. Not that I'm tempted to anyway, and I'm sure he feels the same.

As I watch him leave the bar without a goodbye or a glance over his shoulder, I can't help but ask myself what the hell is my life turning into.

chapter 12

JAMES

The next few days are pure, slow torture.

I didn't see her during our session on Friday, since I was away at a work conference, but that didn't stop my mind from spiraling.

For days, I thought about her more than I should have. I thought about that morning in my office, when I told her she wouldn't be able to go back to professional ballet for a few months, and how I could see the struggle behind her eyes as she accepted her new reality. How badly she needed to break down—so I gave her an in.

Once upon a time, I also watched as my dream was lost, washed down the drain, and I vowed to never allow anyone else to fall into that same pit of despair.

If checking in on Maddie when I'm off the clock makes her feel better, then it's a no-brainer.

But that's not all there is to it, not by far, and if I were a better man, I wouldn't let this ember of interest spark to life.

Because I'm an asshole, though, I let it simmer.

I decide to give myself some leeway, just to see what it would feel like to dangle something so forbidden right in front of my watering mouth and never taste it.

Because I won't. I can't.

For two reasons.

Reason number one—she's my patient. I have already crossed multiple lines by accepting her gift, and let's not even speak about the fact that I went to that bar specifically to see her.

And reason number two, perhaps the most compelling and daunting of all—she's *twenty-one*.

For fuck's sake. I don't think I could hit a lower low.

Before, I was one of those guys who frowned upon men who got involved with younger women. What could a thirty-something-year-old want to do with a young woman in her very-early twenties? What could two people so different have in common?

It doesn't matter that, technically, Maddie and I aren't involved. And we will never be. But I can't deny this...this simmer of something, and it's messing with my head.

Because I should have no business making sure she's okay beyond her injury. It's not my place to treat her mental wounds.

"Another root beer?" Graham's dark eyes land on my refilled glass. "That's the second one tonight."

"Congratulations, you can count."

Probably against his will, he throws his head back in laughter. "I'm surprised you like them so much, is all. They taste like shit to me." I can feel his stare on the side of my face. My friend hesitates before asking, "Have you talked to him yet?"

Taking another sip of my poison of choice, I use the drink and the rowdy hockey crowd at the bar as an excuse to delay my response. My hopes that somehow, by some miracle, my friend drops the subject are in vain.

"I wouldn't pressure you for an answer if I didn't think this would be good for you, Jimbo."

"Don't call me Jimbo, Graham Cracker."

"I will until you give me an answer, *Jimbo*."

This son of a—

"No, I haven't. Not planning to either. There. Happy now?"

"I'm just saying, man." He shrugs. "Don't do it for Andrew—do it for yourself."

At the mention of my brother's name, my stomach drops. I slide my best friend a cold, hard look that tells him everything my mouth won't.

"Hint taken," he says, putting the subject to rest.

We eat our greasy burgers, I flag down the waitress—Monica, I recall—for some water this time, and Norcastle's hockey team wins the game to nobody's surprise. A few players get interviewed at the end and say a bunch of stuff I can't even begin to understand. Graham soaks it up like a towel on a puddle, and suddenly I'm ready to go home. Why I agreed to go for a drink on a Tuesday night is beyond me.

I'm about to go up to the bar to ask for our check when a familiar smell hits me out of nowhere. Something clean and flowery.

I could lie and say my heart doesn't start hammering inside my chest. I could lie and say my hands don't start sweating at the prospect of seeing her again outside of the clinic. I could lie, but I'm not a liar. An asshole, sure, but never a liar.

"Doc?" That sweet, raspy voice. That smell coming closer. "Is that you?"

Ignore her, ignore her, ign—

My eyes collide with her hazel orbs, so big and all-seeing, and I find myself trapped. "Miss Stevens."

The little smile she gives me almost manages to take me out completely. "It's good to see you." She turns to Graham, and I freeze.

"Hey, I'm Maddie. Nice to meet you."

I don't imagine the sly look my friend sends my way before giving her his full, undivided attention and his biggest smile.

"Maddie, huh? Name's Graham." He holds out his hand for her to shake. "How do you know Jimbo over here?"

She looks at me and giggles at the nickname, making me want to strangle my so-called best friend to death.

"He's, uh, he's my physical therapist. At the rehabilitation clinic," she explains, and I swear her words light up Graham's eyes. I don't like this one bit.

"You don't say." He rests his chin on top of his hand and scans her face. "Tell me he's an asshole at work too. I'm dying to hear it from the very source."

She chuckles—another stab in my stomach. "He's a little grouchy, but he's all right. He's good at what he does." Just to prove her point, she wiggles her ankle back and forth. "See? Almost brand-new."

It's not and she knows it, but she hides her pain well. It's something I'm yet to master.

"You're in good hands, then, Maddie." My friend smirks over the rim of his bottle, and I've had enough.

"What are you doing here?" It comes out harsher than intended, but I don't correct myself.

She looks taken aback by my tone for a whole second before that easy smile is back on her face. I don't think I've ever seen her look so relaxed.

"I work here. You know this."

I do. Of course I do. I'm losing my mind.

"Doing what?" my friend asks, sounding genuinely interested.

"I used to be a waitress before you-know-what." She shrugs. "Now I'm washing dishes in the kitchen, but I'm grateful Monica allowed me to come back at all. Leaving the apartment is good for me."

"Cheers to that." Graham tilts his beer toward her and takes a sip. "You working now, Maddie? Or do you want to grab a drink with us?" he asks, and the mortification settles in her eyes just as it drops like a heavy rock in the pit of my stomach.

Once again, she covers the shock with a smile that could've easily fooled me if the darkness within me hadn't already recognized hers.

"Thank you, but I still have a couple of hours to go. I just came by because I thought I saw him."

"What a shame." My friend leans in as if he were sharing a secret with her. I don't like it. "I bet you're more fun than this... What did you call him before? *Grouchy* one over here."

Her eyes sparkle with amusement as she looks my way. "I'm tempted, but I really should get back to work. It was great seeing you." Then she smiles at my friend again. "Nice to meet you, Graham. I'll see you guys around."

Just as she's leaving, carefully so as to avoid slipping on the floor slick with spilled drinks, a dangerous thought crosses my mind.

Forgetting the consequences and my inner pep talks about how I should stay away from her outside of the clinic, I launch forward and almost fall off my damn stool. "Wait."

She stops and looks at me over her shoulder, eyebrows drawn together. I'm confused too. That flowery scent fills my nostrils when I get close enough, and I hate myself for basking in it.

The top of her head reaches my shoulder just barely. Our height difference shouldn't make me want to toss her over my shoulder just to hear her laugh, yet here we are.

"Yes?" She arches a half-curious, half-amused eyebrow, and I snap out of it.

"What time does your shift end?"

She glances at the wall clock behind the bar, where Monica sends her a curious glance I guess she doesn't see, since she ignores it. "In an hour and a bit. Why?"

I could spend that time hauling my ass home and binge-watching some show with my cats until I fall asleep, but instead I say, "I'll give you a ride home when you're done."

Her breath hitches, and something twists inside my chest. "You don't have to do that," she says, her voice so low I almost don't hear it.

"I'll be here a while longer with my friend, and then I'll wait for you in my car," I tell her, leaving no room for discussions. Over my dead body is she going back home alone, injured, and so late at night.

But she doesn't seem to share my sentiment. "You can go home, James. I'll be fine."

James. There goes another stab in the heart.

"It's dark, and you won't be able to get away with an injured ankle if something happens." A sudden urge to protect her, to make sure she gets home safe, grips me and doesn't let go. "I'm driving you home, Maddie."

For a moment, she seems to consider it. I really don't want to come off as controlling, but the thought of something happening to her while she's alone and injured...

Get a grip.

"Fine. I'll see you in an hour."

She waves me goodbye and resumes her walk to the kitchen, disappearing moments later.

Back at my table, I barely hear Graham's taunts about how I hauled ass right after a patient to offer her a ride home. I barely acknowledge his dumbass remarks about the kind of ride I probably wish I could give her.

All I can focus on is the way my name sounds on her lips, as if I had any right to hear it.

***

Maddie's shift ended fifteen minutes ago, but I still remember what it was like to work at bars from my college days, so I'm probably looking at another fifteen-minute wait until she comes out. Not that I'm complaining.

There are only two other cars bathing in the darkness of the parking lot, and I can see the silhouette of a man sitting inside one of them. One more reason I'm glad I stayed behind to wait for her.

I let out a tired sigh and rub my eyes, the lack of sleep from the previous nights finally catching up to me. I roll down the window and let the cool air in to avoid falling asleep behind the wheel, but soon it becomes clear I need to get out of this comfortable seat if I want to stand a chance.

Once I step out of the car and rest my back against the driver's door, I scan the parking lot again, stealing furtive glances at the front door of the bar. A few patrons wearing hockey jerseys come out, but still no Maddie.

My eyes fall on the man in the car a few feet away. He's staring at the bar, too, and from out here I'm able to discern a couple of his features—old, balding head, mean scowl. There's nothing particularly threatening about him, yet this weird feeling settles in the pit of my stomach and refuses to go away.

I tell myself he must be waiting for someone. A friend, a relative, a partner. This isn't a dangerous part of town, but the dark is the dark. It's possible we're both acting as very willing designated drivers tonight and nothing else.

But... No. This still doesn't feel right.

My gut is never wrong, and I won't ignore it today of all days.

Before I can overthink it, I lock my car and let my feet carry me toward him at a slow, almost leisure-like pace. If he's dangerous, I don't want him to feel threatened. My six-foot-five height and my grumpy-ass face—as Graham would put it—don't give the best first impression.

As I get closer, I notice his window is down and his left arm is perched on it. Only when I'm almost there does he slide me a look. His dark, wrinkly eyes scan me from head to toe, but he doesn't say anything.

Very well—we'll play by my rules.

"Everything all right?" I ask, hands in my pockets. I keep my voice casual just for good measure.

The man eyes me again warily. "You a cop?" His voice doesn't sound as deep as I expected.

I ignore his question. "I'm curious as to why you've been staring at that door for the past twenty minutes."

He huffs. "I don't know what you're talking about."

I look at the door again when it opens, but it's not Maddie who comes out. Still, I don't want her to see this creep when she does, so I decide to cut our interaction short. "If you aren't waiting for anyone, I'd advise you to leave this parking lot right now."

That manages to rile him up. I can tell he knows he's at a disadvantage here, seeing how I'm standing next to him and he's strapped into a car seat.

"You a cop or not?" he asks again, clearly distressed about that possibility.

"Maybe."

An eternal beat of silence passes between us before he starts the car.

I knew it. Damn it, I knew he wasn't waiting for anyone.

Without sparing me a glance, he speeds out of the parking lot, but I don't return to my car until I've lost sight of his lights down the street. *Good fucking riddance.*

I don't want to alarm Maddie by telling her there might be creeps lurking outside her workplace at this hour, but I'll have a word or two with Monica.

Or better yet—I'll drop by to pick Maddie up when she has a night shift.

As soon as that idea crosses my mind, I realize how insane it sounds. I'm not her friend, her brother, her *anything* to be looking after her like this. I was here today, completely by chance. That's why I offered her a ride, but I can't be going out of my way for her like this.

There are potentially dangerous people lurking out here. Someone could hurt her.

And that possibility burns me alive.

When I reach my car, the door to Monica's opens again, and this time, Maddie walks out holding a take-out bag in one hand. She blinds me with one of those sweet smiles. "I know you've already had dinner, but that was ages ago, so I got you some chicken wings. Is that okay?"

Hell.

Her smile widens, and so does the dark hole inside my chest.

Fuck.

I clear my throat and look away from her. "Let's get you home."

chapter 13

MADDIE

There's something to be said about attraction. Much like resentment, you can't control it—I would know a thing or two about that because I've tried.

I was five years old the first time I felt resentment. I still remember it as if it had happened just last night, instead of sixteen years ago.

When I visited my mother in the rehab center for the first time after moving in with my brother and Grace, a weird feeling sank in the pit of my stomach at the sight of her in that place, away from me. Something heavy and sour I had never experienced before, but I already knew I didn't like it.

It wasn't until much later that I finally noticed everyone around me, at school and at the ballet studio, had a parent whose arms they could run into. A mother, a father, a stepparent—did it even matter?

First, I felt resentment, animosity, and even hatred. Because why did all my friends have a mom and a dad, and I didn't?

Then, the guilt began.

No, I didn't have a mother to read nighttime stories with and teach me how to ride a bike, and I didn't have a father to protect me and play house with me, but I wasn't alone by any means. I wasn't *lonely*. I had an older brother and a sister-in-law who never once hesitated to do all of those things with me and more.

That resentment toward my mother, as the years passed,

turned into resentment toward myself. Because I had people who loved me and worried about me, but I still couldn't close that gaping hole inside my chest. It still wasn't enough to heal. *It isn't.*

She called me ungrateful because of it, and I guess... Well, she was right.

As I lean back on James's pristine car seat after I give him directions to my apartment, I make a mental note to text my friends to go out for lunch one of these days. It's long overdue, and they always manage to keep the monsters at bay.

And I make another, more urgent one, to remind my brain that whatever attraction I feel for the man next to me, it needs to stop now.

He's your much-older physical therapist. You shouldn't think about his arms or hands or beard or handsome face. Stop it.

A car honks behind us, and James finally looks at me, as if the loud sound had woken him up from some kind of foggy mental state. He nods toward my take-out bag. "You can eat in the car. It'll get cold before we get out of traffic."

Yeah, I don't think so. Have you seen these leather seats? I already feel bad enough that the car is filling up with the smell of spicy chicken wings. "Thanks, but I can wait."

"I insist."

"So do I."

I think he grunts. "You always get your way, don't you?" he asks with no real heat in is voice as he changes lanes, and I really should stop ogling his hands as he turns the wheel. It's not productive at all, and I feel like a class-A pervert.

"I don't know about that, Doc. Last I remember, I'm in this car because you told me to."

"You could have declined."

"I did."

"Hmm. I don't remember that part."

Was that the smallest hint of amusement in his voice?

I must be delirious. Coming down with a high fever or something.

Silence falls over us again, but it's not uncomfortable. We watch people crossing the busy lanes between the cars, wearing their hockey jerseys. It hits me then that the arena is just a few blocks away, hence the traffic. Monica always plays all kinds of sports games at the bar, but I don't really follow any of them, so I have no clue what is going on half of the time.

James breaks the silence between us, which takes me by surprise, considering his usual vow of silence. "I was right about driving you home. Your cab fee would've been insane."

I slide him a look that isn't exactly discreet. Since when do we do casual chatter?

Not that I'm complaining. Of course not.

"It looks like we'll be stuck here for a while," I say, still unsure where we are exactly in our doctor-patient-carpool-buddies relationship. "I never asked you about the conference. How was it?"

He mentioned it to me on a Thursday, letting me know one of his colleagues would be seeing me the next day because he had a conference to attend in another city. The other PT, a guy whose name I don't even recall, wasn't bad at all. But he wasn't James.

He rubs his chin with his fingers. "Dull."

I arch a curious eyebrow. "You're a man of many words."

Is that a smile? It's small and barely there at all, but I swear his lips twitch.

"What do you want me to say? That I had the time of my life and wept at the closing ceremony because it was over? I wish that'd been the case."

I get the hint of mirth in his voice and run miles with it. "Yes, please. And then you can tell me about how you took all the flyers from the conference and made a shrine for them in your bedroom."

"Damn, you caught me."

I smirk. He smirks. Traffic moves.

It takes him a couple of minutes, but finally he gives me a real answer. "I didn't learn much. That's why it was a waste of time. I suspected the company hosting it only wanted us to buy their new line of products, but since the clinic kind of forced me to go, I had no choice."

I frown. "They forced you?"

"They send one or two physical therapists to these conferences every year. I was the lucky one with the golden ticket this time."

Traffic moves again. For a moment, I think we're finally out of it, but then we stop again. Hunger and exhaustion must be clouding my judgment because I ask, like I have any right to know, "Do you like your job?"

He shrugs. "I do." A pause. "Most days."

Seeing how he didn't chew my head off for asking a personal question, I try my luck once more. "Why did you decide to become a PT?"

At that, he stiffens. The only reason I notice is because I seem to have a weird fixation on his hands, which tighten their grip on the wheel. I'm not entirely sure he'll answer, but he surprises me once again by entertaining my nosey ass. "It's vocational, in a way."

I wait for an elaboration that doesn't come. "Is someone from your family a PT as well?" I press.

"No. My parents are both retired now. My mom used to be a baker, and my dad worked at a car repair shop."

I light up at that. "A baker? That sounds like such a dreamy job." I smile to myself. "Did you inherit any of her skills in the kitchen?"

Eyes still on the road, he smirks. "Damn sure did."

And just because I love being a little shit, I say, "I don't believe you one bit. In fact, I bet you can't even tell salt from sugar."

That gets him to look at me. "Why's that, Maddison?"

I scrunch up my nose. "Don't call me Maddison. It sounds too preppy."

"I'll call you Maddison for as long as you keep being a brat."

The air whooshes out of my lungs.

Puff, gone.

That familiar tone of amusement in his voice wraps around my ear and whispers a sweet nothing or two into it, and then it sinks in.

Did he just call me a brat?

And most importantly, why the hell do I like it?

My mind is so blank, I can't think of any mildly imaginative comeback. All I can come up with is: "I'm not a brat."

"I don't believe you one bit," he parrots my words back to me. He turns onto a less busy street, but we stop at a red light. "What were we talking about, anyway? Ah, yes, my dubious skills in the kitchen."

I shrug. "Well, you never denied not being a disaster."

"I'm not the best cook, but—"

"I knew it."

He ignores me, but that hesitant smirk comes back. "I'm decent. A solid eight on a good day."

I do a slow clap because maybe he's right and I'm a bit of a brat. On occasion. "A man admitting his flaws? Impressive."

He arches a skeptical eyebrow. "What do you have against men?"

I pretend to think about it. "Hmm... Where do I even begin?"

He laughs. He *laughs*. An actual, honest belly laugh that sounds so beautiful, I wish I could play it on repeat when I need cheering up, which happens to be most days lately.

"You know what?" He shakes his head with amusement as we finally turn onto a deserted road, and he speeds away. "Fair enough. We are terrible."

"I mean, not all of you, but...some are." I shrug. "In my

experience, anyway."

"Hmm."

Silence falls over us again like a thick, comforting blanket in the middle of the night. The streets around us pass in a quick blur, but I don't feel unsafe with James behind the wheel. There's an air of confidence about him, the kind some would mistake for arrogance, that makes him feel reliable. Like he'd be a good person to call if you're ever in an emergency, and he'd leave everything at the drop of a hat to come to the rescue.

I'd never admit it out loud, but the fact that he stayed behind tonight to drive me home is warming my heart. Yet I can't help but wonder, why on earth would someone who barely knows me do such a thing for me? What's in it for him?

"What's your experience with terrible men?" he asks, and for some reason, his next words make my heart jump. "No boyfriends?"

I sink back into my seat and tighten my grip on the takeaway bag. "No boyfriends." I clear my throat. "What about you, Doc? Did the dating app ever pay off?"

Yeah, that's one question he wasn't expecting, nor does he look too keen on answering. Still, I wait for a reply I'm not sure I'll get. But whatever. It was worth the shot.

"I've been single for a few years," he responds, shocking me into silence with an actual answer. "The app wasn't my idea. It was Graham's."

That feels right, for some reason. I just don't picture him as the kind of guy to pick up girls online.

"I have a bad habit of not deleting stuff from my phone, so that's why I still have it. Had it. It's gone now," he explains.

"That makes sense." I smile at him, holding in ten million other questions floating around in my head.

When was your last relationship?

Why didn't it work out?

Does it mean it's been years since you've last had—

Nope. Not going there.

I don't have any right to ask Dr. Simmons about his sex life. It's not my place to even *think* about it.

I blame my stupid thoughts on the crazy day I've had, but honestly, I'm not sure I believe it. There's something about him that breaks down all my inhibitions, and I don't like it because I can't control it.

When he stops in front of my building, I don't miss a beat. "Thank you for giving me a ride." Still smiling, I take out a container with the chicken wings from the bag. "Pop them in the oven for five minutes, and they'll be as good as new."

He looks at it like it's grown a head or something. "I appreciate it, but you can take it."

I frown, unbuckling myself from the seat. "I got my own here. You don't like chicken wings?"

"It's not that." He presses his lips in a thin line, and when I nudge him with the container, he finally takes it. "Fine. Thanks."

"No problem," I say over my shoulder as I open the door.

Once outside, the cold night air hits me immediately, and I shiver. I'm still unsure why I do it—maybe the cold is affecting my brain. But I lean down to look him in the eye all the same and smirk.

"Enjoy your chicken wings from your bratty patient."

Despite the darkness surrounding us, the light inside the car gives me a first-row seat to his deep, unexpected blush.

I *knew* he was a blusher. Why does that make me incredibly giddy?

chapter 14

MADDIE

I'm drunk. Not from drinking away my sorrows at home or from club-hopping with my friends, but from last night's conversation with James in his car.

I'm drunk on his presence, his words, his whole damn existence—and I hate every second of it.

There's nothing, absolutely nothing, that should interest me about him. Not his reasons for becoming a PT, not his skills in the kitchen, and most certainly not his love life.

He's still my physical therapist, and he could get in real trouble if we crossed the invisible line that seems to draw us a little closer every time we're together outside the clinic.

Not that a man like him would ever be interested in little old sad me. Why would he? He's a grown adult in his early thirties with his whole life figured out and probably planned to a T, and I'm twenty-one, lost, and waiting for a deity I don't even believe in to poke me on the side and tell me, "Hey, look. This is the direction you're meant to take."

We don't belong together.

Plus, what would my brother think if I got involved with a man ten years my senior? He'd have a stroke, that's what would happen.

Luckily, I don't have to worry about that because the most realistic, logical part of me knows once my rehabilitation treatment is over, I won't see James ever again. I'll have no reason to.

He seems like a prudent man who won't jeopardize his job for a twenty-one-year-old mess, and maybe that's what gives me the final push to leave all those thoughts behind and focus on what I truly want. What I wouldn't mind.

I want us to be friendly. Maybe not friends *friends*, the way Kyle and Beth are my friends, but I want us to at least be...cordial. A little more than that, if we could. And I suppose he wouldn't mind it, since he's already gone out of his way to drive me home after my night shift. He wouldn't have done that if he hated me, right?

It's likely that I'm misreading all the very obvious neon signs telling me he does, in fact, not give a shit about me. But that doesn't stop me from pulling out yet another mandala from my tote bag at the end of our session and handing it to him.

He looks at the piece of paper, then at me, and back at the paper. Hesitantly, he takes it. "Another one?" He doesn't sound annoyed, not even surprised. It's more like incredulity.

"This one is a crescent moon," I explain like he doesn't have two working eyes. "It's a bit smaller than the last one I gave you, but I thought you'd like the design."

"You didn't have to give me anything." He stays silent for a moment. Then he says, "I still can't believe you draw these by hand."

"It's not a big deal. Making them relaxes me."

His attentive eyes are on the paper before they dart back up to me. "Have you tried going back to ballet like I recommended?"

Right. Back to business. That's good. That's what we need to do.

He opens the desk drawer to his right, puts the drawing inside, and closes it, all while holding my stare.

"No," I confess. "I don't want to hurt my ankle again."

"You need to return to your normal activities progressively," he simply responds, like he doesn't care for my concerns. "We talked about this in our last session."

We did, and then I pretended he didn't say anything. Oops?

"But what if I make a bad move and have to start all over again?"

I don't think I'd have the mental strength to do physical therapy for a second time—I'm barely surviving the first—but I don't say that. I'm pretty sure he can read between the lines, anyway.

"Don't push yourself too hard, and you'll be all right. You can start with some warm-up exercises and a simple routine."

I look at him for a moment too long before drifting my eyes away, defeated. "Okay. I'll do that this week." Or maybe the next.

I'm hiking my tote bag up my arm when his voice startles me. "What's wrong?"

"Nothing's wrong." The lie rolls off my tongue so easily I should probably check what's up with that.

"Maddie."

Hearing my name from his lips gives me tingles, and I hate myself for it. What happened to Miss Stevens?

"I'll have another pep talk with you if I need to, but a patient is coming in five minutes, so I would appreciate some straightforwardness."

Another pep talk. Right. His last motivational speech is forever engraved in my mind. "That won't be necessary. I already said I'm scared of hurting myself again."

He arches a skeptical eyebrow. "Scared. You didn't use that word before."

"Does it matter?"

"To me, it does."

Stupid heart, stop beating so fast. "Why?" I dare to ask, as if his answer doesn't hold the power to crush me.

And crush me, it does. "Because you're my patient, and I want my patients to go back to the activities I know they still enjoy."

A wave of unfounded disappointment crashes into me. *His patient.*

Of course. I never, not for one moment, forgot the real reason we know each other. The real reason we are still seeing each other almost every day. He's my physical therapist, and our relationship is and should remain strictly professional.

Who cares if he went out of his way to drive me home after a night shift?

Who cares if we saw each other on a dating app?

Who cares if I draw him mandalas and he colors them?

I don't.

Liar, liar, pants on fucking fire.

Fine. Maybe I expected him to have warmed up to me just like I'm starting to warm up to him, but it's okay. One of us has to be the reasonable adult and remind the other that this...whatever this is, has an expiration date. And the faster it approaches, the better.

All this fog in my head will clear once I don't have to see him ever again.

"You're right." I put on the least fake smile I can muster. "I still enjoy ballet, and I don't want to quit because of my injury." There's nothing fake about that statement. "I promise I'll go to the studio either this week or the next."

He nods, satisfied. "Good. I'll see you tomorrow, Miss Stevens."

There it is. Back to normal. Just like it should always be.

* * *

"We'll go with you!"

"Oh my God, Maddie. This is *such* great news."

"Aren't you excited? I am!"

My smile wavers as I lift my fork and stuff my face with some ricotta and pine nut salad. It tastes like nothing, just like everything else I've eaten recently, but I don't care. Eating is the perfect excuse for not talking. For my two best friends to not see the truth in my words now that I've finally learned to hide it so well with my eyes.

But I know better than to expect Beth and Kyle to call it quits so easily.

I don't regret having agreed to grab some lunch with them. Now that I'm safe to leave the house, and my friends' busy schedules were miraculously clear for at least an hour, I couldn't say no. Even if I wasn't in the mood when Kyle texted the group chat just a few minutes after I got home from this morning's session. I wasn't— and I suppose I'm still not—in the mood because I'm a coward who's avoiding the inevitable, which is *this conversation*.

"I feel like I wouldn't know where to start," Kyle muses as he stabs his chicken breast. "It's been so long since we've done an easy routine, you know? I don't even remember what that was like."

"I can give you some ideas," Beth offers. "You could do some of the routines I'm teaching the girls."

Going from professional ballet to kid-level dancing due to being stupidly reckless, hurting myself, and losing my dream job? Sounds great.

And this situation is all the more frustrating because ballerinas getting injured isn't unheard of in the dance world. It happens fairly often—I just never imagined it would happen to me.

Turns out I'm not invincible.

"Thanks, Beth." I smile, but it feels forced, even to me.

"No problem." She takes a sip of her fizzy water. "You could rent one of the studios on Glenn Avenue. It's less than twenty bucks an hour."

"I will do that." I don't bother telling her I've already booked one for next Monday, because I need a change of topic more than I need my next breath. "Hey, does Polina have a new girlfriend or something? I saw something on social media, but I didn't want to pry."

And just like that, the conversation shifts to the latest gossip, something that always works as a distraction. I love my friends—they're my rocks—and I know damn well my recovery process would've been a whole lot more miserable and lonely without their constant check-ins, video calls, gossip updates, and visits. I just can't talk about my future—or lack thereof—right now. They would understand if I explained it to them, but I don't want to make them feel bad, so deflection it is.

I'm not winning any friendship awards this year, that's for sure.

A little over half an hour later, a loud alarm that startles the whole café blasts through Kyle's phone, a sign that his break is over. He grabs his bag and rounds the table to give me a hug.

"I'll text you guys later. And Mads, let me know how it goes, all right? I believe in you, girl. I know you can do it."

I resist the urge to bawl into his chest. "Don't get all sappy on me, Kyle." I scowl, but I can't hide a smile.

"That sexy doctor of yours would never advise you to do something that'll hurt your ankle. If you don't have faith in yourself, at least have some in him."

He's right. James would never—

Wait a minute.

I almost choke on my own saliva. "Did you just call him sexy?"

My face must be the picture of pure horror, because both of my friends start laughing. Kyle shakes his head, amused. "It was just a guess, but with the way your face is flushing right now, I'd say I'm spot on."

This is getting out of hand. I still have time to hit the brakes before we crash.

"He's not..." Sexy? I sure know he is. "He's not too bad."

Beth squeals, propping her chin on her hands as she bats her eyelids at me. "That means he's hot as sin, Kyle. I have a master's degree in reading between the Maddie-lines. Oh, God, you *like* him." She points an accusing finger at me.

"What? No."

I don't. I can't.

I...don't.

"We'll talk more about this later," Kyle warns me before planting a quick kiss on my cheek, then on Beth's, and waving at us as he walks away. "Don't you dare gossip without me, bitches! Or you'll regret it."

We laugh at his dramatics, but Beth is quick to sober up again. This time, she means business.

"I'm your best friend in the entire world," she starts, and I know this won't end well for me. "Whatever you confess to me right now won't leave this café. Hell, it won't even leave this table. So, what is it? Do you have the hots for your doctor? How old is he?"

I shift uncomfortably on my chair at the reminder that, even if she isn't aware of it, Beth knows exactly what James looks like. She knows his age and even some of his hobbies. And maybe because I've already had this conversation with James himself and it can't get more embarrassing than that, I decide to tell her the truth.

"Fun fact." I lick my lips and play with my napkin, my elbows resting on the table. "Remember that guy you swiped up on, on the dating app? Turns out he's..." It takes everything in me not to wince. "Ah, he's my physical therapist. James. The guy treating my ankle."

If shock had a face, it would look exactly like Beth's. Her lips form a perfect circle, jaw on the floor and eyebrows on the ceiling. It would look comical if I wasn't dying inside.

She shakes her head. "No. Fucking. Way."

I press my lips into a thin line and nod.

Beth covers her mouth with both of her hands and squeals into them, grabbing the attention of a handful of people around us. I roll my eyes and bat her hands away. "It's not a big deal," I shush her. "I mean, it was at first, but I talked to him and we're cool."

Her jaw hits the floor again. "You talked to him about swiping up on him on the dating app? The balls!"

Now that I think about it, maybe it was a bold move after all. "What did he say?" she asks.

So, for the next ten minutes, I explain how everything went down between us and where we're currently at. I even throw the mandalas and the car ride into the mix because why not. If I want my friend's honest opinion, I must be fully honest myself, first.

"Wow." She sits back on her chair once I finish, shoulders relaxing after being so on edge. Seriously, my friends take gossiping as a life-and-death matter—I kind of love it too, so I'm not judging. "That was... I need to think about this for a second."

I gulp down what remains of my Diet Coke. "Don't think too hard. I won't see him again after next week." I'll probably have to meet with him at some point in the next few months to monitor my progress, but maybe not. Maybe another PT will do my checkups.

Beth glares at me like she doesn't fully believe what I'm saying. "I don't know, Mads. What kind of guy stays *hours* in a parking lot so he can get you home safely? Think about it. He clearly feels something for you."

Pity is the first word that assaults my brain.

"He's ten years older than me," I quip.

She shrugs. "So? That's kinda hot."

She's been reading too many romance books. Clearly.

"He has his whole life figured out. His *adult* life," I add.

"So do you."

"I used to." It's out in the open air before I can prevent it.

Beth's eyes soften at my words, and I hate it. I loathe it with all my heart. "Oh, Maddie."

No. Nope. I'm not doing this right now, or ever. I won't have someone else pity me for my own mistakes. "It's fine. I didn't really mean it," I lie, something that has been coming really easily for me these days. It worries me. "I'm just confused about...you know, him."

"Well, I don't think it would be a good idea if you guys hooked up while you're still his patient," she says, as if there was an actual chance of *that* happening. "So just wait until your treatment is over and see what happens. You say you won't see him again, but something right here"—she taps her gut—"is telling me you're wrong."

Maybe. Maybe not. My head hurts just thinking about it.

I stay silent as Beth finishes her lunch, forcing my mind to stay blank. No James, no future, no "what would my brother think," no nothing, but it proves to be a near impossible task.

I'm about to excuse myself to go to the bathroom when I feel it.

A prickle of uneasiness travels down my spine, an uncomfortable tug in my stomach, just like that day at the park.

Feeling safe now that I'm with Beth and inside a crowded place, I gather my strength and look around.

Nobody is staring back at me, but even so, there's something inside me that would just *know* if I saw this person. An instinct, a feeling, something.

I feel nothing. If someone is watching me, they aren't inside the café.

"God." Beth chuckles, pulling me out of my momentary lapse. "Kyle is going to be so pissed he missed this."

chapter 15

MADDIE

I've never truly felt pure, raw dread. Not even when I realized my future had just gone down the drain. No, at that moment, I only felt angry at the world and sorry for myself. A killer combination if you ask me.

According to Sammy and Grace, I grew up a fearless child. Curious, adventurous, never particularly scared of the unknown. And for the first time in my life, I wish I could grab my inner child from wherever she's hiding and force her to do this for me.

Studio B is everything I've been dreading for the past five weeks, compartmentalized into a medium-sized room with a wall full of mirrors and a wheeled ballet barre.

I thought booking the last slot of the day would bring me some kind of inner peace, knowing I could leave a few minutes earlier with the excuse of the studio closing for the day, but I still feel miserable.

Maybe this was a mistake. It sure feels like one.

But no—I spent Saturday's shift money on this studio, and I will make the most of it. Even if I don't last the whole hour, at least I'll go home tonight knowing I tried.

I'll see James tomorrow and tell him I did all I could and that I didn't back down. I don't know why what he thinks is becoming more important to me the more time we spend near each other, but it doesn't bother me. He wants me to do better, and I can't say I don't want that for myself too.

I move toward the middle of the room and set my bag on the floor then sit down and take out my portable speaker. It's been so long since I used it, I had to spend half an hour looking for it this morning.

After my phone is connected to the speaker, I scroll down my ballet playlist, hit a random song, and get on my feet.

My reflection stares back at me in the mirror, and I'm confused by what I see.

Sleek bun, pink tights, black leotard, black skirt, pink ballet shoes. This is exactly how I looked most days through college—an image I'm as used to as seeing myself in my pajamas—and yet I barely recognize the woman in front of me.

Because, under that put-together facade, there's a broken spirit.

There's a girl who, somehow, for some reason, thinks she's never enough.

Not good enough to keep my parents' love and attention. Not good enough to get into The Norcastle Ballet. Not good enough to perform a simple ballet routine for children without having a mental breakdown.

I inhale. Exhale. "Focus, Maddie."

I try. For myself, I try.

Flashbacks from the day I injured my ankle fill my head as I move, but my steps don't falter. I'm being slow, careful, always listening to my body.

I can do this. I was born to dance. Under different circumstances, maybe, but my fate has always been to wear these shoes, to move to the rhythm of this music. I know it deep inside.

Realizing this is exactly where I'm meant to be after all the hurt and self-loathing is a strange feeling—bittersweet.

This is what I wanted, wasn't it? To wear my ballet flats again and dance. Being here, *finally* in my element again, takes some of the weight off my shoulders, and my pace picks up before I force myself to slow down again.

I won't make the same mistake twice.

The piano hits the cords of my heart, the vibrations of the music becoming a part of me. Slowly, the internal spark I've always felt on the dance floor flares back to life. In this moment, it doesn't matter that I missed an audition or that I won't be able to go back to professional ballet for months.

Because *this* is me. *This* is my life. Dancing—in any way that I can. Always.

One moment I'm feeling as light as a feather, concentrating on the sensation of my feet touching the ground. The song ends and a new one starts, equally as moving and beautiful.

And the next, my foot gives out.

And I fall.

I hear myself shouting. What, I can't recall.

All I'm aware of are the tears in my eyes and the throbbing pain in my bad ankle, not as bad as it was the first time but still concerning.

With tears blurring my vision, I crawl until I reach my bag and turn off the speaker. If I listen to one more second of that song, I might go insane.

Chest heaving, I grab my phone and unlock it.

Now what?

I could call Beth. Or Kyle. Or any of my friends who live or work nearby, and I know they'll come to help me.

But there's only one person I want right now. There's only one person I need.

I ignore all the alarm bells in my head yelling at me that this is highly inappropriate, that this is crossing too many lines, that he won't pick up.

I send them all to hell, search his work phone number in my contacts from that one time he called to check on me after my panic attack, and press *Call.*

He said I could call him if I needed him, didn't he?

A beat passes. Two.

"Who is this?"

My throat is dry as sandpaper, and it hurts to even open my mouth. I lick the tears now rolling down my face, but it doesn't help. "J-James."

Not Dr. Simmons. Right now, I need James.

"Maddie, what's wrong?" I hear shuffling in the background. "Are you hurt? Where are you?"

Amidst the panic clouding my head, I manage to rattle off my current location.

"Is it your ankle?" he asks, but I have a feeling he already knows.

I gulp. "I-It hurts."

"*Shit*," he curses under his breath, but I still hear it. It doesn't give me much hope. "I'm on my way, all right? Don't move."

"Studio B," I choke out, wrapping my shaking fingers around my ankle.

I was doing so good, and now it hurts so much. It hurts so damn much.

"Okay, don't move, please." Traffic sounds reach me through the line, and I know he's outside. He's really coming for me. "Stay calm. Everything will be fine, I promise."

"P-Please, hurry."

"I'm getting in the car right now. I have to hang up. Don't move, Maddie. Please. I'll be there in just a few minutes."

"Okay."

When he hangs up, I take a deep breath and dry my tears.

Will this nightmare ever end?

***

JAMES

I've been staring at his message for the past half an hour. He's not waiting for a response, but it doesn't make this invisible pressure go away.

Andrew is nothing if not a persistent bastard, I'll give him that. For three months, he's been asking, and for three months, he's gotten one rejection after another. He knows he doesn't deserve my time, but that doesn't stop him from asking for it. *In his fucking dreams.*

Shadow and Mist are curled up on my couch, oblivious to my current dilemma. Oh, to be a spoiled cat. I pet their small heads—they continue to ignore me—before grabbing my mug of steaming coffee from the kitchen island. My mind goes so fast, I'm basically immune to caffeine by now.

Sipping on the boiling drink, I lean against the island and have a stare-off contest with my phone, currently resting on my coffee table. When I got home over an hour ago, I barely had time for a shower and a quick change into my sweatpants and hoodie before the nightmare began.

You could be honest with yourself and admit you're curious about whatever he has to say.

Yeah, right. And I could also jump off the roof.

Twelve years ago, I promised myself I would never go back to the two people who took everything from me. I wouldn't talk to them, talk about them, or seek them out. And I sure as fuck don't plan to start now.

I'm so deep in my thoughts, it takes me longer than it should to realize my phone is ringing. My *work* phone.

Frowning, I place my mug back on the counter and cross over to the living room area. At first, I think my parents are calling me, which would be weird since Dad called just yesterday. They have both of my numbers, and they sometimes get confused and end up calling the wrong one.

But as I get closer, I notice it's an unknown number.

A sudden, terrible feeling takes over my body as I accept the call. "Who is this?"

For a second that stretches out for too long, I hear nothing. And then her voice, shaky and broken and all wrong, reaches me. "J-James."

My heart stops.

"Maddie, what's wrong? Are you hurt? Where are you?"

My mind is on overdrive. I shoot toward my keys, stuffing them into the pockets of my sweatpants, and I put my workout shoes on.

There's something very wrong about this. And when she tells me exactly where she's at, it dawns on me.

"Is it your ankle?" I ask, but I already know.

"I-It hurts."

I curse under my breath. "I'm on my way, all right? Don't move."

If she does, she'll only make it worse, but I don't tell her that. The last thing either of us needs right now is to be blinded by panic.

"Studio B," she mutters, which I'm guessing is the room she's in. I hope whoever is at the front desk will let me get to her without a hassle, but if they don't, they'll hear me.

There's nothing, absolutely nothing, that will keep me away from Maddie right now.

That realization strikes the organ erratically beating inside my chest. Maybe it should concern me that I'm having such a primal, visceral reaction to her being hurt, but right now my only priority is getting to her.

The only reason I take the elevator is because it's faster than the stairs, but I'm so worried about her, I mess up and end up in the lobby instead of in the garage below the building. When I realize it, I'm almost outside.

Get a grip. She needs you.

"Okay, don't move, please." I hit the elevator button again like I have a personal vendetta against it. "Stay calm. Everything will be fine, I promise."

"P-Please, hurry." Her strained voice sounds pained, and I have to remind myself to take a deep, calming breath.

Why the hell are you freaked out anyway? She isn't your first patient. You're used to dealing with injuries.

I shut my inner voice as quickly as it takes over.

As I reach my car, I tell her, "I'm getting in the car right now. I have to hang up. Don't move, Maddie. Please. I'll be there in just a few minutes."

"Okay."

The streets of Norcastle are a blur as I speed through them. When I stop at a red light, I allow myself a few seconds to dwell on the fact that she called *me*.

I feel a strange sense of protectiveness when it comes to her, and I'm lucky that the light turns green just as I start pondering why.

Glenn Avenue is one hell of a busy street, so I'm convinced some kind of miracle is in the works when I find a parking spot just a few feet away from the entrance of the building. I fly through the revolving door, get on the elevator, and hit the button of her floor.

My luck runs out when some guy at the front desk says, "Sorry, sir, but I can't let you in if you haven't rented a studio."

Oh, for f—

"Look, man, I'm really sorry to put you in this position, but I really need to go inside," I explain hurriedly, already knowing he won't waver. "My... My friend is in Studio B, Maddison Stevens, and she hurt her ankle. She called me for help."

For a second, he looks convinced enough to give in, but then he shakes his head again. "I'm sorry, sir, but I can't let you in for security reasons."

Right. I could be a murderer for all he knows.

Desperate, I grab my phone and do the only thing I can think of—I call Maddie and put the phone on speaker.

She answers instantly. "Where are you? Are you close by?" Her voice sounds so pained, I'm one second away from shoving this guy aside and running to her.

I give him my best dry look, meaning, *See? I told you I had a reason to be here.*

"Maddie, I'm here. I'm at the front desk." The kid, who doesn't look a day over eighteen, gets another murderous look from me. "The guy at the reception desk says I can't get inside without a reservation. Could you please tell him—"

I don't need to finish that sentence.

"Let him in, please!" she begs, and hearing the angst in her voice tears me apart. "I called him because I hurt my ankle. He's my doctor. *Please*."

He swallows, clearly torn between following the company's policy and being ripped a new one first by Maddie, then by me. But he ends up making the right choice. "Okay, you can come in, but remember there are cameras in every room, and I'll—"

"Thanks, man. Appreciate it." I don't have enough time or patience to listen to the rest of his warning. As if I'd ever lay a hand on Maddie. Not that he knows that, of course, so I get it—but I'm in a hurry.

I rush through the hallway until I reach Studio B, and when I finally open the door, my stomach sinks with a feeling of dread I've never felt before.

Maddie is on the floor, dressed in very delicate ballet clothing I don't have the mind capacity to appreciate right now, cradling her ankle. Her beautiful hazel eyes are all puffy and red, and even though she's trying to conceal it, I know she's been crying.

It feels like a stab in the fucking chest.

"James..." Her voice is barely louder than a whisper, but it's enough to snap me right into doctor mode.

I kneel beside her and gently peel her fingers off her ankle. "Let's take a look, all right?" I stay calm for her, talking in a soothing voice. "I'm sure it's nothing."

She stays silent, killing me with every sniffle.

After a few moments of close examination, I find out it's not serious. I shift it around, and she doesn't flinch, which I take as a good sign.

"I'll need to examine it more thoroughly just to make sure, but everything looks fine," I tell her, and her shoulders drop with relief. "It was probably just a little sore from the lack of practicing, and it gave out. Can you stand up?"

She looks at me, and there's a kind of raw fear in her eyes I have never seen in her—and I don't want to ever again. She's strong, resilient, and seeing her like this...

Stop it.

Slowly, she shakes her head. "I'm scared."

I notice her phone, shoes, and a small portable speaker are still on the floor, so I put them all inside her bag and hang it over my shoulder. "I'm going to carry you to my car. It's just at the front. Can I?"

She nods, and I don't let myself think too much about how well her body fits against mine, or the warmth of her skin, or how she rests her head against my shoulder as I carry her outside the studio in my arms.

Forcing myself to remain in doctor mode, I don't look down at her pouty lips or vulnerable eyes. I don't look at that cute button nose resting against the black fabric of my hoodie. Because, if I do, I'll be gone. And I can't afford to be.

"Are you all right, miss?" the guy at the front desk asks when we pass by, alarm in his voice. Now he gives a crap.

Maddie gives him a weak smile and a thumbs-up, a gesture so adorable it makes my chest hurt. "I'm safe now."

Her words are a bullet aiming for my heart.

Safe.

She feels safe with me.

Pride swells inside of me, and so does another part of my body that has no business being so alert right now.

"I just wanted to remind you that the studio isn't to be held responsible in a personal injury case!" he calls out as we reach the elevators.

"I know! I signed the waiver!" Maddie exclaims back just as the elevator doors open, and we get inside. She doesn't sound pissed off, which is impressive, considering the guy almost prevented me from getting to her in the first place.

We say nothing as I carry her to the front seat of my car. Once she's safely inside, I close the door and climb behind the wheel. "To your apartment?"

When she nods, I start the engine. The journey to her apartment is full of silence, which I only break once to ask her how her ankle is feeling. A bit sore, she says, but much better than a while ago. I'm quite confident she didn't sprain it and only moved it too abruptly, but I want to be sure.

"Do you mind if I take a look at your ankle again at your place?" I ask, which for some reason makes my hands all clammy. I tell myself I'm only doing this for her own sake, because she needs the reassurance that her recovery hasn't been compromised.

"Please."

It hurts me that she's hurt. She's been through enough shit with her ballet career, and I suspect there's much, much more pain in that big heart of hers that she hasn't told me about.

I know how it feels. I've been there, and unlike me, she won't fall. I'll make sure of it.

I'll pick her up every time until she learns to stay balanced.

A small eternity later, I park a couple of blocks away from her apartment. When I get out of the car and open the door on her side, she tells me, "I think I can walk."

That would be good. It would give me a better idea on the state of her ankle, and it would prevent my cock from straining my pants while I carry her. Sounds like a win-win situation.

"I'll get your shoes." I notice she's still wearing her ballet slippers, so I reach into the back seat for her bag and pass it to her.

She changes quickly, and I offer to carry it for her again, but she shakes her head. "It's fine, thanks." But she does grab my arm as she walks.

When she lets go to open her front door, I instantly feel cold, and I don't like it. I don't like that she has the power to affect me so much.

I never allowed myself to imagine Maddie in a more private and intimate setting, so I never wondered where she lived. But somehow, as I scan her quaint studio, it very much feels like her.

There's a small kitchen right next to the entrance, with a few odd-looking mugs showcased on the counter that look like modern pieces of decoration more than anything. Then there's a small couch and a coffee table, separated from her bed by a folding screen. Colorful pictures of abstract paintings and plants are scattered all over the place, and it feels cozy. It feels like Maddie.

It also smells like her—flowery with a hint of vanilla.

Sweet, so damn sweet.

I close the door behind us, suddenly very aware that we're alone in a space that might be even tinier than my office at the clinic, and I try not to panic.

"Shall we sit on the couch?" she offers, visibly more at ease than I am.

I clear my throat. "Sure."

She takes one step and curses under her breath. "I need to change out of my tights. You'll want to look at my bare skin, right?"

Now's not the time to think about her skin. "Preferably, yes."

She grabs something from a dresser and disappears behind the only door of the studio, which I assume is the bathroom. "I'll be right back."

I take a seat on her couch and check my phone. No new messages, but I still find myself opening my chat with Andrew. His text from a few hours ago looks back at me, mocking me.

Unknown: Maybe not this week, but what about the next? Let's just talk, James. Think about it.

That's the problem—I think too much about it, and it's the last thing I need.

Maddie reappears a moment later, wearing a sinful pair of sleeping shorts. I look away from the smooth skin of her legs as quickly as my eyes land on it. *Fucking hell.*

"It barely hurts anymore," she says, sounding more enthusiastic now.

She takes a seat and places her foot on the cushion next to me. Without using my fucking brain, I take it between my hands and place it over my lap. I don't miss her slight intake of breath.

"Is this okay?" I ask.

She gives me a small nod. "Yes."

I concentrate on her ankle for the next few minutes, instead of on the nearness of her foot to my cock. As I suspected, it's nothing to be worried about.

"Everything looks fine," I tell her. "You can apply an ice pack tonight and rest for the next couple of days, but I'm pretty confident it won't give you any trouble."

She lets out a relieved sigh. "Thank you. I thought I'd have to start all over again."

"Not necessary." Carefully, I place her foot on the plush rug below the coffee table and stand up. "It was just a scare. Make sure you warm up for a bit longer next time. I'll give you some exercises at the clinic tomorrow."

Her genuine, bright smile makes my heart leap. *This girl.*

I need to get the hell out of here.

But just when I think I can't possibly die harder on the inside, she gets up after me and throws her arms around my middle.

And hugs me.

She hugs me.

Maddie is hugging me.

"Thank you," she says, her voice muffled against my hoodie. "Thank you for coming to my rescue and taking care of me. You didn't have to."

My traitorous arms move around her smaller frame, engulfing her. It feels right to have her here, safe against my chest, and I hate it.

I hate that I don't hate it.

"No problem," I murmur, not entirely sure that she's even heard me.

But when she squeezes my middle, I know she has.

It's only now that I realize a haunting truth—Maddie Stevens, my twenty-one-year-old patient, has me wrapped around her little finger.

chapter 16

JAMES

For a whole week, I try my best to ignore Maddie.

The day after her incident at the ballet studio, I give her a list of safe exercises and take another look at her ankle, but everything seems normal.

I'm glad she called me, but I shouldn't have suggested going to her apartment with her, seeing her space, and I shouldn't have hugged her back. Because, a week later, I can still feel those arms around my body, around my cold heart, and I can't stand it.

But it ends today.

As always, she's my first appointment of the day. I get to the clinic ten minutes earlier than usual, unable to stay at home for another second. In a little over an hour, I won't have to see her ever again.

This is our last session.

I could get one of my colleagues to oversee her checkups, and if I have to do it myself, at least a whole month would've passed. A month in which she'll move on to do other things, and I'll try my hardest to get her out of my system.

Maybe it's because this is the last time I'm seeing her, but when I woke up at 5:00 a.m. today, my brain decided it's had enough of pretending to conceal what I've known for a while—I'm attracted to her.

I shouldn't, and it feels right and wrong all at once, but there's no point in trying to deny the truth anymore.

Maddie sparks something in me, a strange kind of feeling I don't think I've ever experienced. I've had girlfriends in the past—although I'll admit I haven't for a while—but I still remember vividly how they made me feel.

It wasn't like this.

I'm not battling the kind of attraction that urges me to take her on my office desk, even if I'd spread those beautiful legs and feast on her in a heartbeat. But that's not exactly what I feel, hence why it's so confusing.

With her...it's something else.

I finally put a finger on it when I carried her in my arms out of the studio and she told the guy at the reception desk that she felt safe with me. It wasn't the first time I felt those goddamn tingles. No, I felt them when she broke down in my office after I told her she couldn't go back to professional ballet right away; when I felt like I'd die if I didn't wait until the end of her shift to drive her home; when I urged that creep away from the parking lot, scared out of my mind he'd do or say something to Maddie.

It's taken me too long to realize what I feel for her is a strong, deep-rooted sense of admiration and protection.

Because I see myself in her.

Because the darkness in my heart recognizes hers.

I was nineteen when a leg injury ended my NFL career before it even began.

For as long as I live, I will regret not giving it my all during that college game. Many insisted that it was an accident—an opponent who hit me too hard—and that I could've done nothing to prevent it, but it didn't matter.

I didn't make the NFL draft a few months later, and the two people I thought would support me forever proved to be my most ardent enemies.

After a doctor told me I was at risk of losing all mobility in my right leg if I played again, I spiraled.

I dropped out of college, and for the following few months, alcohol became my best friend. It raised every alarm in my parents' heads since I'd never gotten drunk before. Thankfully, they managed to pull me out of it before it was too late.

Seeing a therapist for a while helped me learn how to have a healthier relationship with alcohol and with myself. I'm okay now—I know my limits and when to stop. I can enjoy a drink without becoming a danger to myself or others.

When Maddie told me about her ruined dream of joining the ballet company, I saw myself in her struggle. At the same time, though, I didn't.

Because, even today, I could only dream of being as strong and brave as her. She thinks she's defeated, but a broken person wouldn't buzz with energy at the prospect of going back to their craft, and her eyes wouldn't shine with such raw determination.

I'm sure she thinks her future is over, but I've seen enough of her to know she'll rise. And that's what makes me want to shelter her from all the bad around her, what makes me run at the faintest mention of Maddie being in trouble.

Because, unlike me, she's strong, her heart is kind, and her sheer determination will get her anything she wants.

I smile at the memory of calling her a brat. Her brother might call her "princess," and she might have grown up a little spoiled, but hell—I'd spoil her, too, if I could.

And those dangerous thoughts, that shit, ends right now.

Maddie knocks on the already open door and walks in without her crutches, a shy smile on those beautiful lips. "Hey, Doc."

One last day. Just one more.

"Ready for our last session?"

She hesitates, and I find myself not having an answer either.

Eventually she nods and gets ready to start.

"This is going to sound crazy," she says as she unties her shoe, "but these past six weeks have gone by so quickly. I can't believe I'm fully healed just like that."

My back is to her, and I take advantage of that fact to allow myself a small smile. "That's medical science for you."

She chuckles, and her laughter wraps around my lungs and squeezes so damn hard I can barely breathe. *It'll be over in an hour. Just hold yourself together until then.*

"I suppose you're right." Still with that easy smile on her lips, she walks over to our exercising mat for the last time. "I just thought..." When she bites down on her lower lip, I turn around to check on whatever random papers I can find on my desk. Jesus. "I thought I would never recover."

The sudden turn in her voice, from playful to somber, makes me glance at her. "I didn't have any doubts that you'd make a full recovery, Maddie."

At my words, she gives me another smile. It doesn't escape me I didn't call her Miss Stevens.

"Even after I went out when I should've been resting?"

I don't hesitate. "Yes. Even then."

"Mm..."

I adjust my glasses just to do something with my hands. "Let's get started."

For the next hour, we do some stretches and jumping exercises, and I observe, to my satisfaction, that her ankle is responding well. I still don't think she should risk going back to professional ballet for a few months—and I tell her that—but I'm not worried about it getting worse.

She stays focused on her movements and my instructions and fires question after question about the care instructions. It's obvious she's nervous she'll have to handle the rest of her recovery by herself, so I tell her, "I'll email you a guide and some videos with quick exercises you can do at home every day." And then, because I love torturing myself, I add, "If you ever have any questions or concerns, you know where to find me."

Maddie nods quickly, gratitude written all over her face, and we continue until the alarm on my watch goes off, indicating the end of our very last session of physical rehabilitation.

It's strange. After our hug last week, I'd been craving the relief this moment would bring, the comforting knowledge that my feelings for Maddie would have an expiration date.

But now that the day has finally come, all I feel is this immense confusion and a twinge of bittersweet disappointment.

And it hits me—I'm going to miss her.

For whatever fucked-up reason, I'm going to miss seeing my twenty-one-year-old patient every day—her constant questions and her strong will to get better.

While I'm pretty sure I'm crumbling inside, Maddie looks unfazed as she puts her shoes back on. I busy myself updating her file on the computer and try not to think too hard about the fact that at this time tomorrow morning, I'll be saying goodbye to a completely different patient.

Just like always, you moron.

Yes, patients come and go, and I don't care if I ever see them again. I wish them well, don't get me wrong, but Maddie is different. And it's taken me a very long time to admit it to myself.

She clears her throat, snapping me out of my thoughts. "I thought it would be appropriate to say goodbye with one last mandala."

I look up just in time to see her holding out another one of her impressive drawings. Carefully, I take it as if it were an original Picasso. For me, it has even more value.

"Thank you," I say sincerely, observing all the intricate details. This mandala comes in the shape of a ballerina, and it chokes me up.

"Thank you." Her smile could blind the sun and the stars. "I know this is what you do for a living, but I can't thank you enough for what you've done for me. Not just my ankle, but...everything else too."

She doesn't need to elaborate. I know exactly what she's talking about because going out of my way for her is what turned me into a mess in the first place.

She picks up her bag, getting ready to leave, and I almost stop her until I realize how insane that would be. What excuse could I possibly use?

Hey, Maddie, I know I've been cold to you, but it's only because you were my patient and I was having some pretty conflicting thoughts about you. Do you wanna go out for a drink tonight?

Instead, I choose to be professional and say, "It was my pleasure, Maddie. I'm glad you're happy with the results." I even give her a smile that doesn't hurt too much.

She wasn't supposed to have this effect on me, damn it.

And with one last smile and a curt nod, she walks away. I clench my fists under the table to keep me from reaching out to her and count to ten in my head.

Only, instead of numbers, they are reminders.

She's too young for you.

She'd think you're a pervert.

You are a fucking pervert.

She only sees you as a helpful professional.

Don't ruin this at the last second.

You're not ready to—

"James?"

Fuck.

I unclench my fists. "Yes, Maddie?"

Her fingers are already wrapped around the door handle, but she doesn't turn it. Her hazel eyes scan my face with uncertainty, and when she pulls her bottom lip between her teeth, I'm positive she wants to kill me.

"I know you're only doing your job, but you've done so much

more for me, and I..." She stops, takes a deep breath, and her voice sounds so much steadier when she speaks next. "I'm working at the bar tonight, and I wanted to offer you a free dinner. On the house. If you can't make it tonight, or ever, I'll understand, but it would mean a lot to me if you said yes."

My heart stops, and I can't help but blurt out the first thing that comes to mind. "Dinner with you?"

Her eyes widen, and I immediately realize my mistake. She said she was working. She's obviously not going to have dinner with me.

But then she nods, and heat climbs up my skin. "Yes, with me. I'm sure I can take a break from washing all the dishes."

"I don't want to cause any problems."

She waves me off. "Monica won't mind. I have a twenty-minute break at around eight, so it'll be a short dinner, but I'll be there."

I should say no. God knows it, I know it, the whole world knows it, but every single fiber in my body is begging me to accept.

It's just dinner in a crowded bar on her break, for only twenty minutes. I couldn't possibly fuck this up in that time.

I swear I can feel the ground shifting beneath my feet as I say, "You don't have to, but thank you. I'll be there tonight."

When she gives me that beautiful smile again, I know I'm in trouble.

chapter 17

MADDIE

If you ever, for whatever reason, need the help of someone with a ton of self-control, I'm not your girl.

Dinner. I invited him for dinner. *With me.*

Because, as I was leaving the clinic for the last time, I couldn't fathom the idea of not seeing him ever again. Of not talking to him, not giving him any more mandalas, not looking at that permanent scowl on his handsome face that looks chiseled by the gods.

There, I said it. Whatever.

I knew it wouldn't take much convincing, but it's still uncanny how quickly Monica agrees to extend my break for a little longer so I can have dinner with James.

"You can come a little earlier and finish your shift before you guys have your date," she told me over the phone after I texted her my request.

"It's not a date," I was quick to amend. "Just a thank-you dinner."

Monica made the kind of sound my brother makes after he asks Lila if she did her homework, she says yes—an obvious lie—and he doesn't believe her.

"I can be there at three," I suggested to distract her. If she so much as plants the mental picture of James and me on a date again, I'm not sure I'll survive it.

"Sure, honey. I'll see you then."

James arrives at the restaurant fifteen minutes before I'm

done for the day. And I may or may not start scrubbing the plates a little faster.

When I'm done, I rush to Monica's office at the back and change out of my plain black T-shirt and put on a loose, baby blue sweater that goes just fine with my black jeans and sneakers. It's not the fanciest of outfits, but again, this isn't a date. I'm not making an effort, although that doesn't stop me from fixing my hair and applying some mascara and a bit of lipstick.

After checking my not-so-bad reflection in the mirror, I square my shoulders, nod to myself, and remember I'm not going to war so I shouldn't be so dramatic.

I mean, let's be real for a second. This is James—he's seen me at my worst, during a panic attack. I have nothing to worry about.

The bar is loud and crowded, as it's a Friday night, but it's impossible to miss him. His blue eyes—*have I unconsciously matched my sweater to his eyes?*—are glued on the TV, but as soon as I step out of Monica's office, they land on me like a missile on a target.

And I gulp.

Despite my usual confidence, my knees wobble at the sight of the trimmed beard that makes him look so much older, and my palms start sweating when I take in his black sweater with a roll neck.

Get it together, Maddie. This is not the first time you've seen a man in a roll-neck sweater.

It's not, but it's the first time I want a man to take it off. Would it be so wrong to imagine him shirtless now that he's not my physical therapist?

Yes. He's still ten years older than you.

Right. That.

I shake my head, forcing myself to snap out of it, and make my way toward the booth he's at. With a smile that hopefully doesn't give away my nerves, I sit next to him and then recoil once

I notice my leg is pressed against his. "Hi."

"Hey."

I don't know whether the half smirk on his lips calms me down or makes me even more anxious.

My hands find the menu, and I pretend to scan it, even though I know it by heart. "So, guess what?"

"Hmm." He puts his arm around the back of our booth, his fingertips almost touching my shoulder, and I take a deep breath.

You're overreacting. His arm must be tired, that's all.

I turn my head and give him one of my biggest smiles so he sees I'm not being weird about our close proximity. "My boss allowed me to clock in early, so I'm done with my shift."

That half smirk is still in place and his signature frown is gone, which throws me for a loop. "Is that right?"

"Yep."

His eyes don't leave mine as he takes the menu away from my grip with the hand resting on the table. "Good. I like to take my time when I'm eating. Go slowly."

My breath hitches at the innuendo that I'm pretty sure isn't even one. My hormones must be on crack, because why am I imagining James's head between my legs right now, seeing firsthand how slowly he can eat?

For fuck's sake.

This isn't happening to me. I'm not having a sexual fantasy about my ex-physical therapist who is a decade older than me and happens to be sitting right here. I refuse to believe it.

"I liked the chicken wings you got me the other day," he comments casually, scanning the menu as if he hadn't just turned me into jelly. "What should we order this time? I trust your judgment."

Yes, Maddie, how about you focus on real food and nothing else?

"The pulled pork sandwich is good," I offer once my heart has calmed down enough to allow me to have a normal conversation like any sane person would. "The chicken quesadillas too."

He thinks about it for a moment. "The sandwich sounds good. What are you getting?"

It's not like I can think properly yet, so I say, "The same."

He nods. "Soda?"

"Sure."

Monica arrives at our booth just in time to take our orders, and while James tells her what we want, I can't help but feel self-conscious by our age difference again.

That beard makes him look older, and even if I physically look older than twenty-one, I'm still worried about what people think when they see us together.

I know it's stupid. Who cares what others think?

Plus, it's not like we're *together*. We're just two people hanging out at a bar. Big deal.

"You there?"

I blink. "Yeah, yes. Sorry. Did you say something?"

That smug smirk almost kills me. "I asked if your ankle is giving you any trouble."

"Nope. Everything's fine." I smile back. "I'm going back to waitressing next week, in fact."

"That's good. Will you be taking more shifts?"

Monica comes back with our sodas and throws James a wink that makes me blush. That woman isn't subtle at all. I clear my throat. "If I can, yes. The tips are great, and I don't want to keep living off my brother." It comes out before I can help it. I don't want him to think I'm a leech, but again, that's the truth, so why keep hiding it?

"I remember your brother coming with you to the clinic that first day. Does he live in the area?"

"That'd be him. And no, he lives in Warlington, a few hours away. That's why he stopped coming to the clinic," I explain.

For a moment, I'm afraid James doesn't care and I'm oversharing, but he keeps asking me questions.

"What about your mother?"

My stomach jumps. "What about her?"

James rubs his jaw, and I can't help but follow the movement. Seriously, I must be coming down with a fever. I don't think it's normal to be attracted to somebody's hands this much.

"I remember you mentioning her once. She couldn't take you to the clinic?" he asks but quickly adds, "Sorry if I'm overstepping. Feel free to tell me to fuck off."

An honest chuckle escapes me. "It's okay. My mom and I don't see each other much." I take the straw on my soda between my fingers and play with it. "I grew up with my brother, actually."

He raises his eyebrows. "Oh?"

I can tell he's curious but is too afraid to ask, so I keep going. I'm not ashamed of the way I was brought up. "He took me in when I was four. He was thirty. I lived with him and my sister-in-law—and then with my niece too—until I moved out here when I was eighteen."

"Wow," he breathes. "I don't even know where to start. I have too many questions."

I smirk. "Shoot."

He moves his arm from the back of the booth and laces his fingers over the table. We're so close, I can smell his aftershave, and now I want to climb him like a tree. *Great.*

"So," he starts. "When I saw your brother, I thought he was your dad. No offense. He just looks older."

"He's forty-seven," I tell him. "I was born when he was twenty-six. And before you ask, yes, my mom was very young when she had him. Sixteen, to be exact. Technically, my brother is only my half brother, but neither of us like to acknowledge it." I smile at the thought of Sammy. "He's much more than a brother to me. He had to be."

"I can imagine." He scans my face like he's looking for something. "What's his name?"

"Samuel, but everyone calls him Cal because his last name is Callaghan. But I call him Sammy."

"That's a lot of names for one man," he teases.

"He doesn't mind." I smile. "Any other questions?"

James doesn't hesitate. "Why did you move in with your brother in the first place?"

Against my will, my lips press into a thin line, but I force myself to tell him this. I want to do it, damn it. For whatever reason, I want him to know all of me.

"My mom used to have issues with alcohol."

He listens attentively, and even when Monica comes back with our sandwiches, he doesn't make a move to eat his.

"My brother was always around because my mother was unreliable. Well, and because he loves me, I guess."

"Of course he does," he assures me, even though he doesn't know my brother or what our relationship is like. I appreciate it nonetheless.

"When I was four, my parents got into a big fight, and my father left. I haven't seen him since, but that's beside the point." I take a deep breath. Strangely enough, I remember everything about that day. "My mother got drunk in our living room after putting me to sleep, but she was crying very loudly, so I woke up. I got upset that my mom was crying, and I rushed to help her because I thought she was dying. And when I was running toward her, I tripped over an empty bottle she'd left around, hit my head against the coffee table, and... Well, see for yourself."

I pull my hair back to show him the right side of my hairline, where a tiny scar is still visible.

He hisses. "Shit, Maddie."

"I know." I give him a sad smile.

He reaches up to touch it, and when his thumb makes contact

with my skin, it lights up something inside me. Something that has never been awoken before.

His eyes find mine as he brushes the hair away from my scar. Zipping electricity passes between us before he draws back.

"What happened after that?" he asks, stealing a fry from my plate.

I glare at him and steal one of his, which makes him laugh.

"Social Services got involved, and long story short, my mom went to rehab, and I moved in with my brother and Grace—his now wife. My mom tried to get me to move back with her when she got clean, but apparently I had really bad separation anxiety from my brother, so they agreed that it would be best if I stayed with him."

"Do you see your mom often?"

"Not much," I admit. "She... We aren't the best at keeping in touch, but I saw her not long ago. As you know."

He nods. "You looked upset that night."

"I was." I don't want to elaborate, so I don't. He doesn't press either, which I appreciate more than he knows. "Let's eat before these get cold," I suggest.

"I've got more questions."

I arch an amused eyebrow. "And here I thought you were a silent grouch. Take a bite and I'll answer."

He chuckles again, deep and husky, and it's one of the most beautiful sounds I've ever heard.

It's also a sound that makes me press my legs together to alleviate some of the discomfort there, but I'd rather not focus on that right now.

"So, your questions," I prompt once I've taken a couple of bites from my sandwich. His is halfway gone already, the monster. "I thought you were a slow eater?" I tease him.

He gives me a look I can't read. "I'm starving tonight."

Oh, God.

He continues, "But yes, I have another question. You moved to Norcastle at eighteen?"

"For my ballet degree, yes."

"And you moved here alone?"

I shrug. "The school had dorms for students, and I was all for it. I didn't want to make anyone move here for me." I wouldn't make them change their lives for me. Again.

"That's impressive," he says. "You weren't scared to move to a whole new city by yourself so young?"

"I was so excited." I smile at the memory of my first day. "All I wanted was to study ballet and be the best I could be, so I didn't care if I had to move out. I tend to make friends really fast, as you're well aware—Graham and I are pretty much inseparable now."

"Sure you are," he deadpans, but he's smirking.

He follows the fry I steal from his plate with his eyes as it disappears inside my mouth.

"Are we friends, James?"

He takes the last bite of his sandwich and swallows it down with his soda. Now is his turn to steal not one but two of my fries. This means war. "I don't know if I want to be friends with a thief."

"You must hate yourself, then."

Something passes over his gaze, but he's quick to blink it away. "I don't befriend my patients."

"*Ex*-patient."

"Same thing."

"But you drive them home after their shift ends?"

He lets out a deep breath through his nose, his cheeks flushing. "You're a menace."

I make a show of batting my eyelashes at him just to piss him off. "But am I also your friend?"

He pretends to think about it. "Only because I get free mandalas."

"Of course."

It should feel weird, I realize, to joke with him. Not too long ago, he refused to say more than a couple of words to me, always keeping it professional, and now... I can almost believe we're really friends.

Or, at the very least, he doesn't fully despise my company.

For the next hour, James keeps asking me questions about ballet and my time at college. It doesn't hurt to talk about it anymore, not as much. He doesn't bring up my ballet-related plans for the future, which helps.

I also ask him what he studied in college—physical therapy, no surprise there—and about growing up in Norcastle. Conversation flows easily between us, and before I know it, a different waitress has come back with our check.

"Let me pay for it," James insists, already taking out his wallet.

"Put that thing away." Without thinking, I shoot out my hand until it covers his. Warm, calloused skin meets mine, and something akin to nerves settles in my stomach. When breathing doesn't come so easily anymore, I pull away. "I told you it was my treat, didn't I? So let me pay."

"You don't have to."

"I want to."

He scowls but puts his wallet back in his pocket. "Brat."

"Grouch."

His only answer is some kind of growl that doesn't sound entirely human.

I take care of the bill while he goes to the restroom, and soon enough we're outside.

"I'm driving you home," he says as he closes the door of the bar behind us, the cold night air freezing my nose the second I step outside. "It's nonnegotiable."

I chuckle. "Okay." I don't feel like taking the metro this late at night, anyway. Now that I can walk, taxis or Ubers are no longer an expense I need.

We are walking toward his car when his hand suddenly comes to rest against the small of my back. I stiffen at the unexpected touch, but I also feel grounded. When I tilt my head to look at him, though, his jaw is so tight I'm afraid he might shatter all his teeth. "James?"

He doesn't look at me, his gaze lost somewhere in the darkness of the parking lot, as he asks, "You see that car over there? The white one." He rattles off a model I'm familiar with.

"Yes," I whisper for some reason. Suddenly I don't feel so grounded anymore. "What's wrong?"

"When I was waiting to drive you home the other day, he was here too."

A shiver of awareness travels down my spine, as if someone were burning their gaze into it. It's the same feeling I got when I thought I was being watched in the city.

"I went up to him and told him to fuck off. He thought I was a cop, so he did. My warning might have expired, though."

I frown. "You talked to him?"

"Yes."

"James, that could've been dangerous."

"I don't care." His hand on me feels heavier, hotter. "I don't want him lurking outside your workplace, Maddie. Not when he might be a danger to you."

Butterflies take flight in my stomach, and I force them to die immediately.

He doesn't mean anything by it. Anyone with common sense and a good heart would want to protect a young woman from a creep.

But as we pass by the mysterious white car, something inside me pulls me toward it.

Like a puppet being led by an invisible string, I turn my head toward the man sitting behind the wheel, bathed in shadows.

And I know.

I know it's him.

The man who—

No. It can't be. It can't fucking be.

I move away from James so abruptly I almost trip over my own two feet.

He calls my name, but I barely hear him.

The only reason I know my heart is beating is because I'm still alive and I am able to keep walking. Otherwise, I would've thought I was dead and had gone to hell.

Because as I close the distance between me and his car, my eyes fall on the last person on this planet I ever expected to see again.

The first man to show me I wasn't enough.

The first person to leave me and never look back.

No matter how many years have passed, I would recognize that face anywhere. It's the one I see in my nightmares.

I stop.

He rolls down the window.

It's him, but I still ask.

A part of me doesn't want this moment to be real.

But I know it is, and my whole world crumbles.

"Dad?"

chapter 18

MADDIE

"Maddie!" James's voice comes from somewhere not far behind me, but I don't react.

I can't.

My body is floating in a bubble of shock and anger that I can't burst.

This is a nightmare. You've fallen asleep, and you'll wake up any moment now.

Only, when my nails dig into my palms from how tightly I'm closing my fists and reality is still here, it dawns on me that this moment is truly my worst nightmare come to life.

"Maddison? Is it really you?" the man in front of me asks, making no effort to exit the car.

I'd forgotten the sound of his voice, and a prickle of uneasiness travels down my spine at the sight of someone I thought was dead.

He sure acted like *I* was.

My name sounds rotten and wrong coming from him, and I don't respond.

My head is frozen in time, prisoner of the last memory I have of my father. Him, yelling at my mother while he thought I was asleep. Pushing her away from the door. Letting her fall to the ground, hurt and scared and confused. His eyes on me as he left.

James's arms wrap around my middle as he pulls me against his chest. I'm numb, but I still feel his warmth. I still feel his agitated breaths against my back. "Who is this?"

Under any other circumstances, his hands splayed against my stomach would make me melt, but now I only feel sick. Sick of living in an endless nightmare I created all on my own.

"I saw you the other day," Pete sneers at James behind me, as if my father was entitled to even be in my presence in the first place.

He's not. He's really fucking not.

Seventeen years have gone by, and he's still as disgusting as I remember.

"You my daughter's boyfriend or some shit? Aren't you too old for her?"

"I'm not your daughter," I spit out, ignoring his assumptions. He has no right to ask, no right to *look* at me after all this time.

Sammy tried, he really tried to prevent this very thing from happening, but this burning hatred I feel for my father is something I'd never blame my older brother for—the skunk in front of me is the only one responsible. No offense to skunks.

"Damn sure are, kid." He slides his glare toward me.

I stand a little taller, not wanting him to see how unsettled his undivided attention makes me feel.

"Raised you for four years. Been looking for you for seventeen."

Raised me?

The usually still pool of anger that sits at the pit of my stomach—and has been growing and growing since I became a teenager who finally understood what kind of cards I'd been dealt—roars to life.

"Raised me?" I let out a dry chuckle that makes me sound nothing like the person I am. I've turned into a cold, cruel, unforgiving creature, nothing like the woman my brother fought so hard to raise. But then I look at the man in front of me, and the guilt disappears. "You have some fucking nerve claiming that."

My father frowns. "Language—"

"Shut your mouth," I growl, the loose grip I have on my sanity slipping through my fingers *quickly*.

"Hey. Let's calm down, yeah? He's not worth it," James murmurs into my ear, holding me closer. He turns to my father, speaking to him over my shoulder. "She doesn't want to see you. Get the fuck out of here before I call the cops."

But my father doesn't even look at him. He doesn't give me the privilege of escaping his harsh stare. "Maddie, listen to me."

"I have nothing to say to you, Pete."

I'm well aware that my whole body is shaking and I can't breathe normally. I don't want him to know he has this effect on me. He doesn't deserve to, and I hate myself for being curious about what he has to say after all these years. I shouldn't, *damn it*.

He left us. He left me when I was a child, when a little girl needs her father the most, for reasons I never knew. And do I want to find out now? Do they even matter?

I grew up with a roof over my head, food on the table, and more love than I could've ever asked for. I'm happy, loved, taken care of. I don't need him, and I never will.

"I tried to come back, you know that?" he continues, ignoring me.

I shake my head and pray to gods I don't even believe in to keep my tears at bay. "I don't care."

I don't. I may have once, back when I was naïve enough to believe my father left because he loved me. Just like my mom did, I thought he wanted me to grow up with my brother because he was my best chance at a healthy upbringing.

But it's bullshit.

Pete didn't look back, not once in seventeen years. Years ago, when I was willing to give him the benefit of the doubt, I told myself he'd left because he loved and respected me enough not to hurt me, knowing he couldn't be the father I needed.

But no. He left because he never wanted me, and he never gave a fuck about me.

Now is his turn to chuckle. The sound is sarcastic and bitter, and I already know I'll hear it in my nightmares for as long as I live. "He didn't tell you. Doesn't fucking surprise me."

"Who?" I shouldn't entertain him. I *shouldn't*, and I hate myself for giving in so easily. This is what he wants, damn it, but I can't take my words back.

I watch as his mouth turns into a mocking, bitter smile. He thinks he's holding a piece of life-changing information over me, the kind that will turn the wheel of fate in his favor, doesn't he?

"Your brother. I found him, found *you* years ago and asked to see you, but he had full custody and wouldn't allow it."

A small pang of disappointment in Sammy for keeping this to himself hits me for a fleeting second. And then I come to my senses. "Do you seriously think you can come out of nowhere after seventeen years and talk shit about my brother?"

I know I'm raising my voice when James pulls me closer, but I don't care. I've been keeping this inside for years, and he's going to hear me.

"What's your endgame here, Pete? Make me hate him and turn to you? Good luck with that. You're nothing to me. *Nothing*. You're not my father, and I couldn't be happier that my brother kept me away from you all those years ago. You don't deserve me. You never did, and you sure don't deserve me now."

He blinks once, his expression not cruel but not welcoming either, and that's all the emotions he shows, like a psychopath. To be fair, I'm not entirely sure he isn't one.

I know nothing about my father. I don't know where he's been for the past seventeen years, what trouble he's gotten himself into, if any. He could've *murdered* someone for all I know.

I've never been more grateful to have James with me.

"I know I've made mistakes," Pete has the nerve to say. "I'm a changed man, Maddie. I've been working really hard on myself all these years, trying to become a better man. I realized I wasn't a good dad, but I promise I'm ready to be the father you deserve."

"Oh, *now* you're ready? How convenient." I cross my arms as best as I can with James's hands still on my stomach. He doesn't let go, and I'm thankful for the anchor that is his presence. "Tell me how you found me. You've been following me around, haven't you?"

"I didn't know how to approach you best," he confesses.

Never in a million years would I have guessed *my father* was stalking me. I guess my life really is a shit show.

"I saw an article in the newspaper about a ballet show a few months ago. Your picture was there with your name."

The summer recital. Our college organizes one every summer for dance students, right before graduation, and it's kind of a big deal. Scouts come to look for talent, as well as agents and other professionals of the world of dance. It doesn't come as a surprise it made the local news, but it feels like a violation that he found out about it. That he found me because of it.

I sober up, set on not letting him see how desperately I want to cry right now. "Okay, thanks for letting me know. You can leave now."

"You don't understand—"

"I understand perfectly." My gaze digs into his, and I take comfort in knowing this may be the last time I look at my so-called father. *Just do this, and it's over. Stay strong.* "You're going to drive away and never follow me again. Do you understand me? Don't you ever attempt to contact me or my family in any way ever again. I have camera footage of your car stalking me outside of this restaurant, an eyewitness, and a police report of child neglect and emotional abuse from years ago that would still hold in court." It probably won't since I'm twenty-one, but I have the feeling he doesn't know this. I have no idea if the cameras outside showed his car, either. Will that stop me from using both as ammunition? Not at all. "So, unless you want to live behind bars for a while, I'd suggest you leave me alone for good."

For the first time since our conversation started, Pete makes an attempt to exit the car. He has his fingers wrapped around the handle when James's hand reaches forward, shutting his door with such a strong force, the car shakes. "Stay where you are," he growls. "Don't come near her."

The blazing fire in Pete's eyes grows. And in this moment, with his anger mirroring mine, I've never felt so disgusted with myself.

You're just like him.

"You her guard dog or some shit?" He turns to me, the cruelty in his gaze making me relive the worst day of my childhood. Of my entire life. "Who is this motherfucker?"

"You don't have the right to ask," I spit out, tired of this whole situation. "Don't talk to him. Don't talk to me. Leave me alone, Pete. I don't want to see you ever again."

He laughs. He full-on *laughs* like a maniac as if any of this were funny.

"I understand now. I've heard about this—daddy issues, is that it? How fucking surprising. What was it, again? When young girls like older men because their dad wasn't around?"

I'm so done. I'm so *done* with this man.

"What are you even saying?" My breaths are agitated, my pulse hammering in my throat. "I *did* grow up with a father. It just wasn't you, and I couldn't be happier about that."

He frowns like I've just personally offended him. "Your brother isn't your father."

"He has more father in his pinky finger than you do in all your body."

For a moment, he says nothing. All I hear is my own nervous breathing and my hammering heart, paired with a sick feeling in my stomach that makes me want to throw up.

I thought I knew what anger felt like, but I was wrong. I was so wrong. My father is so acidic, so damn toxic, I burn just looking at him.

Don't cry. Don't cry now. Not in front of the man who was responsible for so many of your tears.

Without saying a word, Pete starts the car, and an invisible weight lifts off my shoulders. But the tightness in my muscles stays, and so does James's arm locked around my middle.

My father's eyes find mine, mirroring the last time he left when I was four. When he abandoned my mother, hurt and confused, and turned his back on his own daughter forever.

He made that choice. He made that choice for me, and he doesn't get to come back now because he's ready. Fuck that.

When I was four, I felt scared and confused as to why my mother was crying on the floor and why my father was leaving without a word. Now I only sag with relief at the realization that I told him every venomous word I'd bottled up inside over the years and I'll never have to see him again.

I'll make sure of it.

"We're not done here, Maddie," he says. There's an edge to his voice I don't like one bit. I recognize a threat when I hear one. "You're my daughter, and I won't let you get away this time."

"You're the one who walked away, not me." I swallow back my nervous tears, holding them at bay for dear life. "Come near me again, and you'll face the consequences."

A look passes between us, and for a moment, I see myself in his eyes. He's right about something—I'm his daughter, and no matter how hard I try, I can't change that.

You're Sammy's sister. You're not Pete's daughter, not in the way that matters.

Tonight, it sounds less convincing than ever before.

And just like seventeen years ago, Pete Stevens slides his eyes away from me, the daughter he never wanted or loved, and drives away.

The sound of his engine dies away in the distance, and the parking lot drowns in silence once more.

He leaves me wondering if the past ten minutes have really happened or if this is one of my cruel nightmares.

I take a deep breath, but I can't take a second one.

"Look at me, Maddie."

The ground opens beneath me, and darkness swallows me.

My heart is empty, rid of any emotion but the raw, sore wound of the little girl who has been abandoned far too many times, by too many people who were meant to stay forever, because she can't make anything last.

Father. Mother. Dreams.

The logical side of me knows this isn't true. Not completely. My brother and Grace have never abandoned me.

But does it even matter, when this guilt I feel inside is making me push them away? Guilt I feel for having to pause their lives and step in as the abandoned sister who always needs something. All because of her.

I hate you. I hate you. I hate you.

I hate myself.

"Maddie."

My eyes are open, but I can't see.

A strong pair of arms pulls me against a familiar-scented chest, and I hear my own sob before I realize tears are rolling down my cheeks.

"Shh. It's okay, baby. I've got you."

Baby.

My breath hitches, but I ignore how my stomach jumps and my heart rate increases, if only because I have too much on my plate already. It probably slipped out, and it means nothing, anyway.

Instead, I hug him tighter, because if he lets me go right now, I know I'll crumble.

"I took a picture of his car and license plate. We can report him to the police if you want, okay? I won't let him get near you again."

"I'm sorry," I hiccup, hating myself for putting him in this position. We'd just started being somewhat friends, and now this happens.

I shouldn't be surprised something else in my life is going downhill so fast, but here we are.

"You have nothing to be sorry about. None of this is your fault."

"I should... I should have kept walking." My tears taste sour in my mouth.

"No, Maddie, you did what you had to do. I'm proud of you for standing up to him. You were really brave."

His words split me open, and his arms stitch me back together.

James starts rubbing comforting circles on my back, calming my breathing. It's been a long time since I've felt this safe in someone's embrace. "Do you want me to drive you home, or do you need a minute?"

We're not done here, Maddie. You're my daughter, and I won't let you get away this time.

"No," I choke out, shaking my head against his chest. "Don't... Don't leave me alone. I-I can't."

What if he comes back? He admitted to following me around. What if he knows where I live?

"Okay." James grabs my forearms and draws back, putting a small distance between us that feels like miles. "Are you scared of him?"

I don't want to be, but I can't lie to him. I can't lie to myself either. "No. B-But right now, yes."

With the utmost care, the gentle pads of his fingers wipe the evidence of my tears from under my eyes. He rests his hands on my cheeks for a moment, cradling my face, and I burn with the

THE DARKEST CORNER OF THE HEART

heat of a thousand suns.

"I don't want you to be alone either," he whispers, his face only a few inches away from mine. After what feels like a lifetime of heavy silence, he asks, "Do you want to come home with me?"

Every reason in my head for saying no vanishes. *I need him.*

He's not my physical therapist anymore, and I wouldn't care if he were.

He's proved time and again that he cares for me, that he feels *something*, and I'm tired of denying myself what I really want.

"Yes," I breathe out. "I want to go home with you."

chapter 19

JAMES

Seeing Maddie in my apartment should feel strange, I realize as soon as she walks in. The fact that it doesn't only fuels my suspicions that I've gone insane.

And calling her *baby*? That wasn't my brightest moment.

"Oh my God," she gasps as Shadow and Mist jump from the couch where they were napping and start toward her. She kneels and extends her hands for the two cats at her feet to sniff. "Aren't you the cutest little things I've ever seen? What are their names?"

"The black one is Shadow. The gray one is Mist."

"Shadow and Mist? *Are you kidding me?*"

When Shadow, the traitor, rubs against her legs, I almost lose it. "This is a first." I didn't mean for that to come out, but it does in such a low voice, I doubt she's even heard me.

She did. "What do you mean?"

"They're not very social cats." I adopted them two years ago, and they are still reluctant to come close to some of my friends, probably because we rarely hang out at my place. The fact that they warmed up to her in an instant is making me so itchy all over, I don't know where the amazement ends and the confusion starts.

She was my patient just this morning, and she's still too young for me. Sure, she's an adult woman, but an age difference of ten years can't be ignored. *I* can't ignore it.

"Wow," she breathes out, breaking the fog in my brain.

When I look at her, her gaze is on the windows right across

the room.

Norcastle is famous for its tall buildings and skyscrapers, but even I can admit this view is something else—and what sold me on this place.

Floor-to-ceiling windows overlook the river in the near distance, and during the day, the apartment floods with light and poses a homey contrast to the dark wood of my furniture that tends to feel so masculine.

"This view is amazing." The awe in her voice is captivating.

"You should see it during the day," I add before I can stop myself.

She shouldn't be here, damn it. And she definitely shouldn't stay long enough to see the sunrise.

But does that fact stop me from offering her an old hoodie and a pair of sweatpants to change into? No. It should, but it doesn't.

I don't regret any of it. Not for one second. Even when I tell her she can stay in my guest bedroom if she doesn't want to go back to an empty apartment, I don't allow myself to think twice about the choices I am making tonight.

But that doesn't prevent me from hiding away in my bedroom after taking a quick shower. Because, at the end of the day, I'm still a coward.

I left her on my couch nearly forty-five minutes ago with Mist on her lap. And I'm still mustering the courage to go out there and not hug her and never let her get out of my sight again.

If I felt protective of her before, now it's tenfold.

When I found out the man who had been stalking her outside Monica's Pub was her fucking *father*, I had never wanted to kill a man so damn badly.

How dare he show up after all these years and demand *anything* from her? Disrupt her life like this, for no reason but a selfish urge?

For a second, I thought she was going to pounce on him,

and I held her back. I didn't think that one through, apparently, because the feeling of her body against my chest still burns me from the inside out. And now is *not* the time.

Despite everything, I can't help but feel a strong sense of pride. Maddie never once backed down. She told him loud and clear how much of a scumbag he was and how she wanted nothing to do with him. She stood up for her brother and for herself without wavering, and I'm proud of her.

Following her example, I take a deep breath, tug on my hoodie that suddenly seems to fit too tightly around my throat, and exit the safety of my bedroom.

Maddie is still on the couch, a blanket draped over her legs and Mist snoring peacefully on her lap. The sudden urge to snap a picture of them and hang it in every single room of my apartment is so intense, I force myself to count to ten and get a grip.

Her eyes, glued on the TV, slide toward me as soon as I walk into the room. The tight-lipped smile she gives me is so empty, it makes me want to find her father and beat the shit out of him for making her lose her light.

"How are you feeling?" I take a seat on the other end of the couch, putting a safe distance between us. She's already in my clothes and in my apartment—I don't trust myself to not cross any more boundaries.

Mist opens his eye to look at me and closes it a second later, snuggling on her lap again. *Lucky* cat.

Her next words take me aback. "Like shit." She chuckles, but there's no humor behind it. "I think I'm in shock."

"Let me get you something to drink. Hot chocolate?" I offer.

She gives me a funny look. "You drink hot chocolate?"

"Hell yes. But if you don't want any, I could always keep it all to myself."

"I want some," she's quick to say. "Please."

I smirk. "On it."

Once it's ready, I ignore the jolt of electricity that rushes through my veins at the quick brush of our fingers as I give her the steaming cup and sit back down.

"Thank you," she murmurs before taking a sip. "And I'm sorry for asking you to bring me here. Just tell me when you want to go to bed, and I'll leave."

"You didn't ask—I offered," I remind her. I seriously need to peel my eyes away from her lips as she wraps them around the edge of that stupid mug. "You don't want to be alone right now, and I get it. I have a spare room with clean sheets and a small bathroom you can have all for yourself. You're not bothering me at all."

"Promise?" She sounds so unsure, it breaks my heart.

"I promise, Maddie."

Silence stretches between us. The TV is the only sound filling the apartment, but it's not uncomfortable. There's only a dim light in the living room coming from a foot lamp I keep near the couch. The rest of my place swallowed by the shadows. I stare outside the window, at our city that never sleeps, and allow my mind to stay blank.

This Friday alone has felt like a whole lifetime.

It started out with our last session as doctor and patient, after which I accepted her invitation to have dinner together. In that moment, we were just two people getting to know each other on a more personal level without the promise of anything more.

And then, against my better judgement, I brought Maddie home. But I can't bring myself to regret it.

She needs comfort right now, and I want to be the one to give it to her.

She shifts on the couch and pets Mist when he stirs up from his sleep. She's so gentle with him, it's difficult to look away.

"My dad left when I was four," she mutters, shattering our silent bubble.

Her eyes stay glued on the screen as she speaks, but I know

she isn't watching the movie.

"He wasn't a good father. I don't remember him ever kissing me or hugging me or playing with me. He might have, but I don't remember it. He was my mom's boyfriend at the time, and she got pregnant unexpectedly." She takes an uneven breath. "I was an accident. That explains a lot."

"It doesn't excuse a single thing your father did," I tell her firmly, although I'm not too sure she believes me right now. "It wasn't your fault. None of it."

"Honestly, I don't even know why he stayed with us for so long." She shrugs like she can't fathom that someone would stay by her side willingly.

That fucker is lucky he's still alive.

"My mom was too naïve to see how much damage he caused. I don't remember this, but my brother once told me that he kept losing his jobs every few months. Our mom had to pay for everything, so I guess I do get why he stayed after all. He didn't have to lift a finger, and my mom never pressed him about it."

Growing up with parents who loved each other and their children, I can't say I'm familiar with what she's been through. But seeing Maddie broken and on the verge of tears feels like someone is ripping my chest apart and tearing out my heart.

I hate that she still suffers the consequences of a father who never deserved to be one.

I shift closer on the couch until my knee is brushing hers, just so she knows that I'm here and I'm listening. That I won't leave.

She doesn't pull away.

"Even when I was still living with my parents, Sammy took care of me the most," she says, and I can't help but feel respect for her brother. I'm sure it wasn't easy. "He took me to school, to my ballet classes, played with me, paid for my clothes and sometimes even my mom's bills. I feel like his daughter more than I do his sister."

"And is that a bad thing?" I ask softly.

She shrugs and opens her mouth to say something but closes it again. I don't press her. When she's ready to talk, I'll be here to listen.

A car explodes in the movie we're not watching, and she says, "At first I was happy to be with him all the time. With his girlfriend too. I grew up with a great family, friends, and love, which is way more than I could've asked for, given my early childhood."

"But," I prompt.

"But." She gives me a wavering smile and shakes her head. "I feel like such an ungrateful brat."

"Hey." I nudge her knee with mine. "You might be a brat sometimes, but not because of this. Tell me what's wrong."

Another few moments of silence, and then she says, "I feel like a leech."

I frown. "How?"

She shakes her head again, so I nudge her knee once more.

When she finally lets it all out, she breaks me.

"I became my brother's problem when I didn't have to be. And I know what you're going to say—that he loves me and I'm not his problem, blah, blah—and you're right, but just hear me out. He was..." She lets out a deep breath before she continues. "My brother was dating Grace when all of this went down. When he had to get custody of me. They almost broke up because of that, because of *me*. He didn't want to burden her with a child and all that came with it."

"But Grace is his wife, right? They didn't break up," I wonder out loud, hoping I'm remembering correctly.

"No, they didn't break up. Thank God, because I love Grace like a mother, but that didn't make things easier," she explains, her voice laced with sadness. "They couldn't have a normal relationship because there was a child in the mix. They couldn't just go on vacation or go to a party without a babysitter. I noticed those things, James. They said they didn't care about all that and would rather be with me, but it didn't make the guilt go away."

I nod, the picture of Maddie's past and present clearer in my head. "So you felt like a burden."

"I did," she confirms. "They wanted to have kids, you know? My brother and Grace."

"But you said you have a niece."

"Yes, Lila." She smiles at the mention of her. "She's awesome, and I love her more than anything. But they wanted *children*—plural—and they could only afford to have one because I was another kid they had to take care of."

"Wait," I stop her, protectiveness sinking its claws into my chest. "They didn't tell you that you are the reason they didn't have more children, did they?"

Silence stretches between us, and I lose my breath.

If she says yes, if she tells me her own family blamed her for the children they never had, I'm going to lose my fucking mind.

"They didn't tell me anything remotely close to that," she says, and my shoulders immediately sag with relief. But her voice comes out as a whisper, weak and sad, and I don't like it. "They never talked about having more kids after Lila was born, but I remember them saying *children* before they had her. I guess I just assumed they wanted a big family, and I was the reason they couldn't have it."

She shuts her eyes, but she can't hide the pain in them. Not from me.

I move closer until my arm touches hers. "What is it?" I ask, giving her that push I suspect she needs.

Mist, sensing her discomfort, jumps off and disappears down the hall, as if to give her some privacy. When she presses her lips in a thin line, sealing them tightly, and a single tear falls from her eye, I shut down all the alarms blaring inside my head and follow my instincts.

"Maddie, look at me." She opens her eyes but doesn't look away from her lap. Her bottom lip trembles, and I press my thumb against the corner of her mouth for a fleeting moment. I don't know what the hell I'm doing, only that it feels right. "Talk to me. What's making you so upset?"

"It's not important," she whispers, breaking my goddamn heart.

"It is if it's making you cry," I reassure her. "And if it's making you cry, I want to know about it so we can fix it. And if it can't be fixed, I could always break someone's arm or leg."

"James!" she hisses and slaps my arm away.

I chuckle, caught off guard, and that earns me a smile. *Worth it.*

"I'm serious, Maddie. Tell me what's wrong." If she thinks it's weird that her ex-PT just threatened to hurt someone for her, she doesn't say. She doesn't say anything at all.

If she doesn't want to talk right now, I won't force her. Never.

I recognize her pain too well.

The feeling of wanting to open up, to tell someone what's been infesting your heart for so long, but not being physically able to get the words out.

The helplessness that comes with that invisible string made of insecurities, forcing you to stay quiet, to make the pain stay locked until only darkness remains.

I swallow back the distant but still sour memories. Memories I haven't acknowledged in years. Nightmares I haven't been brave enough to relive until now.

Until Maddie.

So I allow the permanent wound in my chest to open, to bleed, to hurt, and I tell her of the time I went to hell and a very different man came crawling back.

"I was about to become a professional NFL player in college when a leg injury ended my career."

She gasps, her eyes now filled with worry. "James..."

"I was told I could lose all mobility in my leg if I ever played football again," I keep going, showing her I can be brave too. I can be vulnerable. "Football was my life. Nothing else mattered, and it ended just like that. I went to a very dark place, and I quit college shortly after that. I went back the following year to get my PT degree, but I lost friends. I lost..."

I won't go there. I can't.

Not yet.

Maybe not ever.

"I lost everything," I opt for, which isn't far from the truth.

"I'm so sorry, James." She places her hand on my knee and gives it a reassuring squeeze before drawing back. I instantly miss her touch, and I hate myself for it. "I know how you're feeling."

"I know how *you* are feeling. I've known all along. That's why, when you broke down that day in my office, I wanted to help you in whichever way I could. I know what that's like, and I wouldn't wish it on my worst enemy. The pain, the frustration, the anger..." I shake my head, but the feeling of hatred I felt for myself all those years ago still lingers. Dormant, but it's there. How I ruined everything, how my brother... "I couldn't let that happen to you."

We fall silent again until she asks in the softest voice, "Is that why you decided to become a PT? To help athletes recover from injuries when you couldn't?"

"Spot on, Maddie." I let out a long, tired sigh. "Spot on."

She stays silent again, but this time not for long. When she speaks next, her voice carries a hint of that light I've missed so damn much.

"Well, you know what? I'm not happy that you went through such a life-altering injury, but I'm happy I had you as a PT." Her hand lands on mine, barely covering it at all, and her smile feels like a hug. "You're a good man, James. Whoever walked away from you because you couldn't play football anymore never deserved you in the first place. Don't forget that."

She has no clue how badly I needed to hear that. All of it.

Before I can think too much about the consequences that don't seem to matter much anymore, I lace my fingers through hers. "You'll figure things out. I'm here if you need me, okay? And I'm not just talking about your ankle. Whenever you want to vent or just pet two really fluffy cats, I'm only a text away."

Because I'm tired of not being there for her when that's all my heart is begging me to do.

She rests her head on my shoulder, and it feels right. It feels so right, I never want the guilt to come back.

"Friends?" she asks.

There's not a single doubt in my soul that this firecracker of a woman who makes all the wrongs feel a bit more right is supposed to be in my life, and I'm meant to be part of hers.

"Friends."

chapter 20

MADDIE

When I wake up at God-knows-what-time, the first thing I notice is that I'm groggy and disoriented. My studio apartment has west-facing windows, so the bright sun warming up my face as I stir awake is a clear indication that I've either slept for fifteen hours or this is not my bed.

I bury my face in the pillow, trying to get away from the blinding light, and a masculine smell I've become very familiar with in the past few weeks hits me all at once.

Yep, last night wasn't actually a nightmare.

I groan my frustrations into the comfortable cloud beneath me as the events of the previous night come crashing down on me.

Seeing my father for the first time in seventeen years. Telling James about my turbulent childhood. Learning about his own troubled past. Almost telling him about her.

Hell.

I'm well aware our conversation isn't over. I left things unsaid, things I want him to know about, but...but I *can't*. The words won't come out, and it leaves a frustrating sensation in the pit of my stomach that makes me want to break something.

Plus, on top of everything that is making my anxiety levels rise like a tidal wave, I need to tell my brother about my father. Pete coming back and stalking me isn't something I can keep from him.

My father said we weren't done talking, that he won't let me get away this time. Whatever he meant by that, it can't be good.

I don't think he'll harm me, but I haven't seen him in more than a decade—and it's not like he was the greatest person in the world when I *did* know him.

I don't know my father, and I don't know what he's capable of. Telling Sammy isn't an option—it's a must.

But I can't do it right now. Not when the memories are still so very recent, not when—

My stomach growls.

Exactly. Not while I'm hungry.

I decide to eat something for breakfast—I'll just say goodbye to James and grab something on my way home—and then I'll call Sammy, when my stomach is full and my head is in the right place. Or at least in a better one.

With a groan, I rub my eyes with the heels of my palms and draw the heavy covers back. Last night, after he told me about his football injury, we stayed up for a bit longer talking about happier memories—my late dog Rocket and James's childhood with his friends in the city. My eyes got droopy sooner than I would've liked, the shock finally wearing off, and we decided to call it a night.

I was so exhausted last night, I only took in the white covers of his guest bed, but now, in the sun, I can see all the details. The floor-to-ceiling windows, looking out on the busy streets of Norcastle and the river only a few blocks away. The queen-sized bed, white and pristine, that feels like a cloud. The lack of family pictures.

There's also a built-in closet and two black nightstands that, paired with the dark paintings on the walls and the charcoal gray rug at my feet, give a very masculine air to this room. All the apartment feels like that—neutral, manly, somber, and kind of impersonal. But not cold. Not soulless.

And it brings me comfort to know within this apartment is

one of the few people I feel one-hundred-percent safe with.

I tug at the long sleeves of his hoodie as I exit the bedroom, suddenly self-conscious about wearing his clothes. The apartment is quiet, and when I reach the living room, only Shadow and Mist are here, bathing in the sunlight.

Luckily, I only stand in the middle of his living room like a total idiot for a couple of minutes until the front door opens and James walks in, wearing training shoes, athletic shorts, and his shirt in his hand.

His shirt is in his goddamn hand.

No matter how many times I blink, the image of a shirtless and sweaty James doesn't go away.

Am I still dreaming?

"Maddie," he breathes out, as if he'd forgotten I was here at all. That would explain his partial nudity. "You're awake."

I clear my throat and try to make my voice sound lighter than I feel inside. "Your bed is comfortable, so that was a struggle." *Sure, Maddie, talk about sleeping in his bed. That'll make things better.* "Where were you?" I ask, quickly changing topics.

"I went to the gym. It's on the building, downstairs." Wow. Talk about living in the lap of luxury. "Do you mind if I jump in the shower really quick? I'm dripping sweat."

Like I haven't noticed.

"Not at all." I smile easily. I'm not dying inside or anything. "Have you had breakfast yet? I can fix us something quick or run to the nearest café."

His grin catches me off guard. I'm not sure I can survive a playful and half-naked James. I might combust.

"I've had breakfast," he says. "Four hours ago."

My eyes almost come out of their sockets. "What do you mean? What time is it?"

"Lunchtime."

Oh, God. "Did I really sleep for that long?" I ask, confused.

It truly felt like I went to bed, blinked, and woke up. "I'm sorry, I should leave. It's the weekend, and I'm sure you have plans."

"Yes, I've got plans," he confirms, making my stomach drop for some dumb reason. "Making sure you eat a proper meal after the long night you've had."

Wait.

What?

"We can order in, or I can make us something. I think I've got some pasta and shrimp in there. Let me check."

"You don't have to do this, James," I'm quick to say. The last thing I want is to be a burden to him, too, all because I had a mental breakdown last night. I don't want him to feel like he has to take care of me now. "You don't have to go all doctor on me. I promise I'll eat. I can even text you pictures of my food if you want."

But he's already disappearing down the hall. "Good try, but you're staying. Have a look at my pantry and fridge and see what you like." He stops right outside his bedroom door, his hand on the handle, and turns his head. "Unless you want to leave."

Do I want to leave? No. Not at all.

Being around James is easy, and I feel like I can be myself and he won't judge me for it. Plus, it may not be a great idea to be left alone with my thoughts right now. If he says I'm welcome to stay, maybe I shouldn't look for a hidden meaning in his words for once.

So, I shake my head and try not to give away how fast my heart is beating right now. "I'd love to stay."

With a satisfied nod, he disappears into his bedroom. As I gather all the ingredients for a shrimp pasta recipe, I try my hardest not to think about those defined muscles under the steaming hot water of his shower.

I fail.

***

"What do you mean you don't rinse your pasta?" This is the most atrocious thing I've ever heard.

James scoops up the fettuccini without rinsing them like a culinary criminal would do. "Because you're not supposed to do that."

I continue stirring the creamy sauce that smells like parmesan and pure heaven. As if he hadn't just told me I'm living a lie. "Says who?"

"Says literally everyone."

I don't believe him. There's simply no way I've been doing this wrong all along.

"Explain," I demand, which makes him smirk. It's barely there, but I watch that mouth tilt like a hawk.

"When you're doing a hot pasta dish like we are right now, rinsing the pasta removes the starch from the surface, which prevents the sauce from sticking," he says, and I hate that it makes so much sense.

"My life is a lie," I mutter under my breath, but he hears me and chuckles, deep and manly and totally not hot. "I feel dumb."

"There's no reason why you should." He places the pasta in both of our bowls and puts the pot in the sink. "The more you know, right?"

"At least I can make a mean sauce." I'm not one to brag, but come on. If I could bathe myself in this cheesy delicacy, I totally would.

James leans in to smell it. When his eyes find mine, his face so close I can't help but swallow back my nerves, he gives me one of his warmest smiles. I don't see those very often, so I make sure to treasure it.

"Just when I thought you couldn't be more talented."

Jesus. He isn't making this any easier.

This, meaning not thinking of him as more than my former PT who I happen to have great chemistry with.

Nothing will ever happen between you.

"It's a great sauce, I'll give you that." I focus on the pan, careful to not let him see the very stupid and obvious blush on my cheeks. "But I don't know about talented."

"You dance, you draw, you cook..." James shrugs like it's all, in fact, very easy to understand. "If that isn't talent, I don't know what is. I think the sauce is done. Here, let me."

His fingers brush mine as he lifts the pan and pours it over our pasta bowls. My mouth waters at the smell, and maybe at the sight of those strong hands too. Sue me.

Once our food is done, we sit at the kitchen island and dive in. A moan escapes me as I take the first bite, and I close my eyes in pleasure. "Wow. We make a great cooking team," I say, twirling some more pasta with my fork. "We should sign up for one of those TV contests."

He arches an amused eyebrow. "Do you think we would win?"

"I'm very competitive," I admit. "And they love a sob story more than anything. I have quite the experience with those."

I didn't mean for the words to come out. The last thing I want to do right now is talk about last night. I'm afraid I've dampened the mood, but then James says, "I don't think I would last a week. I'd probably burn the first thing I put in the oven."

"Dramatic much?"

"I wish. I'm good at stuff like this, but for some reason, ovens and I don't get along. I'm so glad you didn't suggest that we make a pizza."

I chuckle at the mental picture of James cursing at his burnt pizza. "Now I kind of regret it. I would've gotten some good material to tease you with for a while."

He glares at me, but he's unable to hide the amusement glinting in his eyes. "You're a menace, you know that?"

I fake an innocent shrug. "I had no idea."

"Your turn." He nudges my arm. "What's one dish you always burn?"

"Would you believe me if I said I've never burned anything?"

"No."

"Well, it's true." I give him the side-eye. "Not everyone is as talented as me, though. I get it."

"Brat."

"So you keep saying."

"So you keep proving me right."

I laugh, and the conversation shifts toward that one time I kind of burned something in the kitchen. Grace and I were baking some cupcakes for my brother's birthday, but we accidentally forgot about them while they were in the oven. In my defense, I was more intrigued by the book I was reading than by my brother's culinary present, and Lila had been born just a few months before, so Grace was busy with her.

But James still teases me about it, and I find comfort in the easy friendship we're building brick by brick.

When we're done eating, I offer to do the dishes, partly because I feel like it's the least I can do for him after he let me stay the night, and partly because I'm a coward.

I know I'm delaying the inevitable. I'll have to tell my brother about Pete sooner than later, and the responsible, good sister side of me tells me it has to be today.

Once the dishes and the kitchen are clean, I get dressed in last night's clothes and find James looking through his phone. He sits on the couch with his legs open and one cat chilling on each of his thighs.

I chuckle at the adorable picture in front of me, and he looks up.

"What's so funny?"

"You three." I smile. "It's so obvious that they love you."

He smiles down at them and scratches their fluffy little heads. "They're my babies."

Thump, thump, thump.

There goes my heart.

It shouldn't feel illegal to imagine him holding a baby, a real one, against that naked chest I so blatantly ogled earlier, but it does. It really does.

I shake my head, willing the heart-melting mental image to go away. "I just wanted to thank you for everything. For last night, for today... Um, everything."

He frowns and places the cats on the couch so he can stand up. "You're leaving?"

It hits me then—this isn't a "Goodbye, I'll see you later." This is a "Goodbye. I probably won't see you again."

Because even if I'll still see him for checkups, it won't be the same. At the clinic, we aren't Maddie and James, but Miss Stevens and Dr. Simmons.

We aren't the kind of people who cook together, or joke with each other, or stare into the other's eyes for far too long.

But what are my options? Tell him that I want to spend more time with him, doing whatever, because everything is easy and fun when we're together?

He probably has other more interesting plans that don't involve hanging out with someone ten years younger than him and more family drama than a soap opera.

"I should call my brother," I tell him, trying not to focus on the warmth of his body, so close to mine. "I have to tell him about last night."

He tips his head once in acknowledgment. "How are you feeling about seeing your father again?"

Isn't that the question of the century?

I feel betrayed, hurt, empty, afraid. I feel many things I can't find a name for, but most of all, I feel exhausted, so that's what I tell James.

My father's been a ghost for many years, and now he's shown himself when I thought I'd never see him again for as long as I lived.

"But I'll manage. My brother will know what to do."

"Call me if you need anything," he says, so firm and serious I want to believe him. I want to believe he'll always be there for me, but I can't. "I mean it, Maddie. I'll text you from my personal number so you can have it."

I nod and give him a smile, unsure of what else to do. Hug him? He doesn't strike me as an overly touchy person, and I've already crossed that line once.

"I'm here for you as well," I offer with sincerity. "Take care, yeah?"

His eyes pierce mine, looking for something I'm not sure he'll find. "Text me when you get home safe."

My heart melts into a gooey puddle. Nobody has ever worried about me like this aside from Sammy and Grace. It feels good to be appreciated, but I don't allow myself to dwell on it too long.

It never lasts. You make sure of it.

So, with a smile and a goodbye, I exit the comfort of James's apartment for the very last time.

chapter 21

MADDIE

I changed into my loungewear as soon as I got home, right after texting James.

> **Me: Just got home. I'll probably take the longest nap known to humankind now, lol**

A moment later, an unknown number texted me. I immediately knew it was him.

> **James: You mean like this?**

Then he attached a picture of Shadow and Mist all cuddled up on his couch.

> **Me: Sooooooo cute**

> **James: Can't argue with that. Take it easy today, Maddie**

As soon as I read his last text, I threw myself in bed, covered my shivering body with blankets, and dialed my brother's number.

I don't want to do this, but if I'm not brave right now, I know I'll never be.

The phone rings once, twice.

"Princess?"

A weight I've been carrying for far too long leaves my shoulders the second I hear my brother's voice.

"Sammy," I breathe out, relieved to hear his voice. It feels like a lifetime since the last time we spoke, and now I need him more than ever.

"What's wrong?" he asks, all his fatherly instincts kicking in right on cue like they always do.

That breaks me.

My brother doesn't deserve any of this. He's been through enough in his life, starting with a mother who was too young when she had him and a father who left before he was even born.

He loves me, and I love him, and I couldn't be more grateful that I grew up with him, but I still hate this.

I hate that I'm his problem.

When will I let him live his life and not make him worry about his little sister, who can't seem to look after herself?

Tears run down my cheeks, chasing an endless finish line, and I break down.

"Maddie. Talk to me." He never calls me by my name, and it only makes me cry harder, knowing that I'm making him upset. "Did you get hurt again?"

Not in the way he's imagining.

He won't see this coming, and it will break him too.

Why can't we live in peace? Is it because of me?

Of course it's you.

"Pete," I hiccup. A deafening silence greets me from the other line, and I can only imagine what's going through his head. "I saw him last night. H-He came...for m-me. To see me. He found me."

"Fucking hell," I hear him mutter under his breath, and then he's moving. "Wait a second, okay? Don't hang up."

I hear a door closing, muffled voices, and then my brother speaks again. "You're on speaker now. Grace and I are here. Tell us what happened, princess." His voice sounds softer, probably because his wife has calmed him down.

I sniffle. "Where's Lila?"

"She's at a friend's birthday party," Grace answers. "Are you okay, sweetheart?"

We're not done here, Maddie. You're my daughter, and I won't let you get away this time.

My father's cruel words grip at my chest and force me to speak.

I tell them about how he waited for me outside of Monica's Pub, about how he'd been following me around for a while. I tell them he wasn't aggressive, but that he was adamant in keeping in touch when I told him I didn't want to.

Throughout it all, I can feel my brother's simmering rage from the phone. Grace does most of the talking, and I know it's because he's losing his mind.

"Did he threaten you in any way?" he finally asks, venom lacing each of his words.

"Not explicitly, but I think he'll try to contact me again, even though I said I didn't want to."

"Do you feel physically endangered?"

"No."

I don't. Going by what James told me, I suspect my dad has had a few unpleasant encounters with the law over the years. That would explain why he left that day when he thought James was a cop and why he paled when I threatened him with telling the authorities.

"He told me he was ready to be a father to me now," I tell them.

Sammy snorts, but there's no humor behind it. "That fucker."

"Do you want to stay in Warlington with us for a while?" Grace offers, as I suspected she would.

"No. I promise I'm fine here."

The last thing I want is to intrude in their lives again now that they've finally gotten rid of me. And it's not like I feel unsafe here. Sure, I was shaken up last night, but I truly don't think Pete will do anything to me. Sammy told me himself once—he's all bark, no bite. He remembers him better than I do.

"I don't want you to be alone," my brother says firmly.

"I'm not alone. My friends are here, and I see them every day." It isn't exactly the truth, but I do speak to them every day. And I've been seeing James a lot, although I guess that's over. "I promise I'm fine here. I just wanted to tell you that I've seen him and he wants to rekindle our relationship—something I refuse to do. You don't have to worry about me."

"We'll always worry about you, princess." My brother's words warm my heart and make me feel like shit at the same time. "I trust your judgment, all right? But if he talks to you again, you're coming back home."

"No, I'm not. I'm an independent woman with a job, Sammy, and a future I want to figure out *here*. I won't run home just because some loser can't take a hint. He won't dictate what I do or don't do with my life. If he comes back, we'll let justice take care of him."

Silence greets me from the other line until Grace says, the smile evident in her voice, "Well, you heard her."

My brother sighs. I can't see him, but I know he's running a tattooed hand across his face. So dramatic. "Fine. But I want you to text me every day after you wake up and right before you go to bed. Nonnegotiable."

I smile at his protective antics. He'll never change, and I love him for it, but my poor Lila is in for a long ride. "Okay, *Dad*."

He grunts. "I'm serious."

"So am I."

"Okay, you two." Grace takes over the phone. "Pete has always been harmless, but we haven't seen him in years. There's no way to know if he's become...dangerous."

I don't bring up what my father told me about Sammy—that when he reached out to him to see me, my brother denied him. I have no idea when that happened or what went down, but I don't want to find out in this conversation or over the phone. I've had enough drama in the last twenty-four hours to last me a couple of decades, thank you very much.

"I understand," I concede. "But I promise I'm fine."

"Were you alone when he ambushed you in the parking lot?" my brother asks.

Heat climbs up my cheeks, and I'm glad they can't see my face right now. "No, I was with a friend. He took a picture of his car and license plate."

I know Sammy like the back of my hand, and it's painfully obvious he's zeroing in on that "he" as if his life depended on it. "Good thinking."

I clear my throat to hide the embarrassment. "I'll call you if anything else happens."

"Okay, sweetheart. Thank you for telling us right away," Grace says, and I want nothing more than to hug her right now. She used to give me the best cuddles when I was a little girl, and I miss them like crazy.

"We love you," Sammy says. "Please text me as soon as anything happens, and know that you're always welcome here, okay?"

Instead of bringing me comfort, his words make me feel even guiltier. He wants me to come home, and I don't want to intrude.

Push, pull, push, pull, until the rope snaps in half.

"I love you guys. Give Lila a big kiss for me."

"Will do. Bye, princess."

When we hang up, the sudden silence in my apartment

overwhelms me for the first time. It's not that I'm scared for my life after knowing my father wants to contact me again, but I realize I don't want to be alone anymore.

Until today, I've never had any issue being by myself. Yes, I love my friends, but "me time" has always been a priority.

But now...

Now I want to share some of that time with somebody else. With someone I can be myself around, ugly side and all.

Without thinking of the consequences, I open our text thread again.

> **Me: Do you think my ankle would be fine on a hike?**

My phone buzzes with his reply only a minute later.

> **James: An easy and short one, yes. Why do you ask?**

> **Me: I miss nature and want to test my ankle**

> **James: I know a couple of good spots. I can send you the location if you want.**

Remembering his profile description on the dating app, I muster all my courage and text him back.

> **Me: What if you come with me instead?**

A minute passes, two. The typing bubbles appear and disappear twice before his one-word reply comes through.

James: When?

Me: Tomorrow morning?

Another infinite pause.

James: I'll pick you up at 9 am

chapter 22

JAMES

I give up. I surrender.

There's no point in lying to myself anymore. Not when I always ignore the warning flags waving in front of me, anyway.

I can't stay away from Maddie. I don't want to.

Every day I crave seeing her beautiful, attentive eyes and that smile that could light up a whole room just by her walking in. I long for her fiery personality, and I wish to crush all her demons so she can shine brighter.

Maybe I'm sick in the head. I haven't ruled that out completely. She's still twenty-one, and I'm not a day younger than thirty-one, which isn't the closest of age gaps.

And despite it all, I can't keep pretending that my soul doesn't call to hers.

As I wait for her to come out of her building at nine in the morning on a Sunday, I know I can't act on my feelings. She's still figuring out what she wants to do with her career, and I don't want to interfere. She's young, and I refuse to hold her back if she decides her future isn't in Norcastle anymore.

Wherever these feelings came from, they will leave just as easily. After all, I'm not built for healthy relationships.

I hear a light tap on the passenger window, and I snap out of my thoughts to see that sweet face I've missed way too much.

It's only been a day.

I unlock the door, and she climbs in, not looking like her

ankle is giving her much trouble. "Good morning." Her smile doesn't waver as she straps herself in, and it's the most genuinely happy I've seen her in weeks. "Phew, it's cold."

"Morning." I turn on the heater and pull out of my parking spot. "It'll be even colder in the mountains. Did you bring water and food?"

"Yes and yes," she says. "I might not be an expert hiker like you, but I have Google."

Right. I forgot I included hiking as one of my hobbies in that damn dating app. Well, I didn't, although that fact is still true. *Fucking Graham.*

"How often do you go on hikes?" she asks with a genuine interest that I find adorable.

"Every few weeks, I reckon. I try going at least twice a month."

She lets out a low whistle. "You weren't joking when you said you liked hiking."

"Have you ever gone on one?"

"Last year I went with my friends from college. Clark Hills, just an hour away. Are you familiar with the trail?"

I nod. "Walked it three times. We're not going there today."

"Oh?" She looks at me with interest shining in her eyes. "Where are we going?"

I smirk, pulling onto the highway. "It's a surprise."

"You're going to kidnap me, aren't you?"

"You caught me. You make too good of a parmesan sauce. I can't just let you run free like that."

Her laugh lights up something dormant within me. It opens a curious eye, then another, and blinks.

No. Stop.

The ride to the trail lasts forty minutes, during which we make casual talk that isn't at all uncomfortable and she sings along to some of the songs on the radio. Being with her is dangerously addictive, and even though it's hardly begun, I don't want this day to end.

Since it's early on a Sunday morning, there's no traffic, and we arrive at the trail when no other cars are in the parking lot.

Maddie looks out of the window, eyes full of wonder as she takes in the endless sea of green and blue. "Wow," she breathes out.

Wow, indeed, I think as I look at her.

"We're really going to reach the lake?" she asks.

"Sure thing. It's only a couple of miles away and it's mostly flat, so your ankle should be fine." I kill the engine and take my jacket and backpack from the back seat. "Shall we?"

The deserted trail threads to the leaf-covered forest, and Maddie marvels at every cloud and tree as we start our hike. Our boots meet the rain-quenched path, and for the first time in too long, I breathe easily.

I've gone on this hike once before, years ago, but I'd forgotten how stunning the scenery is. Too bad I can't take my eyes away from the girl beside me.

"Oh, look!" Maddie points at a nearby tree. "That's a black-capped chickadee," she beams, stopping near its trunk.

"A what now?"

She uses her hand to block the faint sunlight filtering through the treetops. "A bird. See it?" She points again, and I squint my eyes, following the direction of her finger. "It's a small one. It has a black-and-white head, and the rest of its body is mostly gray."

A chirping sound reaches us just as my eyes land on the little thing. "I see it."

"It's so cute." She smiles up at the bird as if it could see her, as if it could appreciate her softness the way I'm doing right now. *Unlucky bird.*

We keep following the trail in silence, not wanting to disturb the sounds of nature around us and only stopping once to drink some water. I ask about her ankle at some point, and she tells me it's not bothering her.

As we walk, it dawns on me that I haven't been outside like this in a really long time—probably since my friends dragged me on a trip to the lake earlier this year. But it's been months. Maybe I should consider driving up to Bannport, Maine, for the weekend. It's not too far, and getting out of the city by myself would be good for me. Shadow and Mist don't mind the car, so they could tag along.

The thought of inviting my parents crosses my mind for two seconds before I let go of the idea as if it were on fire. I love my folks, and I try to visit them as often as I can, but I can't spend a whole weekend with them. I *can't*, not when they'll use our time together to bring up my brother, and that's where I draw the line. They mean well, I know that, but it doesn't make it hurt any less.

"I can hear you brooding all the way from here," Maddie says, the faintest smile grazing her lips.

She's only a few steps ahead, and I catch up with her in two long strides. "I wasn't brooding."

She clicks her tongue. "Don't lie to me, you grouch."

I come to a halt. "What did you just call me?"

Mischief shines in her hazel eyes. "What has your head all tangled up?" she asks, ignoring my question.

"It's nothing."

"Pants on fire."

"I'm not lying."

She narrows her eyes at me. "Fine, don't tell me." And with that, she gives me a nonchalant shrug, turns around, and resumes her walk.

I catch up to her, this weird sensation in my chest feeling a lot like guilt. "Fine," I concede. "Maybe I had something on my mind."

She shrugs once more, enhancing that uncomfortable sensation. "It's okay, really. You don't have to tell me." She slides a quick glance my way. "I understand if you want to keep things to yourself. You don't even know me that well."

I wrap my hand around her forearm to stop her, but I don't hold her tightly enough to hurt her. "That's not true," I say, honesty lacing every word. "We are friends."

"Are we really?"

I hate that her words feel like a punch in the gut, and I hate that I don't know how to answer straight away.

Are we friends?

Yes, but also no.

I don't want to throw my friends over my shoulder, pin them against the nearest tree trunk, and make them come with my fingers inside their tight heat.

So maybe what I feel for Maddie isn't a friendship in the most traditional sense of the word; maybe not at all.

All I know is that thinking about not seeing her ever again makes me sick. It makes me want to tear the world apart until I find her again, and I don't know what label that puts on us.

But those feelings are too confusing, too scary to put into words, so I simply say what feels true to my heart. "Yes, Maddie. We are friends." I don't let go of her forearm, and she doesn't pull away. "I was thinking about family stuff I have going on."

There. She wanted me to talk, to open up? I don't feel the usual discomfort, but maybe it's because, in the grand scheme of things, I haven't told her anything.

Her features soften all the same, understanding passing between those eyes I could get lost in if I let go of the thin rope holding my sanity together. She gives me a small nod. "Okay. You don't have to talk about it if you don't want to." The birds chirp around us, and the wind picks up as the morning passes us by. "But there's no use in worrying about that right now, is there? You can't fix it at this very moment."

I swallow because I can. "Right."

She presses her lips together, as if she wanted to say something but ultimately decided it wasn't worth it. The somber look on her face disappears just like that, her lips morphing into a smile that could blind the sun above us, and I feel my mood shifting with it. "I need your help with something."

"What is it?"

She surprises me by releasing herself from my grip and grabbing my arm instead, tugging me along the trail. "You're going to help me find a bird. The first one to spot it, wins."

"I know nothing about birds," I say, but I feel my cheek twitching with the beginning of a smile. *This girl.*

"You have eyes. That'll do."

I know she's trying to distract me, but I still say, "Fine," because I'm beginning to think I can't say no to her. That worries me way less than it should. "What bird are we looking for?"

"A red-winged blackbird. It's all black with a red spot on each of its wings—you can't miss it." She eyes me over her shoulder, my arm still clutched in her small hand. "If you lose, I want to stop for donuts on the way back. Your treat."

My lips twitch. "And if I win?"

"If you win, we can do whatever you want."

A fleeting image of Maddie pressed between my hard body and a tree trunk assaults my head. "I'll think about it," I opt for, sounding calm but internally losing my goddamn mind.

"Okay. It's not like you will win, anyway."

The image in my mind morphs into one of Maddie being thrown over my lap, my hand spanking that round ass I've looked at more times than I can count since we arrived.

"Like I said, brat," I mutter under my breath, but not quietly enough that she doesn't hear it.

I feel the loss of her warmth as she releases my arm, only to cross her own over her chest. "Prove me wrong, then, Doc."

That word snaps something inside of me, something forbidden and untamed. Before I know what the fuck I'm doing, I wrap my hand around her high ponytail and pull at it softly.

My mouth lowers to her ear, her heavy breathing reaching my own, and I mutter, "I'm not your doctor anymore, Maddie."

Her hand reaches up until it covers mine, still wrapped around her hair. And then she does something I would've never, ever in my most insane fantasies expected.

Instead of peeling my fingers away, she squeezes my knuckles, as if she wants me to pull harder.

Does she like this?

My head goes on overdrive with the possibility. Just to test the waters, just to see if I've read her all wrong, I pull on her ponytail a little tighter. A small gasp leaves her lips, and the pink shade of her cheeks tells me all I need to know.

"You're not?" she asks, trying to sound casual, but the breathiness in her voice gives her nerves away.

It's so fucking sexy and adorable, I lose the grip on my self-control a little more.

My lips graze the shell of her ear when I speak next, making her shiver. "I don't make a habit of hiking with my patients, no."

"And do you usually pull their hair?" she asks next, gaining that brazen confidence I knew she had in her.

There's my little firecracker.

"Only when they're being bratty, which hasn't happened until now. So, no."

I release my grip on her hair, and her hand lets go of mine. "So, that bird," I prompt, trying to bring back a sense of normalcy between us. And between me and my cock.

Twenty minutes later, Maddie ends up spotting the so-called red-winged blackbird first, which means I owe her donuts on our way back. She squeals excitedly at the prospect of getting her sweet treats after a tiring day, unaware of the fact that I would've bought her those donuts anyway.

We reach the lake by noon and sit on a dry patch of grass near the edge to eat our sandwiches. At one point, I ask her how she knows so much about birds, which makes her laugh. "One of my grandfathers taught me all about them. We would go birdwatching together when I was a kid," she explains.

"Are you close to your grandparents?"

"Grandfathers," she corrects, a soft smile on her lips. "I only have grandpas, not grandmas. And they're married to each other."

It takes a second until it dawns on me. "Wait. Your grandfathers are together? As in—"

"As in they're gay, yes." She smirks.

"That's cool."

"They live in Canada, so I don't see them as often as I'd like, but they're amazing." She swallows the last bite of her sandwich, and I follow the movement down her slender throat. "They're Grace's dads—she's adopted. I'm technically not their granddaughter because Grace isn't my mother, but who cares. Blood doesn't make a family."

I shift on the grass, the uncomfortable feeling at the pit of my stomach not unfamiliar to me. "You don't say," I mutter under my breath.

She catches it. Of course she does. "What do you mean?"

Yes, James, what do you mean?

She must have an idea, seeing how I brought up my family earlier, but she doesn't press. She simply looks at me with an open expression that holds no judgment. She just wants to...listen.

And for the first time, I want to talk.

"I have an older brother. We aren't on speaking terms."

And it doesn't exactly help that my parents keep insisting I should make an effort, that family should forgive each other. They know there's no point, but that doesn't stop them.

After twelve years, they know I haven't forgotten, and I most certainly don't fucking forgive. Not for the things he did to me.

"Can I ask why you don't get along?"

I give her an apologetic smile. "You can, but I'm not going to answer."

She blinks at my unexpected answer then throws her head back and laughs in that carefree way of hers. "Fair enough. Thank you for telling me about him."

"Why are you thanking me?"

She shrugs, looking away. Her fingers slip through the green grass, caressing it softly. "I like knowing things about you is all. So, thank you for sharing what you can with me."

My stomach drops.

She likes knowing things about me. She likes it when I talk about myself. And, so far, she hasn't asked me about the NFL dream I failed to reach. It's like that part of my past doesn't exist to her, and for that I'm grateful.

Forget about the tree trunk—I want to tackle her to the ground, right where she's sitting, and kiss her until I run out of oxygen.

"I like knowing things about you too," I say honestly. "You're full of surprises."

She snorts. "I guess learning about my dad was one of those, right?"

"I didn't think you'd want to talk about it."

Her shoulders rise and fall as her delicate fingers continue playing with the strands of grass between us. "I talked to my brother yesterday. He suggested I go back to Warlington for a while."

My breathing stops. *Warlington*. That's also on the East Coast, but hours away. An eternity away.

"And what did you tell him?" I manage to ask casually, as if my whole body isn't on edge right now.

The thought of Maddie moving away when we've finally seemed to cross an invisible line I can't define but is really, really comfortable, makes my stomach roll with unease. I haven't known

THE DARKEST CORNER OF THE HEART

her for long, but I haven't felt this free, this *relaxed* with anyone since college.

No, scratch that—since ever.

Someone I can share my time with, knowing she isn't seeking anything in return. No hidden agendas. Someone I can talk to, trusting that she won't force me to reveal the memories that still hurt too much to say out loud.

Being with Maddie feels right and wrong at the same time. Allowing myself to get close to her feels like the best and the worst decision I've ever made.

"I told him I wasn't going to let my father control my life," she answers with a definitive resolution in her voice I can't help but admire. For someone who's been through so much, she stands taller than most people would. "I want to stay in Norcastle. My life is here."

I should feel relieved—and I do—but the fact that her brother suggested she move back with him makes a silent alarm go off in my head. "Do you feel unsafe here? Because of your dad?" I ask carefully. Without knowing the answer, I already regret not beating up the motherfucker when I had the chance.

"Not exactly." She brings her knees to her chest, resting her chin on top of them. Her eyes find mine. "My dad is all bark, no bite. I know I'm safe here."

"You are." I hope she understands the meaning behind the hidden words I'm too scared to say out loud. That's she'll always be safe as long as I'm here. "But I want to know how you're feeling."

"I'm..." She frowns, as if she hadn't stopped to think about how seeing her father made her feel. A deep breath later, she continues. "I'm mostly shocked. He left when I was four, and I really thought I'd never see him again. I... I didn't know he had contacted my brother again and asked to see me."

"Your brother didn't tell you that." It's not a question, and I can say I understand why he made that choice.

"I've always assumed he never reached out again. That he moved on with his life... Or that he was dead. I didn't know for sure."

"Are you angry with your brother for keeping it from you?"

It takes her a moment to answer. "No. I don't blame him for wanting to keep me away from him," she explains. "My father isn't a reliable man, and my brother was just protecting me. Pete would've left a second time—I know it deep in my soul. I get why my brother did it, and I'm not angry with him."

"That's very admirable of you, Maddie." On the other side of the lake, a small group of people have gathered to have lunch. Their voices don't reach our small bubble I never want to burst. "Not everyone would see it like that."

"It's just... What's the point?" She lets out a long sigh. "I wouldn't have wanted to see my father anyway, so Sammy did the right thing. I don't want to see Pete now or ever again. I don't want to have any kind of relationship with him. He made his intentions crystal clear when he left seventeen years ago. Pete Stevens isn't and will never be a good man."

Pete Stevens.

That name will remain engraved in my brain until I make him pay for everything he's put Maddie through. I'm not above violence in this particular case.

We stay silent for a while, letting the birds and the sounds of the lake talk for us. The wind has picked up in the past couple of hours, and it's getting colder, but at least the sky is clear. I've gone on hikes with rain pouring down on me, and it's not fun.

I'm about to suggest we start our way back to my car when an alarming thought crosses my mind at high speed. It comes out of nowhere, and I can't shake it off.

I don't know why I didn't think of this sooner. It consumes me, boils me from the inside, and I know I won't sleep a wink tonight if I don't get an answer.

Her eyes are lost on the lake.

"Maddie," I start, grabbing her attention. She turns her head with a hint of a smile I know my next words will vanish. "Can I ask you something about your father?"

Just like I feared, her smile falls. Not by much, and maybe not noticeably for the normal eye, but I've been at the receiving end of those smiles enough times to recognize this isn't a happy one. "Sure."

She doesn't sound too put off by my request, but I still feel the need to add, "It's not an easy question."

"It's fine."

"You said you had some records of child neglect and emotional abuse against him." Just thinking about it makes my stomach turn. When she nods, I ask, "Was your dad ever abusive to you in other ways?"

She sobers up. "What do you mean?"

"Did he ever put his hands on you?"

If she says yes, that motherfucker won't live to see another day. I'll buy her donuts, drop her home, and look for Pete Stevens until I find him. And then I'll kill him with my bare hands.

Luckily for everyone involved, she says, "No."

"You can tell me if he did. I would never judge you or blame you for it," I insist.

"I know you wouldn't." A pause. "I trust you, James. I do, and I would tell you if he had been abusive, but he wasn't. He only yelled at me and shrugged me off sometimes, but he never went far. My brother would've killed him."

Her brother and I see eye to eye, it seems.

A relieved sigh escapes me, and the tension in my shoulders disappears. "Okay. I just wanted to make sure. I can't stand..." *Don't say it.* "Forget it."

The last thing she needs to be aware of is this weird protectiveness I feel for her.

"You can't stand what?" She nudges my knee with hers.

I don't remember her getting this close. We're sitting right next to each other on the grass, our arms almost touching, and I resist the urge to pull her into my lap and hold her there until I make sure she really is okay.

Now isn't the time. It will never be.

"It's not important."

"James," she sing-songs.

I rub my jaw with the palm of my hand, hiding the small smile she always seems to be pulling from me. "You always have to get what you want, don't you?"

Unlike me, she doesn't veil the amusement in her voice. "Come on, big guy, just tell me."

Big guy. I should have more restraint than this, but damn it—it's her. She makes me want to open up in ways I haven't since my injury. Since ever.

Throwing all caution to the wind, I give in.

She wanted the truth? Here it is.

"I can't stand the thought of you being hurt, Maddie. In any way, present or past. It makes me want to hurt whoever hurt you. Badly. Repeatedly."

She says nothing, and I'm afraid I've gone too far.

Who even says shit like that? To a twenty-one-year-old who, just two days ago, was my patient.

I'm sick in the head. There's no other—

Maddie throws her arms around my neck, almost tackling me to the ground. Instinctively, one of my arms wraps around her middle, pulling her closer until she's halfway on my lap.

She's hugging me.

Not slapping me or calling me insane but *hugging* me.

It ends too soon, and before I can even fully bask in her warmth, she pulls away and squats next to me so we are at eye level.

"How are you real?" she asks, out of breath, and I don't answer because I don't know what she means. If anything, she's the unreal one between us. "Thank you for always listening to me."

I'm taken aback, and the only thing I can think of saying is, "Sorry for pulling at your ponytail earlier."

She sits on the grass again. "Don't worry. I liked it."

I stop breathing.

She stops smiling.

"I mean..." She clears her throat, heat rising up her cheeks. I'm lucky my stubble covers mine, because I'm sure they are just as red. "I enjoy teasing you and all that. Being playful. It's lighthearted fun. I like it."

There's nothing playful or lighthearted about what I want to do to you, baby.

"I thought I'd freaked you out," I admit.

"You could never." I can hear the truth in her words, and it calms my heart. Then, she reaches out her finger until she's poking my cheek. "You're blushing."

"I'm not."

I am, and we both know it.

Her smirk is nothing short of mischievous. "I've caught you blushing a few times, you know?" she confesses, shattering all illusions that my cold mask is impenetrable. "For all that grouchy and intimidating exterior, you're actually pretty cute."

Cute. Something not entirely uncomfortable turns inside my stomach.

"Nobody has ever called me cute before," I admit out loud, not sure why I decided that this level of vulnerability was a good idea.

Because it's her.

"Well, you are. The cutest grump I've ever met." That smile, paired with the playful glint in her eyes, is my undoing. "Should we start making our way back? I don't want to be a party pooper, but I need those donuts."

I chuckle, getting up in one easy move and helping her to her feet.

It never fails to surprise me how straightforward she is, how she's never afraid to ask for what she wants, when she wants it. Or how she teases me without shame, and I'm happily powerless against it.

She might think she missed out by growing up without her parents, but the fact that she's become such an incredible, fiery, compassionate woman shows how strong she is, inside and out.

I don't think I've ever admired someone this damn much.

chapter 23

JAMES

We reach my car two hours later, Maddie on my back.

She complained about her ankle about half an hour ago, and I welcomed the warmth of her body pressed against mine and her legs around my waist as I carry her like a bookbag. It's not like she weighs a lot to me, even though she kept insisting that she didn't want to strain my old man's back.

I have never resisted such a potent urge to spank somebody's ass.

She stretches her arms before getting in the car, her background in ballet becoming obvious with her elegant movements. I've never seen her dance, but I have the feeling I wouldn't be able to peel my eyes away from her if I did. It's difficult enough to do it when she does mundane things.

As soon as we get in the car, I take out my phone and open the music app. "Do you mind if I put on one of my playlists?"

She gives me a smile. "Go ahead."

The upbeat notes of a song by Pet Shop Boys fills the car as I drive us out of the parking lot. I watch out of the corner of my eye how she does a little happy dance with her head, and my knuckles turn white from tightening my grip on the wheel. A reminder to my hands not to reach out and tuck that loose strand of brown hair behind her ear.

Eyes on the road. You're going to scare her away.

That daunting thought is enough to keep my hands in place

and my mouth shut. Until she says, "This song is cool. Who's the artist?"

If I weren't driving, I would've turned my head and gaped at her. "Are you kidding me?"

Her carefree chuckle fills the car. "No."

"Are you seriously telling me you don't know who Pet Shop Boys are?"

"I mean, it's not like I'm telling you I don't know who Taylor Swift is. Now that would be a crime," she says. "Also, that's a weird name for a band. Pet Shop Boys? Don't tell me you like the Zoo Guys too?"

My lips twitch with the beginning of a smirk. "You've just insulted several generations and everyone with great music taste."

"Sorry, I forgot you're ancient."

"What does that say about you, then? That you hang out with an ancient man."

She shrugs. "I've always felt for the elderly."

Oh, Maddie. If I weren't behind the wheel right now...

The song ends and another one by the same group starts. "First you say you don't want to strain my old man's back, and then you call me ancient. You do realize I'm only thirty-one, right?"

"Didn't you hear? Thirty-one is the new ninety-one."

"Then I'm afraid we'll be heading straight home. All the sugar in those donuts might kill me."

"But I thought old guys were gentlemen?" she teases. "And what kind of gentleman goes back on their word after making a promise to their most amazing, funniest, most incredible, most attractive, and most charming friend?"

I can't fight the smile anymore. "And that friend is supposed to be you?"

"Graham is great, but I'd like to think I'm at least a tiny bit prettier than him."

"You're beautiful, Maddie."

The words escape me before I can think twice about what I've just said. Because yes, there's no doubt she's the most stunning woman I've ever met—inside and out—but did I have to run my goddamn mouth?

But because I'm not ready for my stomach to drop to the depths of hell when things inevitably get awkward between us, I blurt out the first thing that comes to mind. "If I'm so ancient, why did you want to hang out with me today?"

I risk a quick glance at her, and I find her already looking at my profile with the same relaxed expression as before. As if me calling her beautiful hadn't made her want to exit my car and never see me again.

"I happened to remember you are an expert hiker and wanted to see for myself," she answers, something in her voice shifting. Sounding almost shy.

Maybe it's our banter, or how easy it is to talk to her, but I find the strength to ask the question that has been nagging me since she sent me that text last night.

"You don't think it's weird?" I swallow back the sudden lump in my throat. "That we hang out, I mean."

"Because I was your patient?" I can hear the confusion in her voice.

"Not only that." It all comes down to this, doesn't it? "I'm ten years older than you."

"I know."

I use the little time it takes me to overtake a couple of cars to think carefully about my next words. Because I may be overthinking this. All of it. I've always frowned upon older men hanging out with younger girls, but when it comes to Maddie...

It's just *her*.

I like spending time with her. A lot. Making her laugh, absorbing every small detail about her life, keeping her safe.

"And you don't find that weird?" I ask once again. "You could be hanging out with your friends today."

Friends your age.

"I could if I wanted to. But I wanted to hang out with you," she says, as if it was really that simple. "Does our age difference make you uncomfortable?"

Yes. No. Not exactly.

When she was my patient, sure, because that crossed too many serious boundaries. But now that she isn't entrusted to my professional care, now that I don't hold any power over her...

You're attracted to her. It's still fucked up.

"James?" She pokes my arm with one of her fingers.

"I know we're just hanging out," I start, unsure of where I'm even going with this. "But I feel like... I don't know. Like I'm robbing you from having other experiences. Doing things with your friends a twenty-one-year-old would do. Not hiking with an older man."

She stays silent for so long, I start wondering if she's angry with me. If I've messed up.

Until a tired sigh reaches my ears.

"You want the truth?" she asks, all the playfulness gone from her voice.

I nod, scared of what she's going to say but dying to hear it.

"Sometimes..." She pauses and starts again. "Even when you were only my PT and we didn't hang out like this, it was like... I don't know. I've never felt immature around you, if that makes sense."

"Because you're not," I assure her.

"I don't always make the best choices," she concedes, "but I wouldn't say I'm immature, either. I had to grow up too fast."

"I get that."

The urge to reach out and grab her hand in mine has never been so damn strong.

"What I'm trying to say is that you've always treated me as

an equal."

The organ in my chest soars at that. "Because we're equals, Maddie."

"I've just never related that much to people my age," she confesses. "Not only because of what happened with my parents, but also because I've dedicated my whole life to ballet and that requires discipline. When I was a teenager and my friends attended summer camps or went to the pool, I was at ballet school practicing my ass off."

She doesn't say it, but I hear the silent words anyway.

Only for my dream to be ripped away from me at the end.

Little does she know that's far from the truth. But I don't push, wanting to hear her talk instead.

"And it stayed the same as I grew older. Do you have any idea how many of my friends got kicked out of a class for being hungover after a night out?" She shakes her head. "No, thank you. I've always taken ballet seriously. And I've never been a big fan of parties or alcohol in the first place, because of...you know, my mom."

"So, you don't go out clubbing?" I ask as I take a turn toward the donut shop.

"I used to when I first moved to Norcastle for college, but I only did it during my first year. Just to see what the fuss was all about, but it wasn't that fun for me," she explains. "I enjoy the occasional cocktail, but getting blackout drunk and dancing with sweaty strangers isn't my thing. Been there, done that, have no desire to do it again."

"And that's perfectly okay."

Society isn't always kind to those in their early twenties who don't want to be party animals. Some people will even tell them that, if they aren't going out every weekend, they're wasting their youth. That's not true by any means, and I'm glad Maddie doesn't feel pressured to do anything she doesn't want.

"You're not robbing me of any experiences, James," she says in a firm voice. "We understand each other, and we're friends. The fact that you're a cranky old man doesn't change any of that."

The donut shop comes into view as I let out a sincere chuckle. "I'm glad to hear it."

"Are you okay with being friends with someone younger?"

"It's complicated," I admit, not wanting to lie to her. "We have things in common, sure, but I still feel like we're in different stages of our lives. It's not weird, but it's not entirely normal either."

Some would even say it's fucked up.

But why does being with her feel so right if it's so wrong?

"Jeez, you're acting like we're about to get married or something." She chuckles, and something inside of me jumps. I don't want to think it's my heart. "What stage are you in, anyway? Do you want to travel? Have a bunch of kids? It's not like that would affect our friendship."

Right. Because the thought of having kids with another woman isn't making me sick.

What the fuck are you saying?

"I don't want to travel or have kids right now. I'm happy with my current life." I clear my throat as I stop behind a red car in the drive-through. "And you?"

Her face falls a little. "I want to find my path, is all."

"I know you will."

She hums, unsure. When I turn my head to look at her, at those hazel eyes that are always so attentive, she says, "I'll tell you to get lost if you ever want to hang out and I don't. No experiences will be robbed. Pinky promise."

I don't hesitate as I hold out my pinky, and she wraps her much smaller one around it. "That's all I've ever wanted."

Her touch lingers for a second too long. "Good." She gives me a small smile, pulling away. "Do you know if they have jelly donuts here? With strawberry jam?"

THE DARKEST CORNER OF THE HEART

They do. Which is a good thing because otherwise I would've gone to every donut shop in the state until I found them for her.

Twenty minutes later, the sun is setting as we leave the drive-through. In charge of the playlist this time, Maddie has chosen an old Taylor Swift song when she says, "We need to do this again sometime."

Thump, thump, thump.

"Getting free donuts from me, you mean?" I tease her, adjusting my sunglasses over my eyes.

"That too." I'm not looking at her, but I can hear the smile in her voice. "But I meant going on a hike. We can try one you've never been on before."

"I wasn't joking when I said I've gone on many hikes." I see her face fall from the corner of my eye. It's not dramatic, barely there at all, but it kills me all the same. "But I'd love to do this again. You and me."

"You and me," she repeats, as if she was tasting the sound of us on her tongue. "It sounds good."

Yes, it does.

Music fills the space between us during most of the ride. She's clearly tired, and I wouldn't mind a shower and an early bedtime either. Despite having spent the last few hours with her, though, I'm not ready to say goodbye. So maybe that's why it takes us longer than usual to enter Norcastle, and maybe that's why my car somehow finds itself in the middle of a busy road I didn't need to take at all.

"Can I ask you something?" Maddie asks out of the blue as we stop in traffic.

"I interrogated you earlier, so it's only fair."

"Why did Graham make you a dating profile?"

It doesn't surprise me she doesn't beat around the bush, but my stomach jumps all the same. I'm not ready to share the full story, though, no matter how badly I might want to.

234

When I got injured and lost my career in football, I thought I couldn't possibly go through something worse. And then I did.

They took care of the parts of me that miraculously remained unbroken and tore them to pieces.

It still hurts to think about it, but for completely different reasons. Reasons I will probably never be ready to tell her about. But I can give her this. "Graham thought it had been too long since I last dated someone."

I can practically hear the million questions roaming around in that cute head of hers. "How... How long have you been single for?" she finally asks, her voice shy.

I don't turn to look at her because if I see that innocence mixed with curiosity in her gaze, I won't be able to hold it together.

"My last serious girlfriend was in college. I must've been nineteen or twenty."

Silence stretches between us, but not for long. "Does that mean you haven't...?" She stops herself, but I know what she was going to ask. The pressure in my pants knows it too.

I save her from embarrassment by saying, "I've had sporadic hookups over the years." I don't want to hide that from her, for some reason. "But I haven't had sex in months, if that's what you're asking me. Nine or ten."

"Oh my God," she groans, hiding her face in her hands. "James! I was not going to ask that."

"Sure you weren't." I smirk. The car in front of us moves, and for better or for worse, we're only five minutes away from her apartment. "It's all right, though. You can ask. I'm not offended."

"But I'm embarrassed."

"You're good, baby."

It's not the first time I notice how her breath hitches at the term of endearment, but I don't ask her why. I don't think I'm ready to hear the answer.

I'm also not ready to find out when was the last time she had sex, but I know whoever the fucker was, he didn't deserve an inch of her or her body.

And you do, asshole?

"We're here." Her voice pulls me out of my forbidden daydreams, and so does the sight of her building.

The sun casts an orange glow over the empty street, a calm sight so rare in the bustling city. She unbuckles herself from the passenger seat, and I do the same, not really knowing why. Maybe I'm finally going insane.

Five seconds pass, ten, fifteen, and neither of us moves.

"It feels weird," she starts, her voice low and soothing, eyes glued on the sunset in front of us, "knowing that I won't see you tomorrow, or the day after. Or the day after that."

I swallow past the lump in my throat. For days I've avoided thinking about what I would feel come Monday morning and meeting a new patient, and she's just put it out in the open because that's what Maddie does.

What she thinks, she shares. What she wants, she asks for. What she feels, she admits out loud.

For someone so much younger, I could learn a thing or two from her. Or a million.

"It's going to be weird for me too," I admit. I'll miss her like crazy, but I keep that to myself. "I'm still only a text away."

She slides me an unsure look. "You mean that?"

The fact that there's a tiny fraction of her that thinks I don't, kills me.

"Of course, Maddie." Easier than I thought it would come, I add, "I'll drop by the bar, too, so we can catch up."

Catch up. It feels too clinical, too mundane for us.

I don't want to *catch up* with her, damn it. I want to know every detail of how her days go and share mine. I want to hear her laugh, answer all her questions, buy her all the damn donuts she wants.

I've never felt so weakened yet so empowered by one person, and it scares me to death.

"I would love that."

When she smiles, it snaps something in me. Something that should've never been awakened.

Suddenly, her face is too close.

Her arm brushes mine, melting away the ice walls I've carefully built over the years so that nothing, not a scrape of *anything*, could reach me.

Gone. Just like that.

Here, no rights or wrongs exist. No consequences. Only this raw intensity and need to take care of her in ways I've never felt before.

I want to kiss her.

I want to touch her, breathe her, taste her, feel her in my bones.

She parts those plump lips, her sweet breath mixing with mine.

She's only inches away, that mouth ripe for the taking, and I become blind with need.

"James..." My name falls from her lips like a blessing and a curse.

I find myself helpless, unable to make any sound, afraid I will shatter our fragile bubble if I do.

My head is empty of the usual voices telling me it's wrong, that she's too young, that it won't end well. And I take it as a sign.

My hand is suddenly at the nape of her neck, holding her firmly like I suspect she likes it, when her phone rings.

And the moment is gone.

"I..." She blinks, cheeks flushed, disoriented.

"Your phone," I manage to let out. Tension rolls off my body, and I pull away.

"Yes," she breathes out, and she's quick to get it out of her bag.

She frowns at the missed call on the screen. "It's my brother. I have to call him back, or he'll worry."

I nod, straightening in my seat, away from her again. "I'll see you around," I offer, still trying to understand what the hell has just happened.

"Y-Yes. See you. Thanks for today. I had a lot of fun." She gives me a sincere smile, still flustered, and grabs her things before getting out of the car. "Don't be a stranger."

With a wave, she disappears inside the building, but I don't move for another ten minutes—minutes in which I try to build my walls back up.

It doesn't work.

chapter 24

MADDIE

I should've seen this coming. Few things in my life ever go differently, so why would I trust that this, too, wouldn't fall to pieces sooner than later?

It's me. I caused this. Maybe I should've never suggested seeing each other again or going on another hike. I thought we'd had fun and that he was opening up to me just a tiny bit more. Now I understand I've been a fool.

Because you always ruin things. Because you only talk about yourself and put the weight of your problems on other people's shoulders, and they get tired and leave.

Almost two weeks have gone by with no news from James.

I would know, since I have a phone he hasn't contacted and a bar he hasn't visited like he said he would.

Nothing. Nada. Radio silence.

I worked every day and every possible shift last week, not necessarily because I was hoping to see him but because my ankle finally feels like it's back to normal—at least enough to work for the extra cash. I lost many tips while washing dishes, so I need to make up for lost time.

It's a Friday night and I'm not supposed to be here, but one of the waitresses called in sick, and I was all too happy to cover for her. But, as soon as I walked into the bar nearly two hours ago, I realized my rookie mistake.

Tonight is hockey night, and the bar is *packed*.

Not another soul fits in the crowded booths as patrons order drink after drink and yell at the TV. If their frustrated sounds and not-so-nice words are anything to go by, our team is getting their butts kicked.

I guess not even the great champions of Norcastle are immune to a bit of bad luck. Unsurprisingly, it doesn't make me feel better.

What does make me feel better, though—and a little nervous—is the job interview I have lined up for next week.

Me and job interview in the same sentence. Shocking, I know.

When I called Grace a few days ago, fed up with being stuck and not knowing where to start, we talked about my options. She's been a ballet teacher for years, so I asked her for advice. She explained how classes usually go and how much I can expect to make, and I made a decision.

Finally, I made a decision about my future after almost three months of wandering in the dark and getting too comfortable in the nothingness of it.

I need to get it together. I might have injured myself, and I might have lost the one and only golden ticket to my dream job, but I'm still breathing.

All my bones and muscles are in the right place and recovering, and I will be able to dance again. Maybe not as soon as I would've wanted, but the point is that I will.

Seeing my father gave me a kind of clarity I never expected but sure needed. He hasn't reached out to me again, but he doesn't have to. His purpose in my life is fulfilled.

He reminded me that I could end up like him if I let myself go too far. And although I would never, *ever* abandon my kids or my partner like he did, I could very well fall into the same pit of self-neglect.

All his life, my father stood for nothing. He never tried to make a name for himself, not even a whisper. Seeing what has become of him after seventeen years is the loudest wake-up call I could've asked for.

He wasn't in a better place like he said, I could tell. And I was on my way to that same destination.

So even if my current dream isn't to teach ballet to a bunch of kids, it could be the start of a new road that leads me to my true purpose. I won't know until I try, and staying at home and feeling sorry for myself won't help me at all. I've tried.

Earlier this week, I applied to four different dance studios in Norcastle that were looking for a ballet instructor, and this morning I got the golden call from one of them. With my interview coming up on Monday, I go over every piece of advice Grace gave me on the phone.

Minutes into my shift, though, I find that my mind has drifted to the forbidden topic on its own accord. Again.

I don't understand why James hasn't texted me. Why he hasn't stopped by when he said he would.

Sure, I could've texted him first, broken the ice, whatever. But I didn't because I freaked out after our almost-kiss, and I didn't want to make another big decision after applying to my first dancing job. I've done enough adulting to last me a lifetime.

Ugh.

"Doll!" One of the men at table four hollers at me, demanding to be fed.

Cavemen, all of them. And not in a hot kind of way.

"Hey, doll!" he calls again. I was hoping one of the other waitresses would go to his table by some miracle, but luck isn't on my side tonight.

"What can I get you?" I ask, avoiding eye contact with all five brutes sitting in front of me. They're old, drunk, and more than a little agitated. *Stupid hockey. Stupid TV.*

The guy places the order for the whole table, but not before he ogles the neckline of my top, and I leave as quickly as I came. They're on their sixth beer—seventh if you count the ones I'm supposed to bring them over. I really don't want to be the one to tell them we can't serve them anymore. But everyone is too busy to come to my rescue, so I'll have to woman up.

Placing all their beers and a basket of nachos on my tray, I slither through the crowd, careful not to spill a single drop. It's a miracle I make it to their table unscathed, but then Creepy Old Man Number One—the one who called me a doll—thanks me for being so quick by reaching out his dirty fingers and touching my midriff.

I jerk back, a sudden wave of disgust climbing up my throat, and I see it happen in slow motion—my tray falling, all five beers and the nacho basket spilling over Creepy Old Man Number One and his friends.

The bar falls silent behind me.

Don't cry, don't cry, don't—

"You useless piece of shit! Who the fuck gave you a job?" the man yells, shooting out of his seat to avoid the waterfall of beer spilling from the table onto their laps.

"I'm..." *I'm sorry*, I want to tell him, even though I'm really not.

But I don't get the chance.

"If I were you, I would watch how you talk to her."

That voice.

He stands only a few feet behind me, his eyes darkened with violence as he looks at the man who yelled at me.

He doesn't acknowledge me, doesn't look at me, only steps in front of me like the protective, six-foot-five wall of pure muscle he is.

And I let him. I let him even though a pool of hot anger starts boiling in the pit of my stomach.

I can barely move. I can barely breathe.

I feel Monica's arm come around my shoulders before I hear her voice. "Are you okay, honey? Tell me what happened." She sounds concerned, but I don't answer.

My gaze stays locked on James, who's now drawing the attention of every table around us, hockey be damned.

And the pool of anger grows.

Creepy Old Man Number One says something my ringing ears don't catch, but I hear James's response as clear as if he were whispering it in my ear.

"Get out of here before I make you swallow your own fucking teeth for putting your hands on my girl."

My girl.

His girl.

My body starts shaking from fear or anger, I don't know, and Monica pulls me against her in a comforting embrace that does nothing to calm me down.

No matter how big or tall or strong James is, there's five of them and only one of him. He's alone, and they're dumb and drunk. I don't even stop to think why he's here in the first place. Why now, after two weeks of giving me nothing but his cold shoulder. I can only tremble and watch as the drunk men stand up from their booth, all eyes on James.

Matt comes out of the kitchen a moment later, stopping next to him. "Get the fuck out. All of you. *Now.*"

Another four guys from nearby tables stand up, too, shouting at the drunk men to leave and threatening to call the cops. After what couldn't be longer than a minute but feels like an infinite lifetime, the five of them finally leave without looking back.

As soon as the door closes behind them, the whole bar erupts into a collective cheer, but I barely hear it. Shaking, I untangle myself from Monica's hug.

"Go to my office, honey," she offers, reading my mind.

I need to be alone right now. I need to calm down. I need to breathe.

"Take a break, okay? As long as you need."

I nod absentmindedly, my feet carrying me all the way to the small room with a desk, a small couch, and no windows that makes up her office, and I allow myself to shake with all the anger, disgust, and fear harbored inside me.

I spilled beer on them, but it was an accident. I lost my grip on the tray because he touched me, not because I was being clumsy.

That man *touched* me, and I feel dirty.

Sinking into the uncomfortable chair in front of Monica's desk, I bury my face in my hands and let the tears fall.

Why did he have to touch me?

Why did he have to yell at me?

I don't hear the door opening behind me, and I don't hear it closing again.

But I hear his voice.

"Maddie. Look at me."

And I feel the warmth of his big hands covering my much smaller ones, peeling my fingers away from my wet eyes gently. He kisses the back of each one, slowly, so softly more tears fall against my will.

"You're okay, baby. I'm here."

Through my tear-covered eyes, I see that he's kneeling in front of me, still keeping my hands in his, cocooned.

"You..." I sniffle as the disgust slowly fades away. *I'm safe.* "You're here."

Still holding my hands in his, he wipes away my tears. His gentleness only makes me want to cry harder, and I hate myself for it.

"I shouldn't have left," he whispers as if he could read my mind. "I should've texted you. I should've called you. I'm sorry."

I'm angry at him. I'm angry that he disappeared without a trace, but is it really his fault? When I push everyone away?

So even though I want to give in to that anger, I choose to be the person Sammy and Grace raised me to be.

"Wh-Why didn't you?" I breathe out, my voice calm but shaky.

Maybe he didn't miss me at all. Maybe I'm the only fool between us.

A beat of eternal silence passes between us, and I use that time to bring my breathing back to normal.

"You're safe," James says, ignoring my question but reading the silent worries in my mind. "I promise you're safe. Sit with me on the couch?"

I let him help me up and walk me to the small couch near the door. He sits first, pulling me against his side and shielding me from everything and everyone but the racing thoughts in my head.

He says nothing, and I find that my throat is too dry to speak. The loud voices from the bar filter through the walls, a loud cheer erupting when our team scores.

"I didn't call you because I was terrified."

My head snaps up, heart hammering inside of my chest. My gaze is fixed on his unmoving lips, pressed together in a tight line, and for a moment, I wonder if I've imagined his voice.

"What?" My own comes out as a strained whisper.

James doesn't tilt his head to look at me, keeping his eyes trained forward instead. Deliberately avoiding mine.

And then he says the words I thought I'd only ever hear in my dreams.

"What you do to me, Maddie... You drive me insane."

My breathing stops.

I don't know what to say. If I even trust myself to utter a single word.

James doesn't move an inch. His body is pressed against mine, but it's cold and distant somehow. I don't like it.

"I needed time to think," he finishes, as if that explains everything.

But I've never been more confused.

"About what?" My voice is raspy, nervous, unsure.

"About you."

About me.

What does that even mean?

"I wanted to kiss you the other night. In my car."

His words detonate a bomb inside my heart, reducing everything to ashes.

Then he sweeps the remains away.

"I wanted to kiss you so badly, I was hurting. I am hurting, just thinking about the things I want to do to you, Maddie, and it's not right. None of this is. I shouldn't want you, but I can't stop the pain that comes every time I think I will never have you."

My ears ring, my heart falls to the pit of my stomach, and a deep, unexpected sense of calm falls over my body like a thick blanket.

Nobody has ever told me that it hurts them to think about not having me. And I, too, feel like a piece of this new life I'm fighting to create is missing when he's not near.

"You wanted to kiss me?"

He nods, short and stiff, still avoiding my gaze.

"Do you still want to kiss me now?"

He sucks in a breath. His nostrils flare. That jaw goes tight, locked.

I don't miss it because I can't take my eyes off him.

"What do you think?" he rasps, his voice the lowest I've ever heard it. When he turns to look at me, the ocean in his eyes is a turmoil of hostile waters.

He wants me. He wants to kiss me.

And I want to kiss him so badly, my lips tingle with anticipation, but I don't move.

I barely breathe, waiting for him to make the move I'm too terrified to make myself.

If I leaned in and he changed his mind, pulling away at the

last second, I don't think I could get over his rejection.

Every boy I've ever kissed, every hookup or attempt at a relationship I've ever had, it was never going to end with happiness and wedding bells.

I never allowed myself to feel anything else but mild attraction, the superficial kind, for fear of filling the spot my parents left empty before I even turned five. I've been afraid of chasing that authentic love I always see around me but have never experienced, so I never gave myself permission to feel anything more.

What if I was only trying to fill a spot that could never be filled?

But seeing my dad taught me there's no emptiness to fill because it was never full in the first place.

The love and care my parents were supposed to give me, I got from someone else—Sammy, and then Grace, and then Lila and the rest of our family.

Can I really miss something I've never had? I could, but I'm not going to. I *refuse* to. Not when I have something so precious in front of me, something that feels right and complete for the first time in my life.

I may not have been the luckiest child, but I'm going to make sure I become the luckiest version of my adult self. And it starts with this.

"I want you to kiss me," I whisper, no hint of hesitation in my voice.

I've never asked for the love I think I deserve, but maybe it's time that I do.

Maybe *she* was wrong all this time.

James's breath mixes with my own, our faces mere inches apart. Monica's office is dark, the only light coming from her computer and under the door, yet still I see the hesitation in his eyes. The regret.

"We can't," he says, like it pains him to do so.

Instead of letting my heart crumble like it wants to, I demand, "Why?"

Our team scores again, and the sound of cheers almost muffles his voice, but I hear every word.

"I'm too old for you."

Our age difference is something I have never ignored, but I have never let it control me either. And I won't start now.

"We've talked about this, James. And I'm only asking for a kiss," I mumble, afraid to raise my voice and shatter our bubble. "We're both adults."

He swallows thickly. "And what happens after a kiss, Maddie? Do you think we can stop there?"

"No."

James looks away, lips pressed tight, and lets out a sigh full of frustration. "How are you feeling?"

Confused, excited, anxious, overstimulated.

"Better."

"Then you should go back to work." His words aren't cruel or cold, simply factual. They don't kill me inside or anything.

I'm not looking forward to going back out there, but the fewer tips I make, the more money I'll have to take from Sammy, so I get up from the couch.

I straighten my uniform, about to head out of the door, when his deep rumble stops me.

"Wait for me when your shift ends."

chapter 25

MADDIE

James doesn't take his eyes off me for the rest of the night.

He sits in a far corner of the bar, nursing a bottle of water for a whole hour until our team wins the game and the place clears up.

He spoke loud and clear earlier, and I'm not naïve enough to think he'll miraculously change his mind, although that ember of hope still burns hot.

I'm too old for you, he said, as if I'd forgotten our age difference. Not even for a second.

But I'm not asking the world of him. I'm not demanding a marriage contract or a promise of undying love.

A taste, that's all I want; maybe then I can convince myself it's over.

The bottom line is he's drawing some very clear boundaries, and I should respect them. I'm *going* to. Who cares if I'm old enough to order a drink at a bar? To pay my own rent and be independent? To know what I want—kind of—and be determined enough to go after it? Nobody does because I'm twenty-one. A whole decade younger than him, and I don't see what the big deal is, but I'm also not going to push him.

The fact that I had to grow up faster than other people my age doesn't mean I'm fully mature, I know this. But I also know I grew up in a stable and sensible family that taught me what signs to look out for in people who might want to take advantage of me in more ways than one.

Older or not, James isn't trying to manipulate me. If he were, he wouldn't be fighting these instincts we seem to share.

I guess there's one good thing that came out of the fiasco tonight. All the tables I waited on witnessed the shit show with Creepy Old Man Number One, and they left some extra tips to cheer me up. And I'm not complaining.

Monica also let me off the hook earlier than usual, given that the crowd had visibly lessened after the game ended. Just as I close the door behind me in the break room, ready to get out of this tight top and call it a day, my phone pings inside my bag.

It's a text from James, sent just now.

James: I'm waiting in my car outside

I don't text him back but instead rush to change with my heart beating so fast I'm scared it will stop all of a sudden.

For almost two full weeks, he didn't contact me at all. Not even to tell me he needed some time away. I would've understood. Damn it, I really would have. But he took that choice away from me, the option to decide what I wanted to do with our...relationship? We don't have one, and we never will.

A part of my brain knows I'm being irrational. He came back, apologized, and explained himself. And I get it, but I also can't seem to put out this fire consuming my stomach, filling me with anger like never before.

Because I'm tired of allowing the people who leave to walk all over me when they want to come back. I stood up against my father, holding my ground until he left, and tonight won't be an exception.

Never again. They don't get to walk away and come back whenever they feel ready. That's bullshit.

I grab my things, wave goodbye to Monica and Matt, and

step outside into the cold night air.

Standing against the hood of his car with his bulky arms crossed in front of his chest, James waits for me like he said he would.

His eyes don't leave mine as I cross the parking lot, and I can tell the exact moment he sees it, because I feel the shift too.

I stop before him, mere inches away from the warmth of his body, and say, "You left." My voice doesn't waver. My words don't hesitate to slice him open. "You promised me you'd be there for me, and you left. You *broke* your word."

His massive body doesn't move an inch. Not his arms, not his chest, and not that sharp jaw.

He doesn't even blink, this huge man who's never been short on the intimidating traits. But I don't back down from the coldness behind those beautiful eyes I've gotten lost in more times than I can count.

The seconds go by, then a full minute, and he still hasn't said a word. The lips I confessed I wanted to kiss merely an hour ago are sealed tight.

I wish I could read his mind, but at the same time, I'm too scared of what I'd find there. I wonder if it would sting too much, if it would burn.

If it would break me.

He takes a step forward, then another. And then that hand, that massive hand, is cupping the side of my cheek, cradling it in his warm palm. "Maddie," my name falls from his lips in a single breath, something between a pained whisper and a sigh.

I blink up at him, unsure if I'm even allowed to breathe right now. It doesn't feel like I could, even if I wanted to.

When his forehead meets mine, gentler than I've ever seen him do anything ever before, I melt a little.

And when he speaks again, I melt all at once.

"I'm sorry for hurting you." His voice is low and rough, and

I think his fingers against my skin are shaking a little. But I might be imagining it. "I don't know what's happening to me, Maddie. Why I'm so fucking terrified of this."

I swallow, my throat feeling as dry as sandpaper. "I'm scared too."

"Why?" I feel him frown against my skin.

It all comes down to this, doesn't it?

"Because I make everyone walk away." I swallow again as my heart gallops inside my chest and my pulse drums in my ears. "I made you walk away. I told you we should see each other again, and it freaked you out."

His thumb brushes my cheek, right under my eye, and it's only then that I realize a single tear has fallen. "You didn't push me away, baby. You could never." James shuts his eyes and takes a deep breath through his nose. "I couldn't be more ashamed of myself for having disappeared like that, but I promise it had nothing to do with you or anything you said. You could never make me walk away. *Never*, because I don't want to walk away from you. Do you understand me?"

I gulp, giving him a small nod.

"Who did this to you, Maddie?" The sudden change in his voice takes me aback. "Who made you so untrusting, so wary? Who made you believe you were to blame for other people's actions?"

I feel it then.

It starts on my toes, then travels to my knees, my chest, and finally the jaw he's cradling so gently in his touch.

I start shaking like I've never done before, and it doesn't even take him one second before he pulls me into his arms, against his hard chest, and keeps me there. Soothing me.

His arm wraps around my back, his fingers splayed on my hip as his other hand tangles in my hair. James presses his stubbled cheek against the top of my head as he rocks me back and forth, cradling me like I'm this fragile thing he needs to protect.

And I've never, not in my twenty-one years, felt more shielded.

Maybe that's why I tell him. Maybe that's why I decide to confide in him what I haven't told a soul, not my friends and not my family, not *my brother*. But I want him to know.

I want him to know because this is James. Simply him.

I want to tell him about *her*.

"When I moved here, to Norcastle, four years ago, I went to see a therapist," I start, unable to believe this is really happening. *I'm talking about it, and I'm fine. I'm fine.* "I hadn't been to therapy for two years, but being away from my family for the first time, living so far away... I felt like that was the right thing to do."

His arms tighten around me, giving me the strength I need to keep reliving this hell.

"Our first couple of sessions went fine. She said..." I let out a breath, urging my body to calm down and stop shaking so violently. It doesn't work. "She said some things that upset me, but I let them slide. But as time went by, she started planting these ideas in my head. She explained it in a way that made sense, I guess, and didn't raise any alarms at first."

"What things?" he asks, his voice a growl, but his anger isn't directed at me. I know this.

I bury my head in his chest, just a little closer to his heart. "She said I... That I was being selfish with my family by bothering them with my problems. That they needed a real break from me now that I'd finally moved out."

I will never forget the sharp pain in my chest, like I was dying, in that session.

A muttered "*fuck*" reaches the top of my head.

"She said I should be independent and let them be, let them enjoy their family time. You know, because I wasn't their *real* family."

"That's bullshit," he spits out.

"I know it now." But the damage is done, and the residuals are hard to shake off. So painfully hard. "I told her about how I felt bad that they couldn't have more children because of me, even if they had never told me *anything* remotely close to that, and I know now that isn't the case. But she said my suspicions were correct, and that they would probably have another baby now that I had moved out."

But they didn't. And when I brought it up to Sammy as a joke, he snorted and said, "No, thanks. You and Lila are giving me enough gray hairs to last me a lifetime."

James's fingers massage my scalp as if he is trying to get all the bad memories out himself. "What else did she say?"

"Too much. She said too much." My body has stopped shaking, all but the hands I keep sandwiched between our bodies. "How everyone has walked out of my life because I'm selfish and push them away. She said my mother tried to come back for me, but I didn't let her and instead manipulated my brother with my tears so he'd feel pity and keep me. I had panic attacks for years, just thinking about what a shitty person I was. And I never told my family about it."

"Jesus," he mutters against the top of my head. "I'm so sorry you had to go through that. I hope you know it's all bullshit."

"Sometimes it's difficult to remember," I whisper, inhaling the familiar scent of his spicy cologne. "But I'm trying. Every day I fight against the intrusive thoughts."

"How long did you see her for?"

"About two months. I should've never gone back after the first session, maybe the second, but she was just so...so *cunning*. I feel so stupid now, looking back. I should've known something was wrong way before that."

He squeezes my waist. "The important thing is that you got the hell out of there," he reassures me. "Have you gone back to therapy since then?"

I shake my head. "I can't." What if my next therapist says the same stuff? Would I believe she was right, then? "She ruined it for me."

"But do you *need* therapy now?"

"It wouldn't hurt to go back" is an understatement. Until her, therapy had always worked for me. I used to leave my sessions with a lighthearted feeling in my chest and full of optimism, and now... James pulls away from me, not letting me go completely, so he can look me in the eye. "We'll research options together," he decides then and there, just like that.

I blink up at him just as the hand he keeps on my hip travels all the way to my back and settles there. Like an anchor.

"I won't let her ruin a good thing for you, Maddie. A thing you need." He scans my face with intent, looking for something he seems to find a moment later. "Do you know if she still has her license?"

I shake my head. "I have no idea." It used to make me nauseated just thinking about her, let alone stalking her online. "I know she has a website, because that's how I found her, but..."

"What's her name?" he asks, a new resolve in his voice.

"Why do you want to know?"

"I'll have her license revoked." There's not a single trace of a doubt in his words. Not one, and it brings back that tingle in my spine. "Even if it's the last thing I ever do. Nobody messes with you and lives to tell the tale, baby. Not while I'm here."

Thump, thump, thump.

I wet my lips and notice the way his eyes follow the movement like a hawk. "Her name isn't important anymore."

"It is to me. It is if she hurt you."

"James, it really is all right," I insist one more time.

When he opens his mouth to say something else, I do something I would've never, not in a million years, imagined myself doing.

I press a finger against his lips, so soft under my touch, and he shuts up immediately.

It would be funny if not for the fact that the heat in his eyes has morphed into something less angry and more...hungry. I don't even know how to describe it.

"It's fine." My voice comes out as a whisper. "I'm okay now. I'm trying to go back to the person I was before, and that's all that counts. Okay?"

He nods, silent.

Slowly, too slowly, my finger falls from his lips, settling on his stubbled chin first then on the hammering pulse in his neck. And I can't help it, so I say, "I'm sorry for venting like that. I know you asked me, but—"

"Maddie."

I gulp. "Yes?"

"Stop apologizing."

And then, *and then*, as if he were running out of time and starving all at once, he closes the slim distance between us and presses his lips against mine.

Holy shit.

The throaty growl that leaves him is borderline animalistic. His hands, strong and possessive, pull me impossibly closer to his hard body.

Oh my God.

He pulls at my hair in a way that feels dominant and only slightly painful, drawing out a weak sound from the back of my throat I've never heard before. Before I can overthink it too much, my fingers tangle in his hair, my nails scratching his scalp, and he groans.

He kisses me like he's drowning and I'm his mainland.

There's nothing slow or tender about it, but this kiss is exactly what I need. What my body has been begging for.

It doesn't matter that we're standing in the middle of a

parking lot, where anyone coming out of the bar could see us. I don't care about anything but the all-consuming feeling of his lips on mine.

His teeth pull at my lower lip, and my mouth opens just enough for his tongue to tangle with mine in a sensual dance. His hand finds the naked skin on my back, and before we know it, we're panting for air.

"Look what you do to me," he growls against my skin, pressing my stomach against his hard groin. *He's hard. He's hard for me.* "You drive me insane, baby. Can you feel it?"

"Yes," I breathe out, desperate to feel his friction between my legs. "James..."

He nibbles my ear. "Tell me why this feels so right if it's so fucking wrong."

I pull him away from my neck until we're eye to eye. "Because it's not wrong."

He gulps, the conflict so clear in his gaze I want to scream. And maybe I'm not doing myself any favors, but I say, "Just tonight. Take me home tonight and forget about how right or wrong it feels for one night."

His forehead presses against mine, but he doesn't say a word. He closes his eyes, his breathing labored, and I fear I've lost him before I've even had him.

"James—"

My words die in my mouth, silenced with another searing kiss. I pull at his shirt as his hands find the curve of my ass, gripping it like I've imagined so many times in my forbidden fantasies.

His mouth travels to my neck next, biting and kissing and sucking. A primal part of me wishes he'd leave a mark to let the world know I belong to him.

Heat climbs up my cheeks as he hoists me up, and I wrap my legs around his hips on instinct. "Who's blushing now?" he asks in a raspy, teasing voice, his thumb caressing my reddened cheek.

"Tell me what you need, beautiful."

The words spill out of me unabashedly. "I want to feel you," I pant with need, with desperation, with *ache*. I don't think I've wanted anything more than this.

"Yeah?" he grunts, pressing his hard groin against my soft center. "You want to feel me here?"

"Yes," I breathe out, desperately clinging to him. "Right there. *Please.*"

"Look at you, asking so nicely." His teeth sink into my throat, but not hard enough to hurt. An unabashed whimper escapes my lips. "Get in the car, baby."

He kisses me once more, twice, and then reluctantly sets me on the ground. Our lips meet again, short but not sweet, before his touch leaves my body, and I climb into the passenger seat.

James doesn't utter a single word as we leave for his apartment, his heated promise hanging above us. He keeps one of his big hands splayed on my thigh, a possessive gesture I'm starting to become addicted to, and drives away into the night.

chapter 26

JAMES

My mouth finds hers the second I shut the door behind me with enough force to wake up the whole damn building.

She turns me around until she has me pressed against the hard wood, her cold palms hiking up my shirt and exploring every inch of the firmness of my bare chest. I let her have this moment of control, only because she has no idea what's awaiting her tonight.

She has no idea the kind of beast she's letting loose.

Her fingers tug at my shirt like the vicious little thing she is, and I help her take it off. Her eyes roam my naked chest, getting her fill, before she plants open-mouthed kisses on the base of my throat then lower.

A desperate groan leaves my lips. Somewhere in the back of my mind, I know she's still too young for me and I'm too much of a fuckup for her, but at this moment, all I care about is devouring every inch of her skin. Of *her*.

I want to make her scream, beg, spend her until it hurts to breathe.

"Off," I command, tugging at her top, and she doesn't hesitate before it's lying on a pile on the floor along with her bra. I knead that beautiful ass next, my tongue teasing one of her nipples until I have her squirming. "Up."

She does as she's told, my sweet thing, and wraps her legs around my torso as I carry her to my bedroom. She's so light in my arms, those tits so damn delicious on my tongue and plush in my hands, I press her against the nearest wall and fist her hair, breaking contact with her skin. Maddie gasps, her eyes full of lust.

"You like it rough, don't you, baby." I gently sink my teeth into the sensitive spot at the top of her full breasts and bask in the loud moan I get as a response. "You want me to fuck you hard? To have no mercy on your body?"

She gasps as my fingers find the button of her jeans, unclasping it with ease. "These are coming off," I demand, my own judgment clouded by the need of making her drown in pleasure.

She squirms in my arms until I set her on the floor so she can slide her pants down those athletic legs I can't wait to test the flexibility of. The sight of her black panties, so simple yet so damn sexy, is interrupted by her fingers tugging at my own jeans.

"You have too many clothes on," she says with a smirk, and I'm only so happy to get rid of the barriers between us.

Standing in our underwear, we gaze into each other's eyes for a moment, breathing heavily.

We're really doing this. I'm going to fuck my twenty-one-year-old ex-patient in my bed, and I don't feel an ounce of guilt about it.

My hungry eyes glaze over her perfect curves, from her beautiful eyes to her toes, and only one word comes to mind. "Breathtaking."

Despite the darkness in the room, I don't miss her blush. "You don't look too bad yourself," she muses, her fingertips drawing circles on my chest. They move down and down, so slowly and painfully I make a mental note to punish her for it later, until they reach the hem of my boxers.

When she licks her lips, I lose it. I capture that mouth in my own again, our tongues battling for an impossible victory. I walk her backward to the bed, lowering myself until I'm sitting on the mattress. It's only now that I notice a butterfly tattoo on her ribs, small but intricate and delicate, just like her, and plant a soft kiss on it. "Did you draw this yourself?" My voice comes out rough, but so does hers.

"Yeah," she says before I kiss her skin again.

Mine.

The thought comes out of nowhere, but fuck it if doesn't feel right to call her mine.

My fingers, previously gripping her hips, find their way under the hem of her panties. "Can I take these off?"

She nods, probably not expecting my question, and I hold my breath as I slowly lower the slim piece of fabric down her legs. My mouth waters at the sight of her bareness, just a few inches away from my face.

She's so perfect, inside and out, I don't know what to do with myself.

It's all-consuming, and I'm turning into ashes just thinking about what I'm going to do when this is over. Because I'll never get to have her like this again.

One night. Just one night. Tonight, and then it's over.

Pushing my own thoughts away, I scoot back on the bed until I'm lying on my back and my head is flat against the pillow. She eyes me with interest, still standing at the foot of the mattress, taunting me from a distance. I pat my chest. "Come here."

She arches a playful eyebrow. "You want me to straddle your chest?"

"I want you to sit on my face so I can finally taste that sweet pussy."

Her breath hitches, mouth slightly agape, like she doesn't know every small movement she makes is my goddamn undoing.

But she recovers quickly, climbing onto the mattress first and crawling to me on all fours. I can't take my eyes away from her center as she spreads her legs to straddle my torso, from the way those glistening lips part with her movements.

"I've never..." she starts, looking nervous for the first time since we kissed in the parking lot. "No one has ever..."

Hell. "No one has ever eaten you out?"

When she shakes her head, her confession sends a stupid jolt of accomplishment through my chest, knowing I'll be the first to taste her.

And the only one.

That sounds about fucking right.

"Don't worry, baby." My hands climb up the length of her thighs, leaving a trail of goose bumps in their wake. "I'm going to make you feel good. I promise."

"I trust you." Her eyes gleam with confidence, and fuck if that doesn't make me even harder.

"Come up here," I instruct, helping her climb up until her bare pussy is *right there*, just a couple of inches above my hungry mouth.

I blow some air on it, eliciting such an erotic moan from her, it takes everything in me not to dive in like a man possessed.

I want to take my time with her because she deserves no less than that.

The tip of my tongue finds her outer lips, lapping at them just barely, a caress. She arches her back at the faint touch, so responsive like I knew she would be.

"That's it," I growl.

"J-James," she stammers. Her hands find my hair, trying to take the reins, but I won't let her. Tonight is all about her pleasure, and I don't want her to do a thing but revel in the way my body fills her. "*Please.*"

I plant a soft kiss on her folds, still not parting them, then another one, breathing in her sweet scent. "Tell me what you need."

"Y-Your tongue."

I hum. "This tongue?"

The first taste of her is brutal. Undoing. Everything falls away as my tongue pierces her entrance, immediately finding the wetness of her desire ready for me. She moans so loudly it snaps me into action, letting loose the beast in me. The beast I've tried so fucking hard to control when I'm around her. But no more.

Grabbing ahold of her hips to keep her in place, I bury my face in her heat and welcome the sweet death that finds me when I taste her.

I lap at her, licking all the way up like a man starved as she wiggles above me, my stubble rasping her thighs. Every time my tongue pierces her, she lets out a high-pitched scream I already know I'll never get out of my head.

"God," she pants, gripping my hair and grinding herself on me. "Fuck."

That's it, baby.

I fuck her with my tongue, in and out like I'm planning to do with my cock later, and soon I feel her walls pulsing and contracting around me. She's close, but I'm a wicked son of a bitch. After a few more licks, I haul her up until she's sitting on my bed again, panting and sweating.

"On your knees," I command, gripping my still-covered cock. She notices and tries to pull my boxers down, but I smack her ass in response, earning me a yelp. "Be a good girl for me and lift that ass up."

"What are you going to do to me?" she asks, out of breath.

I grab ahold of her face, cradling her cheek in my hand, and whisper, "I'm going to make you scream until you come all over my cock. Does my pretty girl want that?"

"I want it," she whispers against my mouth. "I need you inside me."

If I had any doubts before, it's clear now—Maddie owns me, consumes me, blinds me of all my senses, except for the innate urge to make her feel good, safe, protected, cherished.

I would give her the whole world on a silver platter if she asked for it, and that realization terrifies me.

I don't know what we're doing besides giving in to a tension that has been building up since the day we met. The moment I saw her for the first time in the waiting room at the clinic, I knew she was going to make me come undone. Because how could she not?

It scares me. It feels too soon, and she's too young. And yet I don't regret any decision that has led us here. Not a single one.

She's everything I never saw coming, and now I can't get enough of her. She's addictive, uplifting, good for me.

And yours for one night. Only one. Don't forget that.

As she positions herself on all fours, I take my underwear off and toss it somewhere on the floor. I grab a fistful of my cock, pumping it up and down, getting it ready to give her the pleasure she deserves.

Maddie looks over her shoulder, her eyes immediately landing on my shaft. Her lips part at the size of my length and girth, but I don't let her think too much about it. "It'll fit."

She only nods, swallowing. My hand finds her round ass perched up for me, and I caress the softness of her skin before smacking her. *Hard.* When she yelps, she gets another one.

"This is what you get—" My grip on my cock roughens, squeezing it as I leave a red mark on her ass with my other hand. "—for being a brat."

She moans, arching her back, begging for more. "Yes."

I lower my head between her cheeks, unable to stay away from that pussy for another fucking second. I spread her wide as I lap at her swollen clit once again, drinking her juices and her whimpers.

"James," she whines, face buried in my pillow as I eat her out from behind. "Your cock. *Please.* I need it so badly."

I take one last lick and pull away, if only because I can't resist it when she begs. "You want me to fill you up?"

She nods so eagerly for it, I can't believe she's real. I can't believe she's here, mine to pleasure. Just for tonight. I wipe the aching thought away with a few pumps of my cock. "Let me grab a condom."

"No condom," she blurts out, making my heart stop. "I'm on the pill and tested negative for everything. Did you?"

Holy shit. "Yes. I've never had sex without a condom."

"Me neither," she admits, her lower lip pulled between her teeth. She looks so innocent yet so goddamn sexy, it drives me insane. "But I need to feel you bare inside me."

I've died and gone to heaven. I'm dead. Gone.

"You need it?" I position myself behind her, grabbing her ass cheek with one hand and lowering my cock to her tight entrance with the other but not breaking that barrier just yet. "Tell me how badly you need this pussy to be filled."

Because who am I to deny her when she's being such a wet dream?

"So bad," she whimpers as I trace my engorged head along her seam, coating my length in her wetness. "I want to be so full of you, I can't breathe."

"Fucking hell," I hiss, unable to take this torture for one more fucking second.

She's *mine.*

And I don't want to be anyone else's.

I fist my cock and position it at her entrance, parting those sweet lips with the head but not pushing it inside just yet.

Suddenly my brain fills with conflicting thoughts, battling for dominance in a war where the only loser will be me.

She's your ex-patient.

You don't deserve her.

She's too good for you.

"James." My name sounds pained as it falls from her lips, and she moves her hips in a way that has my cock sliding up her slit, causing both of us to hiss at the contact. "You're having doubts."

I shut my eyes and try not to focus on the wetness coating my length right now.

"Some," I manage to let out, opening my eyes again but not sliding them toward the lower part of our bodies because I know I won't survive it.

And I don't know why. I had no problem kissing her or eating her out, but for some reason, fucking her suddenly feels like too big of a step. Like it's something neither of us will come back from.

Because once I'm inside her, I know I will never get enough.

"We can stop if you want," she says.

Fuck that.

"I don't want to stop."

She arches an eyebrow, looking at me over her shoulder. "But you won't fuck me?"

I curl one of my hands on her waist. "Trust me, I've never wanted to fuck anyone this badly in my goddamn life."

"Then do it," she says, her voice nothing short of challenging.

She's too young.

You can still back down.

My unwelcome thoughts are interrupted by her hand wrapping around the base of my cock. When she positions the head at her entrance, I lose my fucking mind.

"Just the tip," she whispers. "If it's just the tip, it doesn't count."

I don't move. I barely breathe at all as she pushes my cock inside her until the head is buried. A small sound escapes the back of her throat at the intrusion, and everything in me screams to claim her until my apartment is filled with her moans.

And when I look down and see the tip buried inside her, I curse under my breath. "*Goddamnit.*"

She moves her hips so that my cock slips out then grabs it again and pushes the head inside one more time. "Just the tip," she moans, shattering all my walls. She arches her back, panting. "*Shit*, it feels so good."

I wrap my hand around hers, still fisting my cock. "Just the tip, huh?" I take it out, the sound of her wetness filling the room, and push it back in, just a little bit deeper. "Want some more of my cock, baby?"

"*Yes*," she whimpers.

And because I would do anything for this woman, I push even deeper and watch, mesmerized how her tight grip swallows me from tip to base. It disappears between her bare lips, giving way to a wet warmth I could stay buried in forever.

Her walls clench around me, choking my cock. I can't look away as I take it out then put it back in, slowly, and repeat. I don't think I've ever seen something so fucking erotic.

"*Harder*," she begs, my sweet little thing.

I grab her hip with one hand, a fistful of her hair with the other, and lower myself to her ear so I can whisper, "Does my girl want me to come inside her?"

A desperate whimper leaves her throat. "Y-Yes. God, *yes*."

My restraint shatters. I let go of her hair, taking her hips in my hands, and pound into her as hard as she begged me to. As hard as I've been dreaming of for longer than I'll ever allow myself to admit.

Her whimpers, my groans, my balls slapping against her ass, and the wetness of us fills the dark room, these forbidden sounds I had never, not in my wildest fantasies, dreamt of hearing.

Unable to take the pleasure, she arches her back until she's sitting on my lap, me on my knees, and fucks herself on my cock. My eager fingers pinch her nipples before moving downward to her pulsing clit.

"James," she pants, coating my digits in her wetness. "I can't take it. *Oh, God*. I can't."

"Last chance," I growl in her ear. "Tell me to pull out now, or I'm gonna fill you to the fucking brim."

"Yes, *yes*," she hisses. "Come inside me, James. *Shit*."

Everything around me ceases to exist but the woman in my

arms, jumping over the edge with her hand in mine.

We fall at once. Messily. Loudly. Passionately.

I still inside her, shooting my release just like she wanted. Just like I fucking *needed*.

I paint slow circles on her sensitive clit, helping her come down her own high as I fill every inch of her.

When I gently pull out of her, my eyes lock on her release covering my cock, and I know I shouldn't have looked. I shouldn't have looked at my cum leaking out of her brimming entrance, because that's a sight I will never—I will fucking never—get out of my head.

She falls onto the mattress, exhausted and breathing heavily, and I give her a fleeting kiss on her forehead before disappearing into the attached bathroom in my room. I sort myself out quickly and grab a hot, wet cloth to clean her up.

But just as I'm getting out of the bathroom, I walk into her. She giggles as she collides with my chest, and my arms shoot up around her waist to steady her. "Sorry," she mumbles.

"I was about to go clean you up." My voice comes out soft, gentle, and I don't know why.

This never happens to me. In the years since my last relationship, whenever I slept with a woman, I never did any aftercare. Don't get me wrong, I wasn't an asshole, but the lines were never blurred. The agreement was to fuck—no strings attached—and go home. They took care of themselves after the deed was done, and so did I. Individually.

But now...

Now, I can't bring myself to not make sure she's okay. I need to clean her up, make sure she's comfortable.

"Can I use your shower instead?" she asks, a hint of shyness in her voice as if I hadn't just fucked her raw.

"Whatever you need." And then, because I truly don't know what I'm doing, I add, "Do you want to stay tonight?"

She stills in my arms. For a moment, I curse myself, thinking I crossed a line, but then she asks, "Where will I sleep?" As if she were really considering it.

My hand finds her nape, brushing her skin there with my thumb. "Next to me." I will never know why my voice comes out huskier than usual, why something akin to vulnerability opens up in my chest. *What if she says no?*

She doesn't answer. Not with words, anyway.

Standing on her tiptoes, Maddie captures my lips with hers as I wonder what will become of me once the sun rises.

chapter 27

MADDIE

I went out like a light last night. Exhausted, spent, satisfied, confused, and everything else good and bad in between.

That's the thing about giving in to your most hidden desires, kissing your former (or maybe still current?) physical therapist, and damning the consequences—you end up with messy thoughts.

And a pronounced ache between your legs.

As I stir awake the following morning, slowly and a bit disoriented, the first thought to hit me is the fact that not only did I sleep next to James last night... I slept with him.

No, not slept—we *fucked*. Good. Hard.

And—yep. I'm wearing his clothes. An old shirt and a pair of sweatpants he gave me last night.

I wait for the mortification to overwhelm me, then wait some more, but it never comes. It's a weird sensation, not feeling guilty about going with my heart and following my body's instincts, but I welcome it nonetheless.

How could anyone regret ending up between James's sheets, anyway? It's clear he knows how to use his body, knows how to work mine, and together we simply...exploded. I'd never had that kind of rough sex before, so I can't say I was well-versed in the act of sexual pleasure, but it turns out I'm a quick learner.

The second his tongue was inside me, I lost my mind. I'd wondered for so long how it would feel for a man to devour me as if I were his last meal, and I swear I can still feel the delicious friction of his stubble on the inside of my thighs.

I can't explain what it felt like to sleep with James last night. All I can say is that it felt right, as if a galaxy that was meant to explode was finally torn to pieces.

As I stretch my arms and legs on his king-sized mattress, though, I know he won't feel the same.

Because the bed is empty, and James is nowhere to be found.

Here we go.

I knew this was bound to happen the second he told me he was too old for me last night. But I call bullshit.

Sure, our age gap is something I don't want to ignore, but it's not like we're doing anything *wrong*.

I'm not scared of standing up for myself and getting what I want, of not letting anybody else control me. Sammy and Grace made sure I knew I had the right to freedom, boundaries, and independence since I was a young girl, and I'm not going to forget that now. Not for any man.

Plus, I told him to let go just for one night. He did what I told him to do.

But it's the morning now, which means last night won't repeat itself ever again, age difference or not.

It takes me a minute, but I finally hear something—a shower. Remembering his attached bathroom where I cleaned myself up just a few hours ago, I sit on the mattress, my feet barely reaching the floor from how high the bed is.

The closed door only a few feet away calls for me. Tempts me.

It would be stupid to try...

Try *what*, exactly?

To get into the shower with him? What if he kicks me out? What if, unlike me, he regrets last night?

The truth is that I wanted him last night while the moon was high, and today, while the sun shines behind the clouds, I still yearn for him.

Maybe I will regret this in about ten seconds. Maybe I'm tempting my luck too much. But they always leave in the end, so who cares if I speed up the process?

I hold my head high as I walk toward the closed door then wrap my hand around the handle. *Come on, Maddie. It's not like he'll kick you out.*

It's unlocked.

James stands completely naked and wet in the shower. I don't know why this is shocking to me since, well, it's a damn shower. What was I expecting?

Not those firm, bulking muscles, for one. The darkness and my touch last night didn't do his body any justice, and when I saw him shirtless that one morning, I didn't give myself enough time to appreciate it so openly. He looks like he was carved out by a sculptor, following my exact commands. Because, for the lack of better words, James is a dream. His body is the obvious whole package, but it's what I found inside that makes me want to keep him forever.

And that's a thought I should let go of right now.

He's reliable, loyal, with a dry sense of humor that matches my own, and with a soul so battered yet full of life I could exchange it with mine and not feel any difference.

But even though I'm not meant to end up with him, I'll be selfish and take what I want. Just this once.

As I open the door all the way, James turns around, his eyes finding mine through the shower door. They're not wild or surprised, but they hold a challenge in them. One I'm only too happy to accept.

Without taking my eyes off him, I close the door and lean against it, allowing the hot steam to cling to my body.

He's a sight to behold. The steam in the room doesn't prevent me from seeing how the water runs down his toned chest, down his navel, and past his legs. And when he takes his shower gel and starts rubbing it all over his muscles, I die a little inside.

I don't know what I was thinking when I thought he wouldn't want anything to do with me this morning, that he'd regret sleeping with me at all.

Clearly, I read him all wrong.

Without taking those ocean eyes away from me, he fists his cock and starts pumping it up and down, slowly, applying shampoo all over his generous inches.

I'm not ready for the sight of James jerking off in front of me—jerking off *to* me—but I don't back down.

Holding his stare, I strip down from the baggy shirt and sweats he gave me last night. The tension between us crackles, an ember about to turn into a wildfire.

He doesn't say a word, doesn't stop me as I open the shower door and step under the waterfall with him. I get closer until his engorged head comes in contact with the soft skin on my stomach.

"Came to play?" His voice sounds as strained as it did last night, and it adds to the tingles between my legs.

My answer is to get on my knees.

His breath hisses, and he shuts his eyes. "Fuck."

I don't take my eyes away from his face, silently begging for a taste. Water droplets run down my now wet hair, clinging to my skin as he continues pumping his cock right in front of my face, the warm water getting all the soap off his skin.

It's the memory of last night, of him stretching me wide, drawing out all the pleasure I didn't know I could feel, that makes me desperate for more.

"Please," I beg, my voice barely above a whisper.

He cradles my wet cheek with his other hand, rubbing his thumb on my parted lips. I suck it into my mouth. "You're a needy little thing, aren't you?" he rasps.

I nod, just barely, and he takes his thumb out of my mouth. But his hand doesn't travel too far—it grabs a handful of my hair, securing my head into place. His possessiveness lights a fire inside me.

"I need it in my mouth," I whimper, the desperation between my legs climbing up my throat as I part my lips.

He tugs at my hair, his eyes darkening. "You're gonna let me come down your throat?"

My walls clamp in anticipation. "Yes."

He grunts. "That's my girl."

Still fisting his cock, he rubs the tip on my lips, teasing. But two can play that game.

My tongue finds his wet head, and I give it a tentative lick. He shuts his eyes and groans, only for a moment, before that animalistic gaze is back on my mouth, watching my every move.

Confidence builds up inside me as I gather all his small reactions to my touch. Taking a deep breath, I wrap my mouth around his cock and swirl my tongue around the head. His grip on my hair tightens, and I take him deeper down my throat.

He's so big that I have to stretch my mouth wider to accommodate his length, but I take every inch eagerly. He tastes salty and slightly like soap, and it's his groans and his loss of control that drive me over the edge.

"*Shit*," he hisses, pulling me deeper until my lips graze the short hairs at his base. "You suck my cock so fucking well. I knew you would."

I pull back, breathless, but I can't stay away. I swallow him down again, and again, until I pick up a rhythm we both are comfortable with. I've never felt this urgent desire to have a man in my mouth, like the mere thought of his cock not stretching my throat pains me.

"That's it. Suck it hard."

I bob my head up and down his shaft, gagging on it, saliva spilling down my chin. At one point, both of his hands land on my hair, and he uses his grip to fuck himself on my mouth. It's so hot

I want to tear up.

I don't want him to stop. I need to swallow every last drop of his release, just like another part of me did last night.

Almost like he's reading my mind, he says, voice strained, "I'm gonna come, baby. Last chance to pull out."

I shake my head as firmly as I can, and he curses under his breath.

Somehow I manage to take him deeper, the head of his cock hitting the very back of my throat, and he comes undone.

He pulses into my mouth, filling my throat. He tastes salty with just the tiniest hint of bitterness, and I immediately know I don't want this to be the last time I taste him. *But it will be.*

"Come here." His command is rough, but his hands are gentle as he lifts me up and wraps my legs around his torso.

We're pressed against the shower wall as our eager tongues meet again. His fingers find my soaked entrance, bringing me to yet another orgasm in record time. Who knew sucking him off would almost tip me over the edge?

He sets me down on the tiled floor, and I grab on to his arms for support. One of his hands finds my hip as the other pours shampoo over my hair. Through it all, James is silent, stoic even, and I don't know what to make of this sudden change.

"What are you doing?" I whisper, barely hearing my own voice above the water sounds.

"Washing your hair."

Duh. "But why?"

It should be a question easy enough to answer, yet he takes his sweet time brewing a response.

"Because I want to take care of you."

Oh.

Well, shit.

His fingers massage my scalp as he continues to wash my hair, and I close my eyes and allow myself to just...feel.

For all the roughness of his body punishing mine, he can be a big softie.

He wants to take care of me, and I realize now that I want, more than anything, him to take care of me too. Just as much as I want to take care of him.

Tilting my head back with the utmost care, he rinses the shampoo from my hair and moves on to my body. He massages every inch of my skin, his big hands coated in vanilla-scented soap. He's so clinical about it, it's difficult to reconcile this man with the one who was fucking himself in my mouth just a few moments ago.

He places me under the waterfall of his shower, getting rid of all the soap. And then he kisses my forehead, the tip of my nose, my lips. The kisses are short, gentle, and it makes all the butterflies in my stomach take flight once again.

"Maddie, I—"

He doesn't get to finish that sentence.

The sound of my phone ringing pierces the silence of the apartment. "Sorry," I mumble apologetically, stepping past him to get out of the shower.

I wrap my soaking hair in a towel and my body in a much bigger one, and I go on the quest of finding my phone. When I spot it on the living room floor, it still hasn't stopped ringing. A second later, I understand why they're so persistent.

One look at the caller ID is enough to make my stomach flip.

"Yes?" I answer, hoping my voice doesn't sound as unsure as I feel.

"Maddie?" Grace answers, which only confuses me more since she's calling from my brother's phone.

Suddenly, all the confusion is replaced by panic. "Is Sammy okay? Why are you calling me from his phone?"

There's some background noise on her call, but it's too faint to make it out. "We're all right." She's the one who sounds confused now. "I'm only calling you because he's driving. We're roughly an hour away."

"Maddsy!" I hear my niece's excited voice in the background, and it hits me.

Fuck. Shit. Fuck.

"Right, yes." *No, no, no.* I totally forgot. How could I? "Hi, Lila. I'll see you guys soon. I just woke up and have to get ready," I lie, because the alternative would be my brother having a panic attack behind the wheel.

"Okay, sweetheart. I'll text you when we get to Norcastle, okay?" Grace says.

"Yes, yes, okay. Bye, guys! See you later." I think I sound way more excited than shocked, which is a small blessing.

I hang up just as James exits his bedroom, water still clinging to his bare chest, and wearing nothing but a white towel around his hips. He's looking like a real wet dream—too bad I'm going through a very real nightmare right now.

"My family is visiting today, and I forgot," I blurt out, what I'm sure is a panicked look plastered all over my face.

He blinks then laughs. He *laughs* at me.

"What's funny?" I scowl, taking just a moment to pet Mist, who has just woken up from his nap on the couch. "Don't laugh at me."

"Mmm." He tries to be serious, but his twitching lips give him away. Whatever. I can't even be mad at him—I like seeing him happy way too much. "It's funny that you forgot about your family coming to see you. That seems like an important thing you'd mark on your calendar."

I groan. "I'm so sorry I have to leave in such a rush, but they're only an hour away and I need to get ready."

"Let me drive you home," he offers, sobering up a little.

Absolutely not. What if I accept his ride and my brother sees me exiting James's car? I would rather *die*.

Not because I'm ashamed of being seen in public with him, but come on—who wants their older, protective, super fatherly brother to know they have spent the night with a man? Not me, thanks.

"It's fine. I'll just call an Uber."

I walk past him and grab my clothes, scattered all around his apartment—oops—and get dressed in record time. I can tell he wants to object, so once I'm presentable again, I get on my tiptoes and kiss his stubbled cheek. "Thanks for last night. And this morning." *Thanks for the sex? Really?* "I... I had fun."

His gentle smile eases me. "I had fun too."

"Have a good weekend," I add with a smile.

"You too." His hand finds my cheek and settles there, holding my face like it's the most precious thing he's ever touched. "And I promise to call you later."

I give him a look.

"I mean it this time."

"Aren't you scared anymore?"

His throat bobs with a heavy swallow, and I find mine is clogged too.

"I've never been more scared in my life, Maddie."

***

"And then, and then," Lila says with her mouth full of hamburger meat. My brother scolds her for it, but she doesn't listen. The excitement is too real with this kid. "And then she pushed the cat down the stairs!"

She's talking about our cousin Hanna, who is four and has just discovered the power of chaos. I bet Aaron and Emily are pumped about it.

"Oh, yeah?" I heard this story before when I talked to my uncle on the phone last week, but I still listen attentively. "What about school? How's that going?"

My brother rolls his eyes. "Don't start with that," he says before taking a bite of his own burger.

I frown, confused, but Grace is quick to add, "Nothing bad happened. She just doesn't want to do her homework."

"Homework is *so* boring, Maddsy," she pouts.

"Maddie did her homework when she was your age," Sammy quips, giving me that look. We both know I wasn't a fan of the textbooks, even if I was a good student, but since Lila looks up to me so much, he wants her to believe I was some kind of extremely devoted student. It's adorable.

"I did," I say, nodding to Lila. "But it's okay if you don't find it fun." I lower my voice to a whisper. "It's not supposed to be."

She giggles and pulls at my brother's sleeve to get his attention. "See, Daddy? She agrees with me."

"You two are the reason for my gray hairs. I hope you're proud." He shakes his head, but there's no hiding his smile.

"Well, I happen to like your gray hairs *very* much." Grace leans in to peck his lips, and the look in my brother's face is one I will never grow tired of—infinite love, raw adoration, and pure devotion. It's everything I grew up around, everything I miss every day that I'm away from home.

Lila makes a gagging sound, complaining about how gross her parents are, and we all laugh at her antics. A warm feeling settles in my chest, and I don't think I've ever missed them so much while having them right here. The best part of all is nobody brings up my ankle, my upcoming job interview, or Pete. We've talked about it on the phone, and I appreciate the mental break.

My niece doesn't have school next week, so they're staying the night at a hotel in Norcastle—Lila is staying with me at my studio so we can have a sleepover like we used to do when I was still living at home. Which means that, from lunchtime until dinnertime, she keeps asking when it's sleepover time.

I love her so much.

Since the day is warm and there's not a single cloud in the sky, we decide to take a walk by the riverside. As my brother and niece chat about who-knows-what a few feet in front of us, hand in hand, Grace loops her arm around mine.

She's shorter than me, which I found funny when I was sixteen and left her behind in height. Her blond hair is pulled in a low ponytail, her eyes sparkling with that hint of "I know exactly what you did" that amazes and scares me all at once.

"So," she starts, the beginning of a dangerous smile forming on her lips. "You know, I've been thinking a lot about something you told me a few weeks ago."

"I don't know what you're talking about."

If the amusement in her voice is anything to go by, I'm in trouble. "Don't play dumb with me."

Yeah, no, I actually think I want to do just that.

My sister-in-law sees through everything and everyone. Call it instinct, call it logic, but she always picks up on everyone's mood shifts and hidden worries. My brother and I joke that she has some psychic abilities she keeps from us, but sometimes it feels scarily accurate.

"I don't recall," I lie.

My brother isn't too far away, so she leans in conspiratorially. "I know you do, but let me refresh your mind. Dating app? Some guy you knew?"

Okay. We're doing this.

"If you tell Sammy, I'll literally die on the spot," I warn her. She laughs, but also knows me well enough to be aware that I'm not entirely kidding.

"I'm a closed book, you know that. I promise I won't tell him. Now please, let me in on the gossip. I've been dying to hear it for weeks."

If I give in so easily it's because one, she's persistent, and two, Grace is a weird mix between a mother and an older sister, who

I've never been able to keep anything from. Going to Grace with my problems—especially my boy problems—is like second nature to me.

She's never judged me, yelled at me, or reprimanded me for anything, and instead worked with me to find a solution while telling me why what I did was wrong or dangerous. Where my brother is more prone to overprotective outbursts, Grace is the calm after the storm.

So that's why I know I can tell her. "He's older than me. Like, much older."

"Okay," she says slowly. "How much older are we talking about?"

"He's thirty-one."

She lets out a relieved breath. "Phew. I was afraid you'd say forty or something."

I make a face. "Someone Sammy's age? Ew."

She squeezes my arm. "Well, you know your brother is eight years older than me, so I see nothing wrong with age differences as long as they're reasonable and everyone is an adult—which you are. But tell me more. How did you meet him?"

Yeah, we're not going there. Not yet. "I'd rather skip that part," I tell her honestly. "It's nothing sketchy or dangerous, I promise."

"All right. I trust you." And this, *this* is why she's my favorite person ever. Why I've wished, on more than one occasion, that my mother had been like her. "Tell me about him. Does he treat you well?"

"He does." I tell her about how he picks me up after my shifts, how he cooks for me, how he always asks me about my feelings and validates them. "We went through a similar experience, he and I. I think that's why we connect so much."

"What kind of experience?"

"He got injured right before the NFL draft."

Grace winces. "That must have been hard on him. I hope he's

doing better now."

"He is." At least, I hope so. "I guess what I'm worried about is our age difference."

"Age differences can be tricky," she says thoughtfully.

She should know, since she was twenty-two when she met my brother, who was thirty. But she was finishing college then, had a stable job and plans that aligned with my brother's. I'm not that lucky.

"Is this a serious relationship?" she asks.

"We're just fooling around for now."

It's no secret to Grace that I'm not a virgin. She was the one to give me the talk, saving my brother from having an aneurysm. He's not dumb enough to think I haven't even been kissed—he just doesn't want to hear about it. And to be fair, I don't want to tell him either. Talk about mortifying.

"Well, you're twenty-one and you can make your own decisions as long as you remember to be safe and say no when you don't want to do something," she says, and I give her a firm nod.

I was seventeen when Grace told me about her past, about how she's a sexual assault survivor, and why it was important to her and my brother that I understood I always had the option to say no. That I wasn't and would never be weird or annoying for asking for consent—or to demand it.

They've both helped me to stand up for myself from day one, especially when it comes to intimate relationships. She doesn't want me to go through what she had to endure before she met Sammy.

"As long as he's good to you and you're just having fun, I don't think your age difference matters that much." A pause. I know a *but* is coming. "But"—there it is—"if you both want something more, I think you should talk about it. You're still fresh out of college, figuring things out, and I'm assuming he has a stable job."

"Yes." A job I'm too familiar with, in fact. But she doesn't have to know that part.

"It can work out if you both want to head in the same direction." She slides me a look I can't read. "Do you know which direction you want to take?"

I look away. "I'll see how the job interview goes next week."

"I'm not talking about your career." She stops walking, and I do too. There's firmness in her eyes and in her voice as she says, "Many adults in their mid and late twenties—or even later—change career paths and jobs, and it doesn't have to affect a relationship. It happens. I'm talking about direction in *life*. If you want to stay in Norcastle, if he does, if you want to have kids and when, what he thinks about it... All that important stuff every couple should discuss before entering a serious relationship, especially if there's an age gap between them."

Wow. Okay, that makes sense. It makes *too much* sense.

James and I have loosely talked about where we are now, but what about the future? It's definitely way too many things to consider all at once while taking a leisurely walk by the river with my family on a casual weekend.

Not to mention we have no plans to be together.

Grace must read my panicked look, because she quickly adds, "You don't have to make a decision now. Just think about it. We only want the best for you, Maddie, and we're so proud of you for everything you're accomplishing on your own."

"Not on my own," I blurt out, unable to keep it to myself.

"Yes, on your own," she insists. "Your brother and I will always be here to support you in every way we can, but you are making these decisions for yourself, not us. You moved out at eighteen and have never let us down since. You're responsible and independent, and you take such good care of yourself."

My heart feels heavier all of a sudden. "I didn't sign up for a crying session today, Gracie."

She laughs. "Oh, sweetheart. I'm just excited to see you, but everything I said is true. Your brother feels the same way—we talk about these things. We know you're worried about your ankle and getting back to ballet, but we're sure you will achieve anything you want to. You're Maddie."

You're Maddie.

Is it really as simple as that?

***

"Do you have a boyfriend, Maddsy?"

I look over my shoulder at the little girl sitting cross-legged on the couch, playing a game on my phone as I make two cheesy omelets for dinner. They're not as delicious as my brother's—I still haven't mastered his impressive culinary skills—but Lila never complains about my cooking.

"She'll agree to anything as long as she gets to spend time with you," Grace told me once, referring to my niece's adoration for me, and consequently melting my heart. Lila is my favorite person in the world, so I guess it's a good thing I also made it to her top three.

Placing the first omelet on a plate, my stomach somersaults at the reminder of my morning with James, as well as the previous night. No matter what we did or said, though, the reality is that..."No, Li, I don't have a boyfriend. Do you?"

"Daddy says I can't date until I'm thirty," she says so matter-of-factly I can't help but throw my head back in laughter. Sounds like something my brother would say, all right.

Adding the second batch of beaten eggs to the pan, I tell her, "Your dad is a bit overdramatic."

"That's what Mommy says."

My lips twitch.

We don't doubt that Sammy lives and breathes for us, and we love him for it, but he needs to relax a little. Or *a lot*.

Once dinner is ready, I take both of our plates and sit on the couch next to my niece. She puts my phone away, licking her lips impatiently as I set an omelet in front of her.

We eat in silence, a princess movie we've watched together a million times playing on TV, until Lila blurts out in that out-of-the-blue way only kids can get away with, "Daddy said you were feeling sad about not dancing anymore."

My dinner turns in my stomach. "He did?"

I'm not bothered by it because it's the truth. Lila probably asked, and he didn't want to lie to his daughter. I can respect that.

She nods as she takes the last bite of her food. "You can feel sad, Maddsy. Mommy says it's okay to cry because that means we care a lot about something. Caring about things is good."

Who would've guessed this sleepover was about to turn into a crying session with my eleven-year-old niece? Not me, that's for sure.

I give her a wobbly smile. "Your mom is right. And it's true that I was sad, but I'm feeling better now."

"That's good." She reaches out her hand to grab the glass of water I brought her earlier and takes a sip. Then she suggests, "You can read one of Mommy's books if you feel sad again."

There's simply no way I could love her any more—my heart would burst. She's such a compassionate soul, a precious gift, a literal angel. It never ceases to amaze me how wise she is beyond her years. Her empathy knows no limits, and I admire her for it.

"That's a great idea," I tell her. "Do you still read her books?"

I know my brother and Grace used to read them to her all the time when she was younger, but I'm not sure what their routine is like now that I've moved out.

She's quick to nod. "Yes, I love them. My favorite is the one about my grandpas."

The retelling of Grace's adoption story holds a very special place in my heart, too.

"Did you know that she wrote that book for me?"

Her eyes widen. "No way."

"Yep."

Grace wrote her own adoption book shortly after I started therapy as a child to show me that I wasn't alone, that she knew what I was going through. It was her first book that fell into the bibliotherapy category, and I remember her saying that new twist in her career *felt right*. So much so that she hasn't stopped writing those kinds of books since.

And just like her stories have changed my life and shaped Lila's, I'm sure they've reached countless other kids who needed it.

My niece drops her head on my lap after we're done with dinner, my fingers playing with her blond hair. "It makes sense that it's my favorite book," she says in a quiet voice, "because you're my favorite person, Maddsy."

Don't cry, don't cry, don't cry.

"You're my favorite person too." I bop her nose and get a giggle in return. "Have you thought of writing books like your mom when you grow up?"

She purses her lips, thinking about it. "I don't know. I'm not sure I like writing a lot, but I want to help people like she does."

This is the first time she's mentioning any of this to me, so now I'm intrigued. "People in general?"

Her shoulders rise and fall. "I don't know yet. But I think maybe children." She pokes me in my stomach. "Just like that lady helped you."

It's no secret to Lila that I've been to therapy. Eventually, when Lila got older, she got curious about it. My brother told her that, when I was a kid, Grandma got sick and she couldn't take care of me, and that my dad was gone. Grace then took her time explaining to her what therapy was and why I had to go.

Instead of finding it weird or scary, Lila bombarded me with questions about what it was like to tell a stranger all your secrets and how someone who didn't know you could help you so much.

She's always seemed fascinated by it.

"Helping people, especially children, is a job for very special people. And since you're the most special person I know, I'm sure you'd be great at it and make a big difference," I tell her, my hands still stroking her hair.

She looks up at me with big, inquisitive eyes. "Do you really think that?"

It's with full conviction that I say, "I know it, Li. You're smart and have a great heart—you can do whatever you set your mind to. Don't ever doubt that."

Later that night, as she gently snores on my lap while the princess movie still plays in the background, I decide to channel some of Lila's boldness and grab my phone. Because there's something I've been dying to do all day, and I can't wait any longer.

> **Me: I lied. I don't want to be with you for only one night.**

His reply doesn't take longer than a few moments.

> **James: Looks like we're both terrible liars.**

chapter 28

MADDIE

For reasons I still haven't figured out, the following Friday night I find myself not at my shift at Monica's Pub like I had initially planned, but at a fancy gala at the theater.

A gala hosted by The Norcastle Ballet.

If you pinched me, I don't think I would feel it.

With a floor-length dark blue gown that clings to my body in all the right places—in James's words, not mine—and a pair of kitten nude heels (because my ankle is still not the baddest bitch in town), one would think I'm blending in just fine, but...

Maybe not.

No matter whose face my gaze lands on, what dress or fancy suit, there's something about some of these people that just...

I hate to say it, I really do, but they give me a weird feeling.

There.

It's difficult to describe. This happened once before, in high school, when my friends fell in love with the new transfer, a girl from Chicago, and put her on some kind of pedestal. I was friendly at first, of course, but something about her gave me a weird vibe. It wasn't anything specific, because she was funny and super nice to everyone, but it was there. My friends thought I was crazy—and jealous—when I brought it up, so I eventually let it go.

Two months later, we found out she had been insulting every girl in our class on her private social media accounts. So, there's that.

Now, standing in front of the bathroom mirror as I wash my hands, I ponder the possibility that I'm just going insane. I accepted Kyle's invitation tonight because I felt ready enough to move on, and I vowed to keep an open mind and my sad thoughts at bay.

The fact that I'm getting these weird feelings is a surprise.

"Did you see her dress tonight?"

"Feathers are *so* last year. Someone didn't get the memo."

A couple of feminine giggles come into the bathroom as I finish rinsing the soap from my hands, and a second later, two girls send me a smile in the reflection of the mirror. I only smile back because I was raised to be polite.

One of the girls—a brunette—comes to stand a few feet away from me as the other one—a redhead—disappears into one of the stalls. The brunette takes a red lipstick from her bag and starts reapplying it while she talks to her friend as if she were right beside her and not peeing behind a closed door.

"Not all of us can be graceful on and off the stage," she comments so casually it takes me a second to realize it's not a compliment.

The redhead snickers. "And she isn't even that graceful on the stage to begin with."

They may know I'm a stranger to TNB, or they wouldn't be gossiping right in front of me, I think to myself as I use a paper towel to dry my hands.

"I heard she hasn't hooked up with anyone in two years."

All right. Time to go.

I don't say a thing as I exit the bathroom, leaving those girls behind. What the hell was that? Is this how everyone behaves behind the scenes?

This is all a facade.

Still, being surrounded by people who were supposed to be my work colleagues and instructors feels like one of those strange dreams that leaves you all dazed when you wake up.

The Norcastle Ballet is hosting a fundraiser for a children's hospital tonight, and Kyle wanted me to be his plus one. I was hesitant to accept at first, but James convinced me to take a chance and see how it would make me feel.

"You just want to see me in a fancy dress," I teased him.

He smirked, his strong hands holding my hips like a magnet. "No, I want you to go have fun with your friend. The fact that you'll come home to me later and I'll get to fuck you in that dress is just a plus."

And then he showed me just how badly he needed me, dress or not.

That was two days ago, and ever since my family left after their visit, James and I have seen each other every day. He's picked me up from work every day, either to drop me off at my apartment or to spend the night at his.

Grace's words about our age difference and our expectations for the future have been looming in the distance since she brought it up, but I'm too chicken to broach the subject.

There's no need to do that right now, anyway. We're just having fun. This is casual. No need to complicate things with heavy conversations when I don't even know if he will wake up from this strange daydream tomorrow and decide he would rather be with someone closer to his age. Someone stable. Someone who has her future figured out and crazy savings in her bank account.

I shake my worries off when Kyle introduces me to a couple of his coworkers, two women who don't seem to be much older than us, and we strike up conversation with them until the actual dinner and fundraiser starts.

"Are you having fun?" Kyle asks me after dessert is served. It's some kind of fancy chocolate mousse with hints of orange, and I swear I've just had an orgasm in my mouth.

James won't be too happy about it since he's claimed all of

them for himself.

I nod, although I still haven't fully gotten rid of that weird feeling. "Thank you for letting me tag along."

Kyle gives me a weak smile and shifts on his seat. I know what he's going to say before he even opens his mouth. "I didn't know if I was making a mistake in bringing up this gala to you at all," he confesses, eyes on his mousse. "I didn't want you to think I was flaunting all this around to make you feel bad."

My heart softens at that. "Kyle, no. I know you would never do that." I place a hand on his sturdy shoulder and give him a friendly squeeze. "And I could have said no, you know? I'm happy for you, truly. I'm proud of you for passing the audition, and I can't wait to attend the Christmas show."

The Norcastle Ballet always puts together the most magical performances during the holidays, and I feel like a proud mother just thinking about Kyle up on that stage.

This time, his smile reaches his eyes. "You're the best. I hope you know that."

Once the main part of the gala ends, a DJ comes out and the hall transforms into a dance floor. Kyle is still talking to everyone, being his usual social butterfly self, and I stay by his side because I literally know nobody here.

As I scan the room, I spot the girls from the bathroom gossip session chatting animatedly with a woman wearing a short dress made of black feathers. Huh.

I'm distracted by my phone buzzing in my clutch. A small smile starts forming on my lips, knowing exactly who it is.

James: Are you having fun?

He wanted me to come tonight—he encouraged me, even. Yet his eyes couldn't hide the worry that I would relapse, so to speak, and fall down that pit of self-destruction again.

> **Me: Yeah. The food was amazing, and Kyle fits right in**

> **James: I'm glad to hear it, baby**

I get tingles every time he calls me that. I never thought I would be a fan of that term of endearment, but it sounds sexy coming from him.

His next message is a picture of Shadow and Mist curled up on his legs as he watches TV.

> **Me: You look so cozy. I want to be there :(**

> **James: Just say the word and I'll pick you up**

My heart jumps at his offer. Does he always have to be so chivalrous? Not that I'd ever complain.

> **Me: I can just get an Uber. Don't worry about me.**

> **James: Not possible**

Maybe I should find his protectiveness overbearing, but it brings me a sense of warmth and safety to know he cares about me. That he would go out of his way to make sure I'm okay.

I'm about to text him back when Kyle nudges my arm, and I snap my head up, only to come face-to-face with Suzanne Allard.

Holy shit.

"Maddie, I want to introduce you to one of my instructors, Suzanne Allard. Suzanne, this is Maddison Stevens," Kyle says like he hasn't just rocked my world.

"It's a pleasure to meet you, ma'am." My voice comes out steadier than I could've ever wished for, and so does my hand when I hold it out for her to shake.

The smile she gives me is friendly, warm, and it puts me at ease instantly. "The pleasure is all mine, Maddie. I can call you Maddie, right? I've heard so much about you."

It takes everything in me not to gape at her. "Have you?"

This can't be happening. Surely, *the* Suzanne Allard, one of the best choreographers in the goddamn United States, hasn't heard about me. It's just a form of speech. Right?

"Indeed." She touches Kyle's arm affectionately. "Kyle here has told me all about your time together at ballet school. He spoke about an ankle injury, if I'm not mistaken?"

I exchange a quick look with my friend, and he gives me the most mischievous smirk known to humankind. I don't know whether to hug him or kill him. Maybe both.

I clear my throat. I was lucky enough to find my voice in front of this woman once when I introduced myself, and I'm hoping for a second miracle. "Yes." Good, it's not shaking. I check that my hands aren't either before I continue. "I was meant to audition for The Norcastle Ballet, in fact, but I got injured a few days prior."

Her face is the true depiction of horror. "Oh, dear. I hope it isn't giving you much trouble now. How is the recovery process going?"

"I'm done with physical therapy, and I was lucky it didn't require surgery." My cheeks warm up, but I don't think she notices. "My doctor was the best, too."

More than you'll ever know.

"I'm glad to hear that, Maddie. Are you able to dance again?"

I beam at that. If someone had told me two weeks ago that I would be excited about this, I wouldn't have believed them at all. "I've recently started a position as a dance instructor at a local studio, and so far my ankle isn't giving me any trouble."

That's right. Believe it or not—and I hardly do myself—I got hired right away after my interview on Monday. So far I've only given two lessons at this local dance school that's just a few blocks away from my apartment, but I enjoy it. *A lot*. The girls are around six and seven, and they're the best.

My boss, a forty-something-year-old Russian woman, is one of the nicest people I've ever met. She asked me to take over one of her groups to see how I adapted to the flow of the classes, and so far, I'm loving it.

If this is the path I'm meant to take as I fully heal, I'm not mad about it.

"That is wonderful, dear. But surely you'd want to do something a bit more..." Suzanne starts, a notch forming between her delicately trimmed eyebrows. "How do I put this, *meaningful* with your career, wouldn't you?"

I freeze at her words.

Meaningful?

Meaningful.

Is she saying... Is she saying teaching ballet to children who are at their prime age to start their dancing careers is something *inconsequential*?

Kyle tenses beside me, as if he knows exactly what's going on inside my head right now.

I blink once, twice, because I cannot believe those words have left the mouth of someone who *teaches* for a living. Sure, she teaches at one of the most prestigious ballet companies in the country—maybe in the world—but she teaches, nonetheless.

If I ever dared to dream about having a career in ballet in the first place, it's because someone decided to do something *not* meaningful—apparently—with her life and become a ballet teacher. Grace, specifically.

She was my first ballet instructor when I was four, and the

only reason she didn't become a professional ballerina is because she didn't want to. Her path was meant to go in a different direction, and as a best-selling children's author, I would say it went pretty well.

Maybe my own path was always meant to go in the opposite direction of this, after all.

I'm too stunned to speak, and hurt, too, that someone I held in such high regard would be so...so...so damn *classist*.

I don't get a chance to say anything because she continues, oblivious to how ignorant she's just sounded. "We are actually holding an open audition in the winter. You should consider paying us a visit." She throws me a knowing wink, and my traitorous heart leaps.

"An open audition?" I parrot back. "Aren't auditions invite-only?"

"Usually, yes, but we want to experiment this year," she tells me. "They will only be open for three days, though, so you should keep an eye out. I'm sure there's information about it on our website, or Kyle can remind you."

"Absolutely," he beams, as if he had been presented with the opportunity himself.

"Thank you. I will consider it," I say, still dumbfounded, still breathless, still confused, and still angry.

Is the universe kidding me right now?

She gives me another smile I don't consider all that kind anymore. Not after that one comment. "It was lovely meeting you, Maddie. I will see you on Monday, Kyle. Have fun."

To be honest, I don't recall saying goodbye back to her. But I remember Kyle turning to me, eyes wide and full of excitement, and letting out a silent scream.

"Maddie!" he whisper-shouts. "This is huge. *Oh my God.* Are you going to do it?"

I know James said I shouldn't try my luck in professional

ballet for at least a year, but what if...

"I'll think about it," I decide. His face falls, and I laugh, looping my arm around his. "Come on. You still haven't introduced me to everyone and their mothers."

When James picks me up an hour later, I don't bring up Suzanne Allard or the audition. I don't bring up how weird that comment was, how shitty it made me feel, or how confused I am right now regarding my future.

What if I put The Norcastle Ballet on a pedestal just like my high school friends did to the new girl?

What if it's nothing more than an institution full of classism and inflated egos?

That's not an environment I want to be in, or *work* in, ever.

But Kyle isn't like that, so maybe I'm overreacting. Maybe it's just one bad apple. Or two, or three.

The opportunity to audition in the winter doesn't feel real, anyway. Plus, I already know what James's answer would be if I brought it up.

I'll tell him...eventually. Just not tonight.

chapter 29

JAMES

This wasn't meant to happen. None of it. Ever.

It was supposed to be nothing more than a poor lapse in judgment, a fog that faded before it got thicker.

But, against my will, it morphed into a form of release, a way to get rid of the pent-up tension between us. A one-time thing that wasn't supposed to mean anything to either of us. To me.

Twelve years ago, I promised myself I wouldn't lower my walls ever again.

Twelve years ago, when I was forced to rebuild myself from the ground up, I made a vow to never let anyone in until I was healed. And am I?

Love and relationships have never been in the forefront of my mind. My older brother and ex-girlfriend made sure it stayed that way.

For years, my parents tried to reason with me, probably because they wanted peace in our family. They pushed me toward therapy, and it helped for a while, but I was stubborn and thought I could do the rest of the healing on my own. I couldn't.

Maybe I should consider growing up and booking a session now, because Maddie...

Shit, there it goes again.

I can't stop thinking about her, even when I tell myself this will only end in heartbreak.

The worst part is, I don't want to stop seeing her, kissing her, drawing pleasure out of her, or hearing that laugh that drives me out of my mind.

And every time I tell myself that this is it, that today is the day everything goes to hell, it never does.

I can't tell if I'm relieved or disappointed.

To add to the shit show that is my life lately, Andrew texted me again last night, asking to see me. I haven't responded.

My head is about to explode. I need to get away for a while, to leave the headache that is this city, even if only for a couple of days. But for some reason, a heavy weight settles in the pit of my stomach every time I think about not seeing her.

I promised Maddie I wouldn't leave her, and even though a weekend-long trip to my cabin won't mean I'm abandoning her, I really don't want to go by myself. I don't, and that's a huge problem if I've ever had one. Because never, not once in my thirty-one years, have I felt the need to be *with* someone.

When you grow up with an older brother who couldn't give two shits about you, you learn to be independent if you want to survive. Those habits carried into adulthood, which my mother always insisted was a good thing because that means I wouldn't jump into toxic relationships or friendships. I'm enough, and I'm good and happy and complete on my own, and yet...

My thoughts are interrupted by a familiar brunette coming toward my car. She smiles, and the fog inside my brain dissipates just like that.

It should worry me that she holds this much power over me when I've been working to shield my heart for a decade.

"I'm guessing it went well with the girls today?" I ask, pulling out of the parking lot of Maddie's new workplace. She still takes shifts at Monica's Pub, but tonight I have her all to myself, and I plan to let her know just how much I've missed her.

"I didn't think I would enjoy this job, but here we are," she confesses, happiness shining in her face. "We're already discussing doubling my hours after this month."

Pride swells in my chest. "I knew you'd like it. How do you feel about going back to dancing again?"

I keep a hand on the wheel and splay my right one on her thigh, her fingers tangling with mine just a moment later.

"It's strange. I thought it would feel bittersweet, but..." A shrug. "I'm optimistic. I think teaching will be good for me, even if it's not what I envisioned myself doing right after ballet school."

"Your ankle will make a full recovery." I don't overthink it as I bring her knuckles to my lips. "I'm sorry it's taking longer than you wanted, but I'm proud of you for everything you're accomplishing."

Admiration blooms in my chest and clings to my heart every time I look at her. Never in my life have I ever admired anyone besides my parents and a couple of football players. And I have definitely never been in this much awe of someone so much younger.

The sweetest shade of red spreads on her cheeks. "You're helping me a lot," she says, almost shyly. "You gave me the courage and the push I needed."

"It was all you, Maddie. You already had it in you."

"Yes, but you helped me bring it out," she insists, and I can't lie—it fills me with an overwhelming boost of self-esteem.

After my injury, I dropped out of college and never thought I would go back. I didn't see a meaning to my life, couldn't find a purpose, and then my brother burned the remains. I spent months fucking around at my parents' house, feeling sorry for myself and silencing my sorrows with booze, until my father finally snapped.

He gave me a week to get my shit together, or I would be sleeping on the streets.

And so I did. I got my shit together.

When we reach her apartment, I wait in the car as she gets ready, trying not to think too hard about everything going on in my life right now. I fail.

I know it's insane the second I get the idea. She would never say yes, and it's not like I should ask in the first place. I have no right to, not when we're nothing more than two confused souls wandering hand in hand in the dark, ignoring where we're going. Ignoring what we want, maybe, deep down.

"I'm back," she says, smiling as always, so blinding and so fucking beautiful. I almost tell her. *Almost.*

But then she closes the distance between us and plants a loud kiss on my cheek. When I don't respond, she pokes my arm and gives me those doe eyes I can't resist, and before I know what I'm doing, I blurt it out.

"Do you want to come with me to my lake cabin this weekend?"

She blinks in surprise. That makes two of us.

"Wh-What?" she stammers, probably taken aback just as much as I am for having suggested it in the first place.

Still, I nod because I'm a masochist. "It's only a couple of hours away," I say, like that's a good reason to even consider this.

Her piercing silence mocks me. The easy atmosphere in the car changes, and the weight of her unspoken words weighs down on my shoulders.

"James..." she starts, unsure.

I swallow past the lump in my throat, preparing to apologize for having crossed yet another line.

"I think... I think we should talk."

Fuck me.

Despite the sudden ice-cold feeling all over my body, I find myself nodding along. "Okay."

She shifts on the passenger seat so she's facing me. "What are we doing, exactly?"

If that isn't the question of the damn century.

"What do you want us to do?" I ask. I'm too much of a coward to give her an actual answer.

Maddie doesn't answer right away, and when she does, she says the last thing I expected her to. "I want you to give me a warning before you leave."

The air whooshes out of my lungs. "Why do you think I would ever leave?"

The pain flashing in her eyes would normally make me want to hurt the bastard who put it there—only that, this time, the bastard might be me.

She gives me a small shrug, like none of this is really a big deal. "Everyone does, eventually. Just... Just don't do it in a cruel way. Please."

My heart fucking shatters. My own buckle comes undone, and before I realize it, I've got her face cradled in my hands, eyes locked with mine. It doesn't feel close enough.

"Listen to me. No matter what you want us to be, I would never, ever leave. We talked about this. I freaked out once, and it won't happen again. I don't want to hurt you. That's the very last thing I'd ever do."

She gulps. "You can't promise that."

I search her gaze, and what I find is a sweet soul still not fully crushed by the unfair weight of the world. It will never break if I can prevent it.

"Okay," I concede. I know all too well that people leave and everything ends. I would be a hypocrite to insist otherwise. "I may not be able to promise you I will always be there, but I can promise I will try with everything I've got. I would put myself through hell before I ever think of hurting you, Maddie. Tell me you understand."

"And if you do?" she whispers. "If you hurt me?"

It's at this moment it dawns on me that, no matter how many promises I make or words of reassurance I give her, it will never be enough. And I understand. She's been burned too many times to put her blind trust in someone again.

I know exactly what that feels like, but this isn't about me. This is about a girl who has crawled her way into my ice-cold heart and refuses to let go.

And I don't want her to.

My thumb caresses the soft skin of her cheek. "Words aren't enough—I know that. So let me prove it to you. As your friend, or in whichever way you want me to."

She leans into my touch, the hardness in her eyes melting away. "Is that what you want to be? Friends?"

"You and I both know friends don't make each other come, baby."

Her breath hitches, her cheeks getting that red shade I love so damn much. "I guess you're right."

"I'm not sure I want a relationship right now," I tell her, not wanting to beat around the bush or lie to her.

Before I can add anything else, though, she says, "I don't want one either. I need some space to...figure things out."

I nod along. "I understand."

"But that doesn't mean I want to stop seeing you," she quickly adds. "I have fun with you. I feel comfortable and safe around you."

Safe. There's that word again. Nobody has ever told me they feel safe around me.

"I don't want to stop seeing you either," I realize out loud. No matter how wrong it may feel, nothing could keep me away from this girl. It's too late.

"Good." She gives me a small smile that makes her eyes shine. "Would you be okay with just having fun and...you know, not worrying about labels? I just want to do what feels right, and right now it is to be with you and have fun with you. No expectations."

"No expectations," I repeat like the most sacred of mantras.

I would never hurt her, not in this lifetime or the next, but she doesn't know that. She doesn't trust words or promises that look full but might be drained. So instead of reassuring her with words, I will take care of her through my actions.

"What do you say, then?" I dare to ask again. "Does a weekend trip to the lake sound good?"

She doesn't have to answer. I see it in her eyes.

chapter 30

MADDIE

Agreeing to be nothing more than friends with benefits with James lifted a heavy weight off my shoulders. I should probably not even refer to us as that—no labels, after all. And I'm more than okay with it.

It feels liberating to not have any expectations. That way, it will hurt less when he's gone.

I've grown used to his grumpiness and dry humor, and now it feels like my days last longer when I'm too busy to see him.

But no matter how much I keep telling myself that the non-label we put on ourselves frees us of any pressure, that isn't true. No matter how hard I wish I could feel differently, I dive headfirst into a pit of insecurity and self-consciousness as James and I pull up to a tiny cabin in Bannport, a small town near a lake just a couple of hours from Norcastle.

He wants me here, and I want to be here too. But spending a night in a cozy, romantic cabin in the woods, just the two of us, like a couple would, makes me wonder what I've agreed to. If my heart will even survive it. Probably not.

"I'll get our things from the back," he lets me know. His presence inside the car is replaced by the biting cold outside. I welcome it with open arms, if only to feel something that isn't this crippling anxiety that makes my stomach hurt.

Too bad we will only be gone for a night and Shadow and Mist didn't come on this trip with us, because their purrs would for sure make all these nerves go away. James mentioned Graham checking on them later, so at least I know they will be fine. Me, though? That's another story.

For better or for worse, I don't have much time to overthink this. James comes back, opens my door, and holds out his hand. "Let's get inside. Don't want you catching a cold."

He doesn't want me to—

Stop it, heart. Calm down.

I almost have it under control, but then he opens the door for me with that devastating smile of his, and I lose the reins once again.

"It's not much, but..." he says as we enter the cabin, but I'm barely listening.

This isn't much? Holy shit.

The living room and kitchen are spacious and open, and they look like they came right out of an interior design magazine. The wooden touches and fireplace give it such a cozy vibe, all I want is to cuddle on the couch under a big, thick blanket and never move an inch.

Down the hall there are two rooms, the bedroom and what I assume is the bathroom. He stops at the end of the hallway. "This is where we'll be sleeping."

If I thought the rest of the house was gorgeous, this room is simply *magical*. A four-post bed occupies most of the spacious room, and it looks as comfortable as the one in his apartment. There's a wooden wardrobe and a chest of drawers, as well as a TV mounted on the wall right in front of the bed. A full-length mirror by the wardrobe catches my eye, but my attention is soon pulled to the private deck right outside.

"Wow," I mutter under my breath as I stare into the mountains not far from us.

A strong pair of arms wraps around me from behind. "Do you like it?" James asks, resting his chin on top of my head.

"Are you kidding me? This looks straight out of a movie." I turn in his arms, admiring the way his eyes soften when they meet mine. "Thank you for inviting me."

He places a loose strand of hair behind my ear and cradles my cheek in that big, warm hand of his. "We'll have fun this weekend." He takes my hand and leads me to the door. "There's no food here, so we'll have to venture into town to get a few things."

"Okay," I say, excited about being in Maine for the first time.

He stops right at the door, gazing into my eyes with a raw intensity I don't understand the meaning of. "But I'm taking you out for dinner tonight. If you want."

Ah, shit. Why is he being so sweet?

Why is he making this so...difficult?

But I can't lie to myself. I can't deny what I want anymore. "I'd love to."

The small town of Bannport is only a ten-minute drive from the cabin. As the sunlight slips away behind the mountains, Main Street fills with local people and children laughing, giving it a homey feeling one just can't find in Norcastle. A week ago, I didn't even know this place existed, and now I'm in love.

We end up at a sports bar near the lake called The Lair, and the fact that everything is so casual, so easy, makes me feel better about this whole situation.

Nobody bats an eyelid at us as we take a seat. Our waitress, a bubbly girl with a name tag that reads *Allie* pinned on her shirt who looks vaguely familiar and not much older than I am, doesn't give us any weird looks either. Nobody does.

I'm a hypocrite. For days I've been trying to convince myself that our age gap isn't that big of a deal, since we're both adults who aren't interested in anything more than fooling around and spending some quality time together. But all I can think about is how everyone else is going to perceive us now that we're out in public.

James puts an arm around our booth, his fingers splaying on my shoulder. "You're zoning out. You okay?"

"Huh? Yeah, yeah." I blink out the fog in my brain and turn toward him with a smile. "How come you have a cabin in this town?"

"My family used to visit Bannport every summer when I was a kid, so I have good memories of this place. I bought the cabin on a whim a couple of years ago, but I don't regret it," he explains. I swoon at the mental image of little James with a little grouchy frown. "At first it didn't look as modern, but my dad and I finished up the renovations last summer, and I'm happy with how it turned out."

"I take it you're close to your dad?" I snuggle closer to him until our thighs are touching. If he minds, he doesn't say.

"I have a good relationship with both of my parents," he says as he takes a sip of the craft beer our waitress left on our table impressively quickly after we placed our orders, along with a Diet Coke for me.

"Do they live in Norcastle?"

"In one of the suburbs, yes."

I almost don't ask. The urge to bite my tongue has never been stronger, but I'm nosy by nature. If I have a question, I'm never too self-conscious to let it out, and it doesn't help that I feel so relaxed in his company. So maybe that's why, against my better judgment, I ask, "What about your brother?"

The hard muscles pressed against my body become even harder as they tense. I almost regret asking until a moment passes, then a minute, and finally he says, "We don't get along. You know that."

"Why?" I press before I can talk myself out of it, as if I had any right to ask in the first place.

James extends those long, thick fingers and wraps them around the cold beer, bringing it to his lips and taking a sip.

On instinct, my hand reaches out to his thigh, my fingers drawing calming patterns on his jean-clad leg. I don't think it will soothe him at all, but it's—

"I had a girlfriend in college."

My hand freezes. I did not see that coming. What does she have to do with his brother?

A nauseated feeling sinks to the pit of my stomach, and I hold my breath as he keeps talking, finally unveiling a past I didn't think I would ever learn about.

"Now I know we weren't meant for each other, not by a long shot, but back then we were doing okay. She supported my football career, but—this is going to sound so wrong—only because she could already see herself as a trophy wife or some shit. I'm only saying this because she dumped me the second my injury took me out of the game." A pause. "Well, she dumped me in her mind, at least."

"Oh, James." I recognize the pain of someone you thought would always be there, walking away. Better than most people, I do. "I'm so sorry."

His fingers on my shoulder come lower, to my elbow, as he brings me closer to his body.

"Don't be. She was never for me. She wasn't there for me when my head was a nightmare to be in. That's why I turned to alcohol and lost control until my dad stepped in."

"I'm glad he did," I say softly, my fingers finding his. He gives them a squeeze. "I know what alcoholism does to a person. You're strong, James, for getting yourself out of that situation. It's not easy, and I'm proud of you."

"You're not bothered by it?" he asks, his throat bobbing with a swallow. "Because of what happened with your mom."

"You're seriously asking me if I'm bothered by something that happened in your past a decade ago? Something that had nothing to do with me and that you've clearly recovered from?"

His heavy silence is enough answer for me. It kills me that he may be upset about this, so I give him the truth. "No, James, it doesn't bother me. Not one bit. I'm just happy that you listened to your dad and did something before it got worse. That takes strength, and I meant it when I said I'm proud of you. We all have a past; what counts is that we learn from it and get better."

"Thank you." He kisses the top of my head but doesn't linger. He doesn't add anything else, but I know he isn't done.

Our waitress comes back with a plate of spicy wings and nachos to share, and he doesn't make a move to eat. James simply holds me in silence as the loud noises of the crowded bar surround us.

"Hey." I wiggle my way out from under his arm, enough to hold his face between my hands and give him the soft, reassuring smile I know he needs right now. "It's okay. You don't have to tell me if you don't want to. I was just curious, but I understand if you're not ready to talk about it. I'm not going anywhere."

He swallows, a scared look I've never seen before in those beautiful blue eyes. "Promise me?"

It shatters every piece of my heart that he thinks I would ever want to. "I promise."

It's the push he needs. With another sigh, his walls come crashing down around us.

"We were still together when I found my ex-girlfriend in my brother's bed."

My stomach sinks with a heavy feeling of betrayal that doesn't even belong to me. "What?"

"My brother played baseball in college, so I guess she moved from one athlete to another."

Don't call her a bitch, don't call her a bitch. You're better than that.

"I still had feelings for her, obviously, and my life was a living hell. Now I know I wasn't the most attentive boyfriend during that time, but she could've called things off. Cheating on me wasn't the answer.

"My brother knew I wasn't okay, but he didn't care. He ignored my mental and physical health when I went home, saying I was being a little bitch, that I deserved it for pushing myself too hard because I had a god complex and needed to prove I was the best. We never had a close relationship growing up, but that was the last straw."

My heart hurts for him so much, all I want is to find those two shitheads and...and do *something*. Anger simmers in the pit of my stomach, even though I know it's pointless because I can't change the past. And, as selfish as it might sound, I don't know if I would. Our pasts, both of them, led us here. To each other.

"Can I ask if they're still together?" I'm quick to add, "You don't have to answer. We can stop talking about this."

"I don't speak to my brother, even though he's been texting me for a while now, but my parents update me sometimes. Last I knew, he was working at some marketing firm downtown, but that was years ago. They were still together and living in Norcastle." He runs a hand through his hair before his eyes land on mine, determination—not hurt—flashing in them. "But I *want* to talk about this, Maddie. I need to because I'm tired of letting my past tie my hands behind my back. I don't want to let resentment and pain control me."

I squeeze his hand in mine, hoping I can silently convey how proud I am of him. But just in case, I say, "Thank you for telling me." I plant a feather-like kiss on his knuckles. "I can't... I can't even begin to understand how betrayed you felt, but if it's any consolation, they didn't deserve you, James. Neither of them."

He lets out a deep breath. "I don't think I'll ever forgive him."

"And that's okay."

"He's my brother," he points out, as if that explains it.

"And you're his, but he still did what he did to you. He didn't think of the consequences of his actions, so why should you be compassionate? Has he ever apologized?"

"No. I don't think he ever will."

My mind inevitably wanders to my father and how little sympathy I have for him. If he begged for forgiveness, if he promised to be a better man, would I even consider forgiving him?

I realized I wasn't a good dad, but I promise I'm ready to be the father you deserve.

His words at the parking lot still haunt me. For seventeen years, my father couldn't be the person I needed. The fact that he might be ready now doesn't erase the mistakes and trauma of the past, and for that I could never forgive or forget what he's done. He doesn't deserve it.

And I get the feeling James's brother falls in the same boat.

"But he wants us to talk," he says in that deep voice I love listening to so much. Right now, though, it sounds drained. "He's been texting me for months. I haven't responded."

"Do you *want* to talk to him?"

"No." His answer is definite, cold. "I have nothing to say to him. He was a piece of shit then, and he's a piece of shit now."

"You didn't get along as kids?"

He shakes his head. "He's a couple of years older than me, so he thought he was meant to be the big, strong one. Turns out puberty hit us roughly at the same time, and I ended up bigger and stronger," he explains. "If it sounds like vain shit, it's because it is, but he paid attention to those things. When I started playing football, he suddenly decided he wanted to be a baseball player, but he wasn't good enough."

"Because his heart wasn't in it?" I wonder out loud.

"Of course it wasn't. He only did it so he could compete with me, but he wasn't dumb enough to play the same sport I did. That would only prove how much better I was, and he didn't want that. He's always resented me, even though I haven't done anything to him. So you can imagine how happy he was that I got injured and lost my chance at the NFL."

Anger boils in my chest. Who treats their brother, their own blood, like that?

You should know.

Right. I guess not only fathers can be complete pieces of shit.

"But the fact that I couldn't have a career in football didn't mean he would suddenly become a baseball legend, so I guess he slept with my ex just to do some real damage." He finishes with another sip of his beer. It's now empty, but he doesn't order another.

I press a kiss on his shoulder. "He doesn't deserve you, and neither does she. Not forgiving him and not wanting to see him again doesn't make you a bad person, family or not."

That thick throat swallows. "I know, but—"

"Do you think not forgiving my father makes me a bad person?"

His response is immediate. "Absolutely not."

"So why would not forgiving your brother make *you* a bad person? It's the same thing. They hurt us, and they never showed remorse for it."

For a moment, James stays silent. The only way I know his mind hasn't wandered too far away is because his thumb starts caressing my hand in soft, slow circles.

And then I feel it—a kiss on my temple, followed by his face buried in my neck.

"You bring me so much peace, Maddie," he whispers against my skin. The feeling of his lips pressing a kiss on my neck lights me up inside. "More than you'll ever know. Thank you for always having the right words and not being afraid to say them."

My heart leaps. And, for reasons I still haven't figured out, my voice comes out as a whisper as I say, "You bring me peace too."

"Yeah?"

I nod, my lips finding his in a short, sweet kiss. And if he has any doubts about my feelings for him, I'll show him tonight.

**

It's almost midnight by the time we make it back to the cabin, after playing darts until my stomach hurt from laughing because James, as much as he insists he's not, is quite pathetic at it. But I'd never tell him.

He disappears into the bathroom as soon as we get to our room, and I take a moment to sit outside on the private terrace overlooking the forest and the mountains. The sound of the water turning on reaches my ears as I wrap my jacket tighter against my body. The night air is cold but still not freezing, and I welcome the darkness and solitude of this moment.

We're leaving tomorrow, and I already miss this place.

Our conversation about his brother and ex-girlfriend crawls back into my head as I wait for James to come back. How two people could have such rotten hearts, I don't think I'll ever understand. After all, it's been seventeen years, and I still don't understand why my father acted the way he did.

I admire James for moving on from that situation, even if it still hurts him to think about what they did. That kind of pain doesn't always go away—you learn how to live with it. But the fact that he's moved on and is doing something meaningful with his life gives me hope for myself.

The bathroom door opens in the hallway a little over five minutes later, and I feel him before I see him. His arms wrap around my middle, his stubbled cheek rubbing against mine until I fight back. "Stop," I shriek, laughing. "You're scratching me."

"You don't complain when I scratch you in other places." I slap his hand away, and he laughs. "What are you doing out here?"

"I was just enjoying the view."

He arches a skeptical eyebrow. "You realize it's dark as shit, right?"

I shrug, and he wraps his arms around me again. "That's part of the beauty of it."

I don't mean to sound like some kind of inspirational guru, but I realize it's true. I've always found comfort in the shadows because here I have nothing to prove and nobody to disappoint.

His lips press against my cheek, and I melt against him. "I drew you a bath."

My heart skips a beat. "You did?"

"Mmhmm. Let's get you inside. I don't want you getting sick."

His protectiveness warms me up more than any hot bath ever could, but I don't tell him that. Instead, I silently make my way to the bathroom, only to gape at the display before me.

Not only did James prepare a hot bath for me, but he also lit several candles all around the room and made sure the water had the right amount of bubbles. When I turn to look at him with my heart on my sleeve, I realize my sight is blurry.

"Hey." His voice soothes me, his touch welcome as he carefully wipes away the tears I don't even realize are falling. "Don't cry, baby. Why are you crying?"

"I don't know." A chuckle escapes me, and I shake my head. "You didn't upset me. This is... Wow. Just... Thank you."

"You deserve this and more," he says, his voice turning serious, and I find myself nodding along. "I'll leave you to it, all right? Call me if you need anything. I'll be in the bedroom."

"You don't want to join me?" I ask, suddenly not wanting him to be gone.

He slides the tub a look. "I don't think I could fit in there. But I promise I'll take care of you when you're done, yeah?"

"Okay," I whisper, breathless. The thought of his hands on me again gives me goose bumps. And I know this isn't what I'm supposed to be feeling, that he doesn't mean any of this in a romantic way, but only for tonight, I allow myself to pretend.

So, I do.

I pretend he will never leave.

I pretend we're ready for the next step, that our lives are figured out, that our age difference doesn't matter, that my brother won't judge this relationship.

It tastes like the sweetest of lies.

Knowing what's coming after my bath, I take extra time washing and scrubbing every inch of my skin. James must have added some kind of relaxing oil in the water because, on top of smelling like heaven, it's a struggle not to fall asleep. When the water cools, I wrap a clean white towel around my body and make my way to the bedroom.

Just like he said he would, James is waiting for me in bed, watching TV, still in his clothes. As soon as his ocean eyes find me, though, he turns it off and focuses solely on me.

Wordlessly, he dims the light until only the darkness of the moon filters through the windows. His pants hit the floor first, then his sweater. Only when he's standing in just his black boxers does he move toward the door to close it.

He eyes me like I'm his next meal and he's been starving for centuries.

"Get on the bed, beautiful," he orders in that commanding voice that makes my legs feel like Jell-O.

I've had to pretend to have my life together for a long time, and it's good to let go of control and have him take the reins.

I drop my towel and don't miss how his burning gaze pierces my skin as I wait for him on the bed, just like he wanted me to.

"On your back. Place your head at the edge of the mattress." His voice sounds strained, guttural, and it makes me wonder what exactly he has planned for me.

I'm no virgin, but I'm not exactly...versed in sex either. But I trust him. It's like he knows my body, knows what strings to pull to make it sing.

So I lie flat on my back with my head hanging over the bed,

and I watch as he gets closer, so painfully slowly it kills me inside. When he removes his boxers, his thick shaft springing free *right there*, I lick my lips in anticipation.

I don't know what he has planned for tonight, but I might die if he doesn't shove that cock down my throat in the next five seconds.

Luckily for me, he seems to share the sentiment.

Dick fisted in his hand, he brushes the engorged head along my lips. "Will my girl open up for me?"

He hisses the second my tongue comes in contact with the familiar, salty taste of his skin. Slowly, he eases his cock down my throat, getting it deeper since I'm on my back. "Just like that," he rasps, thrusting in and out of my mouth. "Fuck, baby."

Saliva runs down my face as he fucks himself down my throat, but I couldn't be less focused on that. He looks like a beast, like a man possessed above me. It's a sight so powerful and undoing, I never want to forget it.

I gag and choke on his length, which only turns him on more. Unable to take it any longer, my fingers find my wet folds and part them. I need something to fill me up. *Anything.*

"Fucking hell," I hear him mutter. "That's it. I wanna see how you get yourself off. Show me how wet you are."

I'm pretty sure I'm losing my goddamn mind as I give him my fingers, coated in my impending release, and he sucks them into his mouth with an appreciative hum. "So fucking sweet."

He pumps into me one last time before easing himself out of my mouth. I pant, breathless but so, so turned on I can't see straight.

James climbs onto the bed, pulling me to a sitting position on his lap. His lips find mine right as I manage to slip his hardness between my folds so he can claim what has been his since that first day at the clinic.

With a grunt, he climbs with me on top until his back is

resting against the bedrest, and then he lets loose.

His massive hands grab my ass and part my cheeks as he pounds into me, the only sounds in the room being the wetness between our bodies and my loud moans I don't bother concealing. He fucks me hard and fast, in and out like an animal, and I can barely keep up.

"Look at us," he groans against my skin, and I follow his gaze toward the full-sized mirror right behind us, propped against a wall. "Look how that ass bounces on my cock."

A moan escapes me when I spot our dark reflection in the mirror. He uses those strong arms to impale me on his erection as he pleases, and I'm only too happy to give him my body.

He makes me feel so good, so sexy, so safe and cherished, I wouldn't want to be doing this with anyone else. And then he captures my mouth in his, swallowing all my draws of pleasure as our tongues dance together.

I couldn't pinpoint the exact moment the mood shifts. All I know is that one second, he's pounding into me, and the next, his movements become slow, deep, meaningful.

Or maybe I'm just looking too much into it.

He slows down, and I take advantage to fuck myself on his cock, moving my hips to match his rhythm. His hands hold my waist, pushing me as deep as he can.

When we break our kiss, James presses his forehead against mine, his breaths heavy. "You feel so good, Maddie."

He's never said my name during sex before, and it makes my heart flutter. One of his hands cradles the side of my face, and then he breaks me some more.

"Look at me, baby. I need to see those beautiful eyes as you ride me."

As our eyes collide, something between us sparkles to life.

A feeling I don't want to awaken; something we shouldn't poke. And yet it roars to life with the force of a thousand fires.

I don't want to put a name to it.

I can't.

"I..." he starts, and my insides freeze, even though I keep moving. *Don't be stupid. He will never say that to you.* "Fuck. I need to come inside you so badly, fill you up with my cum. Tell me I can do it. Tell me I can claim you the way I'm dying to."

"James," I whimper, my walls squeezing him until his desperation matches mine. "Yes, yes. Come inside me. I need it. I need it so badly."

We don't even need to go faster before we explode. I come apart in his arms as he fills me with his release, and all at once it hits me.

I'm falling in love with James.

Tragically, completely.

I'm falling for my ex-physical therapist, a man ten years older than me, a man who doesn't even want a relationship.

And it's going to shatter me.

chapter 31

MADDIE

Almost two full weeks have passed since we came back from our trip to James's cabin in Bannport, and for every second of every hour, I've wondered how I got myself into this mess.

I literally had one job—don't fall in love with your physical therapist. *Former* PT. It's not like it makes a difference.

I don't want a relationship. My integrity has been compromised before by too many people who I thought cared about me but ended up breaking me.

It's like I'm damaged, and all people see when they look at me is a person they can have a good time with today and throw away tomorrow.

But most of all, I'm tired. Exhausted, really, of always wondering when the next person I love will leave.

James and I have a good thing going on right now, and I don't want to ruin it with conversations that will lead nowhere. I want to revel in our time together for as long as we have.

And I also want to revel in that banana bread he's baking. Why lie?

"Get ready for the foodgasm of your life," James says way too confidently as he checks our dessert, currently—and hopefully—not burning inside the oven.

I watch him from the kitchen island, head resting on one of my fists. "Mm... I don't know about that. You've set the bar pretty high so far."

While baking might not be his calling (although he refuses to admit this), James is an excellent cook. His pasta dishes have impressed me so far, and so has his ability to craft the perfect hamburger. I would inject his parsley salad dressing in my veins every day if I could.

"With foodgasms, or orgasms in general?" He smirks, the little shit, so naturally I choose to be a brat about it.

I pretend to be interested in my nails. "Definitely foodgasms. Last night was a six out of ten at best."

When he doesn't say a word to my obvious teasing, I know I've got him right where I wanted him.

James checks the timer on his phone before tossing it on the counter and starts towards me, a heated look in his eyes. He holds my hips and hoists me up on the island with ease before wrapping his fingers around the waistband of my leggings and panties and yanking them down my legs. I shriek as he tosses both items of clothing aside.

"I'll show you a six out of ten," he growls.

There's nothing gentle about the way his mouth comes in contact with my sensitive nub, already so wet from one look at the possessiveness in his eyes. *Those damn eyes.*

He laps at my clit, sucking and kissing and piercing my entrance with his tongue, and I throw my head back in utter blissfulness. A strangled moan leaves my throat as he eases his middle finger inside of me, so ridiculously thick the intrusion blinds me for a moment.

I come in record time, shattering in his face as he drinks every drop of my release like he's starved for the taste.

"So"—a kiss on the inside of my thigh—"damn"—another one—"perfect."

Still breathless, I'm about to return the favor when the timer goes off. Before he gets away, though, I grab him by the collar of his T-shirt and press my mouth to his, not minding my own taste on his lips.

He pulls away with the cockiest of grins. "Did that help up my grade?"

I pretend to think about it, tapping my finger on my lips. "Still undecided. I think I need a re-do."

His genuine chuckle lights up something inside of me, and so does the gentle kiss he plants on the tip of my nose.

Without warning, his demeanor shifts. Something new and unknown settles in his eyes, and my heart leaps in my chest.

And then it leaps some more when he says, "I want to take you out."

I stop breathing. I stop functioning altogether. "Out?"

Like a date? I want to ask, but I don't. I don't, because I'm too much of a coward to face the possibility that maybe, just maybe, James's feelings for me are changing too.

You're overthinking this.

"There's a restaurant downtown I've been meaning to try for months. We could go together," he continues, as if he hasn't just shattered all my inhibitions. "My treat."

My treat. Is he for real?

I'm going to pass out.

"Are you free tomorrow night?"

Am I free? Am I—

Okay, Maddie, stop it.

This is quite simple. If I want to go, I just have to say yes. And if I don't feel like it, I can turn him down and we'll go back to normal. Easy.

But I know what I want. I've known for a while now.

So I give him a smile and hope my voice sounds steady as I say, "I would love that."

"Good." When he returns the smile, so soft and gentle, I melt a little more. "I'll pick you up at seven from your place."

As the night and some light rain descend upon the city below

THE DARKEST CORNER OF THE HEART

us, we decide that banana bread and some chocolate milk make a perfect Sunday dinner. Because we're two functioning adults with a perfectly balanced diet, duh.

The horror movie we're watching gets so ridiculously unconvincing (no families ever think of moving out of their haunted house?), I zone out, my mind wandering to a place I considered forbidden not too long ago.

It's been a few weeks since I started my teaching position at the ballet studio downtown, and every day I'm growing more and more attached to my students and the routine in general. Plus, between that and a few waitressing shifts, I make more than enough to be financially independent again.

Sammy insisted that he could pay for everything until I got some savings, but I refused. The second he agreed, I breathed easily again for the first time in months.

It still stings to think about what my injury took away from me—the only difference is that I now realize not all is lost. Much like James told me all those months ago, my life isn't over. It's far from it.

Sometimes dreams take a bit longer to happen, and sometimes they change completely because so do we. For the first time ever, I'm comfortable riding the wave and seeing where it leads me.

Inevitably, though, thinking about my future in ballet brings up something I haven't allowed myself to consider since I went to that event with Kyle. Mainly because I fear what the answer will be.

I had my first checkup only a couple of days ago, and according to one of James's colleagues at the clinic, everything is looking up. We agreed transferring me to another physical therapist would be the right thing to do, since James is too invested in me now and—going by what he told me—could compromise my health.

And I know he said I should wait at least a year before putting that kind of pressure on my ankle again, but maybe...

Surely you'd want to do something a bit more meaningful with your career, wouldn't you?

No matter how hard I try to shake it off, this weird feeling that festered in my chest at Suzanne's harsh words won't go away. It's uncomfortable.

Before the gala, I would've jumped at any—and I mean any—opportunity to join The Norcastle Ballet. And now...

Now what?

The opportunity I've been begging for and never thought I would get back is right here at my fingertips. And this time, it's not my ankle that's holding me back. Not exactly.

"Can I talk to you about something?" I blurt out before my brain can register this is probably not the time. I want to enjoy a drama-free Sunday, thank you very much.

But life has other plans.

James pauses the movie. "Of course you can talk to me. Are you okay?"

Am I?

"Do you remember the night I went with my friend Kyle to that fancy event hosted by The Norcastle Ballet?" When he nods, I continue. "Well, he introduced me to Suzanne Allard, one of the best choreographers in the industry. I was starstruck when we met, but then she said... She said something weird."

His brows furrow. "Weird how?"

I shift on the couch, making sure not to bother a sleepy Shadow napping on my lap. "Kyle had told her about my injury, and she asked me how I was doing. And when I mentioned I was a ballet teacher at a local studio, she said..." Just repeating her words makes me sick to my stomach. "She said she hoped I'd want to do something more meaningful with my life. With my career."

At that, something furious passes his eyes. "*Meaningful?*"

I snort, although I find none of it funny at all. "That was my reaction too. But that isn't all she said." Swallowing, I brace myself for what I already know he's going to say as soon as the next words leave my mouth. "She said they were holding some open auditions for the company this winter," I tell him, still not fully grasping this is real in the first place. "I looked it up on their web page, and the deadline for video submissions is in a couple of weeks."

His features soften, knowing where I'm headed with this "Baby..."

I shake my head, wrapping my fingers around Shadow's black fur. "I know. It's silly to even consider it. Plus, what she said about ballet teaching not being meaningful... I don't know. It rubbed me the wrong way."

He wraps his hand around the back of my neck, giving it a gentle squeeze. "I'm glad you want to know my opinion about these things, Maddie. I'm happy I can help you because that's exactly what I want to do."

The more time that passes, the more I'm convinced this man can't be real.

Maybe that's why you think so, because he's a man, not some boy.

Maybe men are supposed to treat their women like this.

Not that I'm his woman or anything. More like an orgasm buddy.

Yeah. That sounds about right.

"You want to know if your ankle will be okay if you go back to professional ballet now," he states, seeing right through me.

I only shrug. "I know it won't, and..." Another sigh. "I can't believe I'm even going to say this, but meeting Suzanne was like a wake-up call. All night I got the feeling people weren't as genuine as they wanted everyone else to believe, and then she said that. It sounded elitist, you know? And I'm not sure I want to work with people who hold those kinds of values, TNB or not."

His fingers find the little hairs at the nape of my neck. "Have you fallen out of love with your dream?"

He massages my scalp, and the calm he brings me breaks down my walls, the ones I hadn't even noticed were up and ready to...*what*? Protect me from the harsh reality that I thought I knew what I wanted, only to find out not everything is as cotton-candy sweet as it seems?

"Maybe I'm overreacting," I wonder out loud, blinking away the fog in my brain. "I can't judge a whole institution based on my bad impression of just a few people."

He keeps massaging my scalp, and it's the only reason my anxiety isn't through the roof. "But you said people weren't as genuine as they seemed?"

A tired sigh escapes me. "I don't know. I overhead some girls gossiping about someone else, and then I saw them all laughing together as if they were the best of friends. The Suzanne thing too... I just... I don't know."

I know what I'm doing. Deep down, I'm very aware I'm stalling.

Because what if this dream, my ultimate goal for the past decade, isn't for me after all? And not because I'm physically incapable of dancing, but because I've finally taken off my rose-tinted glasses.

A comforting pressure sets on my temple, and I realize his lips are on me. "You could talk to Kyle and ask him what the people there are like," he suggests, his voice as soothing as his mouth against my skin. "Just to get a second opinion from someone who works there."

It's not a bad idea, but... "What if he confirms my suspicions?" I swallow back the lump in my throat.

James, this bear of a man who can calm my heart one second and set it on fire the next, wraps one of his muscular arms around me and presses my body against his warm chest. "Then you'll get to create a new dream."

Heavy rain hits the windows as the seconds pass, then the

minutes. Shadow has long abandoned my lap and is now curled up with his brother, oblivious to the storm raging not only outside, but in my head as well.

For years I've been living in fear, terrified of the day when everything I'd built for myself would come crashing down. And then it happened.

My worst nightmare—losing my dream career before it could even begin—came true. But I'm still alive and kicking, and that should count for something.

Whatever you decide to do next, it will fail as well. That's the way your life goes.

I shut my eyes, willing my former therapist's voice to go away, to free me from her shackles.

It's been close to four years, and the seed of self-doubt and contempt has grown into the tallest of trees, and I can't root it out. I can't.

I can't.

***

JAMES

Maddie is upset, and I understand why. The only thing I can't figure out is why her sadness makes me feel like my heart has been ripped out of my chest.

For nearly thirty minutes, I do nothing but stare at the wall in front of me, cradling her back to my front, holding her there. I wait until she calms down, but time goes by, and her breathing doesn't even out.

My hand reaches for hers, resting on her stomach. "Hey," I murmur in her ear, squeezing her unusually cold fingers. "Do you want to tell me what's wrong?"

Her next words break my heart. "No, it's okay. You didn't sign up for all of this."

"I signed up for you, Maddie. The whole package."

I want it all, I almost say. But I don't.

Because what does that mean?

She shrugs. "We're only fuck b—"

"If you say we're only fuck buddies, I'm going to spank that ass of yours until it turns bright red."

"Don't threaten me with a good time."

I let out a deep sigh. "I only want you to tell me what's going on so I can help you."

For a while, she doesn't say anything, doesn't react. Then, abruptly, she disentangles herself from my arms and changes positions on the couch so she's looking directly at me.

When my gaze collides with hers, all I see is boiling anger behind those beautiful hazel pools that can hide so little.

"Do you want to know what's wrong?" she asks, her voice so agitated I know she's not really asking. So I say nothing as she continues. "A therapist who was supposed to help me improve my mental health *wrecked* it instead. And now, even so many years later, I can't get her stupid voice out of my head, telling me that I'm going to ruin everything good in my life because I'm too selfish to be a good daughter, and a good sister, and a good friend."

I make a move to wipe away the tears that are now running freely down her cheeks, but she pulls away. "Let me cry." Her voice breaks. "I need to cry."

I nod. "Okay, sweetheart. I'm here when you're ready to continue."

It's like she doesn't even hear me. Like she isn't here at all—at least, her head isn't. She barely blinks as she casts an empty stare over my shoulder.

The minutes tick by and no words leave her lips, so I wait. I sit next to her, patiently, forever if she needs me to, until she mutters, "She ruined my life."

Something dark and ugly stirs in the pit of my stomach. "What she did was fucked up, but your life is far from ruined, Maddie. You have full control of it."

"It doesn't feel like it." She shakes her head, but not before letting out a heavy sigh that lets me know just how tired she feels. How defeated.

And I won't have that.

"Maddie. Look at me." When she does, I hold her stare and hope she feels the truth, the commitment in my voice. It's all I can give her. "I know you're tired, baby, I know it. But if you want to do something about her, if you want to file a complaint against her, I'll help you do it. I promise to be with you in every step of the process, okay? Just say the word."

For a fleeting moment, I think she might be considering it, but then she asks, "What's the point? A complaint won't fix the damage she's done to my head."

"I know that." When I reach for her hand, this time, she doesn't pull away. So I lace her much smaller fingers between mine and say, "But if she's still working, she might be doing the same thing to other patients. Don't you want to stop that from happening? Or try to, at least?"

That seems to convince her a little more. "I'll just have to file a complaint?" she asks, her voice so small, it breaks me.

"Then a licensing board will investigate and decide on a punishment—or let her walk away if she's not guilty. It could take a long time, but I'm here for you if you want to do it. Every step of the way, Maddie. I'm not going anywhere."

She stares at our hands, and for an infinite moment, all I can hear is the beating of my heart and the rain outside hitting the windows of my apartment.

And then she speaks.

"I looked her up online a few days ago," she admits, her voice still meek. It kills me that I can't physically take her pain away.

"She posts videos online now, talking about therapy and other stuff I couldn't even sit through."

"Okay," I prompt her.

"I watched her most recent videos, and she had quite a few comments. Most were positive, but there was one..." A pause. "One person said they had gone to her therapy sessions and that she made them feel like their problems were nothing. Like they were being overdramatic. That's exactly what she did to me."

"And you know the name of the person who left the comment? Maybe we can look them up and see if they'd want to file a joint complaint."

But she shakes her head. "It was a random username. But the thing is, I went back to the video the next day and the comment was gone."

My eyebrows shoot up at that. "So she's deleting negative comments?"

"She's silencing people who have the right to speak up if they feel that she hasn't been a good professional. I just hope that person left a review somewhere else, where it can't be deleted."

I give her hand a squeeze. "You're not the only one with a bad experience. You're not seeing things. It's not normal for a therapist to get the same complaint over and over."

"Maybe." She shrugs again, her eyes locked on our intertwined hands. "Would you really help me report her?"

"I'd do it for you if I could. If it meant not seeing you in pain anymore, I would."

A calm expression washes over her beautiful face. And when she wraps her arms around me and buries her nose on my neck, I know I've never felt so fucking complete.

I hug her back, wishing I could wipe away all the hurt in her heart but feeling immensely proud of her for fighting for herself.

"Thank you for always taking care of me," she mutters against my skin.

I shut my eyes and breathe in her clean scent. "You make me want to be a better man, Maddie. I will always take care of you."

And I realize it then, a truth that has been looming over me for months now.

I can't take care of Maddie in the way she deserves because, in a way, I'm not taking care of myself.

I've been stuck in the past for twelve years, hung up on what my brother and my ex did to me when I should've focused on healing myself. *Fully.*

Maddie is... *Fuck,* she's my everything. And I want to be her all.

But I can't do that, I could never give her the happiness she deserves, if I don't move on from this chapter of my life that has dragged on for far too long.

And I know exactly how to put an end to it.

chapter 32

MADDIE

When James suggested we come to a restaurant downtown, I thought he meant something casual. A cute, small place that was cozy and had a terrace or something. I wasn't expecting...this.

This, meaning dressing up in a little black dress and having my makeup done after months of not touching a single eye shadow.

But I'm not complaining.

TNB fundraiser aside, it's been months since the last time I dressed up—for an occasion or just because I felt like it—and it wasn't until today that I realized how much I'd missed it. Blasting music on my headphones as I danced around my apartment, browsing my wardrobe for a cute outfit to wear, choosing pink lipstick for my makeup because I still haven't outgrown my pink-obsessed phase from when I was a kid.

Sue me, but pink rocks.

And although I would've loved to complete the look with my favorite heels, let's not tempt my good luck. A pair of ballet flats I've only worn once (oops) will do.

Just as I was getting ready, my phone buzzed with a text from James. He'd told me he would pick me up from my apartment, so when I see his update, my stomach drops a little.

> **James:** Something came up. Do you mind getting a car to the

> **restaurant and meeting me there?**
> **I'm really sorry. I'll explain later.**

But despite the weird feeling I get from his message, I text him back as if nothing was wrong. Like a coward.

> **Me: No worries. I'll see you there :)**

Smiley face and everything. Ugh.

I try not to let it bother me, I really do, but not even five minutes after my reply, I'm already going at it.

What if he came to his senses and realized this looks a little too close to dating?

Because who takes their fuck buddy to a fancy restaurant just because?

He's going to cancel.

Oh, God, he'll never want to see me again.

The intrusive thoughts don't go anywhere as I get to the restaurant an hour later and there's no James to be seen. And then they only get worse when the waiter gives me a look full of pity and understanding as he guides me to our table. A table for two where I'm sitting all by myself.

Yesterday's conversation replays in my head while I wait for him, the manic way I'm bouncing my leg under the table giving away my anxious thoughts.

Despite how obvious it might seem, I never considered reporting my old therapist to the board until he suggested it. I guess I felt too young, too weak and insignificant to do anything about it. But he said he would help me, so maybe I *should* do something about it.

What he said about not being able to change my past but possibly protecting other people's futures sealed the deal for me.

I don't want anybody else to go through that same thing if I can prevent it. As for me...

James was right about my life not being ruined. Tainted, perhaps, but not ruined.

I can't control or change the past, but I can turn my future into something different. Into something hopeful and meaningful to me.

So that's why, just as another intrusive thought crawls its way into my head when I check the time on my phone and I'm still alone at the table, I push it off a metaphorical cliff.

She doesn't control me anymore.

I'm not some puppet of her unethical ways. I'm not a bad daughter, a bad sister, a bad person. Fuck that.

So what if I've had bad luck in my family life? Had I not grown up in a loving and safe household anyway?

Sammy and Grace might not be my actual parents, but they raised me as such. They give me so much love, and support, and respect, and here I am being ungrateful for it. Just because I feel bad for making my brother pay my rent while I got my degree away from home?

Would I have felt the same way if my parents had been the ones to support me like that?

I'm getting a headache just thinking about all the what-ifs, but this time the guilt doesn't come. I'm not naïve enough to believe it's gone forever, yet this small reprieve feels like the breath of fresh air I've been craving for too long. For now, it's enough.

What is also enough is the time I've been waiting for James.

After glancing at my phone for the umpteenth time and seeing no texts, I decide to reach out to him first. Just in case.

> **Me: Hey, I've been here for 15 mins. Are you going to take much longer?**

Five minutes pass with no reply. Then five, and another five more.

He's half an hour late.

Is he...

Have I been stood up?

Think happy thoughts.

Maybe he's stuck in traffic and can't check his phone, or maybe it died and that's why he can't text me back. Wait, no. That can't be it because my texts have been delivered, which means his phone is turned on and he has reception.

What if there's been an accident?

No. He's fine. He's coming. He's just late.

And that's what I keep telling myself for fifteen more minutes.

I keep lying to myself as the waiter asks if I'm ready to order or if we should wait for someone else.

I keep lying to myself as an hour goes by and James doesn't show up, not bothering to send me a goddamn text apologizing, explaining himself, *anything*.

When I exit the restaurant with an empty stomach and an even emptier heart, I stop lying to myself.

He said he was always going to be here for me, but I should've known better than to believe his false promises.

He left once, and clearly he didn't feel bad about it since he did it again.

As my car reaches my building, my phone rings.

But it's not James.

It's my mother.

chapter 33

JAMES

> Me: Today at 6. You have 30 minutes.

I wish I could say I haven't seen my brother in a decade, but sadly I haven't been that lucky.

For years, our parents forced us to share a space during Christmas, but every other holiday he was going to be at home, I skipped it. My parents understood why, and they never held it against me.

They know what he did, but the *"He's our son too"* excuse never gets old. The only reason I don't hold it against them either is because they mean well. It's not an excuse for them—it's an explanation. That doesn't mean I don't feel like I've been handed the short end of the stick.

He was the one who pushed me away when we were young then again when we were not so young. He was the jealous one, the aggressive brother, the one who couldn't stand the thought of me being good at something he wasn't. *He* was the one who slept with my girlfriend while I was still dating her.

But that doesn't matter anymore, does it?

For all intents and purposes, I'm an only child. And I don't care how bad that thinking makes me look.

When people say, "But he's your brother, and blood is thicker than water," they don't realize they are missing half of the saying.

The blood of the covenant is thicker than the water of the womb is the full quote, and it means that the bonds we make by choice are more important than the people we are bound to by the water of the womb.

Hence why I couldn't give less of a crap if Andrew was or wasn't my brother. If he wanted us to have a relationship, maybe he shouldn't have been a class-A asshole all his life. Just a suggestion.

He asked me to meet him at his workplace, some fancy office downtown he promised would be empty by the time I get there. For once, he's honest.

Everything I know about Andrew's adult life, I've learned against my will. My parents tend to give me updates when we see each other, thinking that my pride is keeping me from asking, when the truth is that he's pretty much dead to me. But I never say that out loud—I want my mother's heart intact.

So that's how I know what to expect when I walk into the marketing firm he works at two minutes after our scheduled time. My eyebrows don't rise, and my facial expression doesn't change when my blue eyes meet his brown ones.

Andrew is broad like me but a couple of inches shorter. He's nothing but arrogant, as seen in the current lopsided smirk on his face, as if this was some laughing matter.

"James," he starts, that haughty voice I was only too happy to never hear again piercing my ears.

"Thirty minutes," I bark, getting closer to what I assume is his desk. "Cut the shit."

I have a date with Maddie in an hour, and I've already told her I'll be running a little late, because this can't wait another day. I want to get this done with, this conversation that should've happened years ago, and go back to my girl and have another more important conversation with her that is long overdue.

Because whatever we're doing isn't cutting it anymore.

I want all of her. Always, from now on and until I take my last breath, and I'm not risking losing her before I can even have her.

I'm brought back to the present moment by the way my brother's face morphs into the icy, cruel one I know all too well. "To what do I owe the pleasure?"

"You'd know, since you've been asking to see me for months."

"Ah, yes. That."

Despite the years apart, I know my brother like the back of my hand. And that's why I know the blow is coming, one way or another.

He hasn't been asking to see me out of the kindness of his heart or to apologize for everything he's done to me. That's not him.

I confirm my suspicions when he reaches into one of the pockets of his suit jacket and holds out some kind of invitation. I already know what it is before he says it, but he lets me know anyway.

"Alexandra and I are getting married this spring, and I wanted to tell you in person. We hope to see you there."

His words settle in my brain, taking shape until I'm positive I understand every syllable. Once I know for sure that my head hasn't come up with something so pitiful, I wait for the anger to come.

I expect to feel angry, but not because he's getting married to my ex-girlfriend. Not at all—any feelings I had for her dissipated into thin air the second I caught her in bed with him.

The anger would come because of my brother, I thought. Because this person who was supposed to stay by my side all our lives, who should've been a best friend to me, is still out to hurt me.

Twelve years of open animosity hasn't been enough for him— he wants more.

And so I wait, for a heartbeat and then two and three, for the rage to come. The need to lash out at him, to punch him in the face, *anything*.

Instead, the only reaction his wedding invitation pulls from me is a genuine chuckle.

I miss how my brother's whole demeanor changes, how his shoulders stiffen and that trophy smile is wiped from his face.

I miss the way he fists his hands at his sides and a muscle ticks on his cheek because I'm too busy *laughing*.

At him.

At all of this...whatever this is.

A shit show, if I had to give it a name.

"What the fuck are you laughing at?" he demands, his chest heaving as if he'd just run a marathon.

I shake my head, my amused smile still firmly in place, and give myself the freedom to look at Andrew, at my older brother, in a new light.

And that's when I see it all.

"This is pathetic, man." I'm surprised there's no heat in my voice, no trace of anything but this amusement that isn't entirely unwelcome. I take the invitation from his grip, and I scan it for all of five seconds before scrunching it up in my hand and throwing it in the nearest trash can. "There. Where it belongs."

"What's wrong with you?" He rushes to retrieve the piece of paper, unfolding it and trying to get rid of all the wrinkles with the heel of his palm. When it becomes obvious he can't do anything about it, he turns to me, and the fury behind his eyes isn't unfamiliar to me. "Fuck you, James. Honestly, fuck you. I was trying to extend an olive branch, but—"

My easy smile disappears, but I don't raise my voice. "It's pretty clear what you were trying to do, and that invitation wasn't an olive branch. It was a failed attempt at a jab."

"A jab?"

"Did you really think I would give a fuck if you married her, Andrew? If you got married at all?"

My throat closes up unexpectedly, and I fucking hate myself for it.

I never pictured myself telling my brother any of this, but then I remember how Maddie handled her father coming back after seventeen years. How brave she was, how strong.

And it's only because of her strength that I say, "You're nothing to me, Andrew. Neither is she. You're no longer my brother, not after all you've done."

"I'm still your brother," he says, agitated, as he takes a step closer. "I don't know what the fuck your problem is. I'm only inviting you to my wedding, and I'm having the decency to do it in person."

Is he on something? He must be.

"*Decency?*" The word tastes sour on my tongue. "If you had any ounce of decency left in you, you would've apologized for being a shit brother all your fucking life. But that would require admitting you've done something wrong, and I don't expect you to be that mature at thirty-three."

He lets go of the wrinkled invitation, dropping it between us, and gets in my face, his breath hitting my mouth as he speaks.

"I have nothing to be sorry about," he sneers. "All you cared about was football, fuck everything else. You always strived to be the top of the class, the top of the team, the top of the fucking family. So what if I took care of your little girlfriend while you were busy crying over a failed career that would've sucked ass, anyway? She sure as hell has no complaints."

"The fact that I failed doesn't make you a winner." My voice sounds loud and clear. "In fact, you're one of the most pathetic losers I know."

One thing about Andrew that hasn't changed since childhood—aside from his pettiness—is his violent temper.

I still have that scar on my left shin from when I was four years old and he was six, and he thought it would be funny to see what would happen if he pushed me down the stairs because Dad said it was my turn to choose what to watch on TV.

It wasn't the first time he pushed me, slapped me, bit me, or punched me, and it also wasn't the last. And all right, maybe I started a couple of fights, but I wasn't the one looking for them.

I'd finished them all, though.

I'd always channeled my anger on the field, not like I had much to begin with. But even if I did, punching my brother when we're both *grown men* isn't an option. We're not a pair of immature brutes anymore, damn it.

But I'm the only one who got the memo, apparently.

I duck Andrew's sloppy punch by mere luck. My mind is still deciding whether this is real, if my brother has just tried to *hit me in the face,* when he strikes again.

"Andrew," I sneer, grabbing his wrist at the last second. "Stop."

He doesn't listen. He pushes me with his other hand, making me stumble backward and slam into a desk. I hear things dropping to the floor, but I don't have time to check the damages because he tries to punch me again.

"How dare you," he half yells between gritted teeth, grabbing me by the collar of my shirt.

I grab his forearms and kick him in the leg until he lets go of me, ripping the top buttons of my shirt as he does.

"Andrew." My voice is calm, although my heart couldn't be beating any faster. Is he really trying to beat me up at his workplace? Has his brain stopped functioning? "This is why you wanted to see me? Don't make me knock out all your goddamn teeth. Stop it."

"Always the strong one, the reasonable one, the *perfect* one," he mocks, the expression on his face nothing short of cruel. "Admit that this is killing you."

At that, I frown. "Admit what?"

His mouth curves into a bitter smile, as if he thought he'd just caught me playing coy. "I knew you loved her. I knew you wanted to marry her, have kids with her. But she didn't love you like that, and it *ruined* you. You could be the star player and the perfect son all you wanted, but you were never going to get the dream girl. She chose me instead because she saw what kind of self-centered piece of shit you were, and you can't live with that."

Did that...

Did that just come out of his mouth?

I didn't imagine it, did I?

"Andrew," I start, unable to believe this shit is really happening. When I look at my brother now, all I see is a stranger. "Tell me you're not about to marry Alexandra to get back at me."

That catches him off guard. His mouth opens, then closes, but I don't let him continue.

"You really are, aren't you?" I let out a low whistle. "I can't say you don't deserve each other, so truly, I couldn't be happier you've found your rotten match."

If he's only been with her for so long to try and spite me, maybe my brother needs more professional help than I'd initially thought.

Not my problem, though.

"You still love her," he goes on, trying to push this narrative we both know isn't working. "Y-You wanted everything with her."

"I might have," I concede, my eyes hard on him. "Twelve years ago, before I realized she wasn't worth my time, let alone my love."

I knew that the second I caught her in bed with him. All those feelings, all those dreams of building a future with her went down the drain in that moment and never came back. Not for one second.

They were the reason I refused to open up my heart again until Maddie came into my life and ripped it open with her bare hands. And now...

Now I'm standing here, entertaining this pathetic excuse of a man I call an older brother, when I should be heading to the restaurant to be with her. To enjoy our date and tell her that maybe this no-labels arrangement isn't working for me anymore.

I want it all, and I want it with her.

Because I've fallen in love with her, and I'm doing this for her. To move on and become the healed man she deserves to have by her side.

What am I still doing here?

I didn't mean for this conversation to take longer than five minutes. He doesn't deserve a second more.

When I reach into my pocket to grab my phone and text Maddie that I'll be late, a firm grip stops me.

"Let me go," I tell him more calmly than he deserves. "I don't want you to go home with a black eye."

"Fuck you," he spits out. "Admit what we both know."

"I have nothing to admit because I don't give a fuck about you or her." My eyes zero in on his, so cold and bitter. "I thought maybe you'd changed after all these years, but you're the same bitter motherfucker I left behind. I don't know you anymore, Andrew, and at this point I don't care to. You're forever stuck in the mindset of a petty twenty-something-year-old, and the sad thing is you're comfortable there. You think you're thriving, don't you? You don't care who you hurt as long as you come out on top, and for that you deserve every fucking miserable thing that happens to you."

In some capacity, I expected it to happen. It might be why I do nothing to stop him as he finally gets what he invited me here to do.

My brother lands a punch on the right side of my face, missing my eye by some miracle, as he starts shouting.

His blow leaves my skin feeling hot, and it stings like a motherfucker, but I don't hit him back.

Because, unlike my older brother, I still have a functioning brain.

And two working eyes that spot a security guard running toward us, yelling at Andrew to stand back.

I taste blood in my mouth, and I already know this isn't going to look good in the morning unless I ice it as soon as possible. But one look at the time is enough to set my priorities straight.

"Sir." The security guard's eyes land on my cheek before he keeps going. "What is going on? Did this man hit you?"

"Yes. Will that be all?"

He gives me a weird look. "I'm instructed to call the police if a physical altercation takes place inside the building. They are on their way."

"That won't be necessary." I don't want my parents to have a heart attack when they hear my brother has been arrested for punching me. "I won't be pressing charges." He deserves it, but I don't have the time.

I have a woman to go back to, and she's more important to me than anything and anyone else. More than any other person in this goddamn universe.

"He is an employee of this company, sir," the security guard keeps going. "The CEO has been contacted and will want to take your statement for company purposes, as well as the police. Please, don't leave the premises until they arrive."

Shit.

I ignore my brother as he tries to convince the security guard I threatened him first, but then I spot the security camera right above our heads and know I have nothing to worry about.

See, that's the thing about dealing with assholes—they tend to be so stupid, they ruin their own lives. You don't have to do a single thing.

When I reach into the back pocket of my jeans and get my phone, my stomach drops. The screen is cracked, and it doesn't unlock. I try to restart it, but it doesn't work.

Fuck, fuck, fuck.

He pushed me so hard against the desk behind me, he broke my goddamn phone.

I glance at the digital clock on the far wall of the office, and I realize I'm already late and have no way of contacting Maddie. The restaurant isn't exactly close by, and I'll never get there in time with all this traffic.

But I could call the restaurant. If someone gave me their phone, I could look up their phone number online and tell them there's been an issue and to let Maddie know.

That's what I'm about to do when a man in a suit bursts through the doors, followed by four police officers.

"Simmons!" he roars, and for a second, I think this man I've never seen before is addressing me until I watch his eyes burn holes into my brother's skull. "What the fuck is going on here?"

The next forty-five minutes are tedious. I remember asking for a phone and a police officer telling me they needed to take my statement first, that they won't take long. But they do.

I also remember how Andrew's boss apologized profusely to me, clearly embarrassed even after I assured him it was all right. And I recall him telling my brother not to bother coming in the next morning, which doesn't feel as good as I hoped it would. Not because he doesn't deserve to lose his job, but because the clock was about to hit eight in the evening, and I still hadn't managed to contact Maddie.

After a paramedic takes a look at my face and forces me to put some ice on my bruise, I already know it's too late.

As I am finally allowed to leave, I don't say a word to my brother. My eyes meet his right before I get in my car. Somehow I knew our story was never meant to have a happy ending. After what just went down, it's become even clearer that he doesn't deserve a second chance.

Some people never do, and we aren't selfish for not giving it to them—family or not.

When people fuck up, they don't automatically deserve to be forgiven just because they have apologized or feel bad about it. The damage is done, and we have the freedom to decide whether that spot they've left vacant in our life can fit them again.

Not that my brother has apologized or ever will, and I'm okay with that. I don't need us to have a relationship now that I know he hasn't changed and he's not planning to.

What I need is Maddie, and something inside me tells me I've already lost her.

***

She isn't at the restaurant. I know this because I drove there, asked the staff, and they told me she'd left twenty minutes ago.

So I get back in my car, check that my phone still doesn't unlock, and do the only thing that feels right.

I drive to her apartment.

When I ring the doorbell downstairs, she doesn't respond.

I do it five more times.

And nothing.

I wait outside for half an hour until a man leaves the building with a dog on a leash, and I rush inside. I'm desperate to see her, to make sure she understands I didn't stand her up. I take the stairs two at a time instead of getting into the elevator to get rid of the pent-up anxiety clinging to my chest.

Breathless, I reach her floor and make a beeline for her apartment. The hallway is quiet, deserted, no sounds coming from any of the units.

I ring her doorbell first and then knock when she doesn't answer. Still nothing.

"Maddie," I call out as I knock again, pressing my ear to her door. I don't want her neighbors to think I'm some kind of stalker, so I keep my voice as quiet as I can. "Maddie, I'm so sorry. I went to see my brother, and... It's a long story, but I got held up and my phone is broken; that's why I couldn't call you. I'm so sorry, baby. Let me talk to you, please."

A minute goes by.

Then fifteen.

At some point, I think I hear water (the tap? the shower?) running inside her apartment, so I know she's there. And when the automatic lights on the hallway turn off, I don't imagine the faint glow coming from under her front door.

She's ignoring me, and it hurts.

But I deserve it.

I should've told my brother to fuck off sooner. I don't regret meeting him, if only because I finally got all that shit off my chest and I'll never see his face again if I don't absolutely have to, but I should've been smarter about it.

Because Andrew isn't worth it, but the woman I love sure as fuck is. And I messed up.

After an hour of pacing back and forth in the hallway, hoping she'll open the door to at least check if I'm still there, it becomes clear she isn't interested. I knock once more, but no answer comes.

I deserve her cold shoulder, I really fucking do, but that doesn't mean I'm giving up.

I don't think about the consequences of her neighbors seeing me and possibly calling the police as I sit down in the hallway, my back against the wall right by her door, and wait. If it takes all night, then this is where I'll be.

My phone is still dead, but I wear a watch to work every day, so I'm not too worried about getting to the clinic late tomorrow morning. I don't have my alarm, but I'm not planning to sleep anyway.

Two hours go by, and I think of Shadow and Mist. It wouldn't be the first time they've been alone at home for twenty-four hours, so I'm not worried. They have water, food, and each other. They'll be fine.

Me, though? I don't think I will.

When three in the morning rolls around and not a single soul has left or entered her apartment, I let out a humorless chuckle.

I really am spending the night in a dark hallway, sitting by the door of a woman I won't survive losing, all because my brother punched me in the face.

By six, I think I'm going delirious when I hear a door opening. I haven't slept in twenty-four hours, so it wouldn't surprise me.

But then a familiar shoe steps into the hallway, then another. I follow those long, beautiful legs until my eyes land on a pair of hazel eyes that stole my breath away months ago and still haven't given it back.

"James?" She frowns. "What are you doing here?"

I have a feeling she knows. There's no way she didn't hear me knocking and calling for her last night, but at this point, I don't care.

She's here, and so am I, and I'm not going to let her walk away.

"Maddie." My voice sounds husky and tired as I get up. "I'm so sorry. Something happened last night, and my phone is broken—"

"Your cheek is swollen," she points out.

It must be because my brain is too tired to function properly, but as soon as it registers she doesn't sound *normal*, I wake up at once.

No, her voice sounds flat. Emotionless. And when I look at her, and I mean really look at her, not even the dim light of the hallway can hide the swelling in her eyes or how red they look.

Then I notice the small carry-on luggage by her side, and my heart drops to the pit of my stomach.

"Maddie—"

"Save it," she says, her voice flat but somehow also cold.

"Whatever you're going to say, I don't want to hear it."

I swallow back the uncomfortable lump in my throat. "I didn't stand you up on purpose, Maddie. I would never do that. I went to see my brother, and things got out of control." When she looks at my swollen cheek, I think she flinches. I'm not sure. "He'd been trying to reach me for months, and I..." *Fuck it.* "I needed closure. I couldn't... I couldn't be the man you deserve unless I moved on. And I want to be worthy of you more than anything else in this world."

For a moment, she says nothing. She doesn't make a sound, and neither do I, afraid of startling her after dropping this bomb.

She shuts her eyes, breathing deeply through her nose, and says, "I'm leaving."

My heart stops.

The looming presence of her luggage haunts me. Surely, she can't fit all of her belongings in that small suitcase. She's not leaving leaving. She can't.

Why not, asshole? Because of you? You failed her, left her, broke your promise.

"What do you mean?" I ask, my voice suddenly a lot quieter and my throat a lot drier.

She doesn't look at me as she says, "I'm going home."

Home.

Not here.

Not with me.

"My mother called."

I find myself nodding along. "Okay."

She must have upset her in some way. They don't have the best relationship, so maybe she promised to meet her but called it off at the last second. Maybe she's upset about that. Maybe her brother asked her to go back home?

But she has a job here now, two jobs that she loves.

Is she leaving forever?

Fuck it, but I'd go after her.

I would upend my entire life if it meant creating a new one with her.

After what feels like an eternity of nothing but a heavy silence, Maddie finally looks at me, and I see a turmoil of emotions hiding behind her eyes.

She's confused, angry, broken.

Because I hurt her, and because someone else did too.

You were supposed to take care of her heart. To protect it.

"Maddie—" I start.

But I don't get a chance to finish before the very last words I expected her to say leave her lips.

"My father is dead."

chapter 34

MADDIE

People have walked out of my life over the years for a number of reasons, but I've never lost anyone.

It's strange, this notion that no matter how much time passes or where you go, there are people you will never see again. Because they're dead.

My father is dead. My father is dead. My father is dead.

The following twenty-four hours after my mother's call don't feel real.

I know I got to the airport only because a taxi dropped me off, and I know I arrived at Warlington because my brother was waiting for me at the gate, but I know little else.

My brain shuts down, my body gives up, and my heart...

I don't think it's working anymore.

A soft knock on my childhood bedroom door wakes me up from the state of nothingness I've been in for the past few hours. James's texts sit unanswered on my phone, but I can't bring myself to feel bad about it.

> **James: Did you get to Warlington safely?**

> **James: Just wanted to send you a picture of Shadow and Mist. They say hi.**

> **James: I'm so sorry, Maddie. I'm sorry you're going through this. I'm here if you need anything at all.**

He left me at the restaurant. He said he was always going to be there, and then he wasn't. His reasons, his explanations... They don't mean much. Not when I can't even feel my own heart right now.

Him leaving isn't something I didn't expect, anyway. I'll survive without him.

But do you want to?

I don't say a word, but my brother walks into my room all the same and closes the door behind him.

It doesn't bother me. Nothing does at this point.

Sammy doesn't speak. He only lies with me in bed, above the covers, and holds my hand in his tattooed, warm one.

My phone pings again. I ignore it.

My brother squeezes my fingers.

After five minutes, or maybe five hours, he asks, "How are you feeling?"

"Empty."

And there's that.

Lila is the next one to open my bedroom door. Much like her father, she doesn't say a word as she approaches us. And when my niece, this little person I would give my life for without question, wraps her arms around my neck and presses her cheek against my own, I break down.

The tears fall, but my father's name isn't written on them.

Instead, I cry for the person I wanted, I *needed*, but never got.

I cry for Lila, who has an amazing dad who loves her more than life itself, and I cry because I don't ever want her to lose him.

And then I cry because I hate crying for my father, that vile man who doesn't deserve an ounce of my sadness.

"It's okay to cry, Maddsy." Lila soothes me like she can read my mind. Given who her mother is, it wouldn't surprise me one bit.

I hear my brother planting a kiss on her hair. "Let me talk to your auntie for a moment, little sunshine."

"Okay, Daddy." She kisses my tears away. "I love you, Maddsy. You're my favorite ever."

A half sob, half chuckle escapes me. "I love you more, Lila."

With one last kiss on my cheek and one on my brother's, she hurries out of the room and shuts the door behind her.

My head finds the space between Sammy's arm and his chest, and I settle there in silence.

"I don't want to cry for him," I finally let out. My voice sounds all raspy and wrong, and I hate the weakness in it.

"It's okay if you do," he says, but it doesn't make it better.

Our last meeting haunts me. I saw him for the first time in seventeen years in a dark parking lot after he stalked me for weeks, and now I will never see him again.

Because he's dead.

My father is dead. My father is dead. My father is dead.

"He..." I start, not really wanting to bring this up, but it's now or never. Now, when my heart feels nothing, I know it can take the pain. "He said he came back years ago. He said you didn't let him see me."

I feel my brother's muscles tense under my body. "He did." A pause. "You were around seven. He came by the tattoo shop and demanded to see you. He was drunk, maybe something else, too, and I told him to fuck off. Threatened him. He couldn't do anything because I had custody of you, so he never bothered to try again."

I nod against his chest. "I-I'm not upset with you. You did the right thing."

My brother's lips brush my forehead in a faint kiss. "I vowed to take care of you the very day you were born, and that man lost the privilege to see you when he left. When he came back... I could tell he wasn't healthy. He wasn't okay in the head, and I refused to let you see him like that. Maybe if the circumstances had been different..."

He runs a hand through his dark hair, his chest heaving with a deep sigh.

"You did the right thing," I repeat, and not only to make him feel better. Not so deep down, I know my father would've abused the privilege of seeing me to hurt me again.

"Thank you for understanding. It means a lot to me."

It sucks. It truly sucks that my brother, abandoned by his own father before he was even born, had to witness his little sister being abandoned by her own too. And it hurts so deeply that Sammy, who has one of the most beautiful souls I've ever met, has to go through this mess with me.

"I hate crying for him," I whisper. "I hated him, Sammy. I hate him."

I fall apart in his arms, but he's there to pick up the pieces. He always is.

Now that I've started talking, I can't seem to stop. "Does it make me a bad person to hate him in death? A bad daughter?" I ask, not sure if I want to hear the answer. I sniffle but don't wipe the tears away. "Is it wrong that I don't feel a difference even if he's gone? He wasn't there for me before, and he will never get to be now."

Sammy hugs me closer. "You're not his daughter, Maddie. You never were—not in the way that matters. You might have his genes, but you're mine. *Ours.* You've never owed him anything, and you sure as fuck won't start owing him now. The fact that he's dead doesn't invalidate your hatred, and it doesn't erase the fact that he was a fuckup who never deserved you in the first place."

Burying my face in the inked rose on his neck, I weep.

I sob, break down and pick myself back up, knowing my family will always be there for me.

"I'm so sorry," I hiccup.

His hand cups the back of my head. "What for?"

The words pour out directly from my heart. For once, I don't want to hold them back.

"I'm sorry that you had to raise me because my own parents couldn't, and I'm sorry that you and Grace almost didn't make it because I was a burden. And I'm sorry that you couldn't have more children because you had to take care of me even after I moved out, because I injured my ankle and flushed my future down the drain. I'm so sorry, Sammy." I stop, breathless, my voice cracking with the last word.

My brother wipes the tears from my eyes with his palms, just like he always used to do when I was a kid. So full of care and love, it only makes me want to cry harder.

"Breathe with me, princess. Inhale. Exhale," he instructs. We repeat the motions until I calm down. "How long have you felt this way?"

My lips tremble as I speak, and so does my voice. "A very long time."

I can't bring myself to talk about my former therapist. Not right now. Not when James...

God, James.

Why did he have to let me down? Why can't I shake off the feeling of betrayal?

My brother curses under his breath and searches my eyes, worry plastered all over his features. "Look at me, Maddie. Listen to me."

I nod, my chest heaving with painful sobs.

"You're my sister, my blood, my *everything*. You were never a burden, okay? Never. Since you were born, all I wanted was to keep you all to myself because I knew nobody would take better care of you than your big brother. You gave me a purpose—you still do, just like Lila and Grace. You three are the only ones who matter to me, and you could never be a burden to anybody in this family. You could never be when we love you so much.

"Grace and I didn't have more kids because we didn't want to, Maddie, not because of you. Money wasn't the reason, nor was it a lack of love to give. We felt like our family was complete, and that decision had nothing to do with you and everything to do with us as a couple, okay? You're one of the most incredible people I've ever known, and I'm not just saying that because you're my sister. You're responsible, fun, generous, driven, mature, a fucking angel, Maddie.

"You didn't flush your future down the drain because it's only about to start, and I'm gonna be there, cheering you on every step of the way. You'll always have a home with us. You'll always have our support, in any way you need, because we know you don't take it for granted and we know you want to make a life for yourself—and you're doing it.

"I couldn't have asked for a better sister. I love you and I'm proud of you, you hear me? We all are, and I will remind you every single day for the rest of my life if I have to."

By the time his speech is done, I'm a mess of tears again.

Deep down I knew all of it, if only because he's shown me all my life that it's true, but I needed to hear it from him.

Today of all days, I needed my brother.

"I love you," I say against his skin, my voice muffled. "I love you all so much. I love you."

He wraps his arms around me, pulling me into a big bear hug that glues all my broken pieces back together.

"Cry for as long as you need, princess. I'm not going anywhere, and Lila would love nothing more than to cuddle with you all day long."

I chuckle, my heart feeling lighter already.

"Tomorrow, at the funeral, I don't want you to hold back. Cry, break something, scream, anything. But allow your heart to bleed because that's the only way to heal."

Healing.

It's been a long time coming for me.

***

Attending my father's funeral sits at the very top of the list of things I never, ever thought I would do.

I mean, up until a few weeks ago, I didn't know for sure if he was still alive, if he was still in the country, or what even was going on with him. And I didn't care either.

My talk with Sammy last night helped immensely in the guilt department. I'm not ashamed to say his words are the sole reason I can stand straight in this cold room of the funeral home, look at my father's closed casket, and admit to myself that I've never missed him, never loved him, and I'm not going to start now.

But the pain is still there, lingering in my heart, and at first, I don't understand why.

My father has never been a real part of my life—more like an abstract figure I longed for until I realized my brother embodied every single quality a father should have.

And I couldn't have asked to grow up in a better family.

Better Place is a misleading name for this funeral home, I think to myself as I take in every detail around me, given how it sits in the sketchiest part of Warlington.

Who organized my father's funeral? Grandparents I've never met? An aunt or an uncle I didn't even know I had? Why did they choose this place?

Who are all these people?

The service won't start for another half an hour, but this room is crowded. There are men and women here, most around my father's age, and they're...crying. Some are holding back the tears; others just stand solemnly.

What the hell is this?

A few people have come up to me since we arrived, asking how I knew Pete. Clearly, my name wasn't one he mentioned around. So I simply said he was a family friend, and that seemed to be enough for his...friends? He had friends.

Friends who had no clue he had a daughter.

Whatever. I can't bring myself to care anymore.

I've been here for five minutes, and I'm already overwhelmed. Maybe it was a mistake to come, no matter how much Sammy insisted I may need the closure. I'm about to turn around to go outside and find him, Grace, and Lila, when her strong perfume invades my nostrils.

"He wasn't a good man," my mother says in a firm voice, eyes on his casket. She stands still, rigid, but not solemnly. "Living with him wasn't easy, but I don't regret it. He gave me you, after all."

Tears threaten to come for the first time today. She shouldn't hold this power over me, a mother who couldn't have strayed further from that role, but I can't deny that my heart doesn't hold the same kind of resentment for her as it does for my father.

My mom was a victim of her own circumstances. Normally I wouldn't feel sympathy for someone who didn't make an effort to be more present once she got sober, but I'm tired of fighting the past.

It's clear that my mother has fought hard to get her life back on track, even if she still isn't the best at rekindling relationships that should've never been broken in the first place.

Unlike my father, though, maybe she does deserve a second chance.

But it won't be today.

"How did he pass?" I ask her softly.

"He was driving under the influence and crashed into a building. Nobody else was hurt."

Good. In that situation, nobody else deserved to die but him. "Under the influence of what?"

My mother slides me a quick look before letting out a tired sigh. "Of the same crap that made him lose his jobs every couple of months when you were younger, Maddie. Cocaine, maybe something else. He got himself involved with the wrong crowd before we met. He was dealing drugs when you were a child, but I didn't know this, and then... I..."

She opens her mouth like she wants to say something else, but the words die in her throat. Instead, her bony fingers find my hand and squeeze it.

I let her because I need this too.

"I'm sorry for everything, Maddie. I will always regret what I made you go through. I hope someday, when you're ready, you'll want to have a conversation with me. A real one."

Tears prickle the back of my eyes, and I nod. Because somewhere not so deep in my heart, I know my mother deserves at least that. A conversation in which the new versions of us can have a chance to meet.

"I will call you," I whisper, my voice too husky, and I swear her whole body sags with relief. "But not today. I...need time."

"Yes. Of course." She squeezes my hand again. "I love you, Maddie. Thank you for giving me a chance."

I don't say it back, but I think she understands I can't. Not yet, but maybe someday.

"I'm going to look for your brother," she says next, and I like the new resolve in her voice. I don't think I've ever heard her sound so confident. "I owe him an apology too."

My mother leaves me at the casket, and only then do I give my tears permission to fall.

This is too much all at once. Too many conflicting emotions clinging to my poor heart, already shattered enough, and I don't want these people to think I'm shedding a single tear for him.

Without thinking, I make a beeline for one of the doors in the room, which leads to an empty hallway. There's a single wooden chair a few feet away, and I sink down on it and bury my face in my hands, letting it all out.

I don't even know why I'm crying.

My mom, my dad, myself.

Everyone at once.

He killed himself in a car accident because he was a fucking junkie, and it makes me sob harder to think I could've ended up like him if my brother hadn't stepped in.

My mother could've ended up like him, too, dead or worse, if I hadn't tripped over that empty bottle of whiskey that night and gotten a head injury. If I hadn't hurt myself and gone to live with my brother, maybe she would've never gone to rehab.

Would I have ended up dead as well? Consumed by alcohol and drugs? Abused and alone?

A loud sob tears up my heart, and maybe that's why I don't hear the approaching footsteps.

But I hear that voice.

"Maddie."

chapter 35

MADDIE

"Maddie."

That voice.

That deep rumble I now hear in my dreams. And surely, that must be what's going on here. Because James is in Norcastle. He's at the clinic, working, and not at some random funeral home on the outskirts of my childhood town, five hours away.

But then I snap my head up, and when my eyes fall on the last person I expected to see today, everything around me stops.

No. It can't be.

I blink once, twice, screaming in my head at this cruel dream to go away.

But I know I'm not seeing a ghost. This isn't my imagination playing tricks on me.

He's here, standing in this empty hallway at Better Place Funeral Home in this forsaken neighborhood in Warlington, and it's real.

He's here for me.

For me.

I don't move from my chair, but I don't need to.

His long, muscular legs close the distance between us until he's standing right in front of me. I don't look at him, my eyes locked on his dress shoes. *He put on a suit to come to my father's funeral.*

My heart isn't doing okay. No part of my anatomy is, if I'm

being honest. The sight of James in a suit should be forbidden, and I don't allow myself to appreciate it.

He left.

But he came back.

The voices in my head are still fighting as he kneels in front of me, his face now at my eye level. My gaze still doesn't move from the ground.

"Pain is an abstract feeling." We haven't seen each other in two days, and I didn't know what to expect. Not these words. "We don't always understand why we feel it, at least not right away."

I think he knows I can't find my own voice right now, my thoughts all messed up and blurry, because he continues in that soothing rumble.

I want to be worthy of you more than anything else in this world.

It's the reminder of his words that makes me look at him, at those warm eyes that tell me so much without meaning to.

"There are people in my life that I hate, Maddie," he continues. "That I loathe with every fiber of my being, but I can't stand the thought of their death. It's confusing and it's frustrating, but I promise what you're feeling is normal. It only shows you have a big heart with room for everyone, even those who never deserved it."

Maybe I don't want to hold space for people who don't deserve it anymore. Maybe I'm tired of always being reliable, being there for people who wouldn't do the same for me.

"We can't control how we react to others or how much pain or love they leave within us." He holds out his hand, twice bigger than my own, in a silent invitation. There are no regrets in my heart as I place my palm on his, and he closes his fingers around my hand, just holding it. "Do you know what's one of the things I admire the most about you?"

I don't answer.

"That you don't waste your time with unworthy people.

Look at your father. You didn't give him a second chance; you didn't fold when he begged to come back. That takes courage and determination, something not many people have when it truly counts. You take what's yours and don't apologize for it. I'm so fucking proud of you for living your life how you want to, Maddie. I'm learning so much from you."

Me? He's learning from me?

His thumb draws circles on my skin, setting it on fire and calming me down at the same time. For a while, neither of us says anything. This part of the hallway is mostly silent, with no loud voices or music coming from any of the rooms. It gives me time to think.

His brother hit him in the face that night. His phone was broken. That's why he couldn't contact you.

He didn't stand you up.

He spent the night sitting outside your door, waiting for you.

"What are you doing here?" My throat burns as I speak. "How did you know where I was?"

"I found his obituary online." He holds my hand a little tighter, his gaze searching every corner of my eyes until his protective urges are satisfied. "I needed to see you. I needed to make sure you were okay. I've been worried sick since you left, and I couldn't wait another second."

"But...but work..."

"I took a day off. Told them it was a family emergency." When his fingers settle on my cheek, cradling it like my face is something precious to hold, I don't pull away. "Why are you out here, crying all by yourself?"

I'm tired. I'm so, so tired.

I'm tired of being on edge all the time, on the lookout for the next person who will walk away from me. Because this is the thing—people have already done it. My parents left me to my own devices, forcing my brother to step in.

My worst fear has already happened, and I survived.

I'm here, aren't I? Whole and proud of myself for never giving up, even when it got too tempting.

And what did I do? I kept pushing, kept meeting new people, kept making friends and living my life. In fear, yes, but no more.

Not when I could lose something that means so much to me. That means everything.

James didn't make it to our date, and it upset me, but he had a good reason for it. He went to speak to his brother, someone he hadn't seen in over a decade, and things took a turn for the worse. I know he's telling the truth because his cheek is slightly purple and swollen under his stubble.

He said he was never going to leave me, and he didn't. He didn't.

It's not fair to punish him for something that was out of his control. Nobody is always going to do what I say, and that doesn't mean they don't love me.

But James doesn't love you. He doesn't feel what you feel.

Burying the unexpected pain piercing my heart, I say, "My mother told me he was killed in a car accident." I don't know what it says about me that I can recite the words back to him without feeling any real emotion. "He was a junkie. Always has been."

His thumb caresses the skin right under my eye, erasing the remains of my dry tears. "How does that make you feel?"

I shrug, unable to tell him because I don't even know it myself. "I got what I wanted, didn't I? I'm never going to see him again."

His eyes look into mine with so much intent, I'm scared of what he'll find there. "He wasn't a good man, and he wasn't a good father," he declares, his voice firm. "Maybe he didn't deserve to die for it, but it happened, and you don't have to feel one way or another right now. You need time to process this."

I give him a small nod, his words caving in. "I'll be okay."

That thumb rubs my cheek again. "I know you will, Maddie.

I know."

"My mother apologized," I blurt out, not really knowing why that nags me more than anything else. "I told her we could talk after... You know, in a few days."

"That's good." He gives me a small but reassuring smile that is so mesmerizing, I wish I could capture it forever. "Tell me what I can do for you."

My poor heart leaps. "You don't have to do anything. I..." I shake my head, still incredulous that this is real life. "Thank you for being here. You didn't have to, but I needed you, and I'm glad you're here."

The softness of his gaze, so contrasting to all his rough edges, ends me. "I need you more, Maddie. Trust me on that."

"I don't think fuck buddies do this for each other," I say before I can even realize what my words truly mean.

James's expression sobers up, making my stomach knot. "No, they don't."

The air around us sizzles with a kind of magnetic electricity I've never felt before.

I can see the shift in his eyes, feel it in my bones, and I know this is where the doubting ends and everything else begins.

The healing, the patience, the excitement. The rest of our lives.

His fingers brush the strands of hair away from my forehead with such care, I forget how to breathe. "It wasn't supposed to happen, was it? This thing between us."

Slowly, I shake my head. "It wasn't."

"But it did." His words sound final but not resigned. Scared, maybe. Cautious. "What do you want to do about it?"

He doesn't need to clarify what he means. I've asked myself that question for weeks, maybe months now, and Grace's words come back to me.

"I don't know if we're on the same page," I admit, my voice so quiet, I don't know how he even hears it. "How do you see yourself in five years?"

"With you."

My heart stops. "Doing what?"

When did his forehead come so close to mine? "I don't care, Maddie, as long as I'm by your side. I know you're twenty-one and have many things to figure out still, but so do I."

The way his demeanor shifts makes an alarm go off in my head. He moves back, a sigh parting his lips. "After what went down with my brother and my ex, I couldn't see myself opening up to anybody else. I didn't want to be in a relationship. And then you happened. You, with your strength and your fire, with that beautiful laughter that makes my heart soar even when I try to anchor it to the ground so it can't get hurt.

"Our age difference could be a problem, maybe, or maybe not. I don't know, Maddie, but I'm tired of fighting this when all I've wanted since I laid my eyes on you was to be in your life. Take care of you, love you like you deserve. And if that means quitting my job to move somewhere else with you, or have a bunch of kids, or adopt a dozen cats, then I'll do it with a smile on my face because it'll mean I get to have you."

I don't think my heart is working anymore.

My throat is dry, my pulse so strong in my neck I wonder if he can hear it.

Is he saying...?

"Shit." I've never seen him so visibly shaken up, but I'm too nervous myself to tease him about it. "This is definitely not the time nor place for this, but I don't want to pretend anymore, Maddie. It's tearing me apart."

My voice comes out as a whisper. "Wh-What do you mean?"

"It means I love you," he declares, inking his words permanently on my soul. "It means I've fallen in love with you, and I'm so scared to fuck this up, I can't think straight. That's what it means."

"James, you're not going to f—"

"I might. I already have, and I might do it again. There's no way to know for sure, but I can't keep lying to myself." He holds my face, and I drop my hands, wrapping them around his forearms. "You're my guiding light, Maddie. You have been since the moment I met you. You're admirable in so many ways, I would lose my breath if I dared list them one by one. Just the fact that you're here today, facing the demons of your past, tells me I have a lot to learn from you. I feel like the luckiest man on this planet when you smile at me, and I want to make you happy, to love and protect you for as long as you'll want me. If you even do."

The only reason I'm able to find my words right now is because he needs them.

And for him, as I now know for sure, I would do anything.

Even the one thing I'm most scared of.

"All my life, I've been terrified of being abandoned again," I admit out loud, maybe for the first time outside of a therapist's office. And it feels so damn good. "I wouldn't allow myself to fall in deep because I needed to protect my heart, but... My heart doesn't need protecting from you. You're worthy of it, James—of *all* of me. Don't ever doubt that again."

If there's one thing my brother made sure I learned growing up, it was to recognize when love is real. To know when the person in front of me wanted to cherish all my rights and wrongs, despite the adversity.

I didn't know what he meant at first, but then I sat back and watched. For seventeen years, I watched my brother love his wife in a way I had only read about in books. I watched him show her how much she meant to him, how easily he would give her the world if she only asked.

I may not have been born into the healthiest of families, but I've always had my guardian angel with me—my brother.

And it's because of the way Sammy and Grace loved me and taught me that healthy, everlasting love is real, that I'm able to look at James right now and see our future unfold before my eyes.

"My heart is yours," I whisper against his lips. "And I want your heart, James, all the dark corners that come with it. Will you give it to me?"

His charged gaze searches mine. "It's always been yours."

The moment our lips touch, every doubt I've ever had about us dissipates. The way he holds me like I'm the most precious thing he's ever had, how his tongue wraps around mine with a promise of forever, how my heart has never felt fuller.

I cling to him, and he holds me closer, deepening our bond.

I'm not innocent enough to think we won't ever face any challenges, but I know, I know we can get through anything together.

Because one way or another, we were meant to be.

"I love you," I whisper against his lips as I pull away briefly, and only because I needed him to hear it.

"I love you. So fucking much. I will love you every moment until the day I take my last breath and all over again in my next life." He squeezes my waist, hugging me impossibly closer, and I melt against him. "I brought you something."

It's the slight change in his voice that makes me arch an intrigued eyebrow. "Oh yeah?"

With an arm still locked around my middle, he pulls away just enough to reach his hand into the pocket of his suit jacket. "It's not... Ah, it's not perfect by any means." Why does he sound nervous? Now I'm intrigued. "It's quite ugly, actually."

"I'll love whatever you give me," I encourage him, hoping he can hear the truth in my words. "Come on, what is it? I'm dying over here."

The faint blush on his cheeks kills me.

And then the folded napkin he hands me kills me some more.

"You don't even have to pretend to like it," he says. "I made it on the plane on my way here, and I know it's shit."

I don't even question why he's handing me a paper napkin in the first place. "So dramatic."

But I'm the one who gets the air knocked out of my lungs when I see what's inside.

He...

Oh my God.

He drew a *mandala*. By hand. In the shape of a heart.

"James, this is..."

"The ugliest thing you've ever—"

I don't give him the chance to finish as I close the small distance between our lips again. He kisses me back without hesitation, bringing me closer until there's no space between us.

Now I understand why my perfectly mapped-out future didn't work out. Why it was never going to.

Everything happened the way it did so we could find each other, be here in this moment, and I will never regret a second of it for as long as I live.

"What the fuck?"

I jolt at the sound of that familiar voice, pushing James away as if he were on fire. He looks at me, confused, before we both turn to the man at the end of the hallway.

The man who looks one second away from killing both of us.

chapter 36

JAMES

Two seconds ago, I was kissing the love of my life, giving her my soul, and now her brother is about to put me six feet under.

Fun times.

I'm not a guy who can be easily intimidated. I have a hard body I haven't stopped building since my football days, and I can rock the hell out of a mean scowl. People don't mess with me because they know better.

The rules don't apply to this guy, though, and I get it.

If I had a little sister I'd been looking after for twenty-one years as if she were my own daughter and I caught an older man shoving his tongue down her throat, I would kill the motherfucker on sight.

I'm lucky I'm still breathing.

Her brother doesn't stop until he's right inside our bubble, now burst and gone. I'm only slightly taller than him, but we are equally as broad, and it's not like that matters much now. Not when he looks like he's going to rip me a new one in about two point five milliseconds.

"What the fuck is this?" he demands, but he doesn't look at his sister. Those dark eyes stay on me. "Who the fuck are *you*?"

"Sammy," Maddie starts, grabbing his arm, but he doesn't back down. It's like he can't even hear her, lost in the pool of rage blazing in his eyes.

I swallow back my nerves as I look at her brother—her

goddamn father in all the ways that count—and manage to find my voice again.

"Sir, I'm—"

I see the exact instant recognition dawns on him, his furious gaze widening just enough to tell me I'm as good as dead.

"You're her fucking physical therapist," he spits out, getting in my face. I don't take a step back. I just let him go at me, because maybe I deserve it after all. "You took advantage of her vulnerability, you fucker? You thought it would be fun to mess around with one of your patients, huh? A twenty-one-year-old girl, for fuck's sake. How old are you?"

"Sammy, stop!" Tears fall down Maddie's soft face, so happy and full of light only a moment ago, and I shut my eyes. If I see her fall apart now, I don't think I will be able to grasp the weak reins I have on my self-control. "It's not what you think. Nothing happened while he was my doctor. I started it, Sammy. *I* did."

"I don't give a fuck who started it. He knew exactly what he was doing, and he didn't stop it," he growls in my face. "I asked you a question, *Doctor.*"

All my doubts and insecurities come crashing down at once with every word that comes out of his mouth.

Because he's right.

What was I thinking, going after a younger woman who was entrusted to my professional care?

I feel sick to my stomach for all of two seconds before I will my eyes open, but instead of coming face-to-face with the raging beast in front of me, they find Maddie's gaze—and I remember.

I'm not sick. I'm not a monster. I've never been.

I'm nothing more than a man who fell in love despite fighting against it. A man who looked beyond his own insecurities and took a leap of faith, all in the name of loving the incredible woman in front of him exactly how she deserves.

And I'm not going to stand here and let her brother, or

anyone else, belittle my feelings for Maddie or try to turn them into something dirty.

She's my light, my world, my everything, and I'm tired of feeling bad about it.

We don't have control over who we fall in love with. The thought is terrifying, but I'm so damn glad it was her.

"Sir," I start again, my voice sounding far steadier than I feel inside. "I would like to speak to you."

"Then talk," he barks.

My gaze slides to Maddie, understanding passing between us. She tugs at her brother's sleeve. "Are Grace and Lila outside?" she asks, and he nods. "I'll go find them."

"The service is about to start."

"I don't care."

She looks at me one last time over her shoulder, and the tiny smile she sends my way is enough to give me all the strength I need to face what is surely going to be one of the hardest but most important conversations of my life.

A country song I don't recognize starts playing from one of the rooms just as Maddie closes the door at the end of the hallway, leaving her brother and me completely alone.

And all right, I may be a tiny bit scared of the venomous words that could come out of his mouth now that we don't have an audience.

Instead of lashing out at me, though, he runs a hand down his tired face and sighs like this whole thing is nothing more than a big inconvenience for him.

"My name is James Simmons," I start, ignoring the way my heart starts hammering inside my rib cage. "I'm thirty-one, and I'm a physical therapist at the clinic Maddie went to for her recovery. I was her doctor, but like she said, nothing happened between us while she was my patient. After that, I transferred her checkups to one of my colleagues so as not to compromise her health. I wouldn't be here today if my feelings for her weren't real, sir. I only have her best interests at heart."

The fire is back in his eyes, ready to burn me alive, but I refuse to let him do it.

"You're thirty-one. What business do you have trying to get with a twenty-one-year-old? Is this some kind of sick joke?"

"My feelings for your sister aren't a joke." My voice comes out firmer, a lot harsher than expected, and his eyebrows rise in response. I don't give him a chance to give me shit for it. "We're both very aware of our age difference, and we aren't planning to ignore it. We've discussed it, have come to an agreement, and we'll go slowly. At her pace—whatever she needs, I will respect it and support her.

"With all due respect, Maddie is capable enough to make her own decisions and stand by them. I will never hurt her or put her in harm's way. Over my dead fucking body will anyone ever hurt her again. I tried to fight it. I thought it was wrong to feel all these things for her at first, but..."

My mind is spiraling, my palms are sweaty, and I can't decipher the look in his eyes right now.

He could be a second away from either sucker-punching me or giving me a hug.

I'm too scared to find out.

Fuck it.

"I know what you mean to her. I know she loves and trusts you above anyone else, and I don't want to hide any part of us from you. This... This relationship started months ago, and neither of us dared to put a label on it. We were aware of our age difference, and we wanted to make sure this was what we wanted. But weeks have gone by, and..."

If that look he's giving me is any indication, I'm a dead man walking.

"She's it for me. We've found something special in each other, a home we never thought we would find in another person, and I'm sorry, sir, but I won't give her up unless she wants me to. She's too important to me. She's my everything."

Now I can die happily, having confessed every truth in my heart to the most important person in Maddie's life.

A heavy weight leaves my shoulders, and my heart rate goes back to normal. Sort of.

But the forty-something-year-old man in front of me, with the mean scowl and impressive tattoos all over his neck and hands, doesn't kill me on the spot. Instead, he asks me one simple question.

"Do you love my sister?"

My voice doesn't waver. I don't hesitate. "Yes. With everything that I am. More than life itself."

Something in his gaze softens before he sobers up again. I mean—he doesn't even know me. I can understand the urge to keep her away from harm and heartbreak, because I feel the same.

"Do you promise to take care of her, be faithful to her, and love her in the way she deserves?" he asks, taking me by surprise. I genuinely thought he was still going to deck me.

"Yes. Forever."

His eyes, the exact shade as Maddie's, scan me up from head to toe.

"I don't know you."

I gulp, standing very still, as he speaks.

"I don't know what kind of man you are. But I know this, James—if you ever hurt my sister in any way, shape, or form... I don't care who or where you are, because I'll find you, I'll fucking end you, and I'll make it look like an accident. Am I making myself clear?"

I can only nod and hope he doesn't change his mind and decide to go through with his threat today.

He lets out another deep breath, some of the pent-up tension leaving his body. "If my sister chooses you, then I have nothing to say about it."

Holy shit. He could've started with that.

After scanning me up and down once more, he adds, "I trust her judgment—we raised her well, after all. And I guess she could've done a lot worse than a physical therapist who flew all the way here to make sure she's okay on one of the most difficult days of her life."

I don't think I've ever been so relieved to end a conversation.

You're living one more day, buddy.

"I know she hasn't had it easy," I add for some reason, as if I still wasn't at risk of getting beaten up. But I need him to hear this. "I don't know how much she's told you, and I don't want to intrude, but I think you should know I was with her when her father approached her."

He raises a questioning eyebrow. "You're that guy?" he asks. "The one who took a photo of his car and license plate?"

"Yes. I was picking her up from work and—"

"You picked her up from Monica's Pub? Why?"

I frown. "Because she gets out when it's late and dark, and I want to make sure she gets home safely."

He nods, and something strange happens. For the first time since he walked in, he doesn't look ready to pounce. He almost looks...approachable.

"That was a good call. The license plate thing." His gaze slides to one of the closed doors behind me. "Doesn't matter much now that the fucker is dead."

His words are harsh, but I can't find it in me to feel sympathy for Maddie's dad. Not when he didn't grace my girl with a single ounce of it.

"I guess it doesn't," I mutter.

Silence falls over us. It's not uncomfortable, but it's not exactly welcoming either. He breaks it with the last words I expected after so much tension.

"I'm sorry I yelled at you earlier." I can see the honesty behind his eyes. Even a hint of regret. "Maddie never said anything about you, so it caught me off guard. I'm protective of her. More than I should be, probably."

"I get it." I give him a curt nod. "We're good." I think. I hope.

"This doesn't mean I like you," he warns, but the easiness in his eyes tells a different story. Much like his sister, he can't hide anything in them. He holds out his hand, and I give it a firm shake. "I'm still keeping you under surveillance."

"I understand."

"And please, cut that sir crap. It makes me feel old as shit," he says next, throwing me for a loop even more when the corners of his mouth tilt up. Just barely, but it's there. "Maddie calls me Sammy, but she's the only one. I go by Cal."

"Cal. Okay. Got it." And why the fuck am I nervous now? "Should we go outside?"

He only nods, and together we swallow the distance between the hallway and the door. With his hand on the handle, he looks at me over his shoulder and asks, "How many times have you picked her up from work?"

I try to remember. "Every time she has a night shift pretty much since I've known her. I try to pick her up from her teaching job, too, but sometimes she gets out before I do."

I don't know what kind of answer I expected, but it wasn't a genuine smile. An *approving* smile.

Without a word, he pushes the door open, and I spot her immediately. Standing in the sunlight with a blond woman and a little girl who looks like a carbon-copy of her, Maddie looks absolutely breathtaking in her black dress and long coat, one I itch to wrap tighter around her because it's freezing out here.

The second Cal and I step out in the open, her head turns, and the expression on her face almost makes me laugh. She looks a second away from throwing up.

"You're alive" is the first thing she says as we get closer.

At that, I can't help but smirk. "Seems like it."

She slides her cautious eyes to her brother. "And you don't look like you are on the verge of a nervous breakdown anymore," she observes. Her gaze pinballs between us. "Have you finally decided to behave like adults?"

Her brother wraps an arm around her shoulders, pulling her against him and kissing the top of her head. "As long as you're happy, princess, I'll be as well. That's all I've wanted for you."

She hums. "I'm not sure I buy it."

"How about all five of us go grab some lunch? Would you be more inclined to buy it, then?" Cal suggests.

Her eyes widen in excitement and relief just as my heart somersaults. "Really?" She turns to me. "Really?"

I nod, an easy smile forming on my lips. "I'd love to."

"Who are you? You're very tall." The little blond girl who I assume is Maddie's niece stares up at me with a frown that looks so much like her father's, it's both terrifying and amusing. "Are you Maddsy's boyfriend?"

"Lila!" the blond woman says. "Don't be rude." She looks at me, a pleading look in her eyes. "I'm so sorry. I'm Grace—Maddie's sister-in-law."

"Nice to meet you." I give her a warm smile. There's a hint of hidden amusement dancing in her eyes, and I wonder if Maddie's told her about us. I go back to the girl in front of me, so small she barely reaches my belly button. "You are Lila, right?"

"Yes. I asked you a question."

Another little firecracker, huh? I like her already.

Maddie, still wrapped in her brother's embrace, only gives me one of her beautiful smiles that lights me up from the inside. And even though we haven't explicitly talked about our relationship status, one look between us is enough to know that what we have is forever.

And it starts here.

"Yes, Lila. I'm Maddie's boyfriend—James," I declare so proudly I swear my heart combusts. "It's really nice to meet you."

And then it combusts a little more when her niece gives me the brightest of smiles. "Do you have games on your phone?" she asks, and I nod. She turns to her aunt. "You can keep him."

That dissipates the remains of the tension between us as we all laugh.

And when I catch Maddie's next words, a low whisper, all the darkness in my heart goes away at once.

"I was already going to."

chapter 37

MADDIE

Ice blankets the streets of Norcastle as the first week of December rolls around.

When I woke up this morning with a big hand splayed against the bare skin of my stomach and a warm body pressed to my back, I instantly knew what day it was. But, unlike last time, my heart doesn't feel heavy and my brain doesn't go down yet another self-pity spiral.

The man behind me is part of the reason why, but mostly it's my own growth that has led me here.

Today is the last day to send my application for the new open audition to The Norcastle Ballet, and I'm not even going to open my laptop. My body isn't ready to go back, and my heart has finally accepted the harsh truth.

The Norcastle Ballet isn't for me.

Call it a hunch, a conscious decision, or both at once. It doesn't matter.

The reality is that the dream I had worked so hard for all my life doesn't appeal to me anymore, and it's okay. My future isn't set in stone, and I refuse to pretend it is for the sake of stability.

The fact that I'm not going to work there doesn't mean I failed. It doesn't mean I drive people away or ruin things for myself—it only means my goals change as I grow, and there's nothing wrong with that.

I'm building a future for myself and leaning on people I

choose and who choose me back. And if the day comes when they don't want to choose me anymore... Well, that has nothing to do with me. Unless I do something truly horrible, it's not my fault if someone walks away. People can make their own decisions, and sometimes those decisions include leaving me behind.

That doesn't mean I'm a bad person, friend, daughter, sister, or girlfriend. It just means I'm not part of their journey anymore, and they aren't part of mine, and we can all move on and thrive.

My new therapist, a lovely woman named Kendra, tells me as much.

I was hesitant to go back to therapy, but after telling Sammy and Grace about everything that went down with my former therapist years ago, my sister-in-law asked her own therapist for referrals in Norcastle.

I hope that witch enjoys the complaint I filed two weeks ago.

Throughout the years, I felt an unreasonable need to prove to my brother that he didn't waste his time, that he didn't make a mistake when he took me in. Because if I took my passion and made it to the top, that would make me more worthy in his eyes.

How sad is that? How *insane*?

Somewhere along the way, I lost sight of what is truly meaningful to me—always doing my best and being able to dedicate my life to this craft. And I did it.

I did it, and I couldn't see it.

I was so blinded by a dream that didn't belong to me. Not for the right reasons.

Weeks of working as a ballet instructor have taught me patience, not only with kids and young girls, but also with myself. And I vow to cherish the opportunity to be able to make ballet my livelihood and make kids fall in love with it just as much as I have, while making sure they don't push themselves too hard.

And if I pair that sweet realization with the love the man behind me shows me every single day, deeply and unconditionally,

I'd say I don't have it too bad.

My life is looking pretty amazing, in fact.

James stirs behind me, his lips dropping to my shoulder as he kisses it. "Morning, baby."

God, his morning voice. Someone put me out of this misery.

"You woke up before your alarm again," I point out, noting how he still has nearly an hour to spare before he needs to leave for the clinic.

He buries his face in my neck, his stubble tickling me the way he knows makes me shriek.

"Stop," I pant, out of breath as he attacks my sensitive skin.

"Or..." He plants a kiss right behind my ear, and I shiver. "I could tickle you somewhere else."

I'm not saying no to that.

James's huge body disappears under the covers, dropping kisses on my skin as he goes. He stops at the hem of my pajama pants, his lips grazing my lower stomach as he pulls my clothes off slowly, so painfully slowly I find myself whimpering his name before he even does anything.

"Perfect," he murmurs against my skin. Then he stops. "I never asked you. What does your tattoo mean?"

My back arches as he plants open-mouthed kisses over the inked butterfly. "It's a reminder that I'm meant to fly away. Find my own path."

His kisses become tender, shorter.

"That I'm meant to transform the pain of my past into hope for the future. A symbol of rebirth."

"And you did," he whispers. "All of it. Because you're amazing, and I love you so damn much."

"I love you too." My fingers tangle in his hair, urging him down. "But please."

He only chuckles. "So impatient."

I groan. "I wouldn't be if you weren't such a tease."

"But I love teasing my girl," he purrs, kissing the inside of my thigh.

"James..." I squirm. "I swear—"

"Shh... I've got you."

When the tip of his tongue parts my wet folds, I shatter. My back arches as I pull him closer, needing to feel his tongue in the deepest part of me.

He grabs my hips, securing me into place as he feasts. The roughness of his stubble and the way he sucks my clit into his mouth, licks my folds, has me over the edge in minutes.

"Mm..." His tongue pierces my entrance as I pulse around him, moaning and begging him for a release I know he won't give me. "So fucking sweet. I can't wait to fill you up. Do you want that, baby? Do you need my cock in this tight pussy right now?"

"Yes," I pant. "God, yes."

"Yeah?" he teases.

"I need your cock inside me. *Shit*," I whimper as he continues to eat me out. "I want it so bad."

James throws back the covers until he's kneeling above me, looking more imposing than ever before. He doesn't even shove his underwear all the way down as he pushes inside me, stretching my walls with his hard girth.

"Fucking hell," he curses under his breath, taking me rough and fast like all he wants is to ruin me.

He sits back in bed, pulling my legs around his torso. From this angle, he hits so deep, I scream. My hand finds my clit, and I finger myself as he watches his cock slide in and out of me.

"There's my pretty girl," he coos. "You take my cock so well. It stretches you nice and good, doesn't it? Fuck, yes. Keep touching yourself like that."

An intense wave of pleasure overcomes me, and I know I won't last long. James knows it, just as he always does, and moves back on top of me until his lips are hovering over mine.

"I love you," he whispers, the softness of his voice contrasting with his punishing thrusts. "I love you so much, Maddie. More than anything. More than life itself."

His words throw me over the edge, but I don't want to fall without telling him, "I love you too. I love you. I love you."

James presses his forehead against mine, his eyes never leaving mine as I fall, and he falls right behind me.

Our kiss is passionate and slow, our tongues intertwining as he brings me closer. He's inside me, around me, in me, and I don't think I could ever feel more loved if I tried.

After he takes me into the shower and makes sure I'm thoroughly clean, he makes us a quick coffee and toast as I cuddle our fur babies on the couch.

He brings it over with an extra kiss to my forehead, and we eat on the couch, enjoying the sunrise above the city.

"What time are you meeting your mom today?" he asks over the rim of his steaming mug.

"Lunchtime," I say, munching on a bite of buttery toast.

"Are you nervous?"

I shrug. "Not really." Not anymore. When I finally texted her last week, she was eager to meet me, which I'm going to take as a good sign. Sammy does too. "I was way more nervous about meeting your parents."

He snorts. "Please. They loved you," he says with a genuine smile as I recall our lunch together last weekend. "My mom can't wait for the holidays so she can bake you all the cakes in the book."

James's parents couldn't be sweeter, which is quite funny, given how grumpy their son is. They didn't bat an eyelid at me being so young, and they sounded interested in my ballet career, so the prospect of seeing them over the winter holidays isn't as daunting as I imagined it would be.

His mother assured us that his brother, Andrew, wouldn't be there. Apparently, he lost his job after he punched James in the middle of his office—who does that?—and he moved away from Norcastle.

"Good fucking riddance," James had muttered under his breath, and I couldn't agree more.

His wedding to Alexandra has been called off, too, according to his parents, and they have no idea if they're still together or if she's still in the city.

And honestly, we couldn't give less of a crap.

Just like I suspected, Beth and Kyle love James. Just yesterday I had to endure hours of their rants about how they totally saw it coming and how amazing we looked as a couple. And when Kyle asked what James was like in bed, I might have pinched his nipple.

The day after we flew to Norcastle from the funeral, he spoke to management at the rehabilitation clinic about dating a former patient. He was ready to change jobs if he needed to, but luckily, we were told personal relationships between doctors and former patients were allowed as long as I never became his patient again. Since I'm not planning on injuring myself again—I've learned my lesson—it works for us.

James's parents and my family are the only people whose opinions truly matter, and all of them approve of our relationship.

Well, Sammy is still getting there, but I know he'll come around.

Lila begs me daily to bring James to our house for the holidays because she thinks he's so cool, so there's that. After we left the funeral home all those weeks ago and had lunch together, he let her play some popular games on his phone. I think that may be the sole reason my brother has warmed up to him, but hey, I'll take it for now.

"I'll be back before you are." I kiss him on his stubbled cheek. "And I'm making lasagna for dinner."

"I'm not above getting on my knees and begging you for it," he says, and I know he's serious. What can I say? I make a mean beef lasagna.

"I'll have you begging later, but for a whole different reason," I tease, which earns me a smack on the butt as I stand up to leave my mug in the sink.

We're not living together—not yet—but sometimes it feels like it. We sleep together every night, usually at his place because of Shadow and Mist, but I don't mind it at all. His place feels like a home to me, even if I still love my apartment and spend time there as often as I want.

He's hinted several times that I'm paying rent for a place I'm only half using, and while he's kind of right, we both agree that we don't want to rush into anything. We know we're in it for the long run, so there's no reason to hurry when we have forever.

Plus, I still need to have a little more independence in my finances before making such a big decision. Our age difference is something we actively *don't* ignore, and it's obvious that James has more financial stability than I do. So until I feel comfortable in that department, we've both agreed it would be better if we kept separate homes.

It feels right to live like this for now, so why should we change it?

He drops me off with a kiss at my apartment before he leaves for the clinic, and while I get ready for work and think about the audition I missed and the mother I'm going to give a second chance to today, I realize something.

For the first time in twenty-one years, I feel like I'm exactly who and where I'm supposed to be.

***

I get a sense of *déjà vu* as I wait for my mother in Monica's Pub, but nostalgia hits me the hardest.

My boss at the dance school was so happy with my performance, she decided to give me more shifts, which meant my days of working as a waitress had to come to an end. It would've been exhausting to juggle both jobs.

Still, I miss this place and the chosen family I found here. As Monica comes up to me with a big smile and asks me about my new job, I realize I'm never going to lose what this bar has gifted me.

Some things stay forever, and this is one of them.

"Maddie." My mother's voice is gentle as she takes a seat in front of me. She even spares Monica a greeting and a genuine smile, and I almost don't recognize the woman in front of me.

Her skin has a healthy glow to it, and she moves with more confidence now than I ever remembered her having. It's hard to reconcile this new person with the memory of the careless and unkempt parent she was while I still lived with her.

"How are you, dear?" she asks, her undivided attention on me. "You look beautiful. Did you do something to your hair? It looks great on you."

She noticed? She can tell the difference?

"I straightened it." Which I never do. I prefer it when my soft waves run wild, but I wanted to put some effort into my appearance today. For some reason. "You look good as well."

She smiles, and it's only now that I notice how much her smile looks like mine.

I'm not bothered by this realization. Not one bit.

"Thank you. I've been happy."

Happiness. That's what it is. That's the secret.

As we wait for our orders, she tells me about how good Dave is to her and how he's encouraged her to go back to school. "It's just a silly diploma." She waves it off as if it weren't the hugest of accomplishments.

"Are you kidding me?" I gape, my shock quickly turning into a proud smile. "That's amazing! What are you studying?"

Is that a blush on her cheeks? "I don't know if it'll ever get me any job—I'm not getting any younger, after all—but it's a certificate for working as a receptionist."

"Oh my God, Mom, that is incredible," I beam. "Do you like it? How are classes going?"

She tells me she's just enrolled in a local community college, so she's still adjusting to being a student again. When she mentions the teachers are really supportive and she's making more friends her age than she ever expected, I almost burst into tears.

My mother was able to finish high school by some kind of miracle, since she had Sammy when she was sixteen. Life hasn't been kind to her, which meant we also struggled growing up.

My brother was able to make a name for himself when a family friend who saw his drawing skills took him under her wing and taught him all about tattooing. If my brother hadn't stepped up, I wouldn't have this good, happy life, but I don't blame my mother anymore.

For better or for worse, she's the reason I'm the person I am today.

And I love this new Maddie with all my soul.

"I'm proud of you, Mom. I'm sure things will look up for you from here on out."

She gives me a small but hopeful smile, as if she were too scared to think she deserves a little bit of luck. "I hope so, Maddie. I really hope so."

As I look at the almost unrecognizable woman in front of me, I realize she did all she could. Consumed by an addiction that started long before I was born, she couldn't give me everything I deserved, but she gave me love. I remember that much.

It wasn't enough, but at least it was something. And at least that love has always been genuine.

She used to pepper my cheeks with kisses until my giggles filled the room, make me my favorite foods when I was upset, and work hard to make sure she kept a roof over my head.

But after I moved in with Sammy and Grace, we progressively lost contact as the years went by, and I've always wondered why.

It's time I get the answers I've been craving for seventeen years.

"Mom," I start, unsure how she's going to take the shift in conversation. We've only talked about positive, happy things until now, but she's the one who wanted to have an honest conversation. So here we go. "Why..." I clear my throat. "Why didn't you visit more when I was living with Sammy?"

I expect her to close off, to stiffen. Instead, her eyes water, and it's a hundred times worse. My hand moves on instinct as it covers hers.

"I'm sorry I caused you so much pain, Maddie."

I don't like how weak her voice sounds. Months ago, I would've rolled my eyes and thought she was playing the victim, but my heart holds no space for bitterness anymore. For the people who truly deserve it, it only holds compassion.

"I was scared to disappoint you," she sniffs. "Your brother took such good care of you. He always has. That's why... That's why I held that stupid, unfair grudge against him. He's such a natural and gave you all the things I never could, and... God. It sounds so wrong."

I squeeze her hand. "I'm not here to judge you. I only want to understand."

She blinks, shocked. "Really?"

"Yes." I nod, more convinced than I've ever been before. "I used to resent you for walking away, for not being a present mother, but...I think I understand where it came from. It doesn't make it okay, but I don't want to live in the past anymore."

Her gaze lowers to our intertwined hands. "You've always been such selfless souls, your brother and you. So strong, so full of love to give. I don't deserve you."

"Yes, you do," I tell her firmly. "Please, Mom, stop punishing yourself for this."

She chuckles, but it's humorless. "It's going to take a while."

"We have time," I assure her. When she meets my eyes, unsure, I nod. "But I want you to reach out to Sammy and apologize to him too. He loves you, Mom. So much, and he doesn't deserve this. You're missing out on an incredible granddaughter too."

"I see her sometimes." This time, her smile is genuine. "It's always Grace who comes with her, though. I've always liked her, you know? She's so good to my children, always has been. She's a great mother to Lila, the kind of mother I would've loved to be for you. But..."

"But you want your son back," I finish for her.

She nods.

"Did you talk to him at the...at the funeral?"

I'm still not used to the idea that my father is dead. He's not present, just like he's never been...but in a different way.

Kendra—my new therapist—says we still have a long way to go until I learn to live with what he did and didn't do, as well as how his death makes me feel, but we're getting there. I'm doing well.

My mom shakes her head. "I went to find him, but I couldn't...I wasn't brave enough to speak to him then."

"You can still salvage the relationship. I know it's scary, but trust me when I say that your absence hurts him. He wants his mom back, and so do I."

She rubs furiously at her eyes, and she leaps from her seat so she's right next to me, hugging me so close to her it takes me right back to my childhood. "Thank you, Maddie. Thank you," she whispers. "I love you so much, dear. I will never forgive myself for hurting you, but I promise to be the mother you've always deserved from now on. If you'll accept me."

Tears fall from my own eyes, and I do nothing to stop them. I'm not ashamed to cry for someone who deserves my sympathy.

It might take a while to build this relationship back up from the ground, but it's not impossible because I don't want it to be.

"I want you in my life, Mom," I tell her, holding her close. "Sammy does too. We love you, and I forgive you. I want to start anew. Do you?"

"Yes. So much." She pulls away, wiping my tears away like she would do when I was a child. "I'm proud of the selfless, loving, giving woman you have become, and I couldn't be prouder to be your mother. Don't ever forget that."

I won't. For as long as I live, I won't.

My mother might not have been dealt a fair hand in the past, but her luck changes now. Our future changes now. And I couldn't be happier I decided to stay by her side to witness it.

***

The moon is already shining above the Norcastle skyscrapers by the time James comes back. He texted me earlier that Graham wanted to grab a drink and watch the hockey game, and I insisted that he spend time with his friend. He still feels bad about leaving me alone at home, but frankly, I'm in my element cooking in his kitchen as Shadow and Mist make sure I leave no ingredients out.

"Maddie?" he calls out as he closes the front door behind him. He appears in the kitchen a moment later, wearing the most handsome of smiles. "It smells good in here."

I beam. "Dinner is ready. I was just keeping it in the oven so it wouldn't get cold."

"Mm." He wraps his arms around my waist and presses our foreheads together. "I missed you. Did you have a good day with your mom?"

Not wanting to break our hug, I place my head on his chest and tell him about second chances and forgiveness, all while he sways us softly in the middle of the kitchen to the rhythm of some silent tune.

He grounds me, calms me, and I know without a doubt now that this is where I'm meant to be. He's the one I was always meant to find, the one I was meant to share this journey of healing with.

"I have something to tell you," I say, my voice firm but shy all at once.

His fingers tangle in my hair as he massages my scalp in the way that always gives me the best kind of tingles. "Do tell."

I draw back as I work a nervous swallow, still in his embrace. "I think I know what I want to do with my life."

His eyebrows shoot up in surprise, a small smile forming on his lips. "Oh, yeah?"

"It's like, a *really* long-term thing, but I'm excited about it."

He presses his forehead against mine, and I don't imagine the pride in his voice as he says, "Tell me about your new dream, baby."

So I do.

I tell him how I don't regret, not for one second, everything I went through to try to get into The Norcastle Ballet, because that path led me to him and this new me.

I tell him how Suzanne Allard's comment made me realize something I didn't even know I had within myself and how my own journey inspired me to be there for others.

"I'm really happy teaching at the studio right now, but I'd love to open my own one day," I confess out loud for the first time, and it doesn't sound silly or far-fetched.

James is looking at me like I've finally figured out an answer he's known for a while.

"I want to offer inspiration to young girls, to teach them to cherish their bodies and embrace the journey, no matter where it takes them."

"That's a beautiful dream, my love."

My love.

It's the first time he's called me that, and my heart reacts accordingly.

God, I love him so much.

"All I want is to prevent other dancers from going through the same thing I did. And I'm not talking about the injury—I'm talking about their own dreams. That no matter what they want to do in the dance industry—teaching others, joining a company, or just doing it for fun—it will be important. That it will be enough," I tell him. "I can't change what happened in my past, but maybe I could change somebody's future."

"That's all that matters," he says, pressing our lips together. "You're a gift to this world, Maddie. I'm so goddamn lucky I'll get to be with you every step of the way, holding your hand. I'm sure you'll make a difference. You already did with me."

He smiles, a smile so soft and full of love, I almost can't believe this incredible man is all mine.

I wrap my arms around his torso again, hugging him against me. "Ugh," I groan, which makes him chuckle. "I didn't think I could possibly love you more."

But I was wrong.

So wrong.

epilogue

MADDIE

Life has a funny way of giving you exactly what your soul needs, even if it's not what your heart initially wanted.

Ten years ago, I pushed myself too hard to pass an audition I thought would lead me to a dream I never wanted for the right reasons.

Ten years ago, life took my father away and gave me a better version of the mother I never had.

And ten years ago, fate put me in the professional care of some sexy man called Dr. Simmons, and I've chosen to put up with (and love) the stick up his ass ever since.

It's important that I remember our love every day, especially at times like this.

"I promise I only looked away for one second. Two, tops," the man in question argues, hands up in the air and everything. The sight of this six-foot-five Greek god being terrified of his bedridden wife would amuse me if I wasn't in so much damn discomfort.

I give him one of my *I don't believe a word you're saying* looks and slide my gaze to the little culprit. "What about you?" I ask as I fight back a grin. He really is a sight to behold. "You don't have anything to say about this?"

Our three-year-old son, Dylan, looks down at his ruined T-shirt and pouts. *That pout.* "I'm sorry, Mommy. The bowl fell from my hands."

James and I exchange a look—he wants to laugh as hard as I

do, if not more. Neither of us can resist The Pout, and Dylan sure knows how to use it to his advantage.

I hold out my hand, and my little man is quick to grab it and hug my arm in the process. "You angry with me, Mommy?"

"I'm angrier with your daddy, if I'm being honest." I mock-glare at my husband, who holds his hands up again.

"I only looked away for a second," he insists. "Shadow and Mist were chasing each other, and I was making sure they didn't break anything."

"Mm." I run a hand through Dylan's messy brown curls and kiss the top of his head. "It's okay. Just tell Daddy to give you more eggs and flour, okay? And change your T-shirt."

"I was just making Gramma's cake recipe." He pouts again, and I melt. "Lila said she liked it last time. I ruined it."

This time, I'm the one who pouts at James. He pouts right back.

I don't know what we've done to deserve such a sweet little angel, but we couldn't be more grateful. He might not eat his veggies just yet, but he's funny and selfless, and that's all we could ask for.

"You didn't ruin it, buddy," James assures him. He sits on our bedroom floor by my side of the bed and rubs Dylan's back. "We have more ingredients and all afternoon to make the cake. Don't worry about it. I'll help you with it as many times as you need."

That seems to work for him. "Lila coming tomorrow still?"

"Of course she is," I tell him, booping his cute little nose. "So will your Auntie Gracie and Uncle Sammy, as well as Gramma, Granny, and Pops. They wouldn't miss your birthday for the world."

His actual birthday was a month ago, but our family couldn't get together until now. Even my mother is coming, and I think she's bringing Dave along. I'll have to check the details with her later.

Instead of answering, Dylan lets go of my arm and presses his cheek against my swollen stomach, something he's been doing since we broke the news that he was going to be a big brother. It's safe to say he's taking the role very seriously.

"Can she sing happy birthday in your belly?" he asks, so full of innocence and love for his unborn little sister, I want to bawl my eyes out.

"I don't think so, but she will sing for you at the top of her lungs next year when she's here," I tell him.

That makes him smile. "Yes! I want to see her face now. Do you want to see her face now, Daddy?"

James's face softens at the mention of our daughter, something he's been doing often since we found out we were having a little girl. I've already caught him talking to my brother a few times about what it's like to raise girls and how Sammy got over Lila and me getting into relationships, so we're definitely in for an intense ride.

If James is overprotective of our family now, I can only imagine how much worse he's going to get when she's here.

Gah. I love him so much.

"I would do anything to see her face now, buddy," he says, a proud smile on his face as he looks at our son, eyes full of raw adoration. "Come on. Let's get you cleaned up, and we'll go back to the cake. Sound good?"

Dylan cheers and gives my belly a loud kiss before taking his eggs-and-flour-stained T-shirt off and running away to his bedroom, all while squealing very loudly.

Once he's gone, we finally crack up.

"Fuck, it's so hard to hold in the laughter sometimes," James whispers, shaking his head with amusement as he stands up. "He's so funny."

"He gets it from his mommy," I tease.

"Yeah, you're both brats."

"But you love us."

"More than anything in the world." Just like his son, he rests his cheek against my belly and holds my hand. "How are you feeling, love?"

"My lower back is killing me," I admit with a small groan. "I can't wait to push this baby out and go back to the studio."

James gives me an understanding smile. It was hard leaving my girls at the ballet studio a couple of weeks ago, but my doctor recommended I rest as much as I can until she's born, so that's what I'm focusing on.

I love having my own studio and teaching aspiring dancers, but my girl is my priority. My family comes first. Always.

"You're doing amazing," he assures me, and it's crazy how his sweet words always make me want to cry lately. Stupid hormones. "Lila called earlier, by the way. She asked if she could bring her boyfriend along to introduce him to us, and I said yes."

"God, finally," I groan. "I've been hearing about this mysterious Oliver for months now. I think Sammy's threatened him once or twice already. I'm not sure he's a fan."

He chuckles. "And what does Grace think?"

"Oh, she likes him." I wave him off. "They met in college, and apparently Grace and Sammy caught them holding hands or something when they went to visit her as a surprise. My brother almost had a stroke."

I smile at the memory of Lila freaking out over the phone as she told me, and I quote, "The most mortifying moment of my entire existence, Maddsy. Please kill me."

"I can't wait to make fun of her some more," I conclude.

"You're evil." My husband—*my husband*—kisses my belly and gets up. Five years have gone by, and I'm still not used to calling him that. "I'm going to check on Dylan. Do you need anything?"

"For you to wrap it up next time," I joke. Kinda.

At least he laughs. "I don't know about that."

"James!" I whisper-shout, reaching out to slap his arm as he laughs like the little shit he is.

When I try to sit up in bed, something weird happens.

A gush of water comes out of my lower area, and I know it's not pee because I still have an ounce of control over my crazy pregnant body.

My eyes widen in realization, and James's face loses all color as he, too, spots my water breaking right here, right now. Just like that.

"Well." My voice sounds way calmer than I expected it would, given the situation. "This is kind of your fault, you know? You and Dylan told her you wanted to see her face, and she's clearly eager to meet her daddy and older brother too."

James opens and closes his mouth several times, like a fish out of water, but nothing comes out.

"I..." he starts, blinking his shock away. "She's coming? We're going to hold our little girl today?"

His voice is all love and devotion, and I smile despite the contraction hitting my abdomen and back. "If we're lucky. But I think she wants her daddy to hold her as soon as possible because she's literally killing me right now."

"Right, right." He snaps out of it, rushing to the other side of our bedroom where we keep my hospital bag. "Dylan!"

"Yes, Daddy?" he calls out from his bedroom.

"Your sister is coming!" His words are met with the loudest scream I've ever heard. "You're going to stay with Uncle Graham and Aunt Sarah today, okay? Only until Uncle Sammy and Auntie Gracie get here tomorrow."

Our son materializes in our room, a little finger pointed at me. "Mommy! You peed the bed!"

Thankfully he's put on a clean T-shirt, so James scoops him up and, with his other hand, helps me out of bed.

"Mommy didn't pee on the bed, buddy. That water means

your baby sister is ready to meet you. We're going to the hospital, and Uncle Graham will pick you up from there, okay?"

He squeals in delight as if I wasn't dying. *Ugh.* I love them with all I've got.

And after our precious Alice is born six hours later and she's asleep in her father's arms as I rest, I know for sure this is the life I was always meant to live.

There's no other place I would rather be, no man I would ever want to build a family with.

I don't regret my past, the things I've said and done, because every significant and seemingly insignificant decision led me to the happiest, fullest version of myself.

Life is a constant battle of choices, and you won't know if you've made the right one until you dare to take a leap of faith.

This was mine.

THE END

acknowledgements

I couldn't keep Maddie's book in the drafts. I have never, ever, felt such a strong desire to write someone's story, to provide closure to both my characters and my readers.

Despite being a child in *The Brightest Light of Sunshine,* Maddie's character had a very unexpected yet powerful impact on me. I kept wondering, "How is all this chaos and unfairness going to affect her when she grows up?" Then I realized I was the author (surprise!) and could actually answer that question and many more.

I hope *The Darkest Corner of the Heart* gave you exactly that—an answer.

And if you still have more questions...Well, let's just say this won't be the last time you'll see these characters.

To my readers. Thank you for allowing me to do this for a living. Thank you for hyping me up behind the scenes, for spreading the word about my work and encouraging others to give it a shot, for giving me the courage I need to keep going. You have changed my life.

To my beta readers, Aurora and Alex. Am I going to thank you for the millionth time for being two of the most supportive people I've met on this journey? Absolutely. Thank you for being there for me in so many ways from the very beginning. Please don't hold it against me if we ever meet and I hug you for twenty minutes straight.

To Alejandri. All my books are for you, even though I better not catch you reading any of them until you turn eighteen (I'm watching you). Don't ever question your worth or doubt how far you will go. *Te quiero más que a nadie en este mundo.*

To *Tía*. Thank you for always being a text away. A million times thank you for encouraging me to keep going when my head got so loud, I almost forgot why I started.

To Alexis. Thank you for not being weird about your girlfriend writing hot fictional men doing the nasty. Thank you for supporting my insane career, for listening to my ramblings, for your patience, for celebrating my wins as if they were your own, for being the best cat dad to our furry girls. You're better than any book boyfriend I could ever write.

Para papá y mamá. Hace diez años me dijisteis que algún día conseguiría ser una autora reconocida y que vendería muchos libros. ¿Me prestáis la bola de cristal? Aunque os prohíba leer mis historias, os dejo que leáis este pequeño párrafo (no os quejaréis de lo generosa que soy) para que sepáis que os quiero mucho y que todo esto está pasando porque soy quien soy gracias a vosotros.

To my agent, Savannah Greenwell at Two Daisy Media, for being a real powerhouse. Thank you for believing in me and the stories I need to tell. You are a true dream to work with.

To my editor Keeley and the whole team at Hot Tree Editing, for being so uplifting and curing my second book syndrome with so much kindness.

To the Team at Books and Moods for bringing my vision to life with this stunning cover.

To the wonderful Meredith and Solange at Page & Vine for working on this book with so much love, enthusiasm, and respect. I can't thank you enough for helping me find my author voice. My characters and I have truly found a home with Page & Vine.

Para Tata y Abue. Siempre.

about the author

Lisina Coney is a New Adult and contemporary romance author with a weakness for heartfelt love connections and happy endings. She believes in creating complex and relatable characters that will make her readers feel less alone in their journeys.

Besides putting her daydreams into words when the sun comes down, Lisina is an avid reader who is obsessed with French fries and tends to force kisses on her very patient cats.

For more information about Lisina's books (as well as some good ol' bonus content), you can visit her Instagram page @lisinaconeyauthor and her website www.lisinaconeyauthor.com

discussion questions

1. What did you most enjoy about this novel?

2. What themes did The Darkest Corner of the Heart strive to convey?

3. If this novel were a movie, who would you cast for Maddie and James?

4. What is your favorite quote in the novel and why?

5. If a playlist for The Darkest Corner of the Heart were made, what songs would you choose?

6. Why do you believe the author chose the title?

7. How did the characters feel relatable to you?

8. What do you feel most attracted Maddie and James to one another?

9. What did the two main characters help heal inside one another?

10. How would you rate the spice level of the novel?

11. What scenes made you blush like James?

12. Have you ever been attracted to a medical practitioner? Tell us more.

13. What surprised you most in the novel?

14. What opinions, if any, changed for you throughout the novel?

15. What side characters did you most enjoy?

16. If you could give Maddie and James a piece of advice, what would it be?

17. Did The Darkest Corner of the Heart melt your heart?

18. Have you read The Brightest Light of Sunshine by the same author?

19. Will you be reading the author's upcoming novel?